**THESE SERIES SLEUTHS THINK THEY'LL
BE GETTING A LITTLE R & R ON THEIR
SUMMER VACATIONS.**

THEY'RE WRONG.

New York Times bestselling author
Shamus Award Winner
MAX ALLAN COLLINS
*Private eye Nathan Heller gets caught up in a lurid double-
murder case in 1940s Los Angeles. . . .*
**"No one can twist you through a maze with as much
intensity and suspense."—Clive Cussler**

SELMA EICHLER
*Manhattan detective Desiree Shapiro witnesses a murder
while vacationing in the Caribbean. . . .*
"A heroine we can embrace."—Joan Hess

TAMAR MYERS
*Magdalena Yoder leaves Pennsylvania Dutch country for a
crime-filled vacation in Charleston. . . .*
**"Tamar Myers has a great sense of humor."
—*Murder Most Cozy***

Edgar Award Winner
DANA STABENOW
*Magistrate Linda Billington presides over a presumptive-
death hearing in the Alaskan bush co* . . .
"A splendid write

age . . .

Agatha Award Winner
JEFF ABBOTT
*Whit Mosley, the justice of the peace in Port Leo,
Texas, meets a vivacious, flirtatious woman—and finds
himself investigating her death the next day. . . .*
"A wonderfully talented Southern writer."
—Sharyn McCrumb

LYDIA ADAMSON
*Cat-sitter Alice Nestleton investigates the supposed suicide
of an eccentric psychiatrist. . . .*
**"The Alice Nestleton mystery series is catnip for all
mystery fans."—Isabelle Holland**

ANN CAMPBELL
*Annie O'Hara and her clue-sniffing German shepherd,
Claudius, sort through rumors of domestic discontent—
and murder. . . .*
**"[A] new crime fighting team . . . that canine lovers and
amateur sleuth fans will adore."—Harriet Klausner**

JOANNA CARL
*In JoAnna Carl's delightful debut, chocolate shop clerk
Lee McKinney develops a taste for solving crimes. . . .*
Soon to be a new series!

EDIE CLAIRE
*Amateur sleuth Leigh Koslow goes on a trip to Niagara
Falls—with deadly results. . . .*
**"Edie Claire writes with style and dash, creating
characters with real pains, aches, fears, and foibles."
—Carolyn Hart**

HAZEL HOLT
Sheila Malory gets cozy with crime in the
Scottish Highlands. . . .
"Mrs. Malory is a most appealing heroine."—*Booklist*

PETER KING
Real-life author—and now fictional detective—Jack London
solves his first case in San Francisco. . . .
**"London is the perfect two-fisted literary hero . . . from
the masterful Peter King."—Stuart M. Kaminsky**

Edgar Award Nominee
JOHN LANTIGUA
Miami-based private eye Willie Cuesta soaks up the sun—
and the crime—in Palm Beach. . . .
"A forceful writer."—*The New York Times Book Review*

SAM McCARVER
Professor John Darnell and his wife investigate a
suspicious death—and rumors of the Loch Ness Monster—
in Scotland. . . .
**"McCarver [gives] much enjoyment to historical
mystery fans."—Harriet Klausner**

ANDY STRAKA
Police detective turned private eye Frank Pavlicek stays
close to his Charlottesville home—only to find
that crime has moved in. . . .
**"A new P.I. who is not drowning in wisecracks. . . .
Straka should be proud."—Robert J. Randisi**

continued on next page . . .

DENISE SWANSON

School psychologist Skye Denison takes a summer job as a lifeguard—and witnesses a very mysterious drowning. . . .

"Skye Denison is the quintessential amateur sleuth: bright, curious, and more than a little nervy."
—Earlene Fowler

PETER TREMAYNE

In ancient Ireland, Sister Fidelma joins a pilgrimage—and finds a newly dead body in a very old grave. . . .

"[Sister Fidelma is] a brilliant and beguiling heroine."
—*Publishers Weekly*

JUDITH VAN GIESON

Rare-book expert Claire Reynier chases down clues to a long-ago crime in the steamy Southwest. . . .

"A savvy and thoroughly likable sleuth."—Margaret Coel

Edgar Award Nominee
k.j.a. WISHNIA

Filomena Buscarsela finds crime on the beaches of South Florida while on vacation with her young daughter. . . .

"[Wishnia] writes with brio, energy, rage, passion, and humor."—*Booklist*

MATT WITTEN

Screenwriter Jacob Burns's family vacation in an idyllic lakeside community turns ugly. . . .

"An up-and-coming comic genius in the amateur sleuth game."—*Sujata Massey*

WAYNE WORCESTER

Sherlock Holmes and Doctor Watson have a most uneventful vacation—until someone keels over in the lobby of their hotel. . . .

"Wayne Worcester has gotten the voices exactly right."—Peter J. Heck

AND THE DYING IS EASY

All-New Tales of Summertime Suspense

––⌇⌇⌇––

Edited by
Joseph Pittman & Annette Riffle

A SIGNET BOOK

SIGNET
Published by New American Library, a division of
Penguin Putnam Inc., 375 Hudson Street,
New York, New York 10014, U.S.A.
Penguin Books Ltd, 27 Wrights Lane,
London W8 5TZ, England
Penguin Books Australia Ltd,
Ringwood, Victoria, Australia
Penguin Books Canada Ltd, 10 Alcorn Avenue,
Toronto, Ontario, Canada M4V 3B2
Penguin Books (N.Z.) Ltd, 182–190 Wairau Road,
Auckland 10, New Zealand

Penguin Books Ltd, Registered Offices:
Harmondsworth, Middlesex, England

First published by Signet, an imprint of New American Library,
a division of Penguin Putnam Inc.

First Printing, June 2001
10 9 8 7 6 5 4 3 2 1

Copyright © Penguin Putnam Inc., 2001

Author's copyrights to these stories can be found on p. 388.

CONTENTS

INTRODUCTION

Summertime. They say that the living is easy, but in the world of detective fiction, life has a way of turning deadly. So we wondered, what happens when private eyes want to take a vacation? Do they pack their guns alongside their suntan lotion? Amateur sleuths are always stumbling upon dead bodies, but would they still search out a killer while sunning themselves on the beach? And what about the past—did the sleuths of yesteryear ever get a day off? These questions, and more, are answered, as twenty of Signet Mystery's favorite writers take their series sleuths on a holiday filled with mystery and mayhem. Each story was written specifically for this collection, so thanks to them all for rising to the challenge.

If you like your mysteries with a cozy attitude, then grab some lemonade and lounge about with stories by Tamar Myers, who sends her feisty sleuth Magdalena Yoder to Charleston, or Edie Claire, who sends the intrepid Leigh Koslow on a trip to Niagara Falls—both with murderous results. Visit the Scottish Highlands with Hazel Holt's Sheila Malory, or take a trip to Scumble River, a small American town with lots of trouble brewing, courtesy of Denise Swanson. Lydia Adamson's amateur sleuth Alice Nestleton is pure catnip, and Ann Campbell shows us the flip side, as German shepherd Claudius once again comes to Annie O'Hara's rescue. And lastly, who can turn down a case involving gourmet chocolate? Thanks to JoAnna Carl, we can have our crime and eat it too!

Private eyes always seem to go from client to client, so who's got time for a vacation? Max Allan Collins revisits 1940s Los Angeles, as Nathan Heller abandons his summer plans in order to investigate an explosive case of murder.

Selma Eichler sends Manhattan P.I. Desiree Shapiro to the Caribbean—and learns there will be no fun in the sun for her. For Willie Cuesta, John Lantigua's hero out of Little Havana, it's a trip to Palm Beach that makes for precarious vacationing. k.j.a. Wishnia also visits the land of sunshine, as Filomena Buscarsela finds mystery on South Florida's beaches. Only Andy Straka's sleuth Frank Pavlicek sticks closer to home—and finds that crime has moved in.

History takes a vacation as well, as Peter King introduces readers to real-life author and now fictional detective Jack London, who finds his plans for a summer break suddenly on hold along San Francisco's Barbary Coast. Sam McCarver takes his detective, John Darnell, (along with wife, Penny) out of England, for a trip to Scotland to debunk rumors of the Loch Ness monster. Wayne Worcester imagines Sherlock Holmes and Dr. Watson taking a break from detecting, while Peter Tremayne travels back to an Ireland of long ago, as Sister Fidelma takes the seventh century's version of a holiday.

Finally, for those of you who like your mysteries with a contemporary spin, check out Dana Stabenow's chilling tale, where the treacherous Alaskan bush takes a backseat to the treachery of mankind. Or visit Jeff Abbott's Port Leo, where Justice of the Peace Whit Mosley learns the hidden dangers of drinking with strangers. Judith Van Gieson lures us to the Southwest, where a visit from an old friend sparks memories of an even older crime. And lastly, Matt Witten takes us to a lakeside community, where a game of volleyball sets the stage for a game of murder.

At Signet Mystery, we're proud of the wide variety of talent on our list, and we hope you enjoy this original collection of stories. So, get ready to sit back and relax and enjoy the summer. And may choosing your favorite story in *And the Dying Is Easy* be the most difficult thing you do all summer long.

Joseph Pittman
Annette Riffle
Summer 2000

SALT ON THE RIM

A Whit Mosley Mystery Story

Jeff Abbott

This story marks the first appearance in print of Agatha Award—winner Jeff Abbott's new character. Whit Mosley is a justice of the peace in Port Leo, Texas. Coming soon is the first novel to feature Whit, *A Kiss Gone Bad*.

The woman mounted the bar stool as if it were a saddled horse, with an immodest swing of her miniskirted leg. Thighs firm and bronzed, perfume that smelled of jasmine. A confident set to her shoulders. Whit Mosley, two stools down, thought: *Hot stuff but she knows it.*

Toni, the bartender, slid a napkin in front of the woman.

"Margarita, please. On the rocks," the woman told Toni. "Salt on the rim."

Whit studied the woman while pretending to poke at the ice cubes in his own margarita. Hair the color of mahogany lay in a thick spill down her neck. Her dress was a neon lime-green, a city girl's party dress, not bar wear for small-town Port Leo. Lightning-strike pretty, a vanguard of the bright-smiled women of the Texas coast's summer season. The ones not hauling screaming sunburned kids in tow, not cooing to moneyed widowers and shaking the Viagra bottle like a baby rattle.

She glanced over her shoulder twice in the first minute at the bar, watching the front door.

Whit chewed ice and watched the television mounted above the bar. The Astros were in a fourth-inning meltdown. He hadn't paid much attention to the game, lost in confessing the boring detritus of his personal life to Toni Packard; she was that old-style kind of bartender, a flesh-and-blood confessional. The woman's arrival threw him and Toni both into silence.

He nearly didn't hear the woman speak to him.

"Hi," she said, and he glanced at her in the mirror behind the bar. "This place is deader than roadkill."

Whit shrugged. "Port Leo in all its glory."

Toni set the margarita in front of the woman. "Run a tab?"

"Sure." She waited until Toni turned away to scribble on a pad. She sipped at her drink, shivered and sighed in satisfaction, and licked the salt from the glass. "Perfect." She nodded at Toni. She turned to Whit. "I thought waterside joints hopped."

"Early in the season." Whit shrugged. "It'll pick up."

"Already has." She gave him a flick of a smile. "I'm Jane."

"I'm Whit," he said.

"The Honorable Whit Mosley," Toni amended, drawing a pitcher of Shiner Bock for a trio of sun-crisped fishermen on the Water's End deck. She was a shameless eavesdropper as well as gentle listener.

"Honorable?" Jane gulped more of her drink, tongued the salt from her upper lip.

"Justice of the peace."

"Ah. The guy who performs marriages for heartsick teen runaways or thrice-divorced optimists."

"Only if they have their blood tests."

"I would never elope without one." Jane took another long haul from her margarita. Her gaze flickered back to him, inviting him to join in the flirting.

Whit was a veteran of summer-tourist flings, with steady regularity from when he was sixteen. Smiling, Yankee-pale girls visiting retired grandparents, bored Dallas debutantes intent on disproving the myth of frigidity, browned fisherwomen brimming with machisma. But he wasn't in the mood this summer for a seasonal complication and he kept his smiles for Jane neutral and cousin-pleasant.

Over the course of the next week at the Water's End, she maintained the flirting: laughing at his jokes, tossing her mahogany mane in a coy preen for the benefit of the few customers when she sat at the bar. He suspected flirting was similar to breathing for her. But when he didn't invite her back to his place, she made no foray of her own. She talked with him but gave the impression—from her eyes darting to the door when the bell jingled—that she was patiently waiting for someone. He gleaned Jane was staying at a nearby condo, that she was from Dallas, and that she didn't want to talk much about herself. Their conversations never lasted long; Whit made his one drink last a watery hour, then walked home. It did not do for judges to drink and drive. Jane would usually be ordering a refill as he left, Toni mixing the margarita in a shaker, dusting the rim of the glass with salt, Jane wiggling fingers toward Whit in a good-bye wave and turning to chat with Toni.

The night before Jane died, Whit saw her perched on her stool, sipping the margarita with all the solemnity of communion wine, watching him leave in the bar mirror.

The Mustang shredded like foil when it smashed into the abandoned pier on St. Leo Bay, the driver's side crumpling, the car half turning in the air before crashing into the shallow water and gouging into the muddy bottom. Blood and gasoline and gulf water mixed, swirling around the wreck in a gaudy, moonlit film.

The paramedics and the sheriff's deputies had fished out the body by the time Whit arrived. He clicked on a flashlight—it was well after midnight—and ran the beam along the corpse.

Jane in death was quite different from Jane in life. She wore another of her too-chic party dresses, lemon-yellow with orange trim. But her body was already stiff, convulsed, as though the warm bay water had been Arctic-cold. Her neck was broken, her chest savaged by the impact. The sour echo of Whit's dinner—tamales smothered in chili and cheese—burned the back of his throat.

He saw her wave good-bye again in the mirror, heard her odd short laugh, remembered the sense that she'd been waiting at that bar like a cat at a mouse hole.

"Jesus," Whit muttered. He checked his watch and made a notation in his JP's notebook.

"I'm pronouncing her dead at 12:50 A.M.," Whit told Billy Nguyen, the young deputy at his side. "Looks like awful quick rigor mortis. How long you think she's been in the water?"

"Don't know, Y'Honor," Nguyen answered. "No one spotted the car until about twenty minutes ago."

Whit pulled out his cell phone and phoned the Water's End, three miles away.

"Toni? It's Whit Mosley. There's been an accident. Jane—the margarita lady—is dead. Car crash."

Stunned silence. "Oh, my God."

"Had she been drinking much tonight?" He had skipped the bar that evening, preferring to watch an old movie on cable.

"No, Judge, I swear. She came in, had one 'rita, ate some stuffed jalapeños, just hung out like she did. I thought that maybe she was waiting for you to show up. I swear."

Jane always seemed to be waiting for someone to show up. "She was staying at Big Cat Beach, right?"

There was a pause. "I think so. But you talked with her more than I did."

"I need to talk to you tonight, I'll be there shortly."

"Okay," Toni Packard said in a small voice and clicked off.

Whit studied the road leading to the bay; the road made a fairly straight line for the last mile. She'd nailed the deserted pier at high speed, at least sixty miles an hour.

Billy Nguyen walked back up the pier road, flashing his light on the ground. Whit joined him.

"Any sign there was another car?"

Nguyen flashed the light across the pockmarked asphalt—coastal Texas weather was hell on roads. "No sign of brakes, no sign of skidmarks, Judge, no sign of debris from the car. But looks like she plowed down those signs"—he pointed at splintered roadway posts that promoted local fishing services and a herbal diet supplement—"on the way to the pier. Somehow she lost control. Or she was drunk or high."

In the bay, the wading deputies affixed a chain to pull the car from the muck. Whit watched them. "I don't even know her last name," he said. "See if there's a purse. Or liquor bottles in the car. I'm ordering an autopsy. Y'all can remove the body now."

Whit watched the mortuary service bundle Jane onto the stretcher, zipping the dark body bag over her torn, lemon-colored plumage.

Whit drove to the Water's End while calling the medical examiner's office in Corpus Christi and telling them a corpse was en route. In Encina County—as in many rural Texas counties—the justice of the peace served as coroner and was responsible for death inquests. Clearly death was caused by the car crash, but vague unease crowded his mind as to what had led to Jane's car ramming into the bay from a completely straight road.

At the Water's End, the neon CLOSED sign glowed in the window. A halo of fat june bugs swarmed the lights. A double knock brought Toni to the door. The bar's janitor, an elderly Vietnamese man, was upending chairs and sweeping the floor with the quiet meticulousness of a priest.

The bar's owners, Bill and Matsy Kidder, sat huddled in a dimly lit booth. Both looked like they had been roused from bed. Whit knew them only by reputation; they were one of those immaculate, graying couples retiring more often to Port Leo these days, swollen with money from Dallas or Houston or Austin. He knew they'd bought the bar barely six months ago, an apparent whim for a distraction other than charity work, fishing, or golf to fill the time.

Bill was hearty for a man in his early sixties, tall, trim, hair nearly gone but handsomer for it. Matsy was a willow; full gray hair pulled into a simple ponytail to show off the simple diamonds in her earlobes and the simple diamond at her throat.

"I called Bill and Matsy," Toni said, her voice strained. "Y'all know Judge Mosley?"

Whit shook hands with them and sat.

"Judge," Bill Kidder said. "I can assure you that woman wasn't drunk. Toni wouldn't let a drunk drive. She's under strict orders to call a cab if there's a problem."

"Or to call me," Matsy Kidder said with civic rightness. "I'll drive a drunk home if need be."

Whit found it hard to imagine Matsy ferrying around boozy fishermen in her Lexus. But he didn't really know these people.

"What time did Jane leave here, Toni?" Whit asked.

Toni tugged at her lip; Whit could see a tremble in her hand. "Around midnight, I think. She was the last customer."

"You didn't shut down then?" Whit asked.

"No," Toni said. "Bill likes for me to keep the place open even if everyone's gone before closing."

The Kidders shifted against the booth's vinyl, as though chafing under this sudden criticism. "Not the point, Toni," Bill said. "People expect us to be open during business hours." He said this in a tone entirely too lord-of-the-manor for Whit's taste, considering said manor was a smallish bar with an oyster-shell lot and weathered deck.

Toni said nothing; she shredded a napkin between her fingers.

"Was there liquor in the car?" Matsy asked. "Perhaps the young woman drank on the way home."

Whit shrugged. "Don't know yet."

"You knew her, didn't you, Matsy?" Toni said quietly. "Pretty brunette, just arrived in town? I was sure I saw you talking with her downtown the other day."

The silence hung above the booth like a ghost. Matsy shook her head. "I don't remember . . . oh, yes, there was a young woman who asked me for directions . . ."

"She always wore a bright dress," Toni said. "I'm sure it was Jane."

"Yes. Bright pink that day. I remember," Matsy said. "She was out for a stroll and asked me how to get to Artists' Row. I told her, she thanked me, I never saw her again." She coughed, once, like a bark, and her gaze narrowed at Toni in ill-concealed annoyance.

Whit frowned. "Is there anything y'all know about this woman or this accident you're not telling me?"

Bill stared at him. "We don't know a blessed thing."

The next morning, at 7 A.M., the condo manager at Big Cat opened Jane's door for Whit and Billy Nguyen. Her sodden purse had finally been found in the wreckage and the address was inside.

The condo looked like a hurricane had blasted through it. Under normal circumstances the decor was typical Gulf Coast rental, ruined by a rum-punch decorator besotted with nautical motif. A fake captain's wheel had been converted into a glass coffee table. A candleholder was made to look like an old schooner, the tapered vanilla candles serving as masts. Hand-painted wooden fish cavorted on the walls in various angling postures, mouths agape with hooks, eyes bugging. Now the decor was stripped from the walls, the couch cushions torn, bookshelves emptied of hardcovers and knickknacks, furniture overturned.

The condo manager, Whit, and Deputy Nguyen stared at the mess.

"The door hasn't been forced." The condo manager checked the lock. He was a balding canary of a man with a trilling drawl and primly folded, wiry arms.

"Christ," Billy Nguyen said. He stepped gingerly through the jumble, exploring the rest of the condo.

"What do you know about Jane Collins?" Whit asked the manager.

"I've had better tenants," the man murmured. "Too many tequila bottles in the recycling bin, too much loud music."

"Many visitors?" Whit asked.

"You mean was she a whore?" the manager said with delicate malice.

"I mean did she have many visitors," Whit said. He felt sure peeking through blinds at comings and goings was in the man's unofficial job description.

"I saw her once with a beefy guy, twentyish, red-haired." He shrugged. "Jane had only been here a week or so."

"How long did Jane rent for?" Whit asked.

"She didn't rent. A Dallas company owns the condo. Atasboro. Big in oil development. They loan it out to employees, clients, whoever they want to treat to a little vacation."

"She work for them?"

"Don't know. Didn't care," the manager said. "She showed up with a key."

Deputy Nguyen returned from the bedrooms. "The same," he said. "Torn apart."

Whit pointed at a blinking answering machine on a kitchen counter. He jabbed the button.

"Hey, Janie-jane," a man's voice said, slushy with ice and whiskey. "Call me if the line's been reeled in. Bored to tears. 555-2378."

Billy Nguyen phoned the sheriff s office to get a location for the caller's number. Whit began to pick through the clutter. After a few minutes, Nguyen joined him. The ransacking had apparently been quick and violent: only larger hiding places had been disturbed. The mattresses and pillows lay ripped open, stuffing spilled in fluffy intestinal twists. Furniture stood away from the walls, drawers emptied.

"It doesn't seem like a burglary," Whit mused. "The electronics are all here. So what did they want?"

He wandered to the bathroom—the tidiest room, the one that seemed least disturbed by the intruders. Makeup, curling iron, stick of deodorant, middle-crushed toothpaste tube, a variety of expensive perfumes. An unmarked white bottle of pills. Whit slipped the pills in an evidence bag.

He returned to the den, stepping over a spill of books on the floor. Books about the sea, mostly, to complement the rental decor. Guides to fishing and sailing, the collected novels of Patrick O'Brien, John D. MacDonald anthologies, a thick tome on Texas maritime history. He picked up the heavy history book, flipped through the pages, noticed that some of the paper felt oddly thick. Random pages were stuck—no, glued together. Whit pried one set of pages free.

"Billy," he called, setting the book down immediately. "Come here, please."

The young deputy stood by him as Whit pointed at the two crisp hundred-dollar bills hidden in the book. He riffled the book, opening each joined page, each one a hiding place for a pair of hundred dollar bills.

He found over five thousand dollars, fresh and hidden.

The sheriff's deputies picked up the young man who'd called Jane—his name was Danny Flanagan—and questioned him about his knowledge of dead Ms. Collins. He'd stayed relentlessly tight-lipped, claiming only that he'd met her at a local bar, hung out with her for a couple of drinks, but barely knew her. Nguyen took fingerprints to see if any matched prints in Jane's apartment. Flanagan said he worked in Tulsa for a consulting company, but a phone call revealed he'd been laid off weeks before.

The oil company that owned the condo, Atasboro, said Jane was a long-time employee—a public relations specialist—who had been given the condo for a month as a reward for superior performance.

Quite a reward, a summer month on the coast, Whit thought, *for someone who wasn't an executive.*

Whit waited until Danny Flanagan was back at his apartment the next morning. He knocked and the door was opened by a rumpled young man, tall, with freckled muscles straining an old polo shirt. Reddish hair stuck up in sleepy cowlicks. The man smelled like spilled whiskey drying in the sun.

"Danny Flanagan?"

"Yeah?"

"I'm Judge Whit Mosley. I'm conducting the inquest into Jane Collins's death."

Flanagan blinked at him; Whit wore khaki shorts, a sun-faded blue polo shirt, and sandals—not typical judicial wear.

"I already spoke with the police. I barely knew her . . ."

"I know. But I'd like to talk to you myself."

Danny gave Whit a look that made him feel as welcome as lice. "Come in."

The apartment was dark and disheveled. A near-gone bottle of Jack Daniel's sat on the coffee table, next to a pile of dog-eared fishing magazines. The cushions on the threadbare, chocolate-colored couch lay crushed from slumber. A new smell of burnt eggs fouled the air. Whit heard the slow gurgle of coffee brewing.

"Rough night?" Whit asked.

"Insomnia. It's a bitch. Especially without cable."

"So what's keeping you awake?"

Flanagan gave him a thin smile. "Marveling at the time small-town authorities have to waste investigating car wrecks."

"Ah." Whit took a seat, uninvited, in a bedraggled armchair. Cracker crumbs rubbed against the back of his legs. "But most car crashes aren't followed or preceded by the victim's condo being ransacked."

"I don't know anything about that, Judge," Flanagan said. "I told the police, I hardly knew her."

"I don't believe you," Whit said mildly.

"Excuse me?" Flanagan, still standing, stared at him.

"I don't believe you," Whit repeated. "People lie all the time, yet they're so outraged when you call them on it. Why is that?"

"Get out of here," Flanagan said. "I don't have to take this crap."

"You know, you lie to the police in an interrogation room, that's bad," Whit said. "But I conduct an inquest hearing, I put you on the stand under oath and you lie, you're in the fun-filled world of perjury. That means jail. No cable there, either."

Flanagan stared at him. "I'm not lying. She was just a casual acquaintance."

" 'Janie-jane' is an awfully familiar nickname."

"She told me to call her that." Flanagan crossed his thick, freckled arms. "We had a one-night stand, okay? I'm little embarrassed about it."

"Why? Were you lousy?" Whit asked.

Flanagan stared at him in surprise. "Screw you."

"Be nice. I sign the arrest warrants around here. Where'd you meet her?"

Flanagan let out a hiss of breath. "That bar she hung out at. Water's End."

"When?"

"Night before she died. Left the bar with her about ten."

"Really? I was sitting with her at that bar till nearly eleven that night. I don't recall your charming face."

Flanagan's mouth thinned. "Why are you harassing me? It was a car crash. I didn't have nothing to do with her or it."

"She had a lot of cash hidden away. Someone wanted something out of her condo. Your message referred to a fish being reeled in. I don't think you were talking about angling out in St. Leo Bay, were you?"

"Yes, I was," he said. "We had planned on going fishing. I can't help it if you got a suspicious mind."

"So tell me about this fish, Danny. What were you baiting the hook with? Jane?"

"I don't know what you mean."

Whit laid down the trump card he'd gotten that morning. "Your PR company in Tulsa, Klee Associates? They told us you got fired for incompetence. I visited their Web site. Saw that Atasboro is a client of theirs. Same company Jane worked for. Same company as owned the condo."

Danny Flanagan shuddered. "I want a lawyer before I say anything more."

Whit nodded. "We can arrange that." He clicked on his cell phone.

The Kidders' home stood along the northern crescent of St. Leo Bay. Oleander framed the entrance to the driveway and dominated the beds and in the summer heat the white petals glimmered like drops of sun. The house was Mediterranean-grand, with marble arches, a curving driveway free of oil spots and gull guano, and a private dock with jet skis and a fifty-foot fishing boat named *Matsy's Joy.* At the end of the dock was an artificial golf green, where every shot would be into the drink.

Whit Mosley stood on the deck with Bill Kidder. The wind off the bay was cool and intermittent, the clouds hanging low, broken by strips of blue sky, an unusual blustery summer's day. A tour boat rumbled past along the open bay, stick figures standing on the back. Early summer tourists. They waved at Bill and Whit. Whit waved back. Bill fumed, holding a driving iron, a bucket of balls to be lost in the bay at his feet. Whit had interrupted swing practice.

"You cannot be serious," Bill Kidder said. "You can't be."

"Our witness claims Jane Collins had been your mistress, Mr. Kidder."

Bill blanched. "Witness? Witness to what? I've never heard of Jane Collins. Known her. Or seen her." He stared at Whit. "I've never cheated on Matsy. Not once."

"Mr. Flanagan doesn't look real bright but he has a head for specifics. He says he and Ms. Collins got to know each other through their work for a Dallas oil company. Apparently when you retired you also retired from keeping Jane Collins as a mistress, and she didn't take kindly to it. He alleges he and Jane came here to get money from you and that you had just started to trickle the funds out to her."

"That young man is a contemptible liar," Bill Kidder said. "I'll sue his ass for slander. And if you make any such allegations toward me, I'll sue you and the county for false arrest."

"No one's arrested you, Mr. Kidder. Yet."

"I love Matsy," he insisted with heat. "I've never cheated on her. Ever. God's truth. And you can't find a thing to connect me, ever, with this Jane Collins." A cell phone rang, beeping the famous strains of the 1812 Overture in annoying electronic chirps. Bill scooped up the phone and spoke low into it.

"Hello. Hi, Toni. What?" Silence. "No, not now. I can't discuss it now." More silence. "Sorry, I'm just not interested. I've made myself clear. I'll speak to you later." He hung up.

"Uppity help," he said to Whit.

"Such a cross to bear," Whit said without sympathy. "Would uppity help apply to Jane, too?"

"If you want to talk to me again, do so through my attorney." Bill Kidder smoothed his bald pate. "I sure as hell don't intend to argue with you over groundless charges."

Whit left. He heard the thwack of a golf ball being launched from the end of the dock, and didn't hear it splash into the swallowing bay.

After an excruciating afternoon adjudicating low-brain traffic court, Whit logged onto the Internet again and returned to the Atasboro corporate Web site. Jane had worked on public relations for the company, and he wanted to see where they had made news.

He found it on an archived press release from two years ago. Atasboro had purchased a smaller, private firm that leased oil exploration equipment called Malone-Kidder, Inc. Bill Kidder was the president. Probably where all the bucks to pay for a bayside mansion and a lifetime's supply of bay-bound golf balls came from. The purchase price for Malone-

Kidder was ten million. Bill gave a frothy quote about how Malone-Kidder and Atasboro made for a superior team. At the bottom of the release was Jane's name, the person the press could call for more details or froth.

So there was the connection. Jane's employer bought Bill's company. They had met, become lovers, and then Jane got dumped and Jane got greedy and Jane got dead.

But there was only five thousand stashed in her condo. Either that paltry sum was all she had bled from Bill thus far, or the intruder had found and taken the rest. If it was Bill, he wanted his money back and his blackmailer silenced. If it was Danny, he'd turned against his partner in crime and taken the money.

The accident had been very, very lucky. Too lucky.

His phone rang. It was Dr. Elizabeth Contreras, deputy medical examiner of Nueces County, the usual performer of autopsies Whit ordered on behalf of Encina County.

"I have your car wreck victim done," she said.

"It's not shaping up as a typical car wreck," he said.

"I see nothing odd," Liz said. "Cause of death was blunt trauma to the head, neck, and chest. Multiple injuries, consistent with the crash. I think she died of that before she could really drown. There's barely a trace of water in the lungs."

"Was she drunk?"

"No. Her blood count was .03. She'd had one medium-sized drink. She'd eaten some fish and rice earlier in the evening, then some stuffed peppers later." That agreed with Toni's account of Jane's behavior in the bar.

"Any signs of drugs?"

"No."

"We found some pills in an unmarked vial at her condo," Whit said. "A pharmacist here says they're Tegretol. Used to control seizures for epilepsy and other neurological disorders."

"I'd like to check with her personal physician on that," Liz said. "But it might explain why she wrecked on a straightaway street, if a bad seizure hit her."

It was a horrible thought. "What about the early onset of the rigor mortis?" Whit asked.

He could almost see Liz shrug. "It's unusual. Odd, in fact. Based on lividity and the condition of her skin, I don't think she had been in the water long at all when the wreck was spotted."

"This woman might have been a blackmailer. You're sure there's nothing odd? Maybe she was brained or killed, then dumped in the car?"

"No. Her injuries match the physical evidence—from impacting against the steering wheel, the windshield. Airbag didn't save her. She died in the car."

He thanked Liz and she told him she would fax a more complete report to him. So much for the inquest, he thought, stepping out from the cool air of the county courthouse into the bright haze of a June afternoon. The earlier clouds had burned off from the sky and the glare made him thirsty. He pocketed his car keys and instead of driving home walked the couple of blocks to the beach and to the Water's End bar. He saw Matsy's Lexus parked in the oyster-shell lot.

It was early for the locals, but a couple of soft, pale tourists sat by the window, sipping at longnecks, watching gulls strafe the waves. Toni wasn't at her usual perch behind the bar and as Whit took a seat he heard Matsy Kidder's voice raised from the back room.

"You better keep a better eye on inventory or you'll be out of a job," Matsy snapped. "I don't intend this place to be nickled and dimed to death."

A moment later Toni came out from the back, carrying a stack of containers of margarita salt, balancing packets of pretzels on top, her face red with anger, her mouth a tight line.

"Queen of Sheba's on a tear," she said. "Matsy does inventory every two days, like I'm gonna rob her blind. I've had it."

"Other bars in town," Whit said.

"Yeah, working for someone else," Toni said. "I'd like to be my own boss for a change." She paused. "Sorry, bartenders are supposed to listen, not vent." She smiled. "The Kidders are not the easiest slavedrivers to work with."

"It's okay. Can I get a Coke?"

"You sure can." Toni poured his soda. Matsy Kidder

emerged from the storeroom, clutching an inventory sheet on a clipboard and frowning. She stopped when she saw Whit, as though a pungently bad odor wafted through the bar.

"Hello," Whit said. "How are you?"

"I'd like to speak to you. Outside," Matsy said.

Whit followed her out onto the deserted deck. The bay breeze was a steady caress, scented with salt. Two sailboats plied the bay and down along Port Leo Beach two toddlers ran screaming as the surf lapped at their ankles.

"Yes?" Whit said mildly.

"You berated my husband this morning."

"Berate. That's a strong verb," Whit said. "I asked him some questions."

"And he said he didn't know Jane Collins."

"He's lying," Whit said. "She worked PR for the company that bought Bill's company. Bill's quoted in a press release Jane handled. Danny Flanagan may be loathsome, but his story is plausible."

Matsy grabbed the back of a chair. "The woman died in a car wreck. It's insane that you're persecuting us."

"Did Jane really stop and just ask you for directions?" Whit said. "I somehow don't think so. The way you answered Toni . . . *bright pink that day*. As though you'd seen Jane other days, in other colors. I suspect the police will be looking into your finances, seeing if there's any money missing you can't account for." He played the bluff out as far as he dared.

Matsy studied him. "Bill and I had nothing to do with that woman's death. Danny Flanagan . . . I would look carefully at him. Assuming you haven't given him immunity."

"So you know him."

Matsy's mouth worked. "This is a private conversation, Judge. Bill and I have done nothing illegal or wrong. Bear that in mind. I would be most appreciative if you would go out of your way to spare my family embarrassment."

"If you know something and aren't telling me, embarrassment is the least of your worries."

Matsy sat, gestured for him to do the same. "I know when to fold, Judge. Bill is more stubborn. I would rather confess to weakness than be suspected of a crime."

Whit sat. "Bill was paying her blackmail?"

"No," Matsy said. "I was."

Whit blinked. "I don't understand."

"Bill and Jane's affair was recent but brief. Bill ended it. I suspect he was racked with guilt. He didn't know that I knew about it. He still doesn't."

"So—if you knew—what was there to blackmail you or him over?"

"We have two grown daughters, both of whom worship their father and would be devastated to learn he cheated on me."

"And you weren't devastated?"

Matsy shrugged. "You want to crack open my chest and see if my heart's still in one piece? It is, but barely. I was very hurt but I am not going to have my daughters hurt that same way. Bill made one mistake in our forty years of marriage. That's forty-years of love and decency against a few weeks of hormonal silliness. I wasn't going to ruin my life and his life and our daughters' lives over Jane Collins." She watched him. "Don't you think forgiveness is a worthy virtue, Judge?"

He didn't answer her question—forgiveness was up to her and no one else. "So Jane came to you or to Bill for money?"

"Me. I hold the purse strings in the family, Judge. My family funded Bill's company." She gave Whit a sour smile. "He's Matsy-made, not self-made. Jane knew that. Bill would have . . ." She stopped.

"What? Killed her on the spot for threatening your family?"

"He has a temper, yes, but he's not a fool."

"And you set her up in the Atasboro condo."

"No. She did that herself. I think she might have her fingers in another husband's pie there."

"And then this car wreck very cleverly eliminates her."

"Lucky for us," Matsy said flatly.

"How much money had you given her?"

"Two hundred thousand. In cash. She was supposed to leave town today and never darken my doorway again."

"But a blackmailer might always come back."

"She seemed quite happy with the money. I believe she

planned to buy a house with it." Matsy frowned. "Blackmails for mortgage. The gall." She stood. "There. I've cooperated with you. I expect your discretion on this, Judge. I did nothing wrong. Neither did my husband. This case should be closed."

"Maybe you wanted that money back, Mrs. Kidder."

"I simply wanted her to leave us alone. As I do you." She turned and left Whit alone on the deck except for a line of gulls perched on the railing, watching for morsels.

Billy Nguyen shook his head. "There's no damage on Collins's car. Nothing to indicate she was sideswiped or forced into the bay. No damage to the brake lines or the steering column. And no damage on Flanagan's or the Kidders' cars as well."

"So Jane Collins hits the jackpot as a blackmailer and then has the bad luck to simply die in a car wreck?" Whit asked. "No. I don't believe it."

"Maybe fate just zapped her in the ass," Nguyen said. "Bad karma."

"You're forgetting that nearly two hundred thousand is missing. Someone had to know her car had wrecked. And had to believe the money was hidden in her condo," Whit said. "You still watching Flanagan?"

"Like a hawk. And according to his lawyer, Flanagan didn't know Jane'd received the money from Matsy yet. She'd told him she was due to get it at the end of the month. I think fair Jane might have been planning a double cross on her boyfriend. That's probably why she didn't let him stay at her nice company condo with her."

"I wonder," Whit said. Deputy Nguyen left.

The beginnings of a headache started to pound in Whit's temples. The ball had not yet fallen in the slot; something was off here. He walked down the courthouse hall to the sheriff's department and into the evidence room. The only relative of Jane's yet found was an aunt in Miami who had evinced little interest in Jane's belongings or her niece's death. So the debris from the wreck was still in the evidence room, bagged. Whit looked through the now-dried bagged stuff: a purse, a ring of keys, a ruined appointment book, CDs of salsa and Euro-trash pop, lemon-colored shoes that went with the dress Jane had died in. The purse. He pawed through it, suddenly thinking of something that should be there. And wasn't. He played with the key ring a moment, counting the keys, thinking of his own vacation. Something was wrong.

The keys. Condo key, car key (partly broken off from the crash), a key marked with OFFICE that probably opened an Atasboro door back in Dallas.

Back in Dallas. The keys were wrong.

He hurried back to his office and made a phone call to a local pharmacy. Then he called Atasboro in Dallas and talked with the corporate human resources director, threatened politely to search their records with a warrant from a Dallas judge, and got a phone number he needed. He made two rapid-fire phone calls and then called Liz Contreras at the medical examiner's office to ask her a simple favor.

Then Whit sat at his desk for a long time, waiting for the phone to ring again.

It was a busier night at the Water's End than the evenings of the previous week, the tourist pace picking up, cars with license plates from Oklahoma and Arkansas dotting the oyster-shell lot. Sport fishermen laid the groundwork for predawn hangovers, gulping Shiner Bock and whiskey. Whit sat in his Ford Explorer and waited. He saw Matsy's Lexus purr into a slot and both the Kidders go inside the bar. He thought Matsy glanced his way across the parking lot in the glare of the mercury lights, but he wasn't sure. Not that it mattered.

Whit waited until most of the bar had emptied before he went in and sat at the bar, not at his usual stool but on the one Jane perched on the last week of her life. The Kidders were nowhere in sight; probably in the back office.

Toni greeted him with a tired smile. "Evening, Judge. What can I get you?"

"Margarita. On the rocks. Salt on the rim," he said.

Toni mixed the drink with deft hands, smeared the rim of a glass with lime, turned the rim in the wide dish of margarita salt, filled the glass with the murky concoction of lime juice, tequila, and ice. "There you go, Judge," she said.

"Thanks," Whit said. He picked up the glass and instead of sipping, poured it slowly onto the bar.

"What the hell . . ." Toni sputtered, mopping at the mess with a dishrag. "What's wrong with you?"

"You were very clever," Whit said. "Very."

Toni Packard stared at him. "I don't know what you mean . . ."

"Jane. She sits here, she drinks late each night, and God knows you're the best kind of bartender, Toni. The one it's so easy to confide in, to tell secrets to. I've done it." He paused. "Did she finally tell you she was waiting for Bill Kidder to show up at his own bar so she could scare him a little?"

Toni mopped at the spilled cocktail, not looking at him.

"You don't like Bill and Matsy. You resent them for buying the bar when you wanted to buy it. And Jane gave you a way to crucify the Kidders and buy the bar, all wrapped up in a nice package."

"Are you drunk? Get out of here," she snapped.

"I worried too much about motive, Toni. Bill and Matsy certainly had a screamer of a motive. Danny Flanagan had motive—all the money Jane was going to score. But I'm guessing you didn't know about Flanagan, and he didn't know Matsy had already paid off Jane. You had no discernible motive; Jane was just a customer. But you had opportunity. You were the last to see her alive. You gave her a last drink."

"She died in an accident."

"The accident wasn't an accident. Oh, you made it look like one, yes. Planting those Tegretol pills in her condo. Making it appear like she had seizure problems, just in case the crash needed an explanation. But Jane had no history of epilepsy or any kind of condition to require such medication—I spoke with her doctor in Dallas. So why would anyone want to fake that Jane had epilepsy?"

Toni stared at him.

"I had the medical examiner's office check again for poisons. They found strychnine in Jane's system. It explains the rapid onset of the rigor mortis, explains how she lost control of the car. She died in agony, Toni, jack-hammering in seizures. It made a tidy explanation for why she lost control of the car, and normally we wouldn't look any harder at a simple car crash." He pointed at the margarita glass. "I'm guessing you put the strychnine in the margarita salt. You probably gave her the stuffed jalapeños as a freebie, all that flavor to cover up the taste of the poison. The medical examiner believes she got the fatal dose fifteen to twenty minutes before she died. So you let her leave and drive a car, knowing she'd be dead in minutes. Then you got rid of that container of margarita salt and nickel-and-dime Matsy chided you about inventory. I called and asked her what she argued with you about this afternoon—she says it was missing margarita salt.

"And Bill told me you've offered to buy the bar back. Insisted on it. You even called him to discuss it when I was questioning him. You mentioned to me that Matsy had met Jane; you wanted to up the pressure on the Kidders just in case we investigated Jane's death harder. That's why you left the apartment in a wreck after you found the blackmail money—you suspected the Kidder connection would quickly emerge and you wanted to watch them squirm. It was your biggest mistake, Toni. We probably would have just treated Jane's death as another driving fatality if her apartment hadn't been ransacked. But with that pressure, maybe the bar would become a liability for them, the publicity, they'd leave town. And the bar would be yours. Bought with the Kidders' own money."

Toni twisted the dripping dishtowel in her hands. "You're insane. This is all conjecture."

"And I noticed that there was a key missing from Jane's key ring. The key to the condo. I thought the house key on the ring was to the condo, but it's to her apartment in Dallas. You don't take your house key off when you're on vacation for a week, you just add a new key on. You didn't have to force anything. She steps to the ladies' room at some point, you get a second alone with her purse, you nab the condo key."

She put down the towel.

"Not that many Tegretol users locally, Toni. I checked with every pharmacy in town. Your brother's an epileptic with a Tegretol prescription. You stole the pills from him and planted them in an unmarked container in Jane's condo. And right now, I've got the sheriff's deputies executing a search warrant of your house. Are we gonna find nearly two hundred thousand dollars there?"

Pain flashed in her eyes and she leaned against the bar.

"Toni?"

She glanced at him, tears rimming her eyes. "Shouldn't everyone have their own little patch of the world? That's all I wanted. All I wanted."

"I know." But Toni's patch now would be a cell, bereft of the ocean breeze and the summer light and the gentle confiding of customers, and Jane's patch would be a grave of packed earth.

Whit led Toni outside and drove her to the sheriff's department.

And for the rest of the summer, he stayed clear of bars.

A CASE OF FELINE PSYCHOPATHOLOGY

An Alice Nestleton Mystery Story

Lydia Adamson

Lydia Adamson is the author of over fifteen books featuring Alice Nestleton. Among the most recent titles are *A Cat With the Blues*, *A Cat of One's Own*, and *A Cat Under the Mistletoe*.

It was so warm and humid that morning, the walls of my loft were sweating; and my two cats were crouched under the overhead fan to get the maximum effect.

I lay on top of a single sheet, almost naked, reading an old *New Yorker* I had found on the bus.

The phone rang about eleven.

"Nestleton?"

"Yes."

Alice Nestleton?"

"Yes. Who is this?"

"Maurice Baum."

I was astonished. Maurice Baum? I hadn't seen or spoken to him in fifteen years. I had totally forgotten this homicide detective who had worked with me on a single investigation during my very brief tenure as an NYPD consultant—their so-called Cat Woman, because the case involved several related murders centered around, what can only be called a feline cult.

"Are you still on the job, Maurice?"

"No. I retired three years ago."

"You sound well."

"I am well. But I need your help."

"You want to become an actor?"

"Never."

"A cat-sitter?"

"This is no joke. I need your help."

"Concerning what?"

"It's hard to explain on the phone. And I realize this is very short notice . . . but can you spare me some time this afternoon?"

"I don't see why not. Where are we going?"

"To Gramercy Park. Can you meet me at the north entrance around 3:00 P.M.?"

"Sure. Are you in trouble, Maurice?" I asked, because there was a strange tension in his voice.

"I'm in trouble intellectually, Alice. If you know what I mean."

I didn't. But I told him I'd be there at three.

In fact I arrived at two fifty-five. He was there already. My, he had aged! He was still a large, darkly handsome man, but his black hair was now mostly white and his body was stooped.

He held out his hand. I shook it. Then I kissed him on the cheek. For some reason I felt tears coming and I choked them back resolutely. We walked across the street and he led me into one of those posh old apartment buildings across from the park.

"Did you win the Lottery, Maurice?" I asked.

"No. I'm just a visitor here."

We took the elevator to the twelfth floor. He took out a key and opened the door to 12C. We entered a small waiting room, some kind of doctor's office obviously. Then through the waiting room into a large, comfortable office. There was a desk, a straight-backed chair behind it, bookshelves along one wall, two large leather easy chairs, and a matching leather couch. On the walls were framed degrees, one of them identifying the practitioner as a psychiatrist.

Maurice sat down heavily on one of the leather chairs and opened the buttons of his suit jacket. He looked like an exhausted white-maned walrus. I sat down on the other leather chair and relaxed in the unaccustomed air-conditioning.

I quipped: "I knew you always thought me strange, Maurice. But a gift certificate to a shrink?"

Baum smiled. "The shrink whose office this was, is dead. Through the door behind me is the rest of the apartment. The dead shrink's sister lives there. She's away now. She lent me the apartment. Her name is Pat. Her brother's name was William Macbride."

Suddenly I heard god-awful mewling and crying.

"That's the Macbride cat, Antonia," Baum said. He got up and opened the door that led from the office to the apartment.

A very peculiar-looking cat sauntered in.

She was large and shaggy with lynx-type ears. Her legs were so furry that she seemed to be wearing ski socks. Antonia appeared to be one-third Persian, one-third Maine coon, and one-third alley cat.

A minute after she entered the room she leaped up on the armrest of my chair and glared at me. I ignored her and gave Baum a look that signified it was time he got to the point.

He did.

"Dr. William Macbride died in this room about three years ago. The room has not been changed. His sister Pat keeps it this way I suppose as a kind of shrine. We know how he died because there was a witness to his death—Kir Silva, at the time a thirty-one-year-old travel agent and patient of Macbride's. Do you remember reading anything about his death?"

"No. Nothing."

"Okay. Here is what Kir Silva told us."

He was interrupted by Antonia, who moved so fast from my chair to his that Baum flinched. Antonia mewed twice, then moved on to the leather sofa where she scratched the wood on the armrests a few times with her front claws, as if it were a scratching post, then curled up on the sofa top.

Maurice continued.

"Silva arrives for the session at four-thirty. She has been his patient for about a year. On this afternoon she begins to talk about her fear of rape, a recurrent theme since her childhood, although she had never been through a rape. She tells Macbride that she has bought a gun to allay her fears. Macbride asks her where she keeps the weapon. Always on her, she says, in her purse. Macbride says he does not allow weapons in his consultation room. She says it's perfectly safe—there isn't a round in the chamber, only one bullet in the cylinder, and the safety is on. He is adamant and demands she put it in the waiting room. She goes outside, leaves her purse in the waiting room, and returns. At around 5:00 P.M. Macbride excuses himself for a minute. The last mail leaves the building around five and he has several letters in the waiting room that have to be dropped down the chute in the hall. He comes back and the session continues."

He paused and lit a cigarette. If I recall, he had stopped smoking a long time ago. The narrative seemed to be fatiguing him.

But he continued.

"At around five-fifteen, Kir, who is now lying on the sofa, hears a strange sound. She sits up. Macbride has her gun and is spinning the cylinder to locate the single bullet. He takes off the safety, presses the barrel against his head, over the right ear, and pulls the trigger. He is killed instantly. Kir runs into the waiting room and dials 911. When she comes back into the office she sees that in addition to the wound to the head there are hideous scratches on Macbride's face—on both cheeks. She realizes that the cat, who was never allowed in the office while the doctor was with a patient, must have sneaked in when she left the office to put her gun in the other room, or when Macbride went into the hall to mail his letters and picked up her gun on his way back. She sits down and waits for the police to arrive. And that was that."

"You mean it was ruled a suicide."

"Yes, of course. There were powder burns on Macbride's hands. And his sister informed us that Macbride had been very depressed lately because of the death of his son in an auto accident in Spain only six months earlier. Macbride's wife had died some years ago."

"How old was Macbride when he killed himself?"

"Fifty-five."

"And you say the patient was thirty-one at the time?"

"Yes, she was."

Silence. We both watched Antonia who was now rubbing her back against a desk leg. I still didn't know why Baum had called me, although it was obvious by now that it had something to do with Dr. Macbride. Antonia left the desk and climbed up on the CD player, which was situated on a lower shelf in the bookcase. She curled up there.

"From what I told you, Alice, doesn't it appear to be cut and dried?"

"Yes."

"Even though it was an obvious suicide, Rothwax and I did a pretty thorough examination of the premises, the files, Macbride's friends and acquaintances, and so on. And we looked into Kir Silva's background. Everything checked out. Position of the body. Powder burns on the shooting hand and on the scalp. None on Miss Silva. A depressed man. Recent loss of a child. Sudden access to a weapon. Everything was right where it was supposed to be. Only two things were a little peculiar."

"You mean the claw marks."

"Yes. That was one thing. But there was something else. A personal eccentricity, if you can call it that."

"Whose eccentricity?"

"Macbride's. He was always dressed the same for every session: a short-sleeved mock turtleneck, rust-colored, and green canvas pants, the kind mechanics wear. In his closet, in fact, we found forty-one identical outfits—turtlenecks and pants. And I mean absolutely identical."

"That is strange," I remarked, "but to be honest I don't see what it has to do with the price of tea in China."

"Agreed. It didn't mean a thing to me either. Just an eccentricity. Anyway, case closed. About six months later I retire. I forget all about Macbride. About a year later I get a call from my old partner. We talk about a lot of things but he drops the fact that Kir Silva is dead. She killed herself in exactly the same way her shrink did, a bullet to the head. And she did it on the anniversary of his death. Do you find that troubling, Alice?"

"I guess I do."

"I certainly found it troubling—for a while. But then it passed, like the flu. Now we come to the present. And I want to thank you for being so patient. About two months ago I was reading a book about people with obsessive compulsive disorders. You know, people who have to return to the apartment twelve times to check that the lights are out. People who wash a hundred times a day and can't seem to get clean. People who have to count to eighty-one by threes before they can enter a revolving door. You're familiar with this kind of behavior, aren't you, Alice?"

"Of course. In the theater it's epidemic. Actors have all kinds of obsessive rituals."

"Right. Anyway, in this book, which I was reading for no reason at all except that since I've been retired I read a lot of strange books, the author says there are many little-known facts about OCD, as they call it—obsessive compulsive disorder—that are now being brought to light. As an example she talks about the life of the French composer Erik Satie. He lived in a tiny apartment that no one was allowed to enter. After he died his closet was found to contain a dozen identical new suits, shirts, collars, hats, and walking sticks. In addition, thousands of tiny scraps of similarly shaped paper were found in the apartment, each one with an exotic symbol relating for some unexplained reason to the Emperor Charlemagne. The author notes that if Satie were alive today he would surely be diagnosed with OCD."

"I see where you're going, Maurice. If Satie had OCD, so did Macbride."

"Yes."

"But so what?"

"Well, consider this. Imagine a person whose thing is compulsive hand washing, the most common symptom in OCD. This young man, let's call him Johnny, washes his hands fifty—a hundred—sometimes two hundred times a day. Now, if John's parents die in a car crash, it doesn't affect his washing ritual. No grief, trauma, joy, no event whatsoever can stop him from washing his hands. And because of this thing he must do, any physical or mental trauma to his own person is irrelevant. He won't commit suicide because then he wouldn't be able to wash his hands anymore. Isn't that funny?"

"You're telling me that people with OCD very rarely kill themselves."

"Right. And once I found that out it dawned on me that I had done a shoddy investigating job."

"How so?"

"I never checked up on those letters, the ones Macbride took out to the hallway to drop down the chute."

"I don't get the significance of that," I replied.

"Well, if he didn't mail any letters, Kir Silva was lying. And maybe her whole story was fabricated. That was the only fact in her story that could have been confirmed or denied by an outside source. All I had to do was question the doorman on duty. He was responsible for gathering the late afternoon chute mail and putting it into the outside box before the last pickup."

"Yes, but you can't be sure he would have noticed or remembered seeing mail from Macbride."

"No. But I should have followed up."

"Even if her whole story was fabricated, Maurice, the powder burns showed the man fired the weapon himself, at close range, into his own head."

"True. But no autopsy was ever done."

Antonia jumped off the CD player, stretched herself a bit, and then hopped back up. She likes music, I thought.

"Anyway, Alice, the case began to obsess me. So I called Pat Macbride and asked her if I could look over the crime scene again. That's when I learned that she hadn't touched one blessed thing in the office. What you see is the last thing her brother saw."

"But the body is gone," I noted.

"Of course. But the cat isn't. And that's why I asked you to come here."

Aha! Enlightenment, finally. I followed up: "For Antonia's sake?"

"No. For justice's sake. Look, when I thought about it long and hard, the claw marks seemed to be the most irrelevant aspect of the case. But then I remembered what you once said when we were working on those multiple murders all those years ago. Do you remember, Alice? At the meeting. You said, 'Since we can't find motive, we ought to look at the cats.' Everyone laughed at you. That's when they started to call you the Cat Woman. But it made sense to me. Each of the victims had a cat."

He stood up suddenly and approached me.

"Do you understand what I'm saying, Alice?" he asked urgently.

Antonia suddenly leaped from the CD player to the vacated chair and began to claw at the leather. This cat needs a scratching post, I thought.

I was beginning to understand why I was there. To profile Antonia in my capacity as the Cat Woman. To tell Maurice Baum why a cat would claw the cheeks of a man who had just murdered himself . . . a man the cat knew and presumably loved.

Baum went back to his chair. Antonia raced off somewhere, out of sight.

"I know it's a long shot," he said, "but it's the only thing we have now. Macbride is dead. Kir Silva is dead. The sister will never give us permission to exhume the body. And even if she did, we don't know what to look for."

"Seminal fluid, for one," I said.

"Why that?" he asked eagerly.

"I don't know. It just came to mind."

"There is no evidence of an affair between Silva and Macbride. And besides, it wouldn't mean anything if they were lovers; you know what I mean, forensically."

"Why is that?"

"Because during suicides there are often involuntary emissions of all kinds. Just like virtually all people hanged vacate their bowels."

Antonia came into view. She sat at the edge of the rug and watched me.

"She looks like a gentle enough cat," Baum said.

"Yes, she does," I agreed.

"Why would she claw a dead man like that? Or if Kir Silva was lying and the cat clawed the shrink before he pulled the trigger . . . why then? Either way, why?"

"It is very uncommon. Cats usually use their claws on us on the spur of the moment, out of fear. If you pick up a cat suddenly, it will probably lash out with a claw."

"This wasn't just a lashing out," Baum said. "The wounds were deep. Let me show you something."

He took a photograph out of his pocket and handed it to me. "Take a look. Oh, but before we get into that, I haven't had any lunch yet. I could get some food delivered. Are you hungry?"

"A bit."

"Maybe I'll go out and bring back some Caesar salads. That okay?"

"Yes.

"Are you uncomfortable staying here alone?"

"Not at all. It's like the lobby of some air-conditioned old hotel in Narragansett—leather chairs and all. It's the closest I'll get to a vacation this summer."

Baum went out for the food. I looked around for Antonia. She seemed to have vanished.

I concentrated on the photo he had given me. It was essentially a crime-scene photo, a close-up of the face and shoulders of Dr. William Macbride as he sprawled dead in his chair.

His hair was matted with blood from the gunshot wound.

And Maurice Baum had not exaggerated the claw marks on his face; they were deep and symmetrical, like a tribal mask of some sort. The cat must have straddled the face and then dug deep.

The really peculiar thing about the corpse was Macbride's enigmatic smile. Rigor had not set in to explain it.

I could almost see the delight on his lips and in his eyes. But of course, it could be a grimace.

Antonia complained loudly. She was back on the CD player.

"I am here to interrogate you, Antonia. May I call you Toni?"

She meowed again and raised her ears.

"We can do this the hard way or the easy way, baby."

Antonia jumped down, dashed across the floor, and landed in my lap. I pulled one of her ears gently.

"Of course," I said to her, "I fully understand that you will never disclose what you saw. But why did you hurt him after he was dead, Toni? Or did you do that before?"

Toni needed a good grooming. There were all kinds of knots in her fur. She let me interrogate and tease and ear pull for another five minutes and then she repaired to the chair behind the desk.

I suddenly felt very uncomfortable about the whole thing. Did poor Maurice Baum really think I was a cat woman . . . and one with magic powers, at that?

Also, alone in that office, I did feel nervous. There was something about the physical space that agitated me, in spite of the wonderful air-conditioning.

The question I had asked Baum . . . about whether there had been seminal emission . . . I really had no idea why I had asked that.

Maybe Antonia had made me uncomfortable. She had acted strange when Baum and I were in the office. But now that I was alone, she was a pussycat in every sense of the word—snoozing peacefully on the chair.

I looked at the photo again. Macbride was still grinning. Poor man. But I knew, contrary to popular belief, that all photos lie and crime-scene photos lie double.

My shoulders were beginning to ache. It could be the un-accustomed air-conditioning creeping into my joints or it could be the first signs of an anxiety attack.

I walked over to the bookcases and began to read titles.

When I got to the section of the bookcase that contained the CD player, I could see that something was stuck between the machine and the wall.

I pulled it out. It was just a CD case that had slipped down there. The title was "Authentic Tango Music."

It was empty. Where was the disc?

I checked the turntable. Yes, it was in there. Ready to be played.

I smiled. It meant—if Baum was right and Macbride's sister had kept the scene pristine—the tango disc had been in the player for three years.

It might also mean, I thought, that the disc was played at that last deadly psychiatric session.

Tango analysis? It was a ridiculous thought. But I played the disc anyway.

Oh, my! The tango in the afternoon! I didn't know whether to laugh or cry at the haunting music.

I picked up Antonia and we danced together.

Someone shouted from outside the waiting room. It was Baum; he obviously had overbought and needed help with his packages.

I shut off the music and let the cat down.

I headed for the door. But something was wrong with me. I was walking very slowly.

Words, images, thoughts, seemed to crowd my brain, impeding every step.

I never reached the door. Now I knew what was being assembled in my head. A kind of logic. Like when you are a child and you're taking a test and those algebraic functions at first seem like a foreign language but then you realize they are only symbols and you can use them and everything falls into place.

They were algebraic functions of a sort:

The tango.

Seminal emissions.

Smiling ravaged corpses.

Cats scratching leather.

Baum entered, slammed the door shut behind him, and dumped the packages on the desk. One of the drinks had already been upended.

"Didn't you hear me calling?" he asked.

"No," I lied. "I'm sorry."

Then I walked up to him and kissed him on the lips.

He pushed me away. "What the hell is the matter with you?" he yelled.

I placed my hands on his face and kissed him again—this time it was what you'd call a punishing kiss. And this time he kissed me back.

From behind us came a horrendous noise. We moved apart, both staring at the source.

The cat was savagely ripping the leather sofa apart with its claws.

"Some cats," I noted casually, "act strange in the face of human sexuality. Did you know that, Maurice?"

"No."

"It appears that Antonia is one of those cats."

"It appears so."

"And all *we* did was kiss."

"What did Macbride do?" he asked.

"You mean, what did Macbride and Silva do," I corrected.

Then I took a piece of paper from the desk and wrote down what I thought they were doing in that office on that day. I am not a prude but for some reason I could never speak *that* word.

I wrote: "Russian roulette during fellation. The man plays the game while the woman fellates."

Baum read the note.

"I never heard of that," he said.

"I did. It provides, I understand, a unique challenge. Fear and pleasure. As long as the male spins the cylinder and pulls the trigger, the pleasure continues. He can stop at any time—both the fear and the pleasure. Or he can play it to the end. Death or orgasm. Whichever comes first. I'm told the game originated in the brothels in Macao that catered to sailors."

"And what does the woman get out of this?"

"Money, if she's a prostitute. Possibly revenge, if she hates the man. On the other hand, if she loves him . . ."

"You can't prove that what you say is what happened."

"No, I can't."

I walked over to the CD player and flicked it on again. "But listen to the music, Maurice. While you're eating your Caesar salad."

It was a very late lunch. But the salad was excellent.

Sometimes the briefest summer vacations turn out to be the most memorable. Dare one say . . . productive?

LET SLEEPING DOGS LIE
An Annie O'Hara & Claudius Mystery Story

Ann Campbell

Ann Campbell introduced readers to her unique sleuthing duo of Annie O'Hara and Claudius, a German shepherd, in *Wolf at the Door*. They appeared again in *Wolf in Sheep's Clothing*.

"Just don't run," Annie O'Hara said.

"Hmm." George Vining eyed the big black dog lying nearby. "You kidding?"

"Claudius will think you're an escaped felon. He used to be a prison guard dog."

"Fine by me," said George. "I don't have a death wish." He backed away a step or two, keeping a wary eye on Claudius, who was busy gnawing a deer antler he'd dug up from under a wild blackberry bush.

It was July in New Hampshire. The sky was bright blue, and the air shimmered in the heat. In the woods behind the Thurston Tavern, it was shady and a little cooler, but not much.

George had been whittling a twig. Satisfied, he whipped the twig around, trying it out. "Know anything about dowsing?"

"Not really," Annie admitted. A few days earlier, with her well showing signs of running dry, she'd called around town, hoping to find someone who'd dig a new well fairly cheap.

As it turned out, Kirk Deitrich, her one semipermanent boarder at the tavern she ran as a bed and breakfast/antique shop, had mentioned that George knew a thing or two about finding water. George being a well-to-do farmer, recently retired, who'd taken up dowsing as a hobby. So, a phone call later, George had arrived, and they'd walked out back to see what he could find in the way of an underground stream.

Her dog, Claudius, had come along, too. Left to his own devices, the big, black huskie/German shepherd tended to get into trouble. At the moment, he was more or less innocently occupied, gnawing on the antler—a state of affairs guaranteed not to last long.

George had already commented on Claudius's powerful energy field—hardly a surprise since the dog was as big as a pony.

They strolled through the woods near her two-hundred-year-old tavern home and arrived at the area of scrubby, dead trees and overgrown thickets.

George said, "I pick up animal thoughts. Your dog would be happier if you fed him a better brand of dog food. More protein. Get him a bed filled with cedar shavings. That'll keep him off your bed at night."

"He seems happy with the status quo," Annie said, thinking how unpredictable George Vining was turning out to be. It seemed he had unplumbed depths, and she wasn't sure she wanted to find out how far they went.

"Hey, no skin off my nose. I'm just relaying what he said."

"Do you dowse animals as a rule?" she asked.

"Yeah, sheep, cows, horses. Whatever. I can find the source of a horse's lameness without picking up the hoof. Did that just last week. As soon as I walked in the stall, the horse told me the hoof was badly trimmed."

"Is that so?"

"Yeah, and that dog of yours is loaded with energy. Not all of it's good. Get a copper amulet to hang on his collar and deflect his bad energy." And this, according to George, wasn't the half of it. There were many kinds of energy. The trick was learning to manage all of it, the good, the bad, and the ugly. "Take that corn field," he went on, pointing at the tasseled rows of corn on the far side of the stone wall. "I bet you get patches where the snow won't melt till late spring. That's because the ground's got negative energy."

"Really."

"That's right."

"And all this time I thought it was because that hillside didn't get direct sun," she said thoughtfully.

They walked on, and within half an hour he'd located two underground streams, saying both should produce more than enough water for her needs. The underground water, George said, was sweet and pure, full of good energy, and should produce for at least the next seventy years. Using his dowsing twig, he then redirected the streams back toward her old well.

Mystified, Annie watched with cautious optimism as he waggled the twig downward, muttering what sounded like mumbo jumbo. But what did she know. He was a professional dowser. This was costing her fifty dollars, and she had every hope the trickle in the kitchen sink would soon become a torrent.

They headed back toward the tavern, and George paused in the shade of a maple tree. "How about letting me cut some of these dead trees? I'd leave this red maple and that big ash over there. They're healthy, but you've got six or ten others that need taking down. Let sunlight in. You'll get better growth, and the forest will improve."

Annie hadn't been born yesterday. George Vining didn't have an altruistic bone in his body, so what was in it for him? Fall was coming, with a cold winter not far in the offing. Cord wood would be in great demand.

She looked him in the eye—not easy because his were squinty and obscured by thick, bushy eyebrows. "What's the deal?"

"I cut the dead trees, clear the brush, chip the worst of it— say, an acre or two. Bring in a truck, cut the downed trees into log lengths, and haul them out. What I don't want, I'll leave where it falls, or cut up. You can sell the wood or use it yourself. Of course, if you sell it, you're liable if someone gets hurt picking it up."

Annie chewed her lower lip. A lawsuit she didn't need. What the heck. If George said the forest would be healthier less a few dead trees, it made sense. "You've got yourself a deal."

"Good. I'll start tomorrow," he said. With a wave of his hand he got in his truck and drove off toward town.

That afternoon she did a load of wash and was thrilled to see a veritable Niagara of water pouring into the machine.

George Vining knew what he was talking about, at least as far as dowsing for water.

On the strength of which, she rushed downtown and bought Claudius a copper amulet at Heavenly Illuminations, the New Age shop. For $14.95, it was guaranteed state-of-the-art, and she had every expectation that his temperament would improve.

When she got back home, she patted Claudius, who was happily napping on the rug. "I don't think for a minute that you emit negative energy, but let's give it a try." She fastened the triangular copper amulet to his collar. "It has the power of the Pyramids." She read him the brochure: " 'Alchemy of Sacred Living, creating a culture of light from the sacred copper amulet. Use the power of the Pyramid to unveil the mysteries of the ages. Unveil the power of your deeper self. Access your past lives. Heal anxiety, anger, and fear.' "

Claudius decided this was baloney. He gave her a cunning look. If it meant he got more attention and goodies, he'd play along. If it didn't earn him extra treats, then Annie would pay in spades. Past lives or no past lives.

With which prophecy of trouble to come, he trotted off happily in the direction of the broom closet. There was a small brush that needed chewing.

By ten o'clock next morning, Annie was halfway through her usual chores. Claudius had been fed and taken for his walk. She let him out into the fenced side yard while she did a quick laundry and washed the kitchen floor.

The morning quiet was usually broken by the sound of birds and Claudius's barking—generally when some hapless jogger chanced by, and his police dog training kicked in. (Every jogger being an escaped felon he felt it his sworn duty to announce to the world at large.)

But this morning, it was different. There was the constant whine of George's chain saw. Just after eight, he'd pulled up in his truck and went straight to work in the woods. The sound of the saw ripped through the warm summer air, punctuated by the occasional thud of a tree hitting the ground. Then more sawing, thumping, and crashing.

Joanne, George's young blond wife, drove up around eleven with a hamper of snacks and liquid refreshment. She waved as she passed the house and drove into the woods. A short while later, she left, then George's truck rumbled away, loaded with logs, only to return an hour later, empty. Then more sawing, trees crashing, the roar of the chipper . . .

Meanwhile, Annie reveled in being able to shower and run the washer at the same time. There was plenty of water now. She kept an eye on Claudius, hoping the amulet and the power of the Pyramids would accomplish a miracle, and that he'd turn into a golden retriever or a Pekingese, at least by nature.

Unfortunately, this didn't happen, at least not that she noticed. It occurred to her that his nature might be more complicated than she thought. Maybe he'd suffered angst in one of his past lives. Maybe his aura needed balancing.

Then midway through the second day of the tree work, around eleven-fifteen, soon after Joanne arrived with her hamper, the chain saw stopped abruptly. All went eerily quiet.

At first Annie didn't think anything of it. There were any number of reasons George could have stopped work: he needed to sharpen the chain, or was clearing brush, or had just stopped for a breather.

But Claudius was standing on his hind legs, whining and staring out the window toward the woods.

Something was wrong.

So she decided to take him for a walk out back and make sure George was okay. Not that she was really worried, she told herself, clipping on Claudius's leash and following him at a brisk pace that had her panting down the back path and around the side of the house.

Five minutes later, she came upon Joanne looking very upset. George had his back to her. He was swearing. A patch of sweat had soaked through his shirt between the shoulders. He turned, and Annie saw that he was holding a bloody T-shirt to his arm.

"My God, what happened?"

"No big deal," he said. "I cut myself. The saw jumped up when I hit a knot. Happens sometimes."

"It's my fault," Joanne confessed. "If I hadn't gotten in the way, you wouldn't—"

"I'm *fine!*" He brushed past them both and went to his truck. He got out a first-aid kit and bandaged his arm, while Joanne continued to worry aloud that he should see a doctor right away. But he insisted he was fine and went back to work.

After another few minutes of wrangling did no good—by now he was cutting up another log and loading it on the truck—Joanne drove off, looking upset.

Annie decided that whatever had happened, George was clearly in no mood for company, so she went back to the house.

She spent the next hour or two taking inventory in the antiques shop in the barn. Occasional customers stopped in, mostly browsers—but she sold a set of copper pots and an old blue-painted cupboard, not exactly big money, but better than nothing.

Meanwhile, Claudius snoozed behind the counter. Once in a while, his back legs scrabbled like mad on the floor and he growled under his breath, reliving his all too few glory days as Rin Tin Tin of the New Hampshire Prison Canine unit.

Later on, after dealing sternly with him over a twenty-five-pound bag of bird seed he'd ripped open and strewn all over the kitchen floor—she yelled and he stared impassively, promising nothing—(the power of the Pyramids was taking longer to work than the brochure had promised), Annie put him in the car and went off to have her hair done at LaKeisha's Salon d'Beauty.

It was impossible to explain having one's hair done to a dog, so she tied him up to the tree out front of the shop and gave him a rawhide bone to chew. Hopefully, this wouldn't take long, half an hour at most.

On the light blue salon wall near the cash register, next to a black and white poster of various fashionable hairdos, was a silver-framed photograph of a lovely woman with dark hair. She was wearing a low-cut dress.

Gloria Estafan.

LaKeisha had cut her hair. The photograph was autographed: "Fabulous! I owe it all to you! Fondly, Gloria."

LaKeisha, herself—Nefertiti with a couple of hundred

pounds added on, fore and aft, possessed a mysterious an-
cestry. Part Caribbean, Creole, African, and Native American, she spoke five languages. Today, she was resplendent in
a pale green silk caftan and matching turban.

Her earrings were gold bows with dangling jade hearts.
Her long nails were painted green, and studded with gold
glitter.

She wagged a plump finger at Annie. "Girl, you got some
serious split ends. If I had hair like that, I'd be wearing a
paper bag on my head."

Unanswerable. "Uh, I'd like a layered cut," Annie said.
"Not too much off. Nothing drastic."

"Hunh. Drastic is what you need, honey."

"Whatever."

LaKeisha believed a woman's hair was her crowning
glory, and that change was good. Blond one week, pink the
next, she saw no reason why her clientele shouldn't follow
her shining example.

"You oughta go blond," she said thoughtfully. "At least
add highlights. It'd make a new woman outta you. Know
what I mean?"

"I like my hair red."

"Well." LaKeisha pursed her lips. "What about highlights?"

"No."

"Fine, but don't go tellin' anyone I do your hair. It'd be
bad for business."

"Okay."

That settled, LaKeisha went to work, efficiently snipping
and combing Annie's rat's nest of red curls. After a little
while, she said, "Hey, I hear you had George Vining out
dowsing for a new well. How'd it go? Did he find water?"

"Yes, I've got plenty now."

"Ol' George knows what he's doin'." LaKeisha snipped
away, gazed at her handiwork, rolled her eye, and sighed
again.

Annie couldn't see the back of her head, but was sure that
by now she was half bald and LaKeisha was standing ankle
deep in red hair.

Meanwhile, Claudius glowered from outside the shop.

He'd finished the bone ten minutes ago. He pushed his nose against the plate-glass window and woofed loudly.

"What on earth is that?" asked LaKeisha, looking around in astonishment.

"My dog," Annie said.

"Well," said LaKeisha, evidently at a loss for words.

"Thank goodness he's stopped barking," Annie said.

Claudius's eyes narrowed infinitesimally. It was a hot day, and the front door of the shop was open. He'd heard every word. He opened his mouth and started barking louder than ever.

"Don't pay him no mind," LaKeisha said, turning the chair around. "That's what he wants. He'll shut up as soon as he realizes he's not going anywhere. Now that wife of George Vining's—Joanne—she's a piece of work, that one. Cut your heart out, soon as look at you."

Claudius kept barking. He was losing patience. He wanted to go home or at the very least come inside and have a treat.

Finally, with LaKeisha's permission, Annie brought him inside the shop. He lay down by the chair and put his nose on his paws.

LaKeisha snipped another inch or two off and said, "That's better. Now we can hear ourselves think."

The woman in the next chair was having a facial. Her face was covered with a thick layer of LaKeisha's special cold cream. She glanced over a copy of *People* magazine, an old one with Puff Daddy and Jennifer Lopez on the cover. As luck would have it, she happened to be Joanne Vining's cleaning lady.

"Joanne Vining's as mean as they come," the woman said knowingly. "Why George married her I'll never know."

LaKeisha laughed. "Like most men, ol' George was thinking with what's below the belt. Won't do him a lick of good when she's done gone and spent every cent he has. He won't have a pot to you-know-what in or a window to throw it out of when she's through with him."

"Exactly," the other woman agreed. "Joanne's family died a couple of years ago. It was quite the scandal. Three accidents and a suicide in a matter of months. The last to go was her sister. She put a cake in the oven, then went upstairs and blew her head off."

"Good grief," said Annie, appalled. Claudius lifted his head and looked from the cleaning woman back to Annie. His big ears twitched.

LaKeisha gave a wise, seen-it-all smile. "No way anyone blows off the back of her head with a shotgun. Can't be done. It was murder, pure and simple. When Joanne buried her sister, she inherited the whole enchilada. Then when the money ran out, she set her sights on poor ol' George. He never knew what hit him."

"I hear Joanne sleeps with anyone who'll ask her and a good many who don't," said the woman in cold cream.

"Like who and how many?" asked Annie.

"Ed Curtis," the woman said knowingly. "Works over at the bank. He's rather good-looking in a cheap sort of way. Then there's Fred McKinney at the Mobil station, the mechanic with the Elvis hairdo. Joanne gets her oil changed a lot." She sighed. "Poor George. He's not long for this world. That land he owns on the other side of town—realtors want it for a big mall. They say he's been offered two million, but he won't sell."

"That'll change once he's six feet under," LaKeisha predicted. She handed Annie a mirror. "You look better than you ought to. It ain't easy, clipping all those itty, bitty, curly split ends. Now don't go using any of that crappy, supermarket shampoo like you been doing. That's what got you into trouble. Use my organic shampoo. I make it outta herbs and roots. It's powerful stuff." It was common knowledge that LaKeisha didn't patronize any of your garden-variety, A.M.A. doctors. She went to a witch doctor in South Lee.

"Oh, uh, I don't know," said Annie, peering in the mirror. Her head did look neater. Several inches shorter, and not a split end in sight. She ignored the disdainful look Claudius was giving her. What did he know about hairdos, anyway.

"On the house," LaKeisha said, handing her a bottle of homemade shampoo. It was pale green, with what looked like a marijuana leaf on the label. "Don't say I never gave you nothin'. So how about doin' me a favor? I like ol'

George. Talk to him about his wife. He'll listen to you. You got a reputation for solvin' crimes."

"Maybe," Annie said. The thought of saying anything to George made her wilt. How do you walk up to someone and say, "By the way, your wife might be trying to kill you?"

Besides, what proof did she have? When you got right down to it, all she had was beauty parlor gossip—which, along with a buck and a quarter, would get her a cup of coffee. So, pondering the likely outcome of interfering in what was essentially none of her business, she paid LaKeisha, added a large tip, and taking Claudius with her, went home.

She washed her hair with LaKeisha's special shampoo, with the result that Claudius tried to lick her ear off and had to be locked out of her bedroom. Whereupon, he sat in the upstairs hall and whined all night long.

In the morning, she phoned LaKeisha. "Are you sure you didn't give me some kind of love potion by mistake?"

LaKeisha laughed. "No, it's shampoo. Didn't I tell you to rinse real good? It's powerful stuff. You don't rinse, half the dogs in town will be chasin' you." While Annie thought that over, LaKeisha said, "Hey, did you talk to ol' George yet?"

"Maybe we should just let sleeping dogs lie."

LaKeisha snorted. "You're gonna let that wife of his get away with murder, that's what you're gonna do!" With that, she hung up.

For the next twenty-four hours Annie continued to brood about what LaKeisha had said, and what, if anything, to say to George, who by now was all but done clearing away the dead trees. Friday arrived, and coward that she was, she still hadn't made up her mind. To add to her discomfort, a small voice in the back of her mind warned that George's accident the other day could well have been an attempt by Joanne to kill him that had gone awry.

The phone rang.

Speak of the devil. It was George. He and Joanne were giving a party. Would Annie like to come? At first she was going to decline, but something in George's voice changed her mind. Maybe he wanted someone at the party he could talk to—someone who wasn't squandering his hard-earned money.

So Saturday night, Annie wriggled into her good black dress, screwed her grandmother's pearl studs in her ears, and locked Claudius in the kitchen with a bone and a bowl of water for the evening. He was nothing if not predictable, and could be counted on to eat anything remotely edible and a great deal that wasn't. She'd learned the hard way, if he could get his jaws around something, he'd swallow it. With the pantry locked and the kitchen counters clean, however, there wasn't much he could get into.

When she arrived at the Vining house, she saw that it was lit up like the Hindenburg before Lakehurst, New Jersey—with guests' cars parked up and down the narrow street. Soft music wafted from the house's open windows.

She squeezed her elderly Volvo wagon between a BMW and a Lincoln SUV, straightened her hair, and checked her lipstick. Then she got out, made sure she didn't have anything on backward, and walked up to the front door.

Inside, Joanne was holding court by the living-room fireplace. Several men were ogling her, and no wonder. Her purple dress was exceedingly skimpy. The hem came to mid-thigh, and the top was held up, barely, by spaghetti straps. She looked as if she didn't have anything on underneath.

"How nice to see you," she gushed, kissing the air by Annie's cheek. "Don't you look nice. Such a change from the jeans and T-shirt you usually wear. Well, cheese, crackers, fondue, and wine are on the table over there. I'm sure you know everyone."

After a little more small talk, most of which was patently insincere on Joanne's part, Annie ambled off to get herself a glass of wine and some cheese and crackers. The fondue, when sampled, tasted peculiar. It was obvious that Joanne had tossed in all the refrigerator leftovers.

The cheese looked edible, at least. Imported Brie and delicious, she decided, selecting another cracker or two. She hadn't had much dinner. Then she went off to talk to George, at the far end of the room, moodily downing a Coors and looking as if he wished he were a million miles away. He was sporting a bandage over his left eye.

"What happened to you?" she asked.

"Funniest damn thing," he said. "I was on my way to town yesterday, and suddenly no brakes. Damn pedal went straight to the floor. My truck hit a stone wall. No lasting damage, though, thank God. Just a headache."

"Good heavens," Annie said. "You could have been killed."

"Well, I wasn't." He smiled, looked a little uncomfortable, and tugged his tie loose. "Joanne's happy tonight, like a pig in clover. Parties are her thing, not mine."

"Where would you rather be?" she asked.

"In the woods, up in a deer blind. Wrong time of year, of course. I've done a lot of bow hunting, although lately I'd rather take photographs." He gave her a sheepish grin. "Guess I'm gettin' old."

Annie sipped her wine and wondered how Joanne felt about murder.

"I've seen some wonderful things in the woods," he went on. "Owls will fly right past you, after you sit quiet for a time. They don't even see you. Foxes, fisher cats, raccoons, deer. Unless the wind's right, they can't catch your scent."

She nodded. "So I've heard."

"A couple of years ago about 2:00 A.M., I was up a tree, and this young buck comes by, eating moss, sweet as you please. Two nubs for antlers, the rest hadn't come in yet. I always hang my bow on a string. It hangs down the trunk of the tree so I don't shoot myself by mistake. Anyway, the string's hanging down, and this buck walks up and starts blowing it back and forth, playing with it." George paused with a chuckle. "He looked so funny, right below me, playing with that string, I had a hard time keeping from laughing out loud. Then he just walked off after a few minutes. I couldn't shoot him. Fact is, I haven't killed anything since then. Use a camera, instead. I make miniature forest scenes." He gestured toward the back hall. "Come to the den, I'll show you what I mean."

George was a artist. The den walls were hung with display boxes, cunningly lit to reveal the contents. He'd carved each forest animal—so real it was almost frightening—here a gray fox loped through the snow, its tiny tracks leading off into the trees. In the foreground, a bright blob of red in the snow and what looked like hare entrails with more tracks nearby. The tracks led back to where the fox was dragging its prey off to its den.

Another box featured a raccoon in a tall pine tree with a fisher cat below. A third, a red squirrel on an old tree stump. While he chewed pinecones, an owl flew overhead.

"These are wonderful," Annie said, astonished at how lifelike they were. He'd caught each detail exactly.

But the pièce de résistance was the dollhouse in the corner. George and Joanne's home. You couldn't mistake it for anything else. That dark-stained, brooding shape, the central chimney. Two-story, twelve over twelve window panes. The tiny brick walk laid in herringbone pattern to the paneled front door, even the vegetable garden out back.

And inside—Annie walked around to look and stared in amazement. Each detail reproduced, so lifelike it looked real, as if George and Joanne had just stepped away for a moment.

"Had a devil of a time getting the windows right," he said. "Had to make the panes five by seven inches, the way they did back then. The chimney needed the larger-size bricks, like the ones they used before 1750. The clapboards— feather-edged, just like the real thing. The paneling—raised and fielded wainscoting, like that over there." He pointed to the den paneling. "Even got the double-batten front door with the big brass lock."

"It's perfect." Annie examined the four rooms downstairs. The dining room with a tiny corner cupboard and scalloped shelves holding a wee collection of Staffordshire china. The William and Mary–style tavern table with Spanish feet. Windsor chairs, the tin chandelier, the tiny oriental rug.

It was magnificent, a work of art.

The kitchen was no less perfect. Here everything was set for a party. Food displayed on the table and counters, ready to set out for a buffet in the dining room. A turkey on a platter, a roast pig with a wee apple in its mouth. Trays of appetizers, even a fondue.

Upstairs were four bedrooms and two baths. To the left, the master bedroom. Or maybe it was Joanne's, for she was seated at a dressing table, combing her blond hair in front of a mirror. A four-poster bed, brass wall sconces, beautiful clothes peeping from an armoire's half-opened door.

George's own figure stood in the upstairs hall, with his hand on the bedroom's tiny doorknob.

"Wonderful," Annie said, breathing a delighted sigh. "It's perfect."

Naturally, George didn't agree. He felt he needed to fix a few things. "More landscaping in the garden out back. I'll get around to it one of these days."

Late that night when she climbed into bed, Annie found that she couldn't get Joanne out of her head. The admiring glances she'd been getting at the party. Flirting brazenly with other men right under George's nose.

As if he didn't matter.

As if he were already dead.

The next afternoon, and by now thoroughly upset and sure that minding her own business wasn't an option, Annie decided to confront Joanne. She wanted to save George's life. She wanted to keep Joanne from committing murder. Taking Claudius along for reinforcement, she drove over, marched up to the front door, and rang the bell.

Joanne looked surprised at her unexpected appearance, but Annie said she needed to talk.

"What about the dog?" asked Joanne, making no attempt to disguise her contempt for Claudius. What if he lifted his leg somewhere.

"He's a trained guard dog," Annie said flatly, making it clear that if Joanne tried anything, she'd regret it. Soon they were seated in the living room with a pitcher of lemonade and a plate of store-bought molasses cookies.

Joanne's glance strayed to Claudius, who was sniffing the goodies and licking his chops. She frowned.

Annie pulled him away, then on second thought gave him a cookie. Anything to keep him quiet for a few minutes.

"So," said Joanne, looking bored. "Did you need to speak to George about something? He's out back in the garden."

"You're the one I want to talk to," Annie said. There was no point in beating about the bush. "I know what you're up to. If anything happens to George, I'm going to the police."

Joanne's mouth opened and closed, but nothing came out.

Then, her voice a little high and fluttery, she said, "What on earth are you talking about?" All the while watching Annie closely, as if wondering exactly how much she knew.

"I'm warning you. I mean every word."

"You're crazy. I can't imagine where you'd get the idea that I'd hurt my husband . . . that I'd murder him."

"I know what I saw in the woods the other day. George is an experienced woodsman, yet he cut himself. You said you got in his way—"

"Bumped his arm, for heaven's sake. I was holding a log for him—the saw jumped. He told you what happened. He hit a knot."

"What about the truck accident? He said his brakes failed. What did you do, get Elvis to cut the brake line?"

There was an awkward pause. Annie could see Joanne changing her pose from shocked surprise to incredulous outrage. Joanne's hands trembled, and she set her glass down on the table with a bang.

"I've heard just about enough," she snapped. "Get out!" Whatever else she was, Joanne wasn't a good liar.

Annie rose, relieved to be going. "Don't do anything stupid."

"Oh, I'd better not kill George, or you'll do what? Accuse me of murder?"

"That's right."

In short order, Annie found herself out on the front stoop with Claudius, who'd managed a creditable job of licking the cookie plate clean while they were arguing.

The door slammed behind them. Kicked out. Fine. She could live with that. But by now she was determined to see this through to the bitter end. If Joanne wouldn't listen to reason, the only alternative was to warn George.

She went around the side of the house to the backyard. Here George had done himself proud. There were raised beds of carefully tended vegetables, everything neat and tidy. As she walked down the path she heard digging, but he was nowhere to be seen. She had to walk up and down the beds, looking in all directions before she spotted him.

He was digging a new bed in the corner of the garden by

the edge of the lawn. Noticing her arrival, he leaned on his shovel.

"Annie, what's up—how's the dog?"

"Fine, but I've got bad news. Maybe you should sit down."

"What's the matter?"

This was incredibly difficult. She swallowed hard, twice, and said, "Don't take this wrong, but Joanne might be trying to kill you."

"That's ridiculous. She wouldn't hurt a fly."

"Only if it got in her way. Wake up, George, she's dangerous!"

He mopped his brow with his bandaged arm and winced. "What started all this? My accident?"

"More or less. The thing is Joanne's years younger than you; and, I'm sorry, but she has a reputation for sleeping around. It's a small town. People talk. You have money and prime real estate. It's no secret that she wants you to sell."

He scrounged in his pocket for a cigarette and lit up. Annie watched, wondering how long it would take him to get mad and order her to get the hell out, too.

But he just looked depressed, squinting at her through the spiral of smoke. "Well," he said finally, "if it'll make you feel any better, I'll talk to Joanne and get to the bottom of this. Maybe think about changing my will, too. That would put a stop to the gossip. There's no reason to get all steamed up about nothing, Annie. Nothing's happened. I'm hale and hearty and intend to stay that way."

Still worried and with a sinking feeling that she'd made matters worse, Annie left him to his labors in the backyard and took Claudius home. All that night and for the next week or so, she couldn't help wondering if she'd be reading about George's sudden demise in the paper. She scanned the obituaries, but his name wasn't there. Nothing. Things seemed to be at a stalemate.

Then, by the end of August, in the way of these things, it became public knowledge that Joanne had packed up, bag and baggage, and left town.

George made the best of things, and fortunately, the town

benefited as he decided to deed his prime acreage to the Conservation Commission. He also donated the model he'd made of his house to the historical society, where it was displayed with great fanfare at a reception in his honor.

Annie took Claudius. Well, why not. Much to her surprise and delight, he'd been on his best behavior lately. The amulet's Pyramid power must have worked, although he'd ditched it after only a few days. Still, it seemed to have had a residual effect. He hadn't chewed the covers off any books or magazines in at least a week; and he didn't look as if he was thinking swear words at her, at least not to her face.

It seemed as if almost the entire town had shown up for the reception. As Annie made her way through the crowd she spotted LaKeisha, looking larger than life in a bright pink jumpsuit. Her hair was done up in mauve and green cornrows. She had earrings and nails to match.

"I made the cake from scratch," LaKeisha announced with pardonable pride. "Never use mixes. Carrot, real cream cheese icing. Eight eggs. You got a cholesterol problem, don't eat any."

The cake was decorated with a border of roses and spiky green leaves. It said, "Thank you, George."

Annie regarded it with deep suspicion, wondering what else LaKeisha had put in it besides the eggs.

The knife flashed as LaKeisha cut the cake and handed it to the townsfolk, while Claudius sidled up and sniffed with great interest. He was starving. He needed cake. Before long, he'd managed to sneak a piece and was chomping happily.

But Annie had noticed the dollhouse, standing in all its glory on a table nearby. It was just as fascinating as the first time she'd seen it, although a close look revealed that Joanne's little figure was gone from the upstairs bedroom.

George's tiny figure was there, working in the dollhouse backyard among the tiny flowers, vegetables, and raised beds of tomatoes, cabbages, and pole beans.

But the new bed he'd been digging wasn't there, just a tiny, green lawn. Which Annie thought odd, considering what a perfectionist George was about getting everything exactly right.

So where was the new flower bed?

At that point, he walked up and smiled. "How are you and Claudius?"

"Fine," she said. Claudius had already scoffed a second piece of cake and was sauntering around, licking his chops. This was turning out to be a pretty good day. Forbidden goodies at just the right height. He didn't even have to get up on his hind legs to steal them.

Annie, meanwhile, was thinking hard, and she didn't like what she was thinking. No flower bed, which, in a pinch, could have been a handy grave.

They stood there, admiring the dollhouse. George accepting praise, pats on the back, beaming at all the oohs and aahs.

Annie had gone very quiet. Finally, when the crowd thinned and they were alone, she said, "I had it backward, didn't I? It was you all along. You were planning to kill Joanne."

A moment of tense silence, then his shoulders sagged. "She's gone to her cousin's in Boston. You're right. I tried to kill her with the chain saw that afternoon in the woods. I missed, then you showed up before I could finish her off. She thought it was just an accident. And why not, I'm the one who got cut."

"What about the truck accident?"

He shrugged. "A practice run. There's a hill and a bad curve not far from the house. I planned to knock her out first, then put her behind the wheel and jump out just before the truck left the road and hit a tree. Well, I didn't like having to kill her, but what the hell else could I do? She was bleeding me white. But thanks to you, Annie, she found out what I was up to, got scared, and took off. It's better this way. I don't have to murder her. She's out of my life for good and I stay out of jail."

"Well, I can live with that," Annie said.

"Me, too," said George.

Claudius sauntered back to the table and eyed the last of the cake.

"Go on, dog," LaKeisha said, shooing him away impatiently. "There's nothing here for you!"

He decided to try charm, not his long suit, but in this sit-

uation beggars could hardly be choosers. He leered at her and
wagged his tail. He was friendly, very friendly.

"You're some kinda dog, you know that?" With a laugh,
she handed over the last piece, and he swallowed it whole.

THE CHOCOLATE KIDNAPPING CLUE

A Lee McKinney Mystery Story

JoAnna Carl

JoAnna Carl makes her debut with this story, featuring Lee McKinney. Imagine the difficulty JoAnna faced in researching all those delicious chocolates. Lee will appear in her first novel, *The Chocolate Cat Caper*, soon.

People think working in a resort town is like one long vacation. And it might be, if the tourists would only stay home.

I stood behind the counter of TenHuis Chocolade ("Handmade chocolates in the Dutch tradition") and hated the girl on the other side. I'd been working for my aunt and uncle, Nettie and Phil TenHuis, for only a week, and this girl had been in every day, apparently with the sole objective of ruining my life.

Her name, according to her credit card, was Alana Fairchild Hyden. She would have been pretty if she hadn't been so thin. She was about my age—which was sixteen that year—and she had dark hair and big brown eyes, which she emphasized with liner, mascara, and shadow until they dominated her face.

Alana Fairchild Hyden was about the only teenaged customer TenHuis Chocolade ever drew, since Aunt Nettie and Uncle Phil's candy wasn't the kind you'd eat in the movies. Oh, they had some inexpensive items, like a milk chocolate sailboat on a stick, but most of their stock was luxury chocolates and fancy dipped fruits. One bonbon cost as much as two Hershey bars.

But Alana Fairchild Hyden came in every day and bought half a pound of bonbons and truffles, a different assortment every day. She did this, I'd decided, to torture me. She got this smirk on her face, and she went through the whole display case, pointing.

"Now what's that one?"

Since I was new, I'd have to consult the list. "Creamy, European-style caramel in dark chocolate."

"How about the one behind it?"

I'd look at the list again. "Raspberry cream."

"No, the one with the yellow dot."

"Lemon canache."

"Yuk! How about the white chocolate with the little nutty things on top?"

That one I knew, because it was my favorite. "Amadeus," I said. Then I winced. She'd goaded me until I was nervous, and that was when my tongue twisted itself into knots and the wrong word came out. "I mean, Amaretto."

Of course, Alana Fairchild Hyden laughed. "'Amadeus'! How funny! How about the one at the back of that row?"

Back to the list. "Frangelico."

"Frangelico? Just what the hell is that?"

"I'll ask." I turned toward the big window that overlooked the sparkling white room where middle-aged women in white aprons and hair nets produced the chocolates.

"Oh, never mind! You'd think people would train their employees. Give me four of the fudgy ones and four square ones with the white centers. Then I'll have eight of the dark chocolate balls. The rummy ones."

Seething, I put her chocolates—four double fudge and four Bailey's Irish Cream bonbons and eight Jamaican rum truffles—in a little white box with "TenHuis Chocolade" in the corner in classy type, and I tied the box with a blue ribbon. I ran her credit card through the imprinter, then pushed the receipt and the card across the counter.

"Here's your crevasse card." I tried to pretend I'd said it right, but Alana Fairchild Hyden laughed.

"You are such a sketch!" she said.

I tried to look blank. Pleasant would have been more than I could manage. She went out, still laughing, leaving the shop empty, except for the other clerk, Lindy Bradford, and me.

"What a bitch," Lindy said.

I felt crushed, as well as angry. Alana Fairchild Hyden completely destroyed my confidence. It's just a stupid sales clerk job, I told myself, and I can't do it right because I can't talk like a normal person.

"Don't worry about it, Lee," Lindy said. "She acts rude just to cover up her own inferiority complex."

I gulped hard and decided it was safe to talk. "Who is she?"

"Oh, she's one of *the* Hydens. They have that big house at the lake end of Orchard Street. Her grandfather made his money building airplanes. My mother says her mother is trying to spend every cent her grandfather ever made. They're summer people."

In the week I'd been working at TenHuis Chocolade, I'd discovered there were three social classes in Warner Pier— locals, summer people, and tourists. Locals either lived there year-round, or they owned businesses there and spent most of the year in the area. Summer people owned homes—what us Texans would call "cabins," but what these Michigan people called "cottages"—and spent several months there each year. Tourists came for periods ranging from a day to a month and rented rooms in the motels, inns, or bed and breakfasts.

So Alana Fairchild Hyden was a "summer person," not a "tourist." I sighed. "I guess she'll be in every day until I leave in August."

"Who knows?" Lindy reached into the showcase and straightened the Italian cherry creams. "I feel kinda sorry for her, I guess. She always comes in alone." She shot me a side-long glance. "Hey, three of us are going into Holland to the late show tonight. Ask your uncle if you can come. We'll be home by twelve-thirty."

"Not tonight," I said. "But thanks." Luckily, three people came in right then. I couldn't tell if they were tourists or summer people, but I was glad for the distraction. Not that I didn't appreciate Lindy acting friendly. I just wasn't ready to be friendly back. While Lindy told the new customers that we didn't carry candy bars, I stood there miserably and wished I was on the beach. Alone. Without the bag lady I'd seen that morning.

The beach was the best place to cry. That's why I resented sharing it, especially with a bag lady.

The bag lady had scared me. She looked like a homeless old hag, the kind you might see under a bridge in a big city. I hadn't expected to run into someone like that on a Lake Michigan beach, down the road from Aunt Nettie and Uncle Phil's house.

I kept telling myself she was harmless. But I still resented her. As I said—the beach was the best place I had to cry, and I didn't want to meet anybody.

For one thing, I had always lived on the Texas plains. I was used to lots of sky, and Michigan's tall trees made me feel closed in and choked up. But from the beach I could see Lake Michigan stretching west to somewhere beyond the horizon, and it was easier to breathe.

But all I wanted to do down there was sit behind a clump of beach grass and let the tears roll. I had a lot to cry about that summer. I'd lost my family and my friends and been exiled to work in a chocolate factory.

My privacy had gone at the same time. Now I was living with my Aunt Nettie and Uncle Phil, and the walls of their house—which had been built in 1904—were too thin to hide sniffling. If I cried in bed at night, Aunt Nettie would creep upstairs to be sympathetic. If I declined her sympathy—after all, she was almost a stranger to me—they sat downstairs and talked about how unhappy I was. I could hear every word. Why couldn't they leave me alone?

Then there was my stupid speech problem. Every time I opened my mouth the wrong word came out. So the last thing I wanted to do was talk to some scary old lady. I wanted to be alone, and the beach had seemed to be the answer.

I'd pretended I was planning to go out for track and told Aunt Nettie and Uncle Phil I had to run a mile on the beach every morning. I didn't go to work in the chocolate shop until one, when Uncle Phil went in, so that worked.

I would get up when they were eating breakfast—7:00 A.M. or some horrible hour. About seven-thirty Aunt Nettie would head for the factory. Aunt Nettie was a solid, heavyset woman with fair hair and light blue eyes. She was a descendant of the Dutch who settled West Michigan before the Civil

War, and she would have looked right at home in wooden shoes and a winged cap. She supervised making the chocolates.

Uncle Phil was of pure Dutch descent, too, but he was one of these thin Dutchmen with a turned-up nose, the kind Rembrandt used to paint. He had a big desk in the corner of their bedroom, and after breakfast he'd go in there to do paperwork.

I'd wash the dishes, because my mother had told me to be a good girl and help Aunt Nettie and Uncle Phil. And as miserable as I was at their house, I didn't want them to send me back to Texas. This whole thing was my mother and dad's fault, and I didn't want to see them any sooner than I had to.

By eight-fifteen every morning I'd tell Uncle Phil I was going to the beach, and every morning he'd say, "Watch the traffic on the curve." I'd walk a quarter of a mile down the Lake Shore Road, looking carefully both ways before I crossed the road near the blind curve, and I'd turn at the sign that said PUBLIC ACCESS and slip and slide down the sandy path to the beach thirty feet below. Later in the day, I had discovered, the beach could be crowded. But that early the shoreline was still cloaked by the heavy shade from the trees on top of the bank, and there was rarely anyone but me around.

From the public area you could walk on the beach for at least two miles either north or south. Of course, the public area was only about a hundred feet wide, so for most of those miles you were on private property. I didn't think anybody would complain as long as I stayed at the edge of the water and didn't go near the fancy houses on the bluff above, the ones with the expensive views and the major engineering systems of walls and terraces needed to keep the lake from washing the houses away.

Uncle Phil was always telling me that the beach was different when he was my age. In those days, he said, most of the houses were smaller, not so fancy. They were owned by teachers, carpenters, factory workers—people who were willing to rough it in simple little cottages for the summer. Now the area had been taken over by millionaires, I guess.

Uncle Phil had pointed out the biggest house—from the beach it looked like three stories of glass boxed in by redwood decks—and said it belonged to the president of the Lally Corporation. When I didn't act impressed, he told me they owned the company that made my favorite tennis shoes. Cool.

Aunt Nettie and Uncle Phil lived in a house that had been built by my great-grandfather, who was Uncle Phil's grandfather. It was on the inland side of Lake Shore Drive, so we couldn't see the lake. In Warner Pier that meant we gained points with the "locals," but lost points with the "summer people." It was a complicated system.

When I got to the beach I usually walked a quarter of a mile south to my hidey-hole, a niche behind some beach grass in front of the Lally house, and I hid and waited for the tears to come. Instead, on that particular morning this bag lady had walked into my life.

I was sitting with my knees up against my chest and my face down on my knees, and I didn't see or hear her until she spoke.

"Young woman," she said. "Are you all right?"

I scrambled up. For a minute I was sure one of the Lally family had come down, discovered a trespasser, and called the cops. Then I thought the woman must be a trespasser herself.

She looked like a bag lady because she was carrying a big brown plastic trash bag. She wore a hat, the limp-brimmed kind that you can throw in the laundry, but this one hadn't been washed lately. She had on a poplin windbreaker and blue jeans. The face under the hat was weathered, and her eyes were that faded blue that makes people look blind. She was old. Probably at least ninety. (Or that's what I thought when I was sixteen. Later I found out she was in her late sixties that year.)

The old woman shook the bag at me. "Are you all right?"

"Yes," I said. Suddenly I was afraid. She looked so scary, and we were alone on the beach. I blurted a question out. "Do you live here?"

She looked sharply at me.

"Am I trashing?" I said. "I mean, am I trespassing?"

A strange smile passed over the woman's face, like a cloud racing past the sun. "I suppose we're both trespassing, but as long as we stay on the beach and don't build a fire, the Lallys aren't likely to complain. And I certainly hope you're not trashing. Getting rid of trash is my goal in life. I only wish it were the Lallys' goal."

She bent, picked up a beer car, and chucked it into her sack. Then she gestured in the direction of the big house high on the bank above us. I looked up, and I could see a young guy standing at the window. He was staring at us, not moving. "That son of theirs is staying there alone—judging from the alleged music that blares over the neighborhood and from the cars that block the road. His parties overflow onto the beach. I find amazing things."

She looked at me narrowly. "You're sure you're all right? I always wonder about girls I find outside the Lally house. But you look healthier than the skinny little dark one I saw last week." Her weathered face scrunched up into a dried apple.

I looked at my watch. "I'm fine," I said. "I don't have anything to do with the Lally house. But I'm going to be late to walk. I mean, to work. I mean, I've got to get hum. Home." I jumped over a clump of beach grass to get past her, and I headed up the beach at a trot. Which showed how scared I was. I'd never have called Uncle Phil and Aunt Nettie's house "home" normally.

I guess I was panting when I got back to the house, because Uncle Phil asked me if anything was wrong.

"No," I said. "But there was an odd woman on the beach. She looked like a bag lady."

Uncle Phil laughed. "You must have run into Inez Deacon. She'll think that's hilarious."

"Who is she?"

"She's a retired teacher. She lives in that little gray house right before the curve. She had heart surgery several years ago, so the doctors told her to walk several miles a day. She picks up trash as she walks."

I thought about that. "I guess that's a good thing to do. But she looks sort of scary. Don't tell her I said so!"

"I won't. I'll introduce you when I have a chance."

The next morning, however, I introduced myself. I'd been hiding out behind the beach grass again, and this time Mrs. Deacon scrunched on the sand, so I heard her coming. My Texas grandmother—my dad was a Texan—insisted on teaching me old-fashioned Southern manners, so I came out and introduced myself.

"I wondered if you weren't Phil's niece," she said. "They were excited about having you up for the summer."

"They're being awful nice to me."

"Are you meeting any young people, Lee?"

"Well, there's Lindy Bradford. She works in the store."

"I know Lindy. She's no intellectual giant, but she's a nice girl."

"She's really cute."

"Yes, Lindy is cute, and she has a bubbly personality. Of course, she'll never have your looks."

I was astonished. My "looks" consisted of long skinny legs, a flat chest, narrow shoulders, and eyes and mouth so pale they might as well not have existed. If I had a good feature, it was my hair—a light blond that didn't need "touching up."

I must have gaped, because Mrs. Deacon frowned. "Surely your parents have told you you're going to be a beautiful woman, Lee. They've been remiss if they haven't. You're going to have the sort of looks that attract attention, and you should be prepared to deal with the problems that brings."

After that I adored Mrs. Deacon. I began to look forward to running into her. We'd chat about the birds on the beach and about the interesting rocks that the lake waves uncovered. Sitting on a driftwood log and looking out at those waves, I was able to tell her that my parents were getting a divorce, and that when I went back to Texas I'd be leaving the little town where I'd always lived and moving to Dallas, where my mother had a new job in a travel agency. I'd have to go to a new school that was eight times bigger than my old one, and I'd have to make all new friends. Mrs. Deacon assured me I would be able to do it, and for practice she suggested I accept the next invitation I got from Lindy.

Sometimes Mrs. Deacon and I talked so long I didn't have time to hide behind the grass and cry.

Work began to go better, too. Uncle Phil discovered I could add right, even if I couldn't talk straight, and he started allowing me to balance the cash register when we closed at 9:00 P.M. I learned to pronounce the shop's name as "Ten-Ice," which wasn't quite the way Uncle Phil did it, but was closer than "Tin-Hahs," the way my Texas mouth wanted to shape the word. I memorized all the bonbons and truffles, and I could rattle them off without saying "model Pyrenees," instead of "mocca pyramid" or "Midol liquor," instead of "melon-flavored Midori liqueur."

Except when the customer was Alana Fairchild Hyden. I couldn't say a word to her without stumbling over my tongue. Lindy knew how she affected me, and she tried to wait on her, but Alana would refuse to select something until Lindy was busy. Then she'd ask me a lot of questions in a loud voice and laugh when I goofed.

The last time she came in, I almost cried. After she left Lindy shook a fist at the door. "I hate that girl!" she said.

I parroted the advice Mrs. Deacon had given me. "I try not to waste my time hating her," I said, though a little voice inside admitted that I did hate Alana. "How does she get the money for all this candy?"

"Oh, her family's got all the money in the world, I guess. Her mother's in Europe this summer. With a boyfriend."

"Then who's she staying with?"

"I think there's a housekeeper."

"How does she eat that much chocolate and stay so thin?"

Lindy shrugged. "I don't know? Bulimia?"

The thought of someone eating the beautiful chocolates Aunt Nettie and the ladies worked so hard to make and then vomiting them up—well, it was nauseating. That made me feel a little bit sorry for Alana for real, not just pretending. But I almost wished she'd fall off the balcony of her family's big house and break her neck.

So I felt guilty the next day when I heard she'd been kidnapped.

There are no secrets in a town of twenty-five hundred, even when it grows by ten thousand tourists and summer people. The police and the FBI might keep Alana's kidnapping out of the newspapers and off the television, but the Hydens' housekeeper told the man from the lawn service, and within an hour everybody up and down Main Street knew.

The housekeeper hadn't missed Alana until about 8:00 A.M., when she got a phone call demanding ransom. She thought the call was a prank until she found Alana's bed empty and her sports car sitting at the foot of the drive with the door open, the headlights switched on and the battery dead.

"My brother says he saw Alana in the Dockster at 2:00 A.M.," Lindy told me excitedly. "It looks like they snatched her when she got home."

"I guess Alana won't get her chocolates today," I said.

Lindy and I were silent after that. In a way I felt a kinship with Alana. Her mother had shuffled her off to the big house in Warner Pier and ignored her for the summer while she went to Europe with a boyfriend. My mother had shuffled me off to an aunt and uncle in Michigan to work in a chocolate factory while she started a new job and got a divorce.

The difference was that the Hyden housekeeper obviously didn't care what happened to Alana, and my aunt and uncle did care what happened to me. They didn't let me hang out at a place with a reputation like the Dockster's until 2:00 A.M. They didn't let me run wild with an expensive sports car. When I cried at night, they worried about me, even if it annoyed me. Even my mother and my dad, I admitted, each called me once a week, even though I knew neither of them had any money for long-distance bills that summer.

And like all the TenHuis Chocolade employees, I was allowed two pieces of candy a day. I ate them, and I was not tempted to vomit them back up.

Aunt Nettie, Uncle Phil, and even my mother and dad came out looking pretty good next to Alana Fairchild Hyden's family.

I tried to express this the next morning, when I met Mrs. Deacon on the beach, right under the Lally house. "I do appreciate Aunt Nettie and Uncle Phil," I said. "But it's hard to tell them. It seems like nothing I say comes out right."

"So write them." She picked up the remains of a small,

white box, then turned to me and gestured with it. "If you can't tell people something face-to-face, then write it out. That way you can work it over until it suits you."

"Maybe."

"They'd be thrilled."

We might have gone on, but someone yelled at us from above.

"Get out of here!"

I looked up and saw the Lally boy leaping down the stairs toward us. The morning was cool, but he wore no shirt or shoes, just a pair of jeans. He was taking the stairs two at a time. His long, greasy hair was flying in the wind, and he continued to shriek at us.

"Scram! Get lost, you bitches! Get off our beach!"

Mrs. Deacon stood her ground, and I couldn't leave her. She merely looked at the Lally boy until he got to a little railed deck at the top of the final flight of stairs that led down to the beach. He stopped there, still cussing at us. Mrs. Deacon kept looking at him with a politely attentive expression, and he gradually quit talking.

"Young man, I wanted to thank you for omitting your usual music last night," she said.

"Get out," he said again. This time his voice was a low growl.

Mrs. Deacon nodded regally. She stuffed the little white box she was still holding into her trash bag, then stooped and picked up a beer can, revealing a blue ribbon that was embedded in the sand under it. She added the beer can and the blue ribbon to her trash sack, then walked slowly in the direction of the public access area, stopping to pick up more refuse—a soft-drink can, a package that had once held bratwurst, one flip-flop, a pleated candy cup, a potato-chip sack. I picked up a few things as well, and we meandered up the beach. I pretended I didn't notice that the Lally boy was still on the deck, glaring after us.

"He sure is rude," I said.

Mrs. Deacon shook her head. "I hate to think of what he's done to that house." We trudged up the path to the road, separated, and went to our homes, watching carefully for traffic on the blind curve.

The next morning was wet, but I wrapped up in a sweat-shirt and a rain jacket and headed for the beach as usual. I was just getting near the blind curve when I heard the roar of a car's engine. It was drawing closer, and it sounded as if it were gaining speed. The sound scared me. Ahead I saw Mrs. Deacon come to the end of her driveway. She looked toward the sound, and she stopped, too, waiting for the car to pass. I jumped into the bushes and got clean off the road. Both Mrs. Deacon and I were being careful to give the roaring car all the room it needed.

When the car came around the curve I saw that it was an old model, big and boxy and some dark color. It was gaining speed. I stood still, braving the possibility of poison ivy in the bar ditch, and waited for it to go by.

I will never forget what happened next. As the car drew near Mrs. Deacon, it swerved, ran up over the edge of the road, and came up into her drive.

It hit Mrs. Deacon a glancing blow. She went flying into the air, arms and legs lopped out like a rag doll.

I'm sure I screamed, but I must have stood still. The next thing I remember the car had gone past me. Then I was run-ning, running toward Mrs. Deacon and shrieking. "Help! Help! Help! Oh, someone! Help!"

Mrs. Deacon was lying in her own shrubbery. I had the sense not to touch her, and I ran to the nearest house, a neat white frame house between Mrs. Deacon's and Uncle Phil's. The woman who lived there called the ambulance, then got Uncle Phil, and the three of us waited for the sheriff's deputies and the rescue truck. I knelt beside Mrs. Deacon. I put my hand over hers, and I sobbed.

"He did it on purpose," I said. "He did it on purpose."

Later, at the Holland hospital, I repeated that to the sher-iff, and he nodded seriously. "I'm afraid you're right," he said. "The tread marks show that the car went right up into the driveway, and there's no sign he tried to put on his brakes. If you could just describe the car . . ."

But I couldn't say much about it. It was a big, old car and a dark color. I hadn't gotten a look at the driver.

Mrs. Deacon was still unconscious when the sheriff came and told us that they'd found a big, old, dark-colored car in a ditch a mile up the Lake Shore Drive. It had a dent in the right front fender. Unfortunately, it was a car that had been reported stolen an hour before Mrs. Deacon was hit.

"First that kidnapping, and now this," the sheriff said. "I tell you, Phil, maybe we have too many summer people and tourists around here. The tracks and all—well, it does look as if he stole the car and deliberately ran Mrs. Deacon down. But why would anybody want to do that?"

At 6:00 P.M. Mrs. Deacon's daughter got there from Detroit, and Uncle Phil and Aunt Nettie made me go home with them. I took a shower and got in bed, and for once I didn't object to Aunt Nettie coming in and talking to me after I got in bed. Mrs. Deacon was her friend, too. We grieved together.

"Why?" I said. "Why on earth would anybody want to hurt Mrs. Deacon?"

Aunt Nettie repeated the refrain. "Why, why in the world should something like this happen?"

Then I heard Uncle Phil come in the kitchen door. He was muttering angrily, and Aunt Nettie hugged me and went down.

Of course, I could hear every word she and Uncle Phil said. "What on earth are you grousing about, Phil?"

"I went over to check Inez's house, the way I told her daughter I would, and some dogs had gotten in her trash. They tore open some of those bags she collects. I'll have to go back in the morning and pick up the rest."

"Oh, Phil! And after what happened this morning."

After what happened this morning.

Somehow the words electrified me. What happened this morning was that somebody tried to kill Mrs. Deacon—and they might well have succeeded. And none of us could think of any reason for anybody to want to harm Mrs. Deacon.

But one person had threatened her. The Lally boy. I didn't even know his name. But he had run down the stairs and screamed at her, ordering the two of us off his family's bit of beach.

Mrs. Deacon and I had walked along that stretch of beach every morning for weeks, and he'd looked down at us from his three stories of glass, and he'd glared, but he'd never so much as come outside before. What had we done the day before that made him so angry? What had been different? And did this have any link to a pack of dogs tearing up the trash sacks that Mrs. Deacon filled on the beach?

Had Mrs. Deacon found something on the beach that had caused the Lally boy—or someone—to attack her?

Well, I'd been with her when the Lally boy came down and cussed at us. I didn't see anything odd. Just potato chip sacks, beer cans, boxes . . .

Oh, lordy! All of a sudden I remembered, and I sat straight up in bed. There had been one odd thing. Actually, two odd things. Maybe three.

But the idea seemed too fantastic. If I told the sheriff, he'd think I was crazy. He'd have to get a search warrant to check it out. And he'd never have the nerve. He'd have to have good evidence before he could search the Lally house.

If there was just a way to prove my suspicions were right.

I pictured the Lally house, with its entire lake side one big wall of glass. And I decided that anybody who lived in a glass house would have no secrets at night.

Downstairs Aunt Nettie and Uncle Phil had moved into their bedroom, and then Uncle Phil turned on the shower—the loud, old shower with the pipes that knocked. I slipped out of bed and into clothes—some black jeans, a navy sweatshirt, and a heavy jacket. I tied a black scarf on my head, took my tennis shoes in my hand, and walked softly down the stairs. The shower would cover any noise I made.

I crept out the kitchen door, put on my shoes, and started for the beach at a run. I wasn't going near the Lally house. I was simply going to look at it from below.

I was terrified of course. The trees. Those tall, scary Michigan trees were being tossed by the wind and might be hiding who knows what. I walked right down the middle of the Lake Shore Drive, staying as far as I could from the threat of bushes and trees on either side of the road. When I got to the access path, I slid down it.

The moon was nearly down to the western horizon and was behind a layer of clouds. Its reflection made a path on the water, but it was a faint path. The lake surf was fairly high. Lake Michigan surf never gets like the Pacific, of course. But that night the waves were coming in fast, one right on the heels of another, and they were noisy.

I told myself that was lucky. If the Lally boy was outside, he wouldn't be able to hear me. And it was too dark for him to see me. However, I found out that I couldn't see him either. The house was lighted from top to bottom—all three stories—but from the beach I was looking up at it, and all I could see was ceilings. I'd have to get closer.

I eyed the stairs that led up from the beach. Did I dare go up them? Then I really would be trespassing.

I stifled a laugh. Trespassing? If I was right, the Lally boy had tried to kill Mrs. Deacon. What was trespassing compared to that? I started up the stairs.

The first dozen steps led up to the deck on top of the wall, the wall that was the first line of defense against the lake's winter waves. After that the steps were stone, and they switched back and forth, crisscrossing the terraced hillside. The whole flight must have been sixty feet high.

Each floor of the house, including the basement, had a deck overlooking the lake. As my head came up even with the basement floor, I stopped and looked in. I saw nothing. Nobody. The house wasn't wide, and I could see into every room. The entire lowest level was empty. I tiptoed on up the stairs, to the deck that was outside the first floor, again stopping with my head just over floor level, so that I could see in, but hoping that my low profile would help keep me invisible from inside the brightly lighted room. And then I saw the Lally boy.

Two rooms opened off that deck, and he was in the left-hand one, a large L-shaped room with a dining table in the narrow section. Living-room furniture in the larger section was grouped around a big stone fireplace. A door opened in the back wall of the dining area, and I could see kitchen cabinets and appliances through it. The area was a mess, as Mrs. Deacon had predicted. The living room had been decorated in a heavily rustic style, with animal heads on the walls, chairs made out of sticks of wood, and furry throws on the floor and the couch. Now every surface was covered with beer cans, and take-out sacks and pizza boxes were tossed under the dining table.

My first impression of the Lally boy was that he must be crazy. He was walking up and down, gesturing wildly, his face furious, talking to himself. I couldn't hear him; the noise of the waves and the thick glass windows blocked the sound.

Then he turned around and strode across the room. He reached over the back of a long, off-white couch that faced the fireplace, and he yanked at something angrily.

The head of Alana Fairchild Hyden appeared. He was holding it up by the hair.

I nearly had a heart attack. For a minute it looked as if her head had been severed from her body. Then she threw up her hand, and I realized with relief that she was alive. She'd been lying on the couch, and the Lally boy had reached down, grasped her hair, and yanked her to a sitting position.

As I watched, he swung his other hand back and slapped her face. He slapped it again. Then he let go of the hair, and she fell out of sight again.

Well, he might not have decapitated her, but she sure was in danger. I'd done a report on violence against women for social studies. "Escarole," I said, barely breathing the word. "I mean, escalate.. The violence is likely to escalate."

I needed to get help quick.

I started to edge down the stairs, but the Lally boy suddenly swung around, crossed to the window, and looked out at the lake. He was staring right at me.

I froze. Then he turned his back, and I decided that he hadn't seen me. He walked back to the couch, but this time he didn't hit Alana Fairchild Hyden again. He simply stood looking at her. Then he walked out of the living room. Within a second or two he appeared in the other room that faced the lake.

It was like watching TV with the sound turned off. I could see clearly as the Lally boy walked slowly into the room—it was a luxurious bedroom—and crossed to the bedside table. He opened a drawer and looked inside. Then he slowly reached inside and pulled out a pistol.

I was mesmerized. He sat on the edge of the bed, holding the pistol and staring at it. It was as if a balloon were flying in the air over his head, just like a cartoon. And the words in the balloon said, "Should I kill her?"

I will say that his face was bleak. He didn't want to kill her. Then his face hardened, and the balloon's words changed. "I've got to do it," the words said.

He laid the pistol on the bed, then crossed to a closet. He opened the door and began to toss boxes off the shelf. My dad had a pistol, and he kept the pistol one place and the clip another. Could the Lally boy's dad do the same thing? Could he be looking for ammunition?

Suddenly I was sure Alana was going to be dead within the next few minutes. Her only chance was to run. And she didn't know she was in immediate danger.

Luckily, the stairs led up to the end of the deck away from the bedroom, so I was able to tiptoe up without being seen and tiptoe across to the door to the living room. If it had been locked—but it wasn't. I opened it a foot—enough to let me in, but too little to make the sound of the waves louder inside the house. I ran lightly across the room.

"Alana! Alana!"

Alana didn't move. At first I thought she couldn't hear me because of the waves. But when I shook her, she still lolled on the couch limply. She was unconscious.

What could I do! She was skinny, true, but she was too heavy to carry. I needed to run for help. But I couldn't just leave her there to die.

The fur rug gave me the idea. I ran around the couch and yanked the cushions out from under Alana, then put them on top of her. I tried to leave her a little space for breathing. Then I draped the fur rug over the seat of the couch.

Did it look as if Alana was gone? I could only hope so.

I ran back to the door to the deck, slid the door open, and edged outside. I shut the door gently, then headed for the stairs to the beach.

Behind me, I heard a yell. I couldn't tell if the Lally boy had found Alana, or if he had seen me. I didn't stop to find out. I started racing down those terraced stairs. Back and forth, switching across the slope. I was afraid to go straight down, through the ivy and other plants, so I stuck to the steps. But I ran.

Behind me I heard the door open. The Lally boy was coming. Then I heard a terrific bang, and I knew he was shooting at me.

By then I was on the little deck at the bottom of the stairs. I fell flat, just as a second shot was fired. Then I slid backward down the final stairs to the sand. When I felt the sand under my toes, I stood up and began to run up the beach.

The trees and shrubs along the bank hid me, I deduced, and the Lally boy would have to run down all those stairs before he could see me. I meant to be long gone by the time he got to the bottom. I ran for home as fast as I could. But considering the sand I was running in, that wasn't too fast.

Still, I was more than halfway to the public access path when I heard the Lally boy yell behind me and knew he was at the bottom of the stairs. I ran on. He chased me. I could see the clump of trees that marked the path up to the road. I aimed for them, and I ran. I swung around the last driftwood log and went up that path, clawing the sand with my hands.

Suddenly I was out in the middle of the road, pounding toward Aunt Nettie and Uncle Phil's house. Behind me, I heard the Lally boy come out at the top of the path. His feet scrunched on the gravel of the parking area, and I hadn't reached the curve yet. I knew he'd be able to see me.

I ran to the edge of the road and cowered among the trees— those threatening Michigan trees that had frightened me so much. Now they looked like a fortress where I could hide. I hugged a tree, blessed the dark, and stood absolutely still.

But he had heard my footsteps. He knew which way I had gone. So, running and then walking, he came toward me. I didn't even breathe.

"Where are you, baby?" he said. "What's all this dumb stuff? Come on out, Alana."

Alana? He thought I was Alana? For the first time I remembered I had covered my hair with a black scarf. He had looked into the living room and been momentarily fooled by my ruse of hiding Alana under the couch cushions and the fur rug. Then, as I ran away from him, I had looked like Alana.

"Come on, babe. We're gonna make this work. We'll get the money. Come on."

Get the money? Alana was going to get the money?

So she'd been a party to her own kidnapping. Why wasn't I surprised?

The Lally boy came up even with me. "Alana? Come on, honey."

I huddled behind my tree, hiding my hands and face in it, exposing no part of me that wasn't dark.

He walked on. Now I was behind him. I still didn't move.

"Alana? Come on!" He sounded exasperated. He was at least thirty feet farther on, almost into the dangerous curve, the curve just before Mrs. Deacon's drive turned off the Lake Shore Drive.

"Dammit! Come out, you little bitch!"

I pictured him swinging his pistol around, looking everywhere for Alana. I just hoped he'd stay where I could hear him, so I'd know where he was.

He was still out in the middle of the road at the blind curve, muttering and calling for Alana, when Mrs. Deacon's daughter's car came around the curve, hit him, and knocked him into the same bush where her mother had landed that morning.

Again I ran to the neat white cottage next door, and again the woman who lived there called the sheriff, an ambulance and Uncle Phil.

"Call two ambulances," I told her. "Alana Fairchild Hyden is down at the Lally house, and I think she's been beaten up pretty bad."

I ran back to the Lally house—this time on the road. The front door was unlocked, luckily, and I was able to pull the couch cushions off Alana before she smothered. Then the door opened behind me, and I screamed.

It was Uncle Phil. I threw my arms around his neck. "Oh, Uncle Phil! I'm so glad it's you!"

The sheriff scolded me, but he didn't deny that the evidence that had made me suspect the Lally boy was involved in Alana Fairchild Hyden's kidnapping was too slight for him to have used as a basis for a search warrant. An empty candy box, a scrap of blue ribbon, and a screwed-up candy cup from the last box of candy Alana had bought were not much to go on. Especially when someone had stolen them from

Mrs. Deacon's trash bag, and I was the only person who knew they existed.

Mrs. Deacon lived. She was in the hospital several weeks, but Uncle Phil let Lindy and me drive into Holland to see her.

Alana lived, too. She admitted she had connived at her own kidnapping. It was plain even to a nut like her mother that she had done it to get attention. Alana got a suspended sentence, and her mother promised to go into therapy with her. They sold the Warner Pier house, and they didn't come back there again.

The Lally boy—it turned out his name was Brian—died. His family hadn't known he was at the Lake Michigan house. He was supposed to be at an Outward Bound camp.

Mrs. Deacon came home from the hospital the day before I went back to Texas. I took her some candy, plus a casserole Aunt Nettie had made.

"Lee, you've had an exciting summer," she said. "And if you hadn't noticed the TenHuis box, the ribbon, and that little candy cup, I guess Alana Fairchild Hyden might be dead."

"TenHuis chocolate is not the kind of thing you usually take to the beach," I said. "So when somebody attacked you, then tore up your trash—well, it was just a simple reduction. Alimentary, my dear Mrs. Deacon."

NEVER NECK AT NIAGARA
A Leigh Koslow Mystery Story

Edie Claire

Edie Claire is the author of *Never Buried, Never Sorry, Never Preach Past Noon*, and the upcoming *Never Kissed Goodnight*, all of which feature amateur sleuth Leigh Koslow.

U p until now, the morning had been almost perfect.
Leigh Koslow had begun her day by gorging on an all-you-can-eat breakfast buffet at the hotel (heavy on the bacon and complete with pastries), then atoning for it with an ambitious bike ride. Exercise was ordinarily anathema to her, particularly during a weekend vacation, but for the trail that ran alongside the Niagara River upstream to Fort Erie, she made an exception. She loved Niagara Falls. There was something about the thunder of the rushing water and the coolness of the rising mist that always lifted her spirits—and her energy level. This particular bike trail, with the calm upper Niagara on one side and a spread of spacious, large-windowed homes on the other, was her favorite. The slight grade going up was almost undetectable—even to a biker as out of shape as she was; yet going down, it proved a faithful ally. The mild May weather of southern Canada was divine, the crowds were still sparse, and if she weren't biking alone, life would be perfect.

But it was near perfect. After all, she wasn't really alone. Her new hubby had been at the hotel when she had left, and he would be there when she got back. Sure, he would be busy with some crazy convention in between, but she could deal with that. After all, it wasn't as though this was *supposed* to be a romantic weekend—it was merely another of the boring political junkets he was frequently attending; one that happened to be in a location worthy of her tagging along. Since they had returned from a fabulous ten-day honeymoon cruise in the Mediterranean only a few weeks ago, she could hardly complain.

Until just now, that is, when the peculiar noises had awakened her, and she was forced to wonder once again what the heck was wrong with her karma.

Her ride complete, she had loaded her bike onto its rack on the Cavalier (which she'd cleverly parked for free at the nature preserve), then headed off to stake out a place to recuperate. The preserve was gorgeous, and wonderfully peaceful in the off-season. Water from the river had been diverted into a series of greenish-blue lagoons, which wound in picturesque fashion around shady, bridge-connected islands filled with wildlife and secluded footpaths. At the height of summer, this spot would be teeming with extended families from every imaginable culture—or at least those with traveling money. Unfamiliar scents would drift up from the barbecue grills as grandparents rested on blankets and children and teens swarmed over rocks and under waterfalls in the shadow of NO SWIMMING ALLOWED signs. But on this happy morning, the only other visitors she'd seen were an older couple picnicking and a middle-aged bird-watcher with binoculars.

She had headed for the interior of the largest island, and had soon found the ideal spot for some quality meditation. At least, that had been the plan. But once she had settled herself comfortably in the lower limbs of an obligingly built maple tree, sleep had taken over. She was, if not athletic in any way, an expert tree climber, and it wasn't the first time she'd communed with nature above ground. Nodding off in the process was a new twist, but then she was a newlywed.

How long she'd been dozing when she heard them, she had no idea. But she couldn't have been snoring loudly, or they never would have chosen the location they'd chosen. And they most certainly wouldn't be doing what they sounded like they were doing.

She twisted her head ever so slightly downward, wincing sheepishly as she cast one eye in the direction of the noises. Moans, groans, giggles, and heavy breathing—they were all there. It sounded like two people were a few yards away from her, doing some communing of their own. If she was lucky, there would be enough cover of foliage between her and them that she could get away unnoticed. If not, she at least hoped they were early in the process.

It only took one eye to remind her she wasn't the lucky type. The couple were lying on a large blanket by the base of the tree, and their clothes were not.

She shut her eyes tight, wondering briefly if Canada had such a charge as involuntary voyeurism. The situation might be considered amusing—*if* it were happening to someone else. But all she could feel was mortification, and her options were limited. She couldn't get down without being seen. And if there was one thing worse than spying on two people making love, it had to be explaining why afterward.

The sounds from below escalated, and she grit her teeth. What she really wanted to do was stick her fingers in her ears and hum, but movement was too risky. She wasn't directly above the couple, but any little shift could catch their eyes, which could be staring contentedly upward any moment now.

Finally the sounds ceased, and Leigh breathed a quiet sigh. For the sake of both her increasingly aching back and her sanity, she could only hope that the twosome had someplace to go—and soon.

"You know, Roger," came a young woman's voice, "I'm not sure it'll be as much fun when we don't have to sneak around."

A man's voice, which sounded at least a decade older, responded sleepily. "Sure it will."

Leigh groaned inwardly. Pillow talk, too?

"Today's the day!" the woman continued, her voice bobbing as if she was up and getting dressed. "You're sure everything's all set?"

The man merely grunted.

"Roger!" the woman chastised, her tone turning sharp. "Don't even think of doing a half-assed job of this. We're not talking about another loaded Nikon here. The consequences—"

"I'm aware of the damned consequences," the man replied peevishly. His voice had also started to jiggle in space, which Leigh hoped meant they were both getting decent again. She allowed both eyes to open.

The man was facing away from her, pulling a pair of khaki shorts over neon-orange boxers. His back and legs were generously covered with dark brown hair, which would have given him a rugged, animalistic look if it weren't for the large bald spot visible on the top of his head. And though he was far from obese, a hefty ring of blubber had settled around his middle, evidently sometime after he had purchased the khaki shorts. "The thing's been planned for months, Ash," he continued, struggling to zip up. "It's set. Now quit harping on it."

"Ash" was quiet for a moment, looking at him. Her generously proportioned body was now covered with a pink halter top and short shorts that would have been more appropriate on a giddy teen than the savvy twenty-something she appeared to be. "You mean you've been dragging your feet for months," she said accusingly. "And now they're getting cold."

The man groaned. "Don't start that again! If you don't believe me, just wait and watch the papers. Or better yet, get a police scanner. It'll be over by midnight. Make nice entertainment for tomorrow's *Maid of the Mist* passengers."

"God, you're cold," the woman said playfully, leaning down to fold the blanket.

The man laughed. "*Me,* cold! Who wanted to make sure she wasn't wearing anything valuable first?"

The blanket hit him square in the face and wrapped partway around his neck. "I'm just being practical," she answered with a half smile. "*I'm* not married to the bitch."

A stab of pain shot through Leigh's distorted spine, but she barely noticed. The pillow talk—and her stomach—had taken a disturbing turn.

"Not much longer, babe," the man said soothingly, tucking the blanket under one arm and pulling the woman to him. "It'll all be over."

She kissed him, long and lewdly, and Leigh shut her eyes again. After a moment, the woman giggled in a coquettish tone. Evidently she could live up (or down) to her teenybopper outfit whenever she chose. "You really think they'll spot her from *Maid of the Mist*?"

"Nah," the man said jovially, "By tomorrow dear old Marjory will probably be bobbing around in the whirlpool."

Leigh fought back images of a woman's corpse being sucked under the rough waters that circled downstream from the falls. Surely they were just joking. The two shared another laugh and—from the sound of it—another kiss, as Leigh struggled to keep the bile down in her throat.

Then the woman's voice turned serious again. "Don't mess this up, Roger," she said quietly. "You know I don't like giving ultimatums, but this was the only way. You run the business with me, or there is no business to run. Remember?"

The man answered just as softly, but even with her eyes closed, Leigh could sense a deep anger simmering beneath his words. "I know exactly where things stand," he said slowly. "And you know perfectly well that blowing the whistle now means big money down the drain. *Your* money."

"Ah," said the woman wistfully, "*my* money. I like the sound of that."

The two moved off, their words and the woman's giggles being increasingly muffled by both their footfalls and the sudden, stiff breeze. It was safe for Leigh to move now, but for a moment she simply sat, the wind robbing any remaining warmth from her body. The hairs on the back of her neck stood stiffly at attention, and her mouth was so dry her tongue seemed glued in place.

His wife, she thought with grim amazement. He was going to kill his wife. If he didn't, sweet Ash the chameleon was going to blow the whistle on their affair. Then he would be out of business—a business she wanted a piece of.

Grabbing the limb with stiff hands, she relaxed her back and let the rest of her body slip off the branch. She hung only a second to break her fall, then jumped to the ground. Adultery. Extortion. *Murder*. The last word resonated painfully in her muddled head. She sank down at the base of the tree, careful to avoid the spot with the X-rating, as the conversation repeated itself over and over in her mind. Was someone named Roger really about to kill someone named Marjory, or had she imagined it? Misinterpreted it? Could they have just been joking?

That didn't seem likely.

Her knees knocked as she sat, and a shiver rocked her shoulders. She couldn't just sit here. She had to do something, didn't she?

With difficulty and without a plan, she struggled to her feet and started walking. It didn't matter if they saw her now, she reasoned. They'd have no idea that she had witnessed their conversation, much less their other indiscretion. She would merely be another sightseer.

Her steps quickened, and by the time she reached the path at the edge of the island, she could see them ahead clearly. They were walking arm in arm, the woman alternately laughing and laying her head on his shoulder. As they crossed one of the lagoon bridges and strode toward the almost empty parking lot, Leigh doubled back on the path and walked farther along the island, heading for a different bridge. She had just finished crossing it when the van the two had boarded roared past her on the narrow road.

Jumping quickly to the curb, she strained to read the license plate, but was frustrated to find the numbers a blur—and her driving glasses in the Cavalier. Though she was only mildly near-sighted, license plates traveling at high speeds were beyond her discernment. Fortunately, a bold, black logo on the side of a full-sized passenger van was not. And she now knew what she had to do next.

Pay a little visit to Purple Mist Tours, Inc.

Niagara Falls, Canada, wasn't a difficult place to navigate in, provided it wasn't a summer evening. Then the streets became so clogged with pedestrians of every shape, size, and nationality that just getting from one light to the next took the nerves of a surgeon. Since Leigh had no such nerves, she was happy for the light crowd, and the fact that Purple Mist Tours, Inc. (whose address was conveniently listed in the phone book) was right on the main drag. She steered the Cavalier past the horseshoe falls and into the tourist area, past wax museums, haunted houses, and a plethora of souvenir shops, to the relatively plain storefront whose sign read PURPLE MIST TOURS, INC./HOT NAILS. She parked and walked in.

A narrow staircase ran straight up from the entrance, stenciled letters and a giant arrow on the wall announcing it as the path to Purple Mist Tours, Inc. Those wishing to increase the temperature of their nails, on the other hand, had merely to make a left. Leigh began the climb.

Through another door at the top of the stairs was a dimly lit reception area with a single counter and two uncomfortable-looking chairs. Serviceable quarters for a small tour company, she thought, but they hardly screamed "big money." A hefty woman with long, stringy dark hair smiled at her curiously. "Hello. Can I help you with something?"

"I'm here to see Marjory," she answered simply. She had been hoping that Roger's wife worked in the business, but if not, she figured she could at least wrangle a home phone number. And that, unfortunately, was about as far as she had planned.

The woman's casual smile told Leigh she had gotten lucky. "She's in the back. You a friend of hers?"

Leigh nodded. Given the circumstances, she figured it was a white lie, at most.

"Go on in, then," the woman said cheerfully, opening a gate at the edge of the counter. Leigh thanked her and walked through it to the closed door behind marked PRIVATE. She opened the door hesitantly, rapping on it gently at the same time. "Excuse me? Marjory?"

The door opened on a spacious office that was lavishly decorated in hues of soft ivory, a sharp contrast to the stark reception area. Plush, spotless modern furniture appeared to have come right out of the plastic, and the walls were lined with what looked—to Leigh's admittedly untrained eye— like original artwork. "Yes. Can I help you?" The woman who stood up was every bit as carefully and tastefully put together as the room. Her crisp coral-colored suit was without a crease, her stylishly short hairdo without a single misplaced strand. Coordinated gold jewelry adorned her neck, earlobes, wrists, and fingers, successfully conveying that "have money—will spend" aura that retailers drool over. She was pretty in a stately sort of way, her age betrayed by the prominent crow's-feet that peeked out through her heavy makeup.

"I, um . . ." Leigh hadn't prepared a speech. Since there wasn't any good way to say what she had to say, she took a deep breath and winged it. "Your husband's name is Roger, right?"

The woman's carefully plucked eyebrows lowered instantly. "Yes. What of it?"

From the look on Marjory's face, Leigh had to wonder if she had encountered many other young women claiming familiarity with her husband. "I don't know him," she said quickly, tensing. I just overheard something he said this morning, and I thought you ought to know about it."

The woman's calm face broke into a carefully controlled smile. "My dear," she began, "I appreciate your sense of moral righteousness. Really, I do. But what my husband does, and with whom, doesn't concern me in the least."

Leigh tried to keep her jaw from dropping. She knew that women with such attitudes existed, but she'd never met one. She hoped her husband hadn't either.

"Is there anything else?" Marjory asked politely, clearly ready to be relieved of her unwelcome visitor.

"Yes," Leigh exclaimed, flustered. "I didn't come here to tell you your husband was fooling around." He was, of course, but it was hardly the point of her visit. She took another deep breath. "I came here to tell you that I think he's trying to kill you."

The woman's smug features dissolved, and for a brief moment, Leigh could see fear flash across her dark brown eyes. But just as quickly, a look of calm confidence returned. "That's ridiculous," she answered softly. "What exactly did you hear?"

Leigh repeated an edited version of the conversation, and grew increasingly uneasy as she did so. Roger had told Ash that her blowing the whistle now would cost them money, and Leigh had assumed that was because once his wife found out about the affair he would lose his half of the tour business. But given Marjory's liberal attitude toward matrimony, that theory didn't wash. So what exactly was Ash threatening to blow the whistle on? Leigh looked into Marjory's carefully concentrating face. Perhaps Roger had been cheating on his wife in more ways than one. Had he been stealing from his own company? Or was there something shady about Purple Mist Tours in general? And if so, did Marjory even know about it?

The walls of the office seemed suddenly closer, and Leigh's fight or flight mechanism kicked in. If there was something illegal going on with Purple Mist Tours, she had no desire to know about it. Marjory was on her own. "That's all I know, I'm afraid," she said quickly, rising.

Marjory's face went blank, and she sat down heavily in her svelte office chair. The reality of what Leigh was saying appeared to have finally sunk in. "I can't believe this," she said weakly. "I really can't believe it."

"I'm sorry," Leigh offered helplessly.

"We should call the police," Marjory said weakly. "Shouldn't we?"

Leigh nodded. She knew she had to call the police, she just hadn't yet. Warning Marjory had been priority one, and far more effective, because the cops wouldn't do squat anyway. They would simply give her the standard speech about not being able to prosecute people for *potential* crimes, write up a report to placate her, and send her on her way. And given her well-established rapport with law enforcement officials—or more accurately, lack thereof—she would probably tick them off royally in the process. Nonetheless, they had to be told. If Roger ever did succeed in his quest, the report could be valuable evidence against him.

"Yes, we should," she answered.

Marjory said nothing for a moment, then announced, more to herself than to Leigh, "I'll call them and get a restraining order."

Leigh smiled. She might just get out of this office and get out of dealing with the police too. "Good idea." She pulled a pen and yellow sticky note off Marjory's desk and wrote down her name and hotel room number. "Have them contact me if they want a statement about what I heard, okay?"

Marjory didn't answer, but sat limply, staring at a spot on the wall. "I was supposed to meet him later today," she said faintly, her face alarmingly pale despite her makeup. "We were going out to dinner. It's—" She stopped a moment, her lower lip quivering slightly. "It's our anniversary."

Blood rushed into Leigh's cheeks, and she squirmed in discomfort. "I'm so sorry," she offered again. "Please be careful. And do call the police right away."

Marjory managed to snap out of her funk and look back at her through moist eyes. "Thank you," she said, extending a cold hand for Leigh to shake. "I appreciate all you've done." She took the sticky note off the desk, folded it neatly, and slipped it into her suit's breast pocket.

"No problem," Leigh answered with a forced smile. She headed for the door, and once safely on the other side took off as fast as her feet would carry her.

For a regular churchgoer like Leigh, sleeping in on vacation Sundays was a real perk, and being in a hotel on someone else's expense account was icing on the cake. She could doze the morning away with preordered blueberry muffins and tea waiting at her bedside, thinking of how nice it was that she had "forgotten" to bring along any work. Being a partner in her own ad agency had its benefits, but feeling constantly guilty about leaving work undone was a pesky disadvantage, and putting a few hundred miles between herself and the unwritten copy was the only cure.

Having been awakened early by hunger, she dove happily into a large muffin. Room service was expensive, of course, and her scrupulously honest public-servant husband would be sure to pay for every morsel she ate out of his own pocket rather than the taxpayers', but it was still worth it. She collected a few crumbs from off the bed sheets and reached for the morning paper to help break the next batch's fall. Then she saw the small headline in the lower right-hand corner, and her appetite dissolved.

WOMAN'S BODY FOUND BELOW FALLS; FOUL PLAY POSSIBLE.

Her pulse pounded in her ears as she read the short article. "The body of a woman was recovered at the base of the horseshoe falls at approximately 11:00 P.M. last night. A search was authorized after numerous sightseers reported watching a large object that might have been a person drifting in the river and going over the edge of the falls near the midpoint. Witnesses claim that the individual was not moving voluntarily at the time, leading investigators to speculate that the woman was either unconscious, or perhaps already dead, when she went over the falls. An investigation is currently under way."

Her stomach lurched painfully in her abdomen. It couldn't be. Marjory couldn't be dead. How could he have killed her, when she knew he was planning to? Hadn't she called the police?

If she had, they hadn't bothered to contact Leigh.

An even sicker feeling suddenly overcame her. If Marjory hadn't called the police, it was probably because she herself was involved in whatever illegal shenanigans Ash was threatening to blow the whistle on. In which case, she had probably never intended to call. She had intended to handle Roger on her own.

Leigh let the paper fall limply in her lap. If she had contacted the police herself, Marjory might still be alive. Guilt washed over her in heavy waves, blending imperceptibly with nausea. She pulled herself out of the bed and started getting dressed. It was too late to save Marjory, but her mistake could still be rectified somewhat. After she told her story to the authorities, Roger and the pink chameleon would be certain to get what was coming to them.

She had finished dressing and had her hand on the doorknob when the phone rang. She flew to it anxiously. "Yes? Hello?"

A man's voice, deep and proper, answered. "Yes, this is Officer Tony Burnett with the New York State Park Service calling. Is this Leigh Koslow?"

Her heartbeat quickened. So. Marjory had called the police after all. The burden of guilt on her chest lifted a little. "Yes, that's me."

"Ma'am, I wonder if you would be willing to come down to our headquarters on Goat Island as soon as possible. We have an individual here who appears confused and disoriented, and we're hoping you might be able to help us identify her. She isn't carrying any ID, but a note with your name and number was found in one of her pockets."

It was a moment before Leigh could speak. Marjory confused and disoriented, on Goat Island? It made no sense, but the primary implication was positive. If Marjory was on Goat Island now, she couldn't possibly have been found dead last night.

Leigh took a deep breath. It was all right. Marjory was alive. Whatever had happened to her between yesterday and this morning—she was still alive. And although Leigh stopped short of being glad that some other woman was dead, she couldn't help but be relieved at not having to drown in guilt for the rest of her life.

"I'll be right there, Officer," she said firmly.

Her hands shook a little as she drove the Cavalier over the Rainbow Bridge back into the United States. Thankfully, it was still early, and the line at customs was short. A tour bus idled up in the queue next to her, and she somehow wasn't surprised to note that it was a Purple Mist. Since yesterday she had noticed two of them driving about, their striking eggplant color making them easy to spot. Like most local tour buses, they shuttled regularly between the U.S. and Canadian falls. But unlike most of the other buses, Purple Mist Tours appeared to cater exclusively to foreign tourists. Both of the buses she had seen yesterday had carried Japanese families, while all the occupants of the current bus appeared to be from India.

A female passenger with a red dot on her forehead stuck a camera up to the bus window and aimed it at the customs booth, and Leigh's mind began to drift to something curious that Ash had said. She was just about to remember it when the radio station she had been listening to began its newscast.

"Police have identified the woman whose body was pulled from the base of the horseshoe falls late last night as twenty-three-year-old Ashley Whitener, a resident of Fort Erie, Ontario. Ms. Whitener was employed as an assistant manager at the Niagara Sun Diner in Niagara Falls, Ontario; she was last seen Saturday morning by her roommate as she left their apartment, ostensibly to go running. Investigators have not yet determined whether foul play was involved in Ms. Whitener's death; autopsy results are pending."

Leigh's mind raced. *Ashley* Whitener. Twenty-three years old. It could be a coincidence, she reasoned. There must be any number of twentyish Ashleys in the area—there was no reason to assume it was Roger's Ashley. If she hadn't first thought the dead woman was Marjory, it would never even have occurred to her.

She drove on, answering the customs agent's questions mechanically as she continued to convince herself that pink-halter Ashley was still alive, well, and committing adultery without remorse. Why shouldn't she be? She was Roger's choice, after all. It was Marjory he wanted out of the picture. Marjory the confused and disoriented . . .

Her hands gripped the steering wheel tightly as she navigated the scenic bridge that crossed from mainland New York to Goat Island, suspending cars above a vigorously churning band of the upper Niagara River. Dangerous rapids surrounded all of Goat Island, a fact that only added to its beauty and fascination. Throw a floating object from the island in any direction and its destination would be the same—over and down. *Way* down.

She located the building the officer had directed her to, parked, and jumped out quickly. She was still about fifty yards from the door when a disheveled woman in a bright-colored suit charged out from around the back of the building, running at top speed. Leigh stared at her curiously for a moment before realizing who she was.

"Marjory!" she called out frantically, giving chase. Where were the officers, and how had she given them the slip? Leigh glanced back over her shoulder as she ran, but saw no one. Confused and disoriented indeed. Marjory appeared to have lost it completely, and in this place if somebody didn't stop her soon, she could be in a good deal of danger.

Leigh continued to follow the fleeing woman, calling out her name and begging her to stop. But Marjory flew on, appearing to hear none of it. When they reached the first bridge to the chain of tiny islands known as Three Sisters, Leigh felt an additional wave of panic. *Not there, please.* Anywhere but there.

On any ordinary occasion, the little islands were one of Leigh's favorite parts of the park. Encased in swirling rapids and edged with huge rocks, the islands had ambiance to spare. But for someone out of control and moving fast, they were dangerous as hell.

"Marjory, stop!" Leigh commanded, but she doubted her voice could be heard over the rush of water that ran under the woman's feet on the narrow bridge. Still seeming oblivious to her pursuer, Marjory plowed onto the first island and headed straight across it to the bridge leading to the second. Leigh kept following, nearing her prey when the woman reached the third island and stopped in her tracks.

Leigh halted a few paces behind her and tried desperately to catch her breath. "Marjory," she panted as soothingly as possible, "take it easy. You don't need to run anymore. Everything will be okay."

A wild-eyed Marjory spun instantly to face her. "Okay? *Okay?* Of course it's not okay! My husband is trying to kill me. He's here, right now, somewhere. He tried it once, and he'll try it again. And it's your fault, Samantha. You had no business sleeping with my husband."

Leigh's panic escalated. The officer hadn't been kidding, Marjory was more out of it than she'd thought, and she herself was quite clearly in this situation way over her head. Instinctively she glanced over her shoulder again, hoping to see a posse of law enforcement officers approaching.

There was no one anywhere, not even another tourist. So early on a Sunday morning, she shouldn't be surprised.

"I'll beat him to it!" Marjory screamed suddenly, her arms flying. She dashed to the far edge of the island and began scrambling onto the boulders. Passing by one of the several prominent signs that forbade that very activity, Leigh cautiously followed her.

"He wants me to go over the falls—" Marjory screeched. "Fine! I'll go over the falls!" She had made her way to a large rock whose lip hung out well over the rushing water. Looking down at the swirling whitecaps, her face suddenly went pale, and she started to sob.

With one last-ditch look over her shoulder, Leigh gave up on waiting for rescuers who knew what they were doing. She could handle one little crazy person, couldn't she? She hadn't grown up in a big family for nothing.

"Marjory," she said soothingly, pulling herself carefully onto the near edge of the rock. "It's all right. Just take my hand and climb down. Roger can't hurt you now, I promise."

But the sobbing woman didn't move. She stood stubbornly on the boulder's far edge, her shoulders heaving. Leigh exhaled loudly, then took a few careful steps forward to where she could just touch Marjory's arm.

In an instant Marjory's hand lashed out and grabbed her wrist with surprising strength, swinging her up and farther out onto the rock. The unexpected motion threw Leigh off balance, and as she struggled to get her feet back underneath her, Marjory delivered a deft blow to her shins that sent her reeling again. She could hear a man's voice shouting angrily, "No, not there!" as she felt herself falling down, down into a heavy, freezing soup that struck her body with the force of a blow.

The breath had been knocked out of her, but with the desperateness of any animal that suddenly finds itself unable to breathe, she nonetheless managed to right her body and pull her head above water. Her limbs felt like lead weights as she flailed to get her bearings. Trying to fight the strong downhill current was futile, but the water's horizontal direction was fickle, pulling her first back toward the island, then out again. She fought to keep her head up and her vision clear, concentrating on keeping the land in sight. She knew without thinking that she had gone in at the top of the island rather than the bottom, and that thought kept her going as she paddled her heavy limbs toward it with all her might.

Only a few seconds had passed before something solid rose up in front of her, and she grasped it for all she was worth. Her face promptly smashed into its side, the sweet texture of tree bark assaulting her bruised lips. She was only a few feet from land now—the fallen tree having stopped her downward movement as the lesser currents helped pull her toward shore. Closer in she could see water only inches deep, sweetly still and placid, as if a toddler could safely splash in it. With the tremendous deeper current still tugging her lower body toward the falls, it was cruel irony.

"Hold on, there," a man's voice called. "Just stay right there and don't move. I'm coming to get you."

The feeling that washed over Leigh should have been re-lief. Instead, it was a chilling fear. She looked up toward shore again, and in between the endless splashes of water that pelted her eyes, she could easily identify her would-be rescuer. It was Roger. Good old hairy. He had tried to kill his wife, he might very well have killed his girlfriend, and now he was trying to save her.

Don't believe it. She stared at the man who had started to inch his way toward her on the fallen log, and every ex-hausted muscle of her body begged her to trust him. But her brain insisted on replaying the sound of his voice. One voice, over and over again, until at last Leigh got the message.

No, not there. It was Roger's voice she had heard just now when Marjory pushed her. And it was Roger's voice, all prim and proper sounding, that had brought her out here in the first place.

Officer Burnette, indeed.

She had been set up—by both of them. He hadn't yelled at Marjory a moment ago because she was pushing Leigh off a rock—he had yelled at her because she was pushing Leigh off the *wrong* rock, into a current that might inconveniently bring her right back in.

Which it had. A situation Roger now had to rectify.

"Hold on tight," he said soothingly, still inching closer along the log. "I'm almost there."

Leigh studied him out of squinting eyes. She wasn't pan-icked. She was far beyond that. She was close enough to cer-tain death that cool acceptance was all she had. Roger would reach her in another few seconds. And what would he do then? Pry her hands off the log? Push her head under with his foot?

No—she thought, eyeing his left hand—he would hit her over the head with the socket wrench he was holding. So much cleaner. No unpleasant struggling or screaming—just another unconscious body going over the falls.

Just like Ashley. Ashley, who had somehow managed to catch on to the shady side of Purple Mist Tours, and had made the fatal mistake of trying to capitalize on it.

A loaded Nikon. That's what Ashley had mentioned, and what the Indian woman with the camera had somehow made her think of. But Ashley hadn't meant loaded with film, had she?

Smuggling. That had to be it. Asian-manufactured drugs, rhino horn powder—who knew? The tour company would make a perfect front for smuggling virtually anything between the U.S. and Canada. No wonder Marjory had hid her decorating tastes behind closed doors. Purple Mist Tours was undoubtedly taking in a whole lot more cash than sightseeing alone could account for.

Enough to kill over.

She looked beyond Roger to where Marjory stood calmly on the bank, all traces of hysteria gone, and the last pieces dropped quickly into place. Roger had never intended to kill his wife. The plans Leigh had overheard at the preserve were just a bunch of nonsense, designed to keep Ashley's mouth shut a little while longer, until he could shut it permanently. Marjory had probably known everything. But neither had counted on a snoopy, do-gooding eavesdropper being in the wrong place at the wrong time.

Roger was at hand, and her fate was in hers. Maybe Marjory had knocked her in accidentally, and maybe Mr. Hairy really was trying to save her. But she didn't think so. And sometimes, a woman just has to go with her instincts.

Thinking no further, Leigh took a deep breath—and let go.

The current swept her under almost immediately, and she had to fight her way up again not once but repeatedly, grabbing a breath whenever a patch of air grazed her cheeks. She couldn't see a thing anymore. Seconds passed, and just as she was beginning to say her last prayer, a sharp pain stabbed her left leg, and a jagged protrusion crashed against her rib cage.

Ignoring the numerous minor pains that broke out on her left side, she struggled toward the object. With the help of the current, her body obligingly rolled partway out of the water and onto the half-submerged stump.

Somewhere, a girl's voice screamed, and a boy's voice issued a heretical exclamation. Strong hands pulled Leigh's torso up and off the waterlogged stump, and her legs met dry land.

"Are you all right? the boy asked loudly. "Where the hell did you come from?"

Leigh opened her eyes. She focused them first on the face of the handsome, shirtless teen who held her, then on the thin girl beside him, who appeared to be wearing the shirt he had lost. It was the mystique of Niagara, she supposed. There was just something about rushing water, danger, and secluded paths that made people want to take their clothes off.

"Hey, you!" the boy called out in the opposite direction. "Can you give us a hand here? This lady's half drowned!" He laid a still-limp Leigh down on solid ground, then turned back to the girl. "Are they coming?"

It took her a second to answer. "No. It looks like they're taking off. How do you like that? Middle-aged couple—too good to get involved."

The boy frowned. "Maybe they're calling an ambulance."

Leigh felt herself smiling. Somehow, she doubted that.

She had just stepped out of a hot bath and into a king-sized terry towel when she heard the door of her hotel suite opening late that afternoon.

"Warren? That you?" she called.

"If it's not, you'd better be surprised," his cheerful voice answered.

"Ramone left an hour ago," she teased. "I thought he might have forgotten his socks."

"Don't see them," he returned casually. "So what have you been up to all day? Finish reading your novel?"

"Not exactly," she answered, slipping out of the towel and into a clean outfit.

"Did you hear what happened at Goat Island this morning?" he asked through the bathroom door. "Some tourist almost went over the falls."

Leigh paused a moment. "Do tell."

"Word from the locals is—" he continued. "Someone stumbled onto a major smuggling ring that the authorities had been trying to locate for months. Apparently a tour company called Purple Mist had been funneling illegal drugs from Asia into the United States through Canadian customs. The police figure their people were posing as tourists and hiding the drugs in camera equipment. Somehow, one of the real tourists picked up on it and threatened to expose them, and got tossed into the Niagara River for her trouble."

"Bummer," Leigh replied, opening the door.

"The owners are being blamed for the death of the woman who went over the falls last night, too," he finished. She walked out into the room, and his eyes widened in alarm. "Leigh!" he said with concern. "What happened to your face?"

She reached a hand up and touched the nasty bruise she'd received from log number one. "Well," she began, looking around for another of the five Mr. Big candy bars she'd bought for herself at the hotel gift shop. "It's like this . . ."

UNREASONABLE DOUBT
A Nathan Heller Mystery Story

Max Allan Collins

Max Allan Collins has been nominated for the Shamus award eight times for his Nathan Heller novels, winning twice. Among the titles in this series are *Majic Man, Flying Blind, Stolen Away,* and the most recent, *Angel in Black.*

In March of 1947, I got caught up in the notorious Overell case, which made such headlines in Los Angeles, particularly during the trial that summer. The double murder—laced as it was with underage sex in a lurid scenario that made *Double Indemnity* seem tame—hit the front pages in Chicago, as well. But back home I never bragged about my little-publicized role, because—strictly speaking—I was the one guy who might have headed the whole thing off.

I was taking a deductible vacation, getting away from an Illinois spring that was stubbornly still winter, in trade for Southern California's constant summer. My wife, who was pregnant and grouchy, loved L.A., and had a lot of friends out there, which was one of the reasons for the getaway; but I was also checking in with the L.A. branch office of the A-1 Detective Agency, of which I was the president.

I'd recently thrown in with Fred Rubinski, a former Chicago cop I'd known since we were both on the pick-pocket detail, who from before the war had been running a one-man agency out of a suite in the Bradbury Building at Third and Broadway in downtown Los Angeles.

It was Friday morning, and I was flipping through the pages of *Cue* magazine in the outer office, occasionally flirting with Fred's good-looking blonde receptionist—like they say, I was married but I wasn't dead—waiting to get together with Fred, who was in with a client. The guy had just shown up, no appointment, but I didn't blame Fred for giving him precedence over me.

I had seen the guy go in—sixtyish, a shade taller than my six feet, distinguished, graying, somewhat fleshy, in a lightweight navy suit that hadn't come off the rack; he was clearly money.

After about five minutes, Fred slipped out of the office and sat next to me, speaking sotto voce.

My partner looked like a balding, slightly less ugly Edward G. Robinson; a natty dresser—today's suit was a gray pinstripe with a gray and white striped tie—he was a hard round ball of a man.

"Listen, Nate," he said. "I could use your help."

I shrugged. "Okay."

"You're not tied up today—I know you're on vacation . . ."

"Skip it. We got a well-heeled client who needs something done, right away, and you don't have time to do it yourself."

The bulldog puss blinked at me. "How did you know?"

"I'm a detective. Just keep in mind, I've done a few jobs out here, but I don't really know the town."

Fred sat forward. "Listen, this guy is probably worth a cool million—Walter E. Overell, he's a financier, land developer, got a regular mansion over in Pasadena, in the Flintridge district, real exclusive digs."

"What's he want done?"

"Nothin' you can't handle. Nothin' big."

"So you'd rather let me hear it from him?"

Fred grinned; it wasn't pretty. "You are a detective."

In the inner office, Overell stood as Fred pulled up a chair for me next to the client's. As the financier and I shook hands, Fred said, "Mr. Overell, this is Nathan Heller, the president of this agency, and my most trusted associate."

He left out that I wasn't local. Which I didn't disagree with him for doing—it was good tactically.

"Of course, Mr. Heller commands our top rate, Mr. Overell— one hundred a day."

"No problem."

"We get expenses, and require a two-hundred-dollar retainer, nonrefundable."

"Fine."

Fred and I made sure not to look at each other throughout my partner's highway robbery of this obviously well-off client.

Soon we got down to it. Overell slumped forward as he sat, hands locked, his brow deeply furrowed, his gray eyes pools of worry.

"It's my daughter, Mr. Heller. She wants to get married."

"A lot of young girls do, Mr. Overell."

"Not this young. Louise is only seventeen—and won't be eighteen for another nine months. She can't get married at her age without my consent—and I'm not likely to give it."

"She could run away, sir. There are states where seventeen is plenty old enough—"

"I would disinherit her." He sighed, hung his head. "Much as it would kill me . . . I would disown and disinherit her."

Fred put in, "This is his only child, Nate."

I nodded. "Where do things stand, currently?"

Overell swallowed thickly. "She says she's made up her mind to marry her 'Bud' on her eighteenth birthday."

"Bud?"

"George Gollum—he's called Bud. He's twenty-one. What is the male term for a gold digger, anyway?"

I shrugged. "Greedy bastard?"

"That will do fine. I believe he and she have"—again, he swallowed and his clenched hands were trembling, his eyes moist—"known each other, since she was fourteen."

"Pardon me, sir, but you use the term 'known' as if you mean in the . . . biblical sense?"

He nodded curtly, turned his gaze away; but his words were clipped: "That's right."

An idea was hatching; I didn't care for it much, but the idea wasn't distasteful enough to override my liking of a hundred bucks a day.

Overell was saying, "I believe he met my daughter when he was on leave from the Navy."

"He's in the Navy?"

"No! He's studying at the Los Angeles campus of U.C., now—premed, supposedly, but I doubt he has the brains for it. They exchanged letters when he was serving overseas, as a radioman. My wife, Beulah, discovered some of these letters . . . They were . . . filth."

His head dropped forward, and his hands covered his face.

Fred glanced at me, eyebrows raised, but I just said to Overell, "Sir, kids are wilder today than when we were young."

He had twenty, twenty-five years on me, but it seemed the thing to say.

"I've threatened to disinherit her, even if she waits till she's of legal age—but she won't listen, Louise simply won't listen."

Overell went on, at some length, to tell me of Louise's pampered childhood, her bedroom of dolls and teddy bears in their "estate," the private lessons (tennis, riding, swimming), her French governess who had taught her a second language as well as the niceties of proper etiquette.

"Right now," the disturbed father said, "she's waging a campaign to win us over to this twenty-one-year-old 'boyfriend' of hers."

"You haven't met him?"

"Oh, I've met him—chased him off my property. But she insists if we get to know Bud, we'll change our minds—I've consented to meet with them, let them make their case for marriage."

"Excuse me, but is she pregnant?"

"If she were, that would carry no weight whatsoever."

I let the absurdity of that statement stand.

Overell went on: "I've already spoken to Mr. Rubinski about making certain . . . arrangements . . . if that is what Louise and her Bud reveal to us tomorrow evening."

"Tomorrow?"

"Yes, we have a yacht—the *Mary E.*—moored at Newport Harbor." He smiled embarrassedly, the first time he'd smiled in this meeting. "Excuse my pomposity—'yacht' is rather overstating it, it's really just a little forty-seven-footer."

Little?

"Louise asked me to invite her and her 'boyfriend' aboard for the evening, with her mother and myself, so we can all get to know each other better, and talk 'as adults.'"

"And you're going along with this?"

"Yes—but only to humor her, and as a . . . subterfuge for my own feelings, my own desires, my own designs. I want you to explore this boy's background—I don't know anything about him, except that he's local."

"And you think if I turn up something improper in this boy's past, it would matter to your daughter?"

His eyes were so tight, it must have hurt. "If he's the male equivalent of a gold digger, won't he have other girls, other women? That would show Louise the light."

"Mr. Overell, is your daughter attractive?"

"Lovely. I . . . I have a picture in my wallet, but I'm afraid she's only twelve in it."

"Never mind that right now—but you should know there's every possibility that these two young people . . . and twenty-one seems younger to me every day . . . really *are* nuts about each other. Gollum may not be seeing anybody else."

"But you can find out!"

"Sure, but . . . aren't you overlooking something?"

"Am I?"

"Your daughter is underage. If I catch 'em in the backseat of this boy's jalopy, we can put him away—or at least threaten to."

". . . Statutory rape?"

I held up two palms, pushed the air. "I know, I know, it would embarrass your daughter . . . but even the threat of it oughta send this rat scurrying."

Overell looked at Fred for an opinion. Fred was nodding.

"Makes sense, Mr. Overell," he said.

Overell's eyes tensed, but his brow unfurrowed some; another sigh seemed to deflate his entire body, but I could sense relief on his part, and resignation, as he said, "All right . . . all right. Do what you think is best."

We got him a contract, and he gave us a check.

"Can I speak with your wife about this matter?" I asked him.

He nodded. "I'm here with Beulah's blessing. You have our address—you can catch her at home this afternoon, if you like."

I explained to him that what I could do today would be

limited, because Overell understood that his daughter and her boyfriend were (and he reported this with considerable distaste) spending the day "picnicking in the desert." But I could go out to the Los Angeles campus of the University of California and ask around about Bud.

"You can inquire out there about my daughter as well," he said.

"Isn't she still in high school?"

"Unfortunately, no—she's a bright girl, skipped a grade. She's already in college."

Sounded like Louise was precocious in a lot of ways.

Around ten-thirty that same morning, I entered at Westwood Boulevard and Le Conte Avenue, rolling in my rental Ford through a lushly terraced campus perched on a knoll overlooking valleys, plains, and hills. The buildings were terra-cotta, brick, and tile in a Romanesque motif.

I asked a cute coed for directions to the student union, and was sent to Kerckhoff Hall, an imposing building of Tudor design with a pinnacled tower. I was further directed to a sprawling high-ceilinged room where college kids played Ping-Pong or played cards or sat in comfy chairs and couches and drank soda pop and smoked cigarettes. Among sweaters and casual slacks and bobby socks, I stuck out like the thirty-eight-year-old sore thumb I was in my tan summer suit; but the kids were all chatty and friendly. My cover was that Bud had applied for a job—what that job was, of course, I couldn't say—and I was checking up on him for his prospective employer.

Not everybody knew Bud Gollum or Louise Overell, of course—too big a campus for that. But a few did.

Bud, it seemed, was a freshman, going to school on Uncle Sam. Other first-year fellas—younger than Bud, probably nineteen—described him as "a good guy, friendly, and smart," even "real smart." But several didn't hide their dislike of Bud, saying he was smart-alecky, writing him off as a "wise guy."

A mid-twenties junior with an anchor tattooed on his forearm knew Bud as a fellow Navy veteran, and said Bud had been a Radioman 1st Class.

"Listen," the husky little dark-haired, dark-eyed ex-gob

said, "if you're considering him for a job, give him a break—he's smarter than his grades make him look."

"Really?"

"Yeah, when you see his transcripts, you're going to find him pulling down some low junk, so far this year . . . but it's that little skirt's fault. I mean, they don't let dummies into premed around here."

"He's got a girlfriend distracting him?"

The gob nodded. "And it's pretty damn serious—she's a young piece of tail, pardon my French, built like a brick shithouse. Can hardly blame him for letting his studies slide."

"Well, I hope he wouldn't be too preoccupied to do a good job—"

"No, no! He's a right fella! Lives at home with his mom and stepdad—he's an assistant Scout master, for Christ sakes!"

"Sounds clean-cut."

"Sure—he loves the outdoors, always going hiking in the mountains up around Chatsworth, backpacking out into the desert."

"His girl go in for that?"

"They go everywhere together, joined at the hip . . . don't give me that look, buddy! I mean, haven't you ever had a female lead you around by the dick?"

"No," I said, and when he arched an eyebrow, I added, "Does my wife count?"

He grinned at me. "Does mine?"

A table of girls who were smoking and playing pitch allowed me to pull up a chair for a few questions; they weren't very cute, just enough to make me want to bust out crying.

"I don't know what a neat guy like that sees in ol' Stone Face," a blonde with blue eyes and braces said. I liked the way she was getting lipstick on her cigarette.

"Stone Face?"

"Yeah," a brunette said. She wasn't smoking, like her friends, just chewing and snapping her gum. "That Gollum gal's got this round face like a frying pan and's got about as much expression."

"Except when she giggles," a redhead said, giggling.

All the girls began to giggle, the blonde saying, "Then she really looks like a dope!"

"She laughs at everything that idiot says," the brunette said. "They hang on to each other like ivy—it's sickening."

That was all I learned at the college, and the effort took about three hours; but it was a start.

Pasadena was the richest city per capita in the nation, and the residential neighborhood where the Overells resided gave credence to that notion—mansions with sunken gardens, swimming pools, and tennis courts on winding, flower-edged, palm-flung streets. The white mission-style mansion at 607 Los Robles Drive, with its well-manicured, lavishly landscaped lawn, was no exception.

Mrs. Overell was younger than her husband by perhaps ten years, an attractive dark-blonde woman whose nicely buxom shape was getting a tad matronly. We sat by the pool watching the midafternoon sun highlight the shimmering blue surface with gold. We drank iced tea and she hid her feelings behind dark sunglasses and features as expressionless as the Stone Face with which those coeds had tagged her daughter.

"I don't know what I can tell you, Mr. Heller," she said, her voice a bland alto, "that my husband hasn't already."

"Well, Mrs. Overell, I'm chiefly here for two reasons. First, I can use a photo of your daughter, a recent one."

"Certainly." A tiny smile etched itself on the rigid face. "I should have thought of that—Walter carries a photo of Louise when she was still a child. He'd like to keep her that way."

"You do agree with this effort to break off Louise's relationship with this Gollum character?"

"Mr. Heller, I'm not naive enough to think that we can succeed at that. But I won't stand in Walter's way. Perhaps we can postpone this marriage long enough for Louise to see through this boy."

"You think he's a male gold digger, too?"

She shrugged. "He doesn't come from money."

"You know where he lives? Have an address?"

"He's here in Pasadena."

I couldn't picture a wrong side of the tracks in this swanky burg.

"No, I don't have an address," she was saying, "but he's in North Fair Oaks . . . where so many coloreds have moved in."

I had been met at the door by a Negro butler, who I supposed had to live somewhere.

But I didn't press the subject. I sipped my tea and offered, gently, "If your daughter is willing to wait to marry this boy till her eighteenth birthday . . . which I understand is many months from now . . . perhaps what you ought to do is humor her, and hope this affair cools off."

The blue and gold of the sun-kissed pool shimmered in the dark lens of her sunglasses. "I would tend to agree with you, Mr. Heller. In time she might come to her senses of her own volition. But Walter is a father who has not adjusted to losing his little girl—she's our only child, you know—and I do share his concern about the Gollum boy."

"That's the other reason I wanted to speak with you, directly," I said, and—delicately—I filled her in on my notion to catch the two in flagrante delicto. I wanted to make sure she wouldn't mind putting her daughter through the public embarrassment a statutory rape accusation would bring.

Another tiny smile etched itself. "We've gotten quite used to Louise embarrassing us, Mr. Heller."

Mrs. Overell thought I might have trouble catching them, however, since they so often went hiking and camping in the West San Fernando Valley—like today. That would be tough: I was used to bagging my quarry in backseats and motel rooms.

As it turned out, Mrs. Overell was able to provide a snapshot, filched from her daughter's room, of both Louise and her beau. They were in swimsuits, at the beach on towels, leaning back on their elbows smiling up at the camera.

Louise had a nice if faintly mocking, superior smile—not exactly pretty, and indeed round-faced, but not bad; and she was, as that ex-gob had so succinctly put it, built like a brick shithouse. This girl had everything Jane Russell did except a movie contract.

As for Bud, he was blond, boyish, rather round-faced

himself, with wire-rimmed glasses and a grin that somehow lacked the suggestion of cunning his girlfriend's smile possessed. He had the slender yet solid build so often seen in Navy men.

I spent another hour or so in Pasadena, which had a sleepy air of prosperity spawned by the many resort hotels, the formidable buildings, the pretentious homes, the bounteous foliage. The North Fair Oaks section did seem to have more than its share of colored residents, but this was still nicer than anywhere I'd ever lived. With the help of a service station attendant—the private detective's best friend in a strange city—I located the home of Dr. Joseph Stomel, married to Bud's mother, Wilhilmina. But I had no intention of talking to anyone there, as yet. This was strictly a point of reference for the eventual tailing of Gollum.

That was Friday, and between the college and the Pasadena run, I'd earned my hundred bucks. I spent all day Saturday with my wife, and friends, enjoying our premature summer vacation.

Then I went back to work Saturday night, though I looked like a tourist in my blue sport shirt and chinos. The camera I had with me was no tourist's Brownie, however, rather a divorce dick's Speed Graphic loaded with infrared film and the world's least conspicuous flash.

It was around ten o'clock when I turned right off State Highway 55, my rental Ford gliding across the low-slung spit over the mouth of an inlet of landlocked Newport Bay, dotted by sails, glistening with moonbeams, dancing with harbor lights. Seaside cottages clustered along the bay shore, but grander dwellings perched on islands in the lagoonlike bay, California-style Riviera-worthy stucco villas, a suitable backdrop for the fleet of yachts and other pleasure craft moored here.

My behind was moored in a booth in the Beachfront Café, a chrome-heavy diner with a row of windows looking out on the dock and the peaceful, soothing view of lights twinkling and pleasure craft bobbing on the moon-washed water. I ate a cheeseburger and fries and sipped coffee as I kept watch; I had a perfect view of the sleek cruiser, the *Mary E.* A few lights were on in the boat, and occasional movement could be made out, but just vague shapes. No different from any number of other boats moored here, gently rocking.

Overell had told me that he and his wife would be entertaining their daughter and her beau aboard the cruiser, having dinner, talking out their problems, perhaps even coming to some sort of understanding. What I had in mind was to follow the young lovers when they left this family powwow.

Since Bud lived at home with his mom, I figured the couple would either go to some lovers' lane to park, or maybe hit a motel. Either way, my Speed Graphic would collect the evidence needed to nail Bud for statutory rape. It's not elegant, but it's a living.

Around eleven I spotted them, coming down a ladder, stepping onto the swaying dock: Bud and Louise. Hazel-haired, taller than I'd imagined her, she did have an admirable top-heavy figure, which her short-sleeved pale blue sweater and darker blue pedal pushers showed off nicely. Bud wore a yellow sport shirt and brown slacks, and they held hands as they moved rather quickly away from the boat.

I was preparing to leave the café and follow them up to the parking lot, and Bud's car—Mrs. Overell had given me the make and color, and I'd already spotted it, a blue Pontiac convertible, pre-war, battered but serviceable—only they threw me a curve in addition to Louise's.

The couple were heading up the ramp toward the café!

Absurdly, I wondered if they'd made me—impossible, since they hadn't seen me yet—and I hunkered over my coffee as the lovebirds took a couple of stools at the counter, just about opposite my window booth.

At first they were laughing, at some private joke; it seemed rather forced—were they trying to attract attention?

Then they both ordered burgers and fries and sat there talking, very quietly. Even a trained eavesdropper like me couldn't pick up a word. Perhaps they'd had a rough evening with her folks, because periodically one would seem to be comforting the other, stroking an arm, patting a shoulder, reassuringly.

What the hell was going on? Why did they need a burger, when presumably that luxury cruiser had a well-stocked larder? And if they wanted to get away from her parents and that boat, why hang around the dock? Why not climb in Bud's convertible and seek a burger joint that wasn't in her parents' watery backyard?

Such thoughts bobbed like a buoy in my trained snoop's mind as the couple sat at the counter and nibbled at their food. It was a meal any respectable young couple could down in a matter of minutes. But forty-five minutes later, the two were still sitting on those stools, sometimes picking at barely eaten, very cold-by-now food, often staring soulfully into each other's eyes. Every other stool at that counter had seen at least three customer backsides in the same span.

I was long since used to boring stakeout duty; but it was unnerving having my subjects so near at hand, for so long a time. I finally got up and went to the men's room, partly to test whether they'd use that opportunity to slip away (again, had they made me?), and partly because after three cups of coffee, I needed to take a piss.

When I got back, Bud and Louise were still sitting on their stools, Louise ever so barely swiveling on hers, like a kid in a soda shop. Frustrated, confused, I settled back into my booth, and glanced out the window, and the world exploded.

Actually, it was just the *Mary E.* that exploded, sending a fireball of flame rising from the cruiser, providing the clear night sky with thunder, hurling burning debris everywhere, making waves out of the placid waters, rocking the pier.

Rocking the café patrons, too, most of them anyway. Everyone except the employees leaped to their feet, screaming, shouting, running outside into a night turned orange by flame, dabbed gray by smoke.

Almost everyone—Bud and Louise were still just sitting at the counter, albeit looking out the window, numbly.

Me, I was on my feet, but then I settled back into the booth, trying to absorb what I'd seen, what I was *seeing*. I knew my client was dead, and so was his wife—two people I'd spoken to at length, just the day before—as that cruiser was already a listing, smoking shambles, sinking stern first into the bay's eighteen feet.

Finally, the couple headed outside, to join the gathering crowd at the water's edge. I followed them. Sirens were cutting the air, getting closer, closer.

Louise was crying now, hysterical, going from one gaping spectator to another, saying, "My father was on that boat! My mother, too! Somebody save them—somebody rescue them— somebody has to rescue them!"

The boyfriend remained at the side of the stricken girl as she moved through the crowd, making her presence blatantly known, Bud's boyish face painted with dismay and shock and reflected flames.

I went to my rental car and got my Speed Graphic. I wouldn't even need the flash—plenty of light.

Snagging shots of the dying boat, and the distraught daughter and her beau, I heard the speculation among the boating-wise onlookers as to the explosion's cause.

"Butane," one would say.

"Or gasoline," another would say.

But this ex-Marine wasn't so easily fooled.

Butane, hell—I smelled dynamite.

Before long, the Coast Guard arrived, and fire trucks, and police from nearby Santa Ana and Orange County Sheriff's Department personnel. The chief of the Newport Beach Police showed, took over the investigation, questioned the tearful, apparently anguished Louise Overell, and promptly released her, and her boyfriend.

Pushing through the bustle, I introduced myself to the chief, whose name was Hodgkinson, and told him I was an investigator who'd been doing a job for Walter Overell.

"A job related to what happened here tonight?" the heavyset chief asked, frowning.

"Very possibly."

"You suspect foul play?"

"Oh yeah."

"Where are you staying, Mr. Heller?"

"The Beverly Hills Hotel."

That impressed him—he didn't realize it was a perk of my security work for the hotel. "Well, obviously, Mr. Heller, I'm gonna be tied up here quite a while. Can you come by the station tomorrow sometime? Tomorrow's Sunday—make it Monday. And if I'm not there, I may be back out here."

"Sure. Why did you let those two kids go?"

"Are you kiddin'? We'll be dredging her parents' scorched

corpses outta the drink before too long. It's only decent to spare that girl the sight of that."

Only decent.

Sunday I took my wife to the beach at Santa Monica—she was only a few months pregnant and still looked great in a swimsuit. Peggy was an actress and recently had a small role in a Bob Hope picture, and even out here her Deanna Durbin-ish good looks attracted attention.

She ragged me, a little, because I seemed preoccupied, and wasn't terribly good company. But that was because I was thinking about the Overell "Yacht Murder" (as the papers had already started calling it). I had sold my crime-scene photos to Jim Richardson, at the *Examiner,* by the way, for three hundred bucks. I was coming out way ahead of the game, considering my client and his wife had been blown to smithereens the night before.

Call it guilt, call it conscience, call it sheer professionalism, but I knew I hadn't finished this job. Walter Overell deserved more for that two-hundred-buck retainer—just like he'd deserved better from that shrewd sexed-up daughter of his.

So on Monday, bright and early, looking like a tourist in sport shirt and chinos, I began looking. What was I looking for? A slip of paper . . . a slip of paper in the desert . . . sounds worse than a needle in a haystack, but it wasn't. I found the damn thing before noon.

Chatsworth was a mountain-ringed hamlet in the West San Fernando Valley that used a Wild West motif to attract tourists, offering them horseback riding and hiking trails, with the ocean and beaches and desert close at hand for lovers of the outdoors—like that Boy Scout Bud Gollum and his bosomy Campfire Girl.

The guy behind the counter in the sparse storefront at the Trojan Powder Company looked a little like Gabby Hayes—white-bearded, prospector-grizzled, in a plaid shirt and bibbed overalls. But he had his original teeth and a faint British accent, which took him out of the running for playing a Roy Rogers or Gene Autry sidekick.

This was the owner of the place, and he was looking at the

photo I'd handed him, taking a closer look than he had at the
Illinois PI badge I'd flashed him.

"That young woman will never drown," he said with a
faintly salacious smile.

"I'm not so much interested whether you recognize her
tits as if her face is familiar—or her boyfriend's."

"I recognize the whole batch of them—both faces, both
bosoms, for that matter. The girl didn't come in, though—she
sat out in their convertible—a Pontiac, I believe. I could see
her right through the front window."

"Did he make a purchase?"

"I should say—fifty sticks of dynamite."

Jesus, that was a lot of dinah.

"This is fresh in my memory," the proprietor said, "because it was just last Friday."

Day before the boat blew up.

"Can anybody stroll in here and buy that stuff?"

"It's a free country—but back in the early days of the war,
when folks were afraid of saboteurs, city and county officials
passed an ordinance, requiring purchasers to sign for what
they buy."

I liked the sound of that. "Can I see the signed receipt?"

Bud had not signed his own name—"R. L. Standish" had
purchased the fifty sticks of dynamite—but I had no doubt
handwriting experts would confirm this as the Boy Scout's
scrawl.

"Some officers from Newport Beach will be along to talk
to you," I told him.

"Fine—what about reporters?"

"Good idea," I said, and used the phone.

Examiner editor Richardson paid me another C-note for
the tip, and the proprietor of the Trojan Powder Company
earned his own fifty bucks of Mr. Hearst's money for providing the exclusive.

I found Chief Hodgkinson at the Newport Beach dock,
where the grim, charred wreckage had been surfaced from
the depth of eighteen feet—about all that remained was the
black blistered hull. The sun was high and golden on the waters, and the idyllic setting of stucco villas in the background

and expensive pleasure craft on either side was turned bizarre by the presence of the scorched husk of the *Mary E.*

Seated in the Beachfront Café across from the blue-uniformed, heavyset chief, in the same booth I'd occupied Saturday night, I filled him in on what I'd discovered up Chatsworth way. He excused himself to pass the information along to a couple of D.A.'s investigators who would make the trip to the Trojan Powder Company.

When the chief returned, bearing a plate with a piece of pecan pie with whipped cream, he sat and ate and shared some information.

"Pretty clear your instincts were right about those kids," he said gruffly but good-naturedly. "It's just hard to believe patricide *and* matricide. Only in California."

"The late Walter Overell was supposedly worth around a million. And, like I told you, he was threatening to cut his daughter off if she married her four-eyed romeo."

"What made you think to go looking for that sales receipt, Mr. Heller?"

"I knew they'd gone 'picnicking' in the San Fernando Valley, and a college pal of Bud's said the loving couple liked to hike up around Chatsworth. Plus, I knew if Bud had been a Radioman 1st Class in the war, he had the technical know-how to rig a bomb. Hell, Chief, Saturday night, you could smell the dynamite in the air—and the murder."

He nodded his agreement. "It's as cold-blooded a crime as I've ever come across. We found thirty-one sticks of unexploded dynamite in the galley, crude time bomb thing, rigged with wire and tape to an alarm clock—second of two charges. Bulkhead kept the larger one from goin' off. Which was lucky."

"Not for the Overells."

"No, the smaller bundle of dynamite was enough to kill 'em plenty dead," he said, chewing a bite of pecan pie. "But it wasn't enough to cover up the rest of the evidence."

"Such as?"

"Such as what the coroner discovered in his autopsies—before the explosion, both Mom and Dad had been beaten to death with a ball-peen hammer we found aboard the ship. . . . That there was no water in their lungs backs that theory up."

"Jesus—that is cold."

A young uniformed officer was approaching; he had a wide-eyed, poleaxed expression.

"Chief," the young cop said, leaning in, "somebody's here and wants to talk to you—and you won't believe who it is."

Within a minute, a somber yet bright-eyed Louise Overell—in a short-sleeved, cream-colored, well-filled sweater and snug-fitting blue jeans—was standing with her hands fig-leafed before her.

"Hello, Chief Hodgkinson," she said, cheerfully. "How are you today?"

"Why, I'm just fine," he said.

"I'm doing better . . . thanks," the blue-eyed teenager said, answering a question Hodgkinson hadn't asked. "The reason I'm here is, I wanted to inquire about the car."

"The car?"

"My parents' car. I know it was left here in the lot, and I thought maybe I could drive it back up to Flintridge . . . I've been staying up there, since . . . the tragedy."

"Excuse me," I said, getting out, and I flashed the chief a look that I hoped he would understand as meaning he should stall the girl.

"Well," the chief was saying, "I'm not sure. I think perhaps we need to talk to the District Attorney, and make sure the vehicle isn't going to be impounded for . . ."

And I was gone, heading for the parking lot.

Wherever Louise went, so surely too went Bud—particularly since another driver would be needed to transport the family sedan back to the Flintridge estate.

Among the cars in the graveled lot were my own rental job, several police cars, Bud's Pontiac convertible, and a midnight blue '47 Caddy that I just knew had to have been Walter Overell's.

This opinion was formed, in part, by the fact that Bud Gollum—in a red sport shirt and denim slacks—was trying to get into the car. I approached casually—the boy had something in his left hand, and I wanted to make sure it wasn't a weapon.

Then I saw: a roll of electrical tape, and a spool of wire. What the hell was he up to?

Then it came to me: while little Louise was keeping the

chief busy, Bud was attempting to plant the tape and wire . . . which would no doubt match up with what had been used on the makeshift time bomb—in Overell's car. When the chief turned the vehicle over to Louise, the "evidence" would be discovered.

But the Caddy was locked, and apparently Louise hadn't been able to provide a key, because Bud was grunting in frustration as he tried every door.

I just stood there, hands on my hips, rocking on my heels on the gravel. "Is that your plan, Bud? To try to make this look like suicide-murder, planned by ol' Walter?"

Bud whirled, the eyes wild in the boyish face. "What . . . who . . . ?"

"It won't play, kid. The dynamite didn't do its job—the fractured skulls turned up in the autopsy. You're about two seconds away from being arrested."

That was when he hurled the tape and the wire at me, and took off running, toward his parked convertible. I batted the stuff away, and ran after him, throwing a tackle that took us both roughly down onto the gravel.

"Shit!" I said, getting up off him, rubbing my scraped forearm.

Bud scrambled up, and threw a punch, which I ducked.

Then I creamed him with a right hand that damn near broke his jaw—I don't remember ever enjoying throwing a punch more, though my hand hurt like hell afterward. He dropped prayerfully to his knees, not passing out, but whimpering like a little kid.

"Maybe you aren't smart enough for premed, at that," I told him.

Ambling up with two uniformed officers, the chief—who had already taken Louise into custody—personally snapped the cuffs on Bud Gollum, who was crying like a little girl—unlike Louise, whose stone face worked up a sneery pout, as she was helped into the backseat of a squad car.

All in all, Bud was pretty much a disappointment as a Boy Scout.

The case was huge in the California press, the first really big crime story since the Black Dahlia. A grand jury indicted the young lovers, and the state attorney general himself took charge of the prosecution.

My wife was delighted when we spent several weeks having a real summer's vacation, at the expense of the state of California, thanks to me being a major witness for the prosecution.

I didn't stay for the whole trial, which ran well into October, spiced up by steamy love letters that Louise and Bud exchanged, which were intercepted and fed to the newspapers and even submitted to the jury, after Bud's "filth" (as the late Mrs. Overell would have put it) had been edited out.

The letters fell short of any confession, and the star-crossed couple presented themselves well in court, Louise coming off as intelligent, mature, and self-composed, and Bud seeming boyishly innocent, a big, strangely likable puppy dog.

The trial took many dramatic twists and turns, including a trip to the charred hulk of the *Mary E.* in dry dock, with Louise and Bud solemnly touring the wreckage in the company of watchful jurors.

Not unexpectedly, toward the end of the trial, the respective lawyers of each defendant began trying to place the blame on the other guy, ultimately requesting separate trials, which the judge denied.

After my wife and I had enjoyed our court-paid summer vacation, I kept up with the trial via the press and reports from Fred Rubinski. All along we had both agreed we had never seen such overwhelming, unquestionably incriminating evidence in a murder case—or such a lame defense, namely that Walter Overell had committed suicide, taking his wife along with him.

Confronted by the testimony of handwriting experts, Bud had even admitted buying the dynamite, claiming he had done so at Walter Overell's request! Medical testimony established that the Overells had died of fractured skulls, and a receipt turned up showing that Bud had bought the alarm clock used in the makeshift time bomb—a clock Bud had given Louise as a gift. Blood on Bud's effects was shown to match that of the late Overells.

And on, and on . . . I had never seen a case more open and shut.

"Are you sitting down?" Fred's voice said over the phone.

"Yeah," I said, and I was, in my office in the Loop.

"After deliberating for two days, the six men and six women of the jury found Bud and Louise not guilty."

I almost fell out of my chair. "What the hell?"

"The poor kids were 'victims of circumstance,' so says the jury—you know, like the Three Stooges? According to the jury, the Overells died due to 'the accident of suicidal tampering with dynamite by Walter Overell.'"

"You're shitting me . . ."

"Not at all. Those two fresh-faced kids got off scot-free."

I was stunned—flabbergasted. "How could a jury face such incontestable evidence and let obvious killers go free?"

"I don't know," Fred said. "It's a fluke—I can't imagine it ever happening again . . . not even in California."

The trial took its toll on the lucky pair, however—perhaps because their attorneys had tried to pit Bud and Louise against each other, the girl literally turned her back on the Boy Scout, after the verdict was read, scorning his puppy-dog gaze.

"I'm giving him back his ring," she told the swarming press.

As far as anybody knows, Louise Overell and Bud Gollum never saw each other again.

Nine months after her release, Louise married one of her jailers—I wondered if he'd been the guy who passed the love letters along to the prosecution. The marriage didn't last long, though the couple did have a son. Most of Louise's half-million inheritance went to pay for her defense.

Bud flunked out of premed, headed east, married a motordrome rider with a traveling show. That marriage didn't last long, either, and eventually Bud got national press again when he was nabbed in Georgia driving a stolen car. He did two years in a federal pen, then worked for a radio station in the South, finally dropping out of public view.

Louise wound up in Las Vegas, married to a Bonanza Air Lines radio operator. Enjoying custody of her son, she had a comfortable home and the security of a marriage, but remained troubled. She drank heavily and was found dead by her husband in their home on August 24, 1965.

The circumstances of her death were odd—she was naked in bed, with two empty quart-sized bottles of vodka resting near her head. A loaded, cocked .22 rifle was at her feet—unfired. And her nude body was covered with bruises, as if she'd been beaten to death.

Her husband explained this by saying, "She was always falling down." And the deputy coroner termed her cause of death as acute alcoholism.

I guess if Walter Overell dynamited himself to death, anything is possible.

AUTHOR'S NOTE: Fact, speculation, and fiction are freely mixed within this story, which is based on an actual case and uses the real names of the involved parties, with the exception of my fictional detective, Nate Heller and his partner Fred Rubinski (the latter a fictionalization of real-life private eye Barney Ruditsky). I would like to acknowledge the following works, which were used as reference: *The California Crime Book* (1971), Robert Colby; *For the Life of Me* (1954), Jim Richardson; *"Reporters"* (1991), Will Fowler; and the Federal Writers' Project California guide. Also, I would like to thank my research associate, George Hagenauer, for calling this case to my attention.

MURDER CAN HURT
YOUR EARS

A Desiree Shapiro Mystery Story

Selma Eichler

Selma Eichler warns us that *Murder Can Spoil Your Appetite*, *Murder Can Singe Your Old Flame*, *Murder Can Kill Your Social Life*, *Murder Can Wreck Your Reunion*, *Murder Can Stunt Your Growth*, *Murder Can Ruin Your Looks*, and *Murder Can Spook Your Cat*. Desiree Shapiro's most recent case is *Murder Can Upset Your Mother*.

"Please, Dez," my secretary and also very good friend Jackie had blubbered.

She was making her plea to me, Desiree Shapiro—the surname having been a gift from my late husband Ed Shapiro. I was born Desiree Soulé, but that was longer ago than I have any intention of admitting to you. Anyway, it's not important. What *is* relevant to this story is that I'm a PI. Just like Ed was.

"I hear Aruba's p-positively gorgeous," Jackie went on. "Well have a lot of fun," she assured me, looking anything but fun-loving.

I mentally shook my head. The way Jackie had been feeling these last few days she wouldn't have been able to enjoy herself in Paradise. And having to watch her in all of her misery, neither would I. Putting that aside, though, I was not the least bit interested in flying down to the Caribbean. I mean, the last time I waded into anything wet was when there was a break in the water main near my Upper East Side Manhattan apartment.

"Are you positive you can't find anyone else to go with you?" I asked as Jackie reached into the tissue box on my desk.

"Yes," she responded tersely after a few healthy honks into the Kleenex.

"And you can't get your money back?"

"No."

I put a silent curse on Derwin, Jackie's (until now) long-time significant other. Or whatever you want to call him. This was supposed to be *their* vacation. But once Jackie had made the arrangements to take over her cousin's time-share for a week—which arrangements, incidentally, had been entered into with Derwin's full approval—that tight-fisted creep had balked at the cost. This led to their exchanging a few words and then to their exchanging a few more words and, finally, to their not exchanging any words at all.

"Maybe Derwin will change his mind," I suggested, trying to be optimistic. And, I swear, not strictly for selfish reasons, either.

"I wouldn't take him back on a silver platter with an apple in his mouth." Jackie rubbed at her swollen red eyes, then gazed at me plaintively. Her final "Please" was so heart-wrenching that . . . well, it wrenched my heart.

And so here I was, a world away from New York City's frenetic pace, trash-strewn, congested streets, and capricious February climate. Instead, I lay stretched out on a chaise lounge on the patio of a two-bedroom suite at The Blue Waters, an elegant four-story resort on beautiful Eagle Beach. Gentle Aruban breezes fanning my prostrate five-foot-two, well-fed-and-it-showed body.

I ground my teeth. How did I let myself be talked into coming to this place?

It was Sunday—our third day on the island—and I have to concede that until a short time earlier, I hadn't found a single thing to complain about. Jackie appeared to be enjoying herself, too. Either she was adapting admirably to life without Derwin or she was a regular Meryl Streep.

At a few minutes before 6:00 P.M., however, The Blue Waters's entire air-conditioning system went kaput. And that was the good part.

Jackie and I had just gone out on the patio to cool off for a while when the phone rang. Jackie went to answer it.

She came back with an announcement. "Derwin is here, in the lobby. He wants me to have a drink with him at the bar. I think I should listen to what he has to say."

"Absolutely," I encouraged.

"I'll only be a half hour or so."

True to her word, she returned within thirty minutes, beaming.

Derwin, it seemed, had been contrite. And, for her part, Jackie had been forgiving. As for me, I was delighted to see her so happy. But then she hit me with the zinger.

Derwin, she informed me, was staying at some run-down hotel nearby—a real dump—and he was thinking maybe he could bunk in here, with us. If it was okay with me, of course, she was quick to add.

Now, it wasn't as if we didn't have plenty of space. And I really don't have anything against Derwin—honestly. It's just that there are other people I'd rather room with—Mel Gibson leaping to mind. (I used to give Robert Redford top priority, only nothing ever came of that, so I've moved on.)

But, naturally, I kept this to myself. "Sure. No, problem." I even stretched my lips into something that could pass for a smile.

Jackie was effusive in her thanks. After which she explained that she had to go help Derwin get his things together. "Why don't you join us for a bite later. Nothing fancy. Derwin isn't very hungry tonight. He, uh, was thinking of McDonald's." At least she had the grace to blush.

Is it any wonder I lay there grinding my teeth?

I must have dozed off after Jackie left. I woke up to an angry voice emanating from the adjacent patio.

"You evidently think I'm an idiot!" a woman was shouting. I sat up, automatically glancing to my right, in the direction of the disturbance. But a profusion of foliage separates The Blue Waters' ground-level accommodations from one another. So all I could see were some bright crimson flowers and a few million leaves.

"Shhh. Calm down, will you?" a second female instructed, her tone fairly even. "You've made a terrible mistake. Why can't I convince you of that?"

"I'm not senile, you know. Although I suppose that's disputable considering that I've put up with you for so long," snapped woman number one. "I'm going inside to dress—I have a dinner engagement. I'll be returning around eleven, and I would strongly advise you to take care of this matter by then. If you don't, I'll be talking to the police first thing in the morning. Do you understand?" Another note or so higher and this last sentence would have been out of human hearing range.

In a moment there were the sounds of a chair scraping, a door slamming. And now: total silence.

I looked at my watch. Close to seven o'clock. I probably should start getting ready for dinner soon myself. The Blue Waters had a nice little outdoor restaurant; I'd have something there. (Needless to say, I'd turned down that tempting invitation to McDonald's.) It was so comfortable here on the patio, though. I leaned back on the chaise lounge—just for a second or two . . . .

It was, I subsequently learned, about fifteen minutes later that I was jolted into consciousness by a piercing scream from the suite next door. "Stop!" the woman cried out. "What are you doing, Eileen?" And then in a voice filled with such terror that at times I believe it will haunt me forever: "No, Eileen! Please!"

And after this, nothing.

I have no doubt it was the fact that I still wasn't fully awake that prompted my uncharacteristic bravery. (Not all PIs are heroic figures, in case you haven't heard. And certainly yours truly has never been accused of excessive valor.) At any rate, my heart somewhere in the vicinity of my navel, I jumped up, hastily untangling myself from the ankle-length print shift that had wrapped itself around my legs.

It was purely adrenaline, I'm sure, that propelled me past all of that shrubbery and onto the patio of the next apartment. I tried the door. Locked. But that adrenaline still working its wonders, I hoisted myself up on the small cast-iron table under the open living-room window and crawled over the sill.

The room was empty.

Could this have been a bad dream?

Then almost of their own volition my eyes darted to the right—and into the master bedroom. And now I began to tremble from the top of my glorious hennaed head straight down to the toes peeking out of my floppy yellow sandals.

You have to understand something. As a private investigator, I'm normally called in *after* a crime has been committed. And while occasionally a homicide has been perpetrated when I've already become involved in a case, never in my entire career have I been an actual witness (even if a couple of minutes removed) to a murder. Stalwart character that I am, I had to gulp three or four times to keep from throwing up.

Directly across the room, a tiny, white-haired figure lay sprawled out in front of the triple dresser, blood oozing from the back of her pale blue silk kimono. Kneeling beside the body was a dark-haired woman of about forty-five or so, her fingers closed around the hilt of a bloody knife.

She looked up—and directly into my horrified eyes.

We shrieked in unison.

"She's been stabbed," the woman said, quite unnecessarily. Then getting to her feet, she stumbled over something lying next to the victim. "A lipstick," she informed me tremulously, glancing down.

I nodded, absently noting the profusion of cosmetics on the dresser.

My voice eluded me for what must have been ten or fifteen seconds. But eventually I managed to croak, "Did you see it happen?" I like to think that being fresh from that tight sleep, my brain wasn't fully functioning yet. Otherwise, how can I justify that it didn't even occur to me I might be interrogating the murderer?

The woman shook her head. "I was in my room when I heard Mrs. Whitman cry out. I ran in here and found her like this." She turned toward the body and gestured. "Except that the knife was protruding from her back. I pulled it out, hoping I could . . . that she would . . . But she was already gone."

And now, catching her own reflection in the large oval mirror above the dresser, the woman appeared to become aware for the first time that she was still clutching the murder weapon. As if suddenly repelled, she thrust it away from her.

"Are you sure she's dead?" I asked, although certain of the answer.

"Yes. I'm a nurse. Or I used to be. But anyway, it's obvious Mrs. Whitman—"

At this juncture there was a loud pounding, followed by a shout. "Hallo-o! Is everything all right in there?"

"No!" I yelled

An instant later a uniformed security guard was at the entrance to the bedroom. His eyes widened in shock. "What's going on?"

He didn't wait for a response. "I'll call the police," he said grimly.

Major Miranda was a good-looking black man somewhere in his late thirties or early forties, with a neatly pressed blue-gray uniform and a very troubled expression. In spite of the air-conditioning's having been restored to service a few minutes earlier, in the short time since he'd introduced himself, the major had mopped his brow at least a half-dozen times. I got the feeling that in this idyllic part of the world he wasn't called upon to deal with homicides all that often.

He had herded the three of us into the resort's conference room. *The three of us* consisting of the knife-holder, a newcomer who wore the knife-holder's same exact face, and myself. We were seated around a large rectangular table, Miranda with pen and notebook in hand.

He cleared his throat before beginning the questioning. "The victim's name was Mildred Whitman. This is correct?" he asked of no one in particular. His tone was somewhat formal and had a pleasant island inflection.

The newcomer stopped nibbling on her lower lip long enough to answer. "That's right."

"And you are—"

"I'm—I was—Mrs. Whitman's secretary and companion. Eileen Neesmith."

Eileen!

My hand flew to my mouth before I had any idea it was headed there. But if anyone noticed, they didn't comment.

"You have been with Missus Whitman how long?"

"Seventeen years."

"You were residing in her apartment?"

"Yes, both my sister and I. We shared a bedroom."

He turned to her twin. "And you are obviously the sister."

"Yes."

"Your name, please."

"Neelie Dodd."

The policeman's eyes went to the blood-dappled, white cotton T-shirt. "Neelie," he repeated with the trace of a smile. "Yes I see." By now I was sufficiently calmed down to recognize that the good-sized gold pin just above the woman's left breast proclaimed that this was indeed Neelie, the name written entirely in flowing, lowercase script, a tiny diamond dotting the "i."

"You have also been with Missus Whitman for this long a time?" Miranda asked.

"No, just since her stroke, which was a little over six months ago. Eileen sent for me. I'm a physical therapist, and Mrs. Whitman required physical therapy. She still does—that is, *did*—but to a much lesser extent."

The major transferred his attention to me. "And you occupy the suite as well?"

"No, I'm in one-E, right next door. I was on my patio when it . . . when it happened. I ran over because I heard the victim screaming."

"Your name is—?"

"Desiree Shapiro."

"Thank you." He addressed himself to the twins again. "One of you was in the apartment when Missus Whitman was stabbed?"

"I was."

"Ahh, Ms. Dodd. Please. Precisely what transpired?"

"I was lying on my bed, listening to the radio, when Mrs. Whitman began to shriek. I rushed into her room and found her on the floor with a knife in her back. I pulled it out before I realized she was dead."

"You know this for a certainty—that the victim had already passed on?"

"I was a nurse once upon a time."

"Ahh. And upon leaving your bedroom, you saw no one?"

"No. The killer either raced out while I was still in my room or hid somewhere—maybe behind the sofa—and then sneaked out while I was trying to minister to Mrs. Whitman."

"She screamed, you say. Did she actually *say* anything?"

"I'm sorry, but I couldn't tell you. I had the radio plugged into my ears."

"I don't imagine you are able to be more specific." The policeman directed this to me.

I glanced over at Eileen before responding. I'm ashamed to admit that my knees were shaking. (I mean, I'm supposed to be a *professional,* for God's sake.) "As a matter of fact, Major, I *can* be more specific. This may not be exact, but it's close to it. Mrs. Whitman said, 'What are you doing, Eileen?' And then she cried out, 'No, please, Eileen.' "

Eileen Neesmith appeared stunned, her face drained of its color. "That's not true!" she protested shrilly, glaring at me. A few seconds later she turned to Miranda, her voice tightly controlled now. "She must have misunderstood."

"Perhaps so," he agreed.

The woman continued to make her case. "After all, it isn't as if she were right in the apartment."

"Ahh, but Missus Whitman's bedroom window was wide open," he pointed out, almost apologetically. "Due to the failure of the air-conditioning, I would surmise. Also, the accommodations are not very far apart, Ms. Neesmith."

I tossed in my two cents worth. "Besides, Mrs. Whitman's room faces my patio."

"But I wasn't even there!" Eileen wailed.

"Then, please, where were you?" Miranda asked.

"I was so uncomfortable when the air-conditioning shut off that I went for a walk along the beach. When I reached Costa Linda"—she named a neighboring resort—"I realized how thirsty I was. So I stopped in for a drink."

"And after this?"

"I came home."

"At what hour did you leave your apartment?"

"A little after six."

"And you returned—when please?"

"It must have been going on seven-thirty—I didn't get in

until a few minutes before you arrived. I do know that it was five after seven when I left the bar—I'm sure of that because I checked my watch. Listen, Costa Linda is about a mile from here, right? So I couldn't have made it back in time to . . . to do what this . . . what Ms. Shapiro"—she sent me a positively lethal look—"is accusing me of."

"There is perhaps someone who can attest that you were at Costa Linda until just past seven?"

"Actually, there is." Eileen Neesmith's troubled expression suddenly vanished—then promptly reappeared. "At least, I hope so. At around quarter of seven this couple from Michigan sat down next to me at the bar, and we chatted for a bit. Her name was Jane, and she was small and dark, a little on the plump side. I don't recall the husband's name, but he was short and skinny, with a gray ponytail. I'd guess they were both in their early fifties. Anyhow, it's possible—isn't it?—that they'd recall what time I left. Maybe the bartender would, too—Celeste, her name was."

Miranda's tone was noncommittal. "Yes, it is possible."

"Try to find those people, *please,*" she entreated.

"We will do our best," the policeman promised. He turned to Neelie. "You can confirm that your sister left the premises at approximately six o'clock?"

"Yes, I can," she responded angrily. "Listen, anyone could have entered that suite and stabbed Mrs. Whitman. The security guard found the front door ajar when he came to investigate. Obviously, Ms. Shapiro didn't hear what she thought she did, that's all."

"This is conceivable." Miranda shifted his focus to Eileen again. "Tell me, Ms. Neesmith, did you lock the front door when you left for your walk?"

"Yes, of course. At least, I'm fairly certain I did. I always do."

"If that's the case then Mrs. Whitman let somebody in," Neelie suggested quickly. And anticipating the next question: "No, I didn't hear anyone knock. I told you—the radio."

Nodding, Miranda pushed back his chair. "I will want to see you all again tomorrow—I will be here in the afternoon sometime. If you leave your rooms I would appreciate your advising the desk clerk where I may locate you. In the meantime, Ms. Neesmith, it would be helpful if you could provide me with a photograph of yourself to present at Costa Linda."

"I'm sure I can dig something up," Eileen told him.

"One of the officers will accompany you to your suite." He glanced at Neelie. "I would suggest you return there now as well, Ms. Dodd, so that you can both collect whatever items you will need until the morning. I have made arrangements for you ladies to occupy temporary quarters tonight in order to allow my people to complete their examination of the crime scene."

He rose then, and Neelie followed suit. I was about to do the same when Eileen grabbed my wrist with icy fingers. "Why are you doing this to me?" she demanded. But apparently regretting this decidedly unfriendly gesture, she immediately released the wrist and covered her face with her hands. "I don't understand," she mumbled. "I just don't understand." And dropping her head to the table, she sobbed.

At Miranda's request, I went to the police station with him to give a statement. My apartment was empty when I got back.

Hope surfaced. Perhaps Derwin had decided to stay put. Then I noticed his clothes strewn all over the sofa.

It was close to eleven o'clock by then. And I was starved. As much as the murder had shaken me, it had had zero effect on my appetite. (But then, few things do.) By that time, though, I was too spent to even think about going out to eat. Fortunately, there were some salami and Brie in the refrigerator.

Jackie came in—alone—as I was on my way into the kitchen. Hope resurfaced. "Where's Derwin?"

"Still at the Alhambra Casino. He thinks he has a hot slot machine."

I raised an eyebrow.

"It's a nickel machine," she clarified, responding to the eyebrow.

Of course.

Suddenly she noticed that I was wearing the same thing I'd had on when she left. "You never went out to eat! Are you okay?"

"Yes, I'm fine." But I have a feeling I didn't sound too convincing. Because as I was about to reach for the refrigerator door handle, Jackie inserted herself between me and my salami and Brie.

"Tell me what's wrong," she demanded.

Well, knowing Jackie as I do, I couldn't even imagine her taking "later" for an answer. My sustenance would have to wait.

"I was lying on the patio . . ." I began.

On Monday I was actually out of the apartment before 9:00 A.M.—which is practically unheard of for me. And on a vacation, no less. But I had a murder to stick my nose into now. After all, simply because I wasn't being paid for my services didn't mean I could just ignore such a terrible thing, did it?

There *was* an upside to Derwin's staying here, I'd concluded last night. This epiphany immediately following Jackie's ten-minute lecture on the merits of minding my own business (an almost impossible charge, as you can probably appreciate). You see, with Derwin available to keep her occupied while I sniffed around . . . well, God bless the man, I say.

The coffee shop on the premises was almost empty. But one of the twins was seated in a booth in the rear.

Her fork was poised to attack an omelet when I made my way to the back. I quickly scanned the woman's chest for a clue to her identity—just as she raised her eyes.

Damn! No name pin.

She smirked when she realized what I was doing. "I don't *always* make it easy for people," she informed me, sampling the omelet.

This was Neelie.

"In fact," she continued, "my sister probably wears her pin more often than I do mine." Then in almost the same breath: "I hope you'll join me for breakfast."

"Thank you." I slid into the booth, and almost simultaneously a waitress appeared. The pancake order had barely left my lips when Neelie confronted me. "Listen, Ms. Shapiro—"

"Desiree."

"Desiree," she echoed perfunctorily. "I've been wanting to speak to you alone. You say it was 'Eileen' you heard Mrs. Whitman call out. But couldn't it have been 'Irene,' for instance?"

I gave the suggestion some careful thought. "It could have been, but I'm almost positive it was 'Eileen.'"

"*Almost* positive isn't positive," Neelie apprised me caustically.

"I don't suppose I can argue with that."

"Well, I hope you'll convey your uncertainty to Major Miranda."

"I'll be completely up-front with him. But why are you asking if it might have been 'Irene' Mrs. Whitman shouted? Do you know an Irene who had a reason for doing away with your employer?"

"No, I'm only making a point, that's all." And she took another bite of her breakfast.

Now, I didn't believe I'd been mistaken; I heard what I heard. Still, if there was even the most *infinitesimal* chance that I was wrong . . . I mean, the last thing in the world I wanted was to be responsible for an innocent person's being arrested for murder.

"Look, I'm sure the police won't be relying on my evidence alone." I said it as much to reassure myself as to pacify Neelie. "They'll investigate your sister's alibi thoroughly. Maybe someone can corroborate that she was at Costa Linda until five after seven."

"Oh, come on. You don't really think anyone would be able to pinpoint the time like that."

I'd had this same thought, but it wasn't something I was prepared to admit to. "You never know. And if that *is* the case, regardless of my statement, Ms. Neesmith will no doubt be off the hook." Just then something occurred to me. "Uh, your sister wouldn't happen to be a jogger, would she?"

Now, I fully expected a heated denial, maybe even accompanied by a nasty little snarl. I was totally unprepared for Neelie's hearty laughter. "My sister a *jogger*? That'll be the day."

Well, this was a woman after my own heart—presupposing, naturally, that Neelie was telling the truth. I mean, my own favorite form of exercise is a hike from the refrigerator to the kitchen table, preferably with a dish of Häagen-Dazs macadamia brittle in hand.

I recoiled in a kind of horror when I realized I'd been comparing myself to someone who—if I could believe my own ears—had stabbed an old lady to death last night.

It was a little after two. Jackie and Derwin had gone into town. And I was reclining on a lounge chair in a sparsely occupied section of the pool area, protected from even the sliver of a sun ray by something that, here in Aruba, they call a hut. The thing had a rounded thatched roof of dried palm leaves set onto a sturdy mahogany pole and, if you ask me, it looked more like an outsize umbrella. Anyhow, I was decked out in my new bathing suit—the first one I'd had on since the days I actually looked good in a bathing suit. Which was when I was around three. Of course, if it hadn't been for Jackie, I wouldn't be wearing one now.

The week of our trip she'd invited herself to accompany me to Woman of Substance, where it had been my intention to pick up a few resort-type articles of clothing. Well, the fact is, while I'm comfortable with the way I look, I don't go out of my way to acquire the sort of apparel that makes me appear practically the same size horizontally as I am vertically—bathing suits heading up that category. Somehow, though, Jackie had manipulated me into trying on this little number. And I have to admit the skirt really played down my hips. Plus, the built-in bra did what was required for the one part of my body that isn't equipped with its own padding.

At any rate, lying there going over the crime, I began to get the strong sense that I was overlooking something. Something important. Maybe if I—

"Hey." A little blond boy in red swim trunks was staring down at me, his hands on his hips. "That's a silly hat," he critiqued.

To be truthful, I thought my new wide-brimmed straw chapeau was quite spiffy. Which is why I insisted on keeping it on even when this was totally unnecessary. Like now. "I'm disappointed that you don't care for it," I said sarcastically.

"Well, I don't. I *hate* it. And it makes you look ugly, too. Uglier even than you are."

Sweet. I briefly considered drowning the darling child, but there were witnesses around. Besides, it would mean I'd actually have to get my bathing suit wet.

"My mother's prettier than you," he informed me. And when there was no reaction: "Even the lady who lives next door to us is prettier than you. And she's the ugliest person in the world."

I was toying with the idea of wetting the suit after all when a tall blond woman of about thirty materialized alongside my chair.

"I'm so sorry. I closed my eyes for a *second*—and Sheldy was gone. I don't know what I'm going to do with this son of mine. I hope he hasn't been annoying you."

"Oh, no, he's a lovely boy."

I thought she eyed me with suspicion before responding with an uncertain, "Thank you."

Once she'd schlepped her progeny away I began to review the tragedy again.

But whatever it was that I'd been trying to grab hold of pre-Sheldy remained beyond my reach. *Relax will you?* I instructed myself. *Let it alone, and it'll come to you.*

I had no sooner begun to follow my advice when someone tapped me on the forearm. I half expected to see a pesky little kid in red trunks again. But it was Major Miranda standing over me this time, the silver chevrons on his shirt—there were four on each shoulder—almost blinding in the sunlight. "They told me at the desk that I would find you here. Do you think you could accompany me inside? It would only be for a short while."

"Sure."

He ushered me into the same room in which he'd set up shop last night.

The instant my bottom made contact with the chair he said, "I must commend you, Ms. Shapiro. This was a very brave thing, rushing next door the way that you did. A little foolish perhaps, but brave. The management received a number of calls from others who heard the woman being attacked, but no one else attempted to come to her aid."

I preened at the words. "Well, I'm a private investigator. That kind of thing more or less comes naturally to me," I lied.

"Ahh, I see." Then, his forehead furrowing, Miranda stroked his chin for a bit before laying the groundwork for the coming question.

"It appears that Missus Whitman had been spending the month of February in Aruba for many years," he began. "And during this time she acquired a number of friends on the island. I spoke with some of those people this morning. And they all said to me the same thing: Missus Whitman was extremely fond of her secretary. Not only that, but they informed me that the deceased had become quite disillusioned with Ms. Dodd in recent weeks. Since Ms. Dodd was the secretary's sister, however, Missus Whitman was attempting to tolerate the woman—at least until she regained her full physical capabilities. This, according to her friends, she anticipated should not take very much longer."

And now he lowered his voice to a level not much above a whisper. "But within the last four or five days a valuable ring and broach belonging to Missus Whitman were stolen from the bedroom safe. The two ladies who had been closest to the victim told me that while Missus Whitman admitted to having no actual proof it was Ms. Dodd who committed the theft, she was, nevertheless, convinced this was the case.

"That is the reason I must ask you: Are you absolutely certain of what you heard when the murder occurred?"

"Look, I wouldn't want to stake my life on it—or Eileen Neesmith's, either, for that matter. I mean, I suppose that I *could have* made a mistake—although I honestly don't believe that I did. Still, since I can't totally rule it out, I hope you're going to try to substantiate Ms. Neesmith's alibi."

"Police officers are checking into this now."

"What about the murder weapon—is it being tested for fingerprints?"

Miranda came close to glowering at me. "Of course. We are not totally backward here, you know."

"Oh, I didn't mean . . . It was a rhetorical question, honestly."

He peered at me skeptically for a moment, then hunched

his shoulders as if to shrug off the slight. "I seriously doubt we will learn anything of significance from that knife, however. In the event you did not recognize it, it is standard equipment in all of the kitchens at The Blue Waters. So if, in addition to Ms. Dodd's fingerprints, we should find Ms. Neesmith's prints, for example, it would hardly be proof that she stabbed her employer." At this juncture the major leaned across the table. "Now I would like to share with you an idea I had last evening."

"Yes?"

"Perhaps what you heard was actually Missus Whitman shouting to her killer, 'What are you doing?' And then, immediately after this—thinking that Ms. Neesmith might have returned—the 'Eileen' was the victim calling out to her trusted companion for help. The 'No, please' that followed was directed at the assailant again. And the second 'Eileen'—this was the victim's final appeal to Ms. Neesmith to come to her assistance." There was a question mark in the gaze that fastened on me.

"I'm sorry. But what you're proposing isn't the way it sounded."

Miranda was obviously disappointed. But at least I had something else for him to chew on. "There's one other thing you should know. It just might tie in with the theft of the jewelry."

"Ahh." The policeman cocked his head expectantly.

"A little earlier that evening, around seven, I overheard Mrs. Whitman arguing with a woman on the patio. Mrs. Whitman hollered that if something or other wasn't taken care of by the time she got back from dinner, she would contact the police. She didn't specify the something or other, though."

"And the woman to whom she was speaking? What did *she* say?"

"I don't recall the words, but the take-away was that Mrs. Whitman was accusing her unjustly. Until now, I had pretty much assumed that the deceased had had this confrontation with Eileen. But . . . well . . . in view of what you've just learned, I'm not so sure anymore. It could be that Mrs. Whitman was demanding that Neelie arrange to return the stolen jewelry to her."

"That is certainly a possibility, Desiree. I may call you Desiree?"

"Please."

"And I am Raymond."

For a brief time after this Miranda sat there quietly, stroking his chin again. I was about to present him with another theory—the only one that seemed to make any sense at this point—when he gave voice to it on his own. "Of course," he murmured, as much to himself as to me, "it is also conceivable that the two sisters conspired to kill their employer."

"You may have something there."

But almost at once Miranda had second thoughts. "Still, Ms. Neesmith was Missus Whitman's secretary for many years—seventeen, I believe. And they had a close relationship. So why would she suddenly take part in this terrible crime? I—" He broke off abruptly. "Oh, I don't know," he muttered irritably.

"Perhaps her sister prevailed upon her to participate in the robbery, and then things got out of hand," I offered.

"Mmm," was all the response I received.

"Or it could be that Eileen recently discovered that she'd been named her employer's beneficiary. Mrs. Whitman," I reminded him, "appears to have been a very wealthy woman."

"I imagine this *could have been* the motive." It was delivered grudgingly. "In any event, I have been attempting to contact the attorney of the deceased. I hope to speak to him tomorrow."

"Good. We'll see what he has to say."

"Yes," Miranda agreed. "We will see."

I left the conference room smiling to myself. The man had all but deputized me. Evidently he was interested in picking the brain of a hotshot New York City PI. Well, I had no intention of apprising him of a background that included shadowing randy spouses, tracking down missing dogs and cats, and even—but only once—locating somebody's pet boa constrictor. (The thing had crawled into the radiator and ended up in the building's heating system. But unfortunately, by the time I found him, he had gone to his reward.)

Anyway, I figured it was time I put a few questions to Eileen Neesmith, and I fully intended to try to set up something for that evening. Granted, I must be the last person on earth she wanted to see, but I was counting on curiosity overcoming aversion. When I got back to the apartment, however, Jackie prevailed upon me to have dinner with Derwin and her that night. And, as I've already indicated, she's a tough person to say no to.

We ate at a lovely Italian restaurant—Valentino's, it's called—where I enjoyed one of my best meals here yet. I had to hand it to Jackie. It couldn't have been easy for her to induce Derwin to come to a place where you don't have to carry your own tray.

After dinner I took a cab back to The Blue Waters, while Jackie and Derwin headed for a casino in one of the high-rise hotels on the Palm Beach section of the island.

It was well after ten when I walked into my suite, probably too late to contact Eileen Neesmith. So I decided to devote what remained of Monday to some heavy-duty thinking.

I settled down on the sofa, which was now cleared of all of Derwin's belongings except a single sport shirt and two pairs of socks. Well, I could live with that.

No sooner had I kicked off my shoes when there was a knock on the door. I opened it to find one of the twins on the threshold.

"Neelie?" I ventured.

The woman smiled wanly. "No, the other one." What's that saying about Mohammed and the mountain? "May I talk to you?" she asked softly. "I won't keep you long."

"Of course."

I have to confess that I was a little nervous. But I immediately chided myself for being such a wuss. After all, what was to fear? Eileen knew I'd already given my information to the police.

She took a seat on one of the wicker chairs, and I plunked myself down on the sofa again, facing her. "I'm glad you came, Ms. Neesmith. I've been wanting to speak to you, too."

"Call me Eileen. You *are* familiar with my first name." The second the words were out, she regretted them. "I'm sorry. It's just that this whole thing is so unreal. But, listen, I've been doing a great deal of thinking, and tonight it came to me: the explanation for what you heard."

"Please go on."

She proceeded to echo Major Miranda's theory about Mrs. Whitman's crying out to her for help. "That was the context in which she screamed my name. It *had* to be."

I shook my head. "I'm afraid the phrasing you're suggesting doesn't jibe with how it was said."

Tears sprang to her eyes. "How can this be *happening*? I *loved* Mrs. Whitman. She was like a second mother to me."

"And Neelie—did she share your affection for your employer?"

"Not exactly," Eileen conceded reluctantly. "Ever since her stroke, Mrs. Whitman could get kind of . . . almost imperious at times. And occasionally my sister took exception to her attitude. But, honestly, it was nothing serious. And anyhow, Neelie would never *kill* anyone." There was a pause before she pronounced slowly, "And neither would I." And now, her eyes boring into mine, she put to me, "Besides, what reason could I have had for murdering someone who'd always been so kind to me?"

"I haven't the slightest notion. Umm, were you, by any chance, in her will?"

"I think so, but I'm certain she didn't leave me very much. She has a son and two grandchildren. Also, a brother."

Well, I could probably scratch financial gain. *Unless,* that is, Eileen here would be profiting from the sale of the stolen jewelry. "I suppose you're aware that Mrs. Whitman suspected Neelie of pilfering a ring and a broach from the bedroom safe."

"Yes, but she was wrong. Neelie is no thief."

"You're positive of that?"

"Of course. She's my sister—my *twin*. I know her almost as well as I know myself."

"The missing jewels are quite valuable, I understand."

"Worth over three hundred thousand dollars."

I produced my own pathetic version of a whistle. "I presume the stolen articles were the only ones in the safe at the time."

"Actually, there were a number of other pieces in there, as well."

"Was Mrs. Whitman normally the only one who went into that safe?"

"No, I did, too. But just when she asked me to get something for her, and that was rare, since she almost invariably wore her costume jewelry. I don't know why she even brought the good things here with her. But look, I want to make something clear. Mrs. Whitman kept the key to the safe in the dining-room chandelier. Not a very inspired hiding place, right? Any number of people could have discovered it and committed the robbery."

"I suppose you're right." But I didn't believe it. After all, the culprit had helped her- or himself to only two items. And it seemed to me that someone outside the household would have hauled away the whole kit and caboodle. No, the way I figured it, there'd been a deliberate effort to postpone the theft's being discovered. Which pointed to a perpetrator who (a) was aware of how infrequently Mrs. Whitman wore her jewels and (b) had the opportunity to remove the remaining pieces at any time. "Incidentally, when did you find out that anything had been taken?"

"On Saturday. Mrs. Whitman wanted me to get out this necklace she had offered to lend a friend, and when I looked inside the safe—I can't really explain it—something just *felt* wrong. As if somebody had been in there. So we—Mrs. Whitman and I—did a quick inventory, and then we knew."

"How were you able to conclude that the jewelry hadn't been missing for more than four or five days?"

"Because of the ring," Eileen answered, "a six-carat Colombian emerald set in platinum. Just last Monday Mrs. Whitman brought it to a jeweler in town to discuss having earrings made to go with it. The set was supposed to be a gift for her granddaughter's twenty-first birthday."

Eileen Neesmith left soon after this. And while she hadn't succeeded in persuading me to amend my evidence, she *had* induced me to rethink the likelihood of her having been involved in the theft. I mean, like I said, the very nature of the crime indicated that it was meant to go undetected for a time. Yet here was Eileen alerting her employer to what had occurred. If she were in on it, would the woman have blown the whistle like that?

Uh-uh. I couldn't quite see it. In fact, I couldn't see it at all.

On Tuesday, at just after twelve, I was getting into my bathing suit when the phone rang.

It was Major Miranda.

"I have news," he announced, excitement in his voice. "Can you meet with me now?"

I threw a long shift over the suit, thrust my feet into a pair of sandals, and within five minutes the major and I were once again rendezvousing in the conference room.

"Last Wednesday Ms. Neelie Dodd deposited one hundred and fifty thousand dollars—in cash—into an Aruban bank."

I came out with one of my more urbane responses. "Wow."

"Yes. I also spoke with Missus Whitman's attorney this morning. He was very cooperative. Missus Whitman's bequest to her secretary was twenty-five thousand dollars. A goodly sum. But not, it seems to me, an amount sufficient to induce a person such as Ms. Neesmith to commit murder. Particularly since this will was prepared ten years ago."

"I agree. Assuming, of course, there was no pressing financial need."

"At any rate, we have an excellent idea of the purchaser of those jewels—the fence." The policeman grinned. "It was not difficult to arrive at this individual. Fortunately, there are not a great many members of his profession here on Aruba. I consider it only a question of time—and the proper persuasion—before this gentleman is willing to implicate Ms. Neelie Dodd."

"Well, things have certainly progressed since last night," I observed.

"In some ways. But, I regret, we are at a standstill with regard to the murder. There, Ms. Eileen Neesmith remains the primary suspect."

"What about those people at Costa Linda? Have you been able to locate them?"

"Ahh, the people at Costa Linda. The wife said that, yes, she believes Ms. Neesmith left the premises at approximately seven-oh-five, while the husband insists that it was much earlier. As for the bartender, she does not even recall serving Ms. Neesmith."

He sighed. "So there we are. Missus Whitman still appears to have been killed by the *wrong sister*. And I anticipate that unless we can establish a motive for Ms. Neesmith to have committed the homicide, we may have difficulty even bringing her to trial—irrespective of your evidence."

Now, maybe I was being overly sensitive, but Miranda's tone when he uttered these last few words made this seem a lot like an accusation.

I had to order myself not to take it personally.

An hour later I was sitting at the pool in pretty much the same spot I'd occupied the day before.

By this point I felt the way Miranda did. Nothing in this case seemed to add up. And the thing is, yesterday I had been practically convinced that something critical was eluding me. But, unhappily, whatever it was hadn't shaken me out of a sound sleep to announce itself in the middle of the night.

Maybe if I tried reviewing exactly what I'd been privy to—only this time sans Sheldy—well, who knows?

Once more the tableau unfolded in my head.

I saw myself on the patio listening to the accusations and threats of one woman, the denials of another. After this I dozed off, awakening to screams. Moments later I was next door, in the master bedroom. My mind's eye took in the details: the elderly woman who lay lifeless in front of the triple-dresser, blood on her pale blue kimono. The younger woman who was crouched beside the deceased, a knife in her hand. I watched again as this younger woman, beginning to rise, stumbled over some object. "A lipstick," she informed me. And then she held the knife at arm's length and—

Wait! I pressed the instant replay in my brain, zeroing in on that lipstick. I noted, too, the cosmetics strewn over the dresser, the oval mirror above it.

Of course! Mrs. Whitman must have been applying her makeup when the assailant came up behind her.

Well, so what? I countered after the brief excitement of discovery.

I mean, this didn't change anything at all. I was still faced with a thief—okay, an *alleged* thief—who, it now appeared likely, had been threatened with arrest by her employer and who, it also appeared likely, hadn't lifted a finger to harm the woman. In contrast, there was the devoted secretary/companion to the victim, and it looked as though *she* was the one to stick a kitchen knife into the back of this beloved "second mother" of hers.

Damn that Eileen! And damn Neelie, too, while you're at it!

And this is when it hit me: the crucial fact that had evidently flitted through my consciousness at some point or other and then proceeded to dance away from me—until this very moment.

But at last I had hold of it.

And almost at once I knew that it explained everything.

I made a record-breaking (for me) dash for my suite. Then tearing a piece of paper from the notepad on the end table, I very meticulously wrote something on it:

neelie

Hurrying into the bedroom, I stood in front of the dresser. And now I held the paper up to the mirror, seeing that name pinned to the killer's chest just as Mrs. Whitman had seen it as she was putting on her make-up:

eileen

I have no idea how long I stood there, grinning inanely at the reflection of that small sheet of paper. But finally I went to the phone.

I was about to make Major Miranda a very happy man.

JOURNEY'S END

A Sheila Malory Mystery Story

Hazel Holt

Hazel Holt is the author of eight British cozies featuring Sheila Malory, among them *Mrs. Malory and the Fatal Legacy*, *Mrs. Malory: Death Among Friends*, and *Mrs. Malory and the Only Good Lawyer*. Look for her newest book, *Mrs. Malory and Lilies That Fester*, Summer 2001!

"Oh, come on, Sheila," Rosemary said. "It'll be fun."

"Fun?" I said doubtfully. "I don't think I'd call a coach trip to Scotland with the Antiquarians *fun* exactly."

"Lovely Highland scenery, romantic castles . . ." she tempted.

"I can't leave the animals."

"Nonsense. Michael and Thea will look after them. Anyway, you need a break after slaving away at that book. Do come!"

"What about Jack? Won't he go with you?"

"Oh, Jack!" She dismissed her husband. "You know what he's like—he loathes going anywhere!"

"I don't know . . ."

"Oh, all right, I'll come clean. There are only two tickets left and Mother wants to come with me. If I can say you'll be having the last ticket then she can't come."

"Ah."

"*Please,* Sheila. Think of me having to sit next to Mother for all those miles, listening to her complaining every inch of the way!"

We both considered this scenario for a while.

"Oh, all right, then. I'll come."

After all, Rosemary *is* my best friend.

The members of the Antiquarians are mostly middle-aged or elderly, usually retired with the time and inclination to go poking about in stately homes and "appreciating" antiques. Membership is strictly limited and new applicants have been known to scan eagerly the obituaries column of our local paper, waiting for an elderly member to die and thereby create a vacancy.

"Thank goodness for that!" Rosemary exclaimed, settling herself more comfortably in her seat as the coach pulled away. "Are you sure you wouldn't like to sit by the window? No, right up to the last minute Mother hoped that Phyllis Burton wouldn't be well enough to go so that she could have her seat. But, mercifully, Phyllis recovered in time." She nodded toward an elderly lady sitting near the front of the coach. "Mind you, she still looks a bit frail. I do hope she's up to it."

"Oh, Phyllis is tough as old boots," I said. "It would take more than a touch of bronchitis to keep her from doing anything she'd set her heart on. Poor Doris said she was quite determined to come on this trip even though the doctor said it might not be wise."

Doris is Phyllis's sister and very much under her thumb. I imagine looking after Phyllis in sickness and in health is no easy task.

"Whatever is Mervyn doing?" Rosemary asked.

Mervyn Gray is the secretary of the Antiquarians, a tall, drooping man in his sixties. The job was rather thrust upon him when he came to Taviscombe, recently retired. Societies such as the Antiquarians are always on the lookout for New Blood, since so much of the Old Blood has been curdled, as it were, by acrimony, and it is becoming increasingly difficult to find people willing (and naive) enough to run things. Mervyn was making his way with some difficulty up the aisle of the bus distributing leaflets.

"I know you've all had your itineraries," he said rather breathlessly when he reached us, "but this is additional information I've run off on the computer to fill you in on the background of the places we'll be visiting."

Mervyn is very keen on displaying his computing skills and produces an endless stream of information on absolutely everything. I think it's the only part of his job as secretary that gives him any pleasure, since at all other times he wears a look of perpetual harassment—as well he might since most of the older members of the Society get *their* pleasure from criticizing the organization of any arrangement he may make.

"Why are we going to this Wordsworth place in the Lake District?" Mavis Williams leaned across the gangway and pointed to an item in her leaflet. "We're supposed to be on a trip to *Scotland* for goodness' sake!"

"Well," I said, in a pacifying tone of voice (Mavis can be very tiresome if she thinks she's got a grievance), "since it's such a long journey from Taviscombe all the way up to northern Scotland we're breaking our journey in the Lakes and a lot of people thought it would be a shame not to take the opportunity to visit Dove Cottage while we're there. It's a lovely place," I added placatingly. "I'm sure you'll enjoy it."

"It still seems a waste of time to me. We've only got a week after all."

I gave her a bright smile and turned back to Rosemary who was looking at her leaflet.

"I'm really looking forward to Dunrobin Castle in Sutherland," she said. "It's right on the sea and looks wonderfully romantic in the pictures."

"I quite like the sound of Blair Atholl," I said. "It's near Dunsinane—very *Macbeth*!"

"Oh, dear, is it bad luck to mention *Macbeth*?" Rosemary said. "Or is that only in theater dressing rooms?"

A tug on my arm made me aware of Mavis once again.

"Do you think we're going to be stopping soon? It's ridiculous hiring a bus that doesn't have a toilet for a long trip like this—especially when there are so many elderly people. I do feel that Mervyn should have thought of that."

"I expect we'll be stopping at that service station on the M5," I said. "It's not far now."

There was a crackling sound and a sudden blast of noise. Mervyn had finally got the microphone to work.

"Ladies and gentlemen," he said, "just to let you know that we'll be stopping shortly, so that any of you who want to do so can get out and—er—stretch your legs. We'll be stopping for fifteen minutes so can you please be back in the coach by then."

There was a sharp screeching noise as Mervyn gingerly replaced the microphone and returned to his seat beside the driver.

"Fifteen minutes!" Mavis said in disgust. "I wanted to have a cup of coffee—there won't be time for that! Trust Mervyn Gray to get things wrong!"

"Oh, dear," Rosemary said softly. "Poor Mervyn! He's going to have a dreadful time with this lot!"

"Is his wife with him?" I asked.

"Amy? No. Apparently she refused point-blank, and who can blame her! Anyway, I expect she was quite glad to get Mervyn out from under her feet for a week."

We were all quite tired when we got to the Lake District and all most of us wanted was a good meal and an early night. There was some muttering from certain members of the party about the hotel Mervyn had booked us into (old-fashioned but comfortable) but they would have complained anyway. Quite a substantial proportion of the group set up a bridge game and, firmly turning their backs on the rest of us, soon became lost in their own little world. The remainder of the party sat around the lounge engaging in desultory conversation and yawning.

"I've never been able to understand the rules of bridge," Doris Burton confided in Rosemary. "It's all so complicated!"

"Nonsense!" Phyllis automatically contradicted her sister. "It's perfectly simple if you have any intelligence whatsoever. I used to be a very good bridge player when I was younger, but I would never allow myself to be *obsessed* by it, like some people." She shot a look of contempt at the group at the other end of the room.

"I've never got the hang of it, I must confess," I said to Doris. "I expect you have to have a certain sort of mind—I can't do crosswords either."

"Ah, now there you're really missing something!" Edward Mostyn, an elderly man sitting beside Rosemary on the sofa, broke in. "They are a great source of comfort in times of stress."

"I'm afraid," I said ruefully, "that they are a *cause* of stress to me—my mind goes completely blank!"

"Crosswords are a great waste of time!" Phyllis made another of her pronouncements. "You could be doing something useful or improving your mind with a good book."

"But what," Rosemary inquired provocatively, "would you consider a good book?"

Phyllis looked at her sharply. "I should have thought that would be obvious! Dickens and Thackeray," she said briskly. "*War and Peace,*" she offered.

"Personally," Edward Mostyn said, "I find crosswords highly educational. I have learned many interesting things from crosswords."

Phyllis gave what in someone less refined might have been considered a snort and launched into a monologue concerning her literary tastes, during the course of which I noticed Edward Mostyn switch off his hearing aid.

After a little while Mervyn came into the lounge.

"Early start tomorrow!" he announced, in what he obviously hoped was a breezy manner. "A quick visit to Dove Cottage and then off we go across the Border!"

This reminder rapidly broke up the party and Rosemary and I retired gratefully to our rooms.

Dove Cottage was all I had remembered it to be. Full of atmosphere.

"It's so *dark,*" Rosemary said, "and poky and massively inconvenient! Think of poor Dorothy Wordsworth trying to keep house here!"

"I know," I said.

"And think of all she had to do!" Rosemary said. "Keeping house for William and walking with William and writing out William's poems after they'd been walking. *Listening* to William!"

"And always," I joined in, "knowing that Coleridge might drop in with no notice and require food and a bed and a sympathetic ear. No *wonder* there are all those entries in her journal that end with her lying down in front of the fire with a headache!"

We passed through the house into the garden just in time to hear Doris Burton say that the path up to the summer-house was very steep and did Phyllis really think she could manage it.

Phyllis definitely *did* think, and she made her way very slowly up the path, thereby blocking it for the rest of the party, while Doris hovered behind her making agitated little noises that her sister totally ignored.

As we got back into the coach I noticed that the driver— a pleasant man called Andrew—had to help Phyllis up the steps (help she would normally have scorned), so it was obvious that the extra effort had taken a lot out of her. I mentioned this to Rosemary.

"Typical of Phyllis!" Rosemary said. "Whatever Doris suggests, she has to do the opposite. Mother says they've always been like that ever since she's known them—that was just after the war when they first came to Taviscombe—from Wales, I think. Anyway, Phyllis has always been difficult."

"They've never married?"

"Well, I ask you, who'd want to marry Phyllis! And I don't suppose she'd have *let* Doris marry."

The countryside went rushing by and soon we had crossed the Border and everyone said, "Oh, look!" and pointed out the sign that said Gretna Green and when we passed the sign-post to Ecclefechan Phyllis could be heard telling Edward Mostyn, who was sitting behind her, that that was where Thomas Carlyle was born. He nodded politely but I wondered if he had his hearing aid switched off.

We stopped for the night at Blair Atholl with the promise of visiting the Castle in the morning. As we sat in the lounge after dinner Mervyn Gray appeared with the coach driver.

"Ladies and gentlemen," he said, struggling to make himself heard above the chatter of the bridge players. "Ladies and gentlemen. Just a word. I thought you might like to know that Andrew here, who comes from Scotland—Inverness, is it Andrew?—says he will be happy to answer any questions you may have about the various places we go through whenever we have a break in our journey. So if you have anything you'd like to ask . . ."

Howard Roseby, our local dentist, and his wife Mabel approached the driver and I heard them asking about Killiecrankie, which we would be visiting next day. I was slightly surprised at the length and quality of Andrew's reply, very much fuller and more scholarly than the standard guidebook information I had expected. I looked at him more closely. He was a tall, well-built man of about fifty with graying dark hair and an easy manner. His voice was pleasant with just a faint Scottish accent. Encouraged by the sight of the Rosebys engaged in conversation, several others of the group approached him and soon he had quite a little circle hanging on his words.

"Do you think he's always been a coach driver?" I asked Rosemary. "Or do you think he's a university lecturer moonlighting in the holidays!"

Rosemary laughed. "He certainly seems to know his stuff. Perhaps he used to be a travel courier or something."

"Yes, I expect that's it," I said, but there was something about him—something familiar almost—that puzzled me.

Blair Castle, dazzlingly white against the green Perthshire hills, was magnificent, especially all the Jacobite relics. Mervyn had some difficulty in rounding us all up and getting us back to the coach, since there was so much we all wanted to see.

"Such a pity," Mavis said resentfully, "we didn't have nearly enough time there—I would have liked to walk through the deer park—I knew a week wouldn't be enough for us to see everything properly. I said so at the last committee meeting, but I was overruled!"

"Oh, look!" I said, pointing to a stand of trees on the horizon. "That must be Birnham Wood—I wonder how far it is to Dunsinane?"

This remark provoked a certain amount of speculation and the awkward unfolding of folded-up maps, by which time we were well on our way to Killiecrankie.

"The Soldier's Leap," Andrew said, addressing the small party that had gathered around him beside the coach, preparatory to setting off, "is so-called because it is said that an English soldier leaped eighteen feet across the river to escape the Highlanders who were pursuing him."

There was a murmur of interest from his audience, though Mavis could be heard to say that she, personally, never believed half these tales.

"Now it's quite a fair step, so some of you may not want to go all the way. But it is a very pleasant walk through the woods."

"So what about the battle, then?" Rosemary asked. "Was it here?"

"This river gorge," Andrew said, getting into his stride, "is the site of the battle, to which it has given its name, in the first Jacobite uprising of 1689. The Highlanders won the day but their leader, John Graham of Claverhouse, who you'll probably have heard of as Bonnie Dundee—as in the song 'Up with the bonnets of Bonnie Dundee'—was killed by a stray bullet."

"If I might just say a word . . ." Mervyn edged his way forward to the front of the group. "We have allowed an hour and a half for visiting this site. We really should be in Inverness in time for dinner this evening, and as time is of the essence, I have, therefore, arranged for a picnic lunch—sandwiches and so forth—for you all to eat on the coach as we travel."

This piece of information, previously withheld from the party, provoked an immediate storm of protest, and the people who had been gathered around Andrew turned their attention to Mervyn.

"This is monstrous," Phyllis said. "It was specifically stated that proper provision should be made for meal stops. As it is, we didn't stop for tea yesterday. I was prepared to overlook that, but this really is too much!"

"It might be fun," Doris suggested timidly. "A picnic could be quite fun."

"If you choose to give yourself indigestion," Phyllis said crushingly, "eating sandwiches bouncing up and down in a coach, then that is your affair, but it certainly doesn't suit me!"

"Why don't we all go for a walk to Soldier's Leap," I said soothingly. "I'm sure it will give us all an appetite for whatever Mervyn has provided."

"You may go if you wish," Phyllis said. "But if I am obliged to eat these sandwiches, then I will have them here and now while the coach is not in motion."

Mervyn, hastening to placate her, brought a large basket

containing the food and began to unpack some of the contents.

"Doris!" Phyllis's voice was raised sharply. "Where do you think you are going?"

"I thought I might like to go for a little stroll through the woods . . ." She faltered.

"You wouldn't enjoy it," her sister replied. "It is probably infested with midges. You had far better stay here with me."

"There aren't any midges," Rosemary said as we strolled along the path. "Aren't we lucky."

"It is a good time of the year to come to the Highlands." Andrew had come up behind us.

"The weather is usually good, and as you have said, there are no midges."

He certainly was an excellent guide and I think we were all impressed, not only by his knowledge but also by the easy way he conveyed it.

"Quite a remarkable man," Edward Mostyn said that evening as we sat in the lounge of the hotel in Inverness. "Very knowledgeable. It would be interesting to know more about him."

"Oh, the Scots are always obsessed by their history," Phyllis said dismissively. "It's all they can talk about! Still," she said grudgingly, "he seems capable and polite and a perfectly safe driver."

"Sheila," Rosemary said, "do you feel like a drink?"

As I followed her into the bar she said, "Honestly, listening to Phyllis going on and on—it's almost as bad as having Mother around!"

"She is a bit much," I agreed. "What are you having? Gin and tonic?"

I gave our orders and we sat down by the window. "She *is* tiresome. I don't know how poor Doris can bear it day in and day out."

"I suppose she simply turns off her attention," Rosemary said.

"Like Edward Mostyn turning off his hearing aid!"

Rosemary laughed. "He always does that when he's bored."

"I can't say I blame him," I said. "But it could be dangerous, I suppose, if there was something he really *needed* to hear!"

"Oh, Edward's all right with or without his hearing aid. He's an absolute whizz at lip-reading."

"Really?"

"Yes, he says it's quite fun. And he can always tell what the Queen is saying when you see her talking to people on the television."

I looked out of the window at the seagulls wheeling overhead.

"It's still light," I said. "Even this late."

"Up in the North it barely gets dark at all in the summer."

"I don't think I'd like that, you'd feel all upside-down somehow!"

The next morning we drove across the Black Isle and over the long bridge that spans the estuary at Dornoch, where we stopped for coffee.

Mervyn addressed us all as we stood waiting to get back into the coach.

"Andrew has made a suggestion for a small diversion," he said. "I think you will all agree that it would be interesting. I'll leave him to tell you about it."

"It's just a wee suggestion," Andrew said. "But not far away from here is a place called the Falls of Shin, where you can see the salmon leaping up the falls on their return journey to their spawning grounds."

"That sounds interesting," Howard Roseby said and his wife murmured agreement. Others, taking their cue from Howard, as they so often did, said how much they'd like to see it.

"How long is all this going to take?" Phyllis demanded. "Does this mean we're going to have to do without our lunch again?"

"It's only a wee way," Andrew said. "The scenery is fine around Struie. It's just past Bonar Bridge, you can see it on the map. There's a visitors' centre at the falls and a grand café that serves the freshest salmon you've ever had!"

Phyllis, who loves her food, seemed mollified by this so it was agreed that we should make the detour.

Certainly the scenery *was* splendid and when we drew up

in the visitors' car park everyone, even Phyllis, was in an amiable mood and willing to enjoy the outing.

We walked along the path looking down the steep banks into the river.

"I can't see any salmon," Mavis said.

"We aren't at the falls yet," Phyllis snapped.

But when we reached the falls themselves there were still no salmon to be seen.

"There are other smaller falls higher upstream," Andrew began, but just then it started to rain.

"Well, I'm going back," Mavis said and there was a general murmur of agreement. "I don't see any point in getting soaked to the skin looking for fish that aren't there!"

"Yes," Doris agreed. "The rain is really getting quite heavy. Phyllis, I think we should be getting back."

"Nonsense," Phyllis said. "I came up here to see the salmon and I'm not going back because of a little rain."

"Oh, come on," Rosemary said to me. "Let's go back and have something to eat. It's going to *pour* at any minute!"

With Rosemary leading the way the main party turned and went back the way we had come, only Andrew, with Phyllis leaning heavily on his arm, and Doris set off in the other direction.

"They must be mad," Rosemary said. "Out there in the driving rain looking for fish when they could be warm and cozy in here eating delicious salmon sandwiches!"

"Poor Doris!" I said. "She wanted to come back but Phyllis is so demanding! I hope they'll be all right."

"I imagine Andrew will look after them," Edward Mostyn said. "He seems a very considerate man. I saw him saying to Doris 'Are you sure you're up to it? It's going to be quite tricky.'"

"Saw?" I inquired. "Oh, I see, you lip-read!"

"Yes, it's very useful," Edward Mostyn said. "Though sometimes I overhear, as it were, things I'm not meant to—still I don't think there was anything *there* that was particularly private!"

It was warm and cozy in the café. The salmon was delicious and the coffee very welcome.

"This really is excellent," Howard Roseby said. "Such a good idea of Andrew's, even though we didn't see any fish."

"Perhaps Phyllis and Doris will have seen some," Rosemary said. "I do feel they should be rewarded with *something* for pressing on in all that rain."

"Absolutely ridiculous!" Mavis snapped. "Phyllis was supposed to be dying from bronchitis a week ago and now here she is traipsing about in all this dreadful weather!"

"It's only a bit of rain," I protested. "And there's quite a lot of shelter under those trees. Actually, they have been quite a while. Perhaps they've been waiting for it to stop." I got up and moved toward the shop at the front of the café. "I'm going to look at the postcards over there. There are all sorts of people I promised to send one to and this is the first opportunity we've had to get any."

We were all clustered round the postcard stand when Doris appeared in the doorway. It was evident that she was in some considerable distress—her hair was soaking wet and disheveled, her coat was muddy, and she was obviously fighting painfully for breath.

"Please," she gasped, "please help!"

Howard moved quickly forward and, seeing that she was in a state of collapse, put his arm around her to steady her.

"It's all right, take it slowly. What's the matter? What's happened?"

Doris drew deep, panting breaths and seemed hardly able to speak. Howard led her to a chair at one of the café tables and pushed his wife's half-finished cup of coffee toward her. "Here, drink some of that. Don't try to speak for a moment."

Doris obediently raised the cup to her lips and sipped a little coffee.

"It's Phyllis," she said faintly, "there's been an accident!"

"An accident! What sort of accident?"

Doris shook her head as if to clear it.

"She fell—down that gorge—into the river. Andrew sent me to get help—please go!" She began to cry, at first quietly, then in great sobs.

While the women gathered round Doris in some concern, the men rushed out into the rain in the direction of the river.

"Hadn't we better ring for an ambulance?" Rosemary asked.

The woman behind the counter in the café went over to the phone hanging on the wall and dialed a number.

"They'll be here as soon as they can," she said. "But it may be a wee while. They have to come from Golspie."

After a while we heard some movement in the road outside the café and Howard came in.

"Has anyone called an ambulance?" he asked.

"Yes," Rosemary said, "but it may take some time to get here."

"I'm afraid it won't matter now," Howard said quietly. "Phyllis is dead."

We were all, not surprisingly, very subdued that evening at the hotel. Doris, after speaking to the police about the accident, had refused a sedative.

"I'll just go and lie down for a bit," she said.

My room was next to hers in the hotel annex so I went with her and saw her settled before going back to join the others.

"Is she all right?" Mervyn asked anxiously. "Do you think someone should stay with her?"

"I think she just wants to be on her own," I said. "How is Andrew—it must have been a shock for him too."

"He's very shaken," Mervyn said. "Keeps saying it was his fault, that he should have tried to stop her going so near the edge."

"It's never been easy to stop Phyllis doing anything she wants to," I said, then felt guilty at having spoken ill, as it were, of the dead. "Where is he?" I asked.

"Howard's taken him to the bar to give him a whiskey."

"I must say," I said, "I wouldn't mind a drink myself—it's been one hell of an afternoon!"

When I got into the bar I found Andrew giving an account of what had happened. "I should have been firmer with her," he was saying—not, I felt, for the first time. "But Miss Burton she would go right up to the edge, she was determined to see a salmon, she said, but with the rain the ground was really slippery." He paused for a moment and took a gulp at his whiskey. "She just went over the edge of the gorge," he said. "She must have struck her head on the stones, and by the time I got down to her she was lying in the water. I could see at once that she was dead." He drank the rest of the whiskey. "It was my fault and I'll not forgive myself."

"Nonsense, man," Howard said. "You're certainly not to blame. No one has ever been able to stop Phyllis Burton doing anything she wanted to."

There was a murmur of assent from everyone at the bar.

"Her sister?" Andrew asked. "How is she? It must have been a dreadful shock to her, the poor wee soul."

"She's lying down," I said. "I made her drink a cup of tea—she wouldn't take anything stronger—and I think she just needs to be quiet for a bit."

Howard turned to Mervyn. "What happens now? I suppose we'll have to stay here until the police have sorted things out?"

Mervyn assumed his usual harassed expression. "I really don't know. I suppose so. Are things the same in Scotland? I wonder."

There followed a certain amount of ill-informed discussion about the differences between English and Scottish law and the term "Procurator Fiscal" was bandied about a bit. Eventually Howard said, "Well the police will be coming to see us again tomorrow morning so we'll know then."

"It doesn't look as if we're going to be able to get right up north," Mavis grumbled over dinner. "I especially wanted to see the Queen Mother's castle at Mey and now I suppose there won't be time. I *said* a week wasn't enough!" She turned to Rosemary. "And the food here isn't up to much—this pork is underdone, how is your beef?"

"It's very good," Rosemary said firmly. "But I don't think we should be bothering about the food with poor Phyllis lying dead!"

"Well," Mavis said, "she brought it on herself, you must admit. She was always willful and downright disagreeable if she didn't get her own way."

"Mavis, really!"

"Don't talk to me about poor Phyllis, it's poor little Doris we should be sorry for! Perhaps she can start to lead a life of her own now. If you ask me, it's just as well Andrew was with her. Else I might have wondered if something hadn't snapped and she pushed Phyllis over the edge herself." She looked round the table. "And don't you all look so disapproving. I've always been one to speak my mind and if you're honest you'll agree with me!"

"And of course she's right," Rosemary said when we were drinking our coffee together in the lounge, a gloomy place with dark wood paneling and the obligatory stags' heads and large stuffed fish in glass cases. "Phyllis was a monster and Doris will be better off without her."

"But will she?" I asked. "Phyllis took all the decisions, Doris is going to be absolutely lost without her."

This thought was with me as I went to my room that evening. I tapped on Doris's door and opened it quietly. Doris was lying on one of the twin beds and it suddenly came to me that Phyllis (who would have been sharing a room with her) wouldn't now be occupying the other. As I opened the door she raised herself up on one elbow.

"Are you all night?" I asked. "Is there anything I can get you? Aspirin or a drink of some kind?"

"No, really, Sheila, I'm quite all right. There's a tray and an electric kettle here. I can make myself some tea if I want it."

"Well, if you're sure . . ."

"No, really, I just want to be alone."

As I prepared to go to bed I thought how strange it must be for Doris to *be* alone. All her life Phyllis had been there beside her, this was the first time she had been by herself. Had Doris secretly longed to be alone? It suddenly struck me how composed she was. After that first hysterical outburst she had been quite calm. And, just now, when I had spoken to her, there was a firmer tone in her voice.

I just couldn't get to sleep. Even though it was ten-thirty and I had the curtains drawn I was very aware that it was broad daylight outside and somehow it didn't seem the time for sleeping. I shifted restlessly on my pillow while the events of the day churned about in my mind. Pictures and incidents kept coming back to me. The wild and beautiful scenery, the rain slanting down onto the river, the warmth and coziness of the café suddenly shattered by Doris's dramatic appearance. I heard Phyllis's voice firm and peremptory, insisting on going on and Doris's voice, timid and overruled as usual, protesting. All these things and other thoughts jumbled together until I was in a sort of daze, and then suddenly I was shaken awake by the sound of voices coming from the next room.

I got out of bed, opened the door a crack, and looked out. The corridor was still quite light, and as I watched, I saw Andrew coming out of the room. There was a murmur from Doris that I didn't catch, but whatever it was made him turn back and say sharply, "We're in this together. You have to keep your nerve. Remember—I'm relying on you." With that he closed the door and went off down the corridor.

For a moment I couldn't believe what I had heard. Then suddenly the words that Edward Mostyn had "overheard" flashed into my mind. "Are you sure you're up to it? It's going to be quite tricky."

What were they in together? It could only be one thing. But how could it be? Doris and Andrew were strangers—how could they both be involved in Phyllis's death? It was unbelievable. There was only one thing for it. I put on my dressing gown and went and tapped on Doris's door. There was no reply but I opened the door anyway.

"Doris," I called softly. "Are you awake. I've got to speak to you."

There was a click as she put on the light and I saw at once that she had been crying.

"Doris, what was Andrew doing here just now and what on earth is it all about?"

She uttered a little moan. "Oh, Sheila, I don't know what to do—it's so awful."

I plugged in the kettle and put a couple of tea bags in the teapot. "Just tell me what's happened," I said. "Who *is* Andrew anyway—how do you know him?"

"He's my son."

"What!" I sat down on the bed and stared at her. "Your son? But he can't be . . ."

"It's a long story. Oh, dear, I don't know what you'll think of me . . ."

"You'd better tell me all about it."

I made the tea and poured two cups. Perhaps the sight of something so ordinary gave her confidence and she began to speak.

"It was during the war," she began "when we lived in Wales—just outside Swansea it was. There was an army camp quite near and they used to have dances there sometimes. Phyllis would never let me go—our parents had both died when we were young so Phyllis felt she had to look after me, I suppose. But I was young and a bit headstrong so one night when Phyllis was on duty fire watching at her office, I went to the dance and I met Jack." She looked at me and gave a shy smile. "Oh, Sheila, he was so nice. Very quiet, not like the others. We hit it off straightaway. So, after that I used to meet him secretly, whenever I could get away without Phyllis knowing. We had so little time, they were going overseas almost immediately—so, well, you can imagine what happened."

"Oh, dear."

"By the time I knew I was going to have a baby Jack had gone. I wanted to write to him but Phyllis wouldn't let me. Oh, she was so angry!"

"Poor Doris!"

"She wouldn't let me keep him—the baby, that is—I only saw him for a few weeks after he was born. She wouldn't even let me give him a name!"

"That was cruel!"

"She said I wasn't to think of him—he'd gone a long way away. The minister at the chapel arranged it—said he'd gone to a God-fearing household—those were his very words. Then Phyllis made us leave Wales and go and live in Taviscombe where no one would know us, or know about my *shame,* as she called it."

She was silent for a moment, then I asked, "And you never heard from him?"

"Not until a few months ago. He sent me a letter—you can find out about your real parents nowadays apparently. It was lucky, Phyllis didn't see the post that morning so I was able to keep it secret. He wanted to meet me. Well, I was so flustered I didn't know what to do—but oh, Sheila, I *did* want to see him—to see how he'd turned out, what he looked like!"

"Of course you did."

She gave a little nod. "So I did meet him. In Taunton. I told Phyllis I was going in to match some embroidery silk for her—you can't get that sort in Taviscombe—so that was all right. I went in on the bus and he met me. I was afraid I wouldn't recognize him, but he had such a look of Jack I couldn't mistake him! We went to a café and we talked—there was so much to say. At first he was angry—you see he thought *I* was the one who wanted him adopted. And he'd had such a dreadful life as a child with the people who adopted him. Scottish, they were, and terribly strict. They said he was a child of sin—can you believe anyone could say that to a child!—and that he must pay for the sins of his real parents and if he ever did anything they thought of as wrong, the man beat him with a leather strap. My heart nearly broke when he told me that!"

"How terrible."

"He got away at last when he was eighteen. He became a driver in a haulage firm and traveled around for years. Then he met this girl, Molly she was called, and they got married. But she died last year—cancer I think—she sounded really nice, but there were no children, so then he was all alone. That's when he got to brooding, about the adoption and everything, and so he got in touch with me."

"I see."

"The more we talked, the more we got on. He wanted me to go and set up house with him (he's got a lovely house just outside Inverness—he showed me photos), but I told him Phyllis would never let me do that. He got angry then and went on and on about Phyllis and how she'd ruined both our lives." She sighed. "He was right, really, wasn't he? Well, then I had to go—Phyllis expected me back on the three-thirty bus—so he arranged to come down to Taviscombe. No one would know him there, of course. I said what about his work, but he's done very well for himself and he owns a fleet of coaches, so he could take time off when he wanted."

"A fleet of coaches?" I said. "Oh, I see—our coach is one of his?"

"That's right. When I told him about the trip he arranged to be the driver."

"I thought there was something different about him," I said "He's very knowledgeable."

"Yes, isn't he?" Doris said eagerly. "He's done so well for himself." She paused for a moment. "Well, things *had* been going well, but it's a cash flow thing—Andrew did explain it to me, but I'm so stupid about money."

"I see. He needed money then?"

"It's only temporary, Andrew says. But I have a bit put by and now Phyllis has gone there'll be her money too . . ." Her voice died away uncertainly.

"Andrew pushed her down the gorge and into the river and sent you back to say that it was an accident?"

"Well—yes. I suppose he did, and I was upset, really upset! But you do see how it was, Sheila? He was so angry—not just for himself but for *both* of us. It was all her fault, the terrible times he went through and all I had to suffer. Jack and I might have been married after the war—we might have been a family . . ." She began to cry again.

"Doris, please don't cry. But you do know that what you did—well, what Andrew did—was wrong, don't you? You know that I have to tell the police . . ."

"No—no!" She grabbed my hand. "No, Sheila, you can't!"

"I'm very sorry, Doris, but I really have no choice. It was murder!"

"No, no! Not that!"

I got to my feet. "Look, they probably won't blame *you*. They'll understand . . ."

She shook her head. "No, I can't bear to lose him again! *Please,* Sheila!"

"No, I'm sorry. I really can't."

I went back to my own room and got back into bed, my head in a whirl. Of course I had to tell the police—I'd speak to Howard first thing in the morning (it would be useless to expect Mervyn to do anything) and we'd go to the police station together. I was deeply sorry for Doris, but obviously Andrew had been using her from the beginning. It was Andrew too who had suggested going to the Falls of Shin—though, come to think of it, it was Doris who made sure that Phyllis wouldn't go back with the others by asking her to, knowing that Phyllis would be sure to do the opposite. *Was* Doris totally innocent then? It was all dreadfully confusing. And upsetting. Then there was the question of the money. When Andrew had got his hands on that would Doris herself be safe, knowing what she did? No, obviously I had to tell the police as soon as possible . . .

Worn out by all this I fell into a deep sleep. It was after eight-thirty when I woke up. I dressed quickly and hurried downstairs to the dining room. There I found total confusion and a babble of excited voices. The coach had gone and Doris and Andrew with it.

They found the coach abandoned outside Glasgow. The police are still hunting for Doris and Andrew.

THE BODY IN THE BAY
A Jack London Mystery Story

Peter King

This story also marks the first appearance for Jack London—as a detective. Peter King's first book to feature Jack is *The Jewel of the North*, available Summer 2001.

"Hey, Jack, look at this one!"

In the afternoon sun of San Francisco Bay, the fish glittered silver, wriggling desperately in attempts to return to its own environment. Young Scratch Wilson nursed it through the rippling waves. He was standing now in the small boat, feet planted far apart, and Jack London moved to counterbalance him and hold the tiny vessel steady.

He grinned at his boyhood friend's enthusiasm as the fish swung into the boat and flopped down, still struggling. Scratch sat down, beaming, and bent to pull out the hook. As he did so, he let out a gasp.

"Jack! Over here!" he shouted.

A couple of yards from the stern of the boat, a shape was breaking the surface. It was dark blue, wrinkled, and it turned slowly among the waves, then sank out of sight. The two friends searched around the boat but there was no sign of the apparition. Suddenly Scratch saw it again. He yelled and pointed.

The sun glinted off silvery metal and a blue mass swelled up behind it, changing in shape and twisting away. Jack reached for a gaffing hook and Scratch stepped over to help. Then the two stared aghast as a ghostly white face broke the surface. For a long second they were petrified. The face sank into the water and the blue shape was slowly disappearing too.

Jack reached out and swung. The hook snagged something

and Jack pulled. Scratch forgot his fish for the moment and leaned over to help Jack. He let out a cry.

The two of them pulled it into the boat. It was a jacket, dark blue in color. Two silvery buttons remained on the front and others on the cuffs. Jack looked at Scratch's horrified expression and knew that he was remembering that face—the eyes open in an accusing glare, the complexion leprous-white, soft and blotchy, the skin like ancient parchment.

Both the young men were accustomed to violence but both were shaken by the sudden appearance of that face of death. The bay was getting choppier now as evening breezes from the Pacific Ocean sprang up. They hunted around for the body in the water but at last gave up.

"We'd better get back and report this, Scratch," Jack said and reached for an oar.

Scratch Wilson was always known as "Young Scratch" even though he was five years older than Jack London. The two had been friends for many years. Then Jack, disappointed by his failure to make enough money from selling his stories, had gone to the Klondike to make a fortune in gold and Scratch had gone to sea as did so many young men of their circle.

A chance meeting in a bar on San Francisco's notorious Barbary Coast had led to this fishing expedition. "First holiday I've had in years," said Scratch, downing another beer. "I'm due to sail for the Indies on *The City of Perth* in five days. Let's go fishing." It had been an opportunity to compare experiences now that both were back in their hometown.

Tall, golden-haired, rangy, Scratch was a modern Viking and in appearance a sharp contrast to Jack, who was medium height, thick curly brown hair and bright blue eyes, stocky with broad shoulders.

"Take a rest from the writing," urged Scratch. "Do you good." He smiled at Jack's look of surprise. "Oh, I know all about that. I read that story of yours, 'To the Man on Trail' in *Overland Monthly*. You'll be a great writer one day and won't have time for fishing and holidays."

Jack had agreed and now they walked out of the Grant Street police station having turned in the sodden jacket and told of the body that had got away.

Sergeant O'Halloran had listened and scribbled on a pad of paper but Jack found nothing unusual in his casual, almost callous attitude. Dozens of dead bodies were found every month on San Francisco's Barbary Coast, which had the reputation of being the toughest place on earth. A body in the bay was of no special significance or concern.

The sergeant had examined the jacket with just a flicker of interest. He looked at the stripped front where only two of the silvery buttons remained. It reminded Jack of a story of the Foreign Legion with an illustration of a Legionnaire symbolically stripped of his rank.

"This face you saw—"

They told him again but he merely grunted, took down the names and addresses of Scratch and Jack, and let them go.

Scratch was to meet a girl that evening so Jack went back to his writing. He was collecting his ideas for a story set in the Klondike Gold Rush. He set himself a target of a thousand words a day and needed to make up the time he had spent with Scratch out in the bay. He wrote until well past midnight, slept until midmorning, ate some bread and cheese, and went on writing.

By evening, pleased as he read over what he had written, he headed for the Barbary Coast. As always, the streets were filled with sailors, goggle-eyed visitors, men carrying chalked boards advertising the various establishments, prostitutes, pimps, drug addicts heading for an opium den, gold miners about to be deprived of their hard-earned money, gamblers, laborers, farmers, Gandy dancers from the several railroads nearing completion, men passing out dodgers describing the shows at the bars and theaters, pickpockets looking for a mark, con men looking for a victim, and hard-eyed characters with a loaded sling shot heading for the darker alleys.

Music blared out from dozens of sources, smells of horse manure, beer, urine, cooking food, stale sweat, and kerosene mingled into an indefinable odor. Jack walked past the El Dorado where a couple of buskers tried to pull him in, shouting "Prettiest girls on the Coast!" It claimed to have been the first music hall on the Barbary Coast, having been opened with the first gold from the Yukon.

Jack passed the Billy Goat, owned by Pigeon-Toed Sal who carried a derringer and a heavy wagon spoke and used both frequently. She permitted any kind of crime in the Billy Goat providing she got half the proceeds. She sold whiskey at five cents a large glassful and if the drinker looked as if he had a few dollars, the drink would contain a dozen knockout drops.

A wave of noise hit Jack as he went through the big double doors of Gilbert's Melodeon. Posters outside proclaimed that Eddie Foy was appearing on the stage but Jack knew he had finished his run last week. The air was thick with cigarette and cigar smoke. A card game at one table had two players on their feet and a fight looked imminent. At nearby tables, heads turned, then went back to their cards. Shouted words came from behind one of the heavy-curtained booths on the mezzanine floor where the girl performers entertained customers as long as their money held out. On the stage, a singer was trying to be heard with the help of the five-piece band but it was a lost cause.

A few spaces remained at the bar and Jack squeezed into one of them and signaled for a beer. Gus, one of the bartenders, knew him for Jack was a regular visitor at all the places on the Barbary Coast. Gus brought him the beer.

"Been in the Bella Union tonight, Jack?"

Jack shook his head.

"Charley Doonan's looking for you. Sounds important."

Gus lingered, curiosity written all over his face.

"Can't think why," said Jack. He rolled a coin on the bar. "Better get over there, see what he wants."

The Bella Union had been in continuous existence for sixty years. It had been called the Haymarket Theatre in a period when it attempted to present melodramas for family audiences but the increasing decadence of the neighborhood had driven families away and it had now become the most popular resort on the Barbary Coast.

Gambling continued to be the biggest business, with numerous large rooms upstairs catering to hundreds every night. This money financed some of the biggest shows in the country, sometimes even bigger than New York. The dodgers being handed out on the streets described it as "Unapproach-able and Beyond Competition" and it certainly strove to live up to that claim.

When Jack asked the bartender for Charley Doonan and gave his name, he got immediate attention. He was given a glass of whiskey, "the good stuff" Jack noted, and in minutes Charley Doonan joined him.

The proprietor wore a frock coat, a white shirt with a ruf-fled front, a scarlet and black waistcoat, and lavender-colored trousers. His silky brown mustache was neatly trimmed and curled. He looked like a dandy but Jack knew he was tough and smart and always had a six-shooter within easy reach.

They exchanged pleasantries. Jack had talked to him a few times but it was a slender acquaintanceship at the most and Jack wondered why he was here. Charley ordered whiskeys and said, "Keeping busy these days? I hear you're writing books."

"Yes," Jack said, "it's going very well." He always said that.

"Thought you might do a favor for me," Charley said. He tossed back his whiskey and the bartender promptly refilled his glass. "Could make you some money too."

Jack tried not to look too interested. The last money he had received from writing had been a mere fifteen dollars from *Overland Monthly* magazine and the end of the money was in sight. He had three more stories out but he was well aware of the vagaries of the business and none of them might sell.

"Pleased to help if I can," Jack said diplomatically.

"A lady," said Charley, "got herself into some trouble. She's talked to the police but they can't do anything. I told her about you—how you spent that time as a law officer."

"Only a year," Jack said, "and it was on the Fish Patrol."

"I didn't give her any details," Charley said loftily. "Just said I knew somebody might help her. She's upstairs. Will you talk to her?"

"She's here?" Jack was surprised. "Well, all right."

They pushed through the crowd. The tables were full and the first evening show was about to start. Charley led the way past the stage and up a steep flight of steps. He stopped before a door and rapped. A voice called for him to come in and Jack followed.

"This is the young man I told you about," said Charley.

Jack just stood there, his blue eyes round as marbles. He wasn't listening to Charley's introduction for he had already recognized the woman coming toward him.

It was Lillie Langtry.

She was statuesque with masses of red-gold hair and a flawless complexion that appeared everywhere in advertisements for Pears Soap. Jack had seen postcards of her in every ship he had ever been on, had seen her picture in numerous newspapers and magazines and saw her face every day in the sides of the cable cars and knew that her figure was described as that of a goddess. He agreed.

Charley left and Lillie sank onto a divan, motioning Jack to an armchair opposite. They were in a dressing room, unused at the moment but half filled with racks of clothes.

"Charley tells me you were a law officer." Her voice was low but vibrant. She articulated perfectly, no doubt a result of her theatrical training.

"That's right." Jack managed to find his voice after the shock of meeting this woman who was the toast of England and America.

"He says you are discreet—that's very important to me in this matter."

Jack nodded.

She sat straight, proud and regal yet she succeeded in portraying a woman asking for help. Jack would have done anything . . . "Can you tell me what this is about? Charley didn't say—"

"Charley knows nothing of it." She studied him, then inclined her head minutely. "Yes, I can trust you, I see that. Very well—" She took a breath and began.

"I have been fortunate in making many friends, some of them in high places—"

Jack knew that was true. The "friends" included Edward, Prince of Wales, New York millionaire Freddy Gebhard, Crown Prince Rudolf of Austria-Hungary, Prince Louis of Battenberg, Oscar Wilde, George Bernard Shaw—even Victor Hugo, who bewailed the fact that he was not three years younger (he was seventy-eight). Jack was not a follower of gossip but it was impossible to pick up a newspaper or magazine without reading such stories.

"—and as I travel a lot," she continued, "I receive correspondence from time to time. A man who is prominent in San Francisco wrote me several letters. A few of them were"— she paused and most women would have blushed or dimpled or looked away; Lillie continued to look directly at Jack without a trace of any of these yet she remained intensely feminine—"were, well, imprudent. I guarded the letters carefully, of course"—she shrugged delicately—"but not carefully enough. They were stolen a week ago. The next day, I received a demand for the payment of a considerable sum of money for the return of the letters. Fortunately, I was able to raise the money."

Should have been no problem, thought Jack. According to a story recently in the *San Francisco Chronicle,* when Prince Edward had snapped at her at a party, "I've spent enough on you to buy a battleship!" Lillie had promptly replied, "And you've spent enough in me to float one!"

"You want me to negotiate for you?" asked Jack.

She shook that wonderful head of hair. "Oh, no, I had Carl, my bodyguard, do that already. He took the money to a rendezvous on the waterfront where he was supposed to get the letters. He didn't return and hasn't been seen since."

Jack did not find that too surprising. Her "bodyguard" was obviously in on the scheme and now they had the letters and the money.

Lillie's eyes were on him intently. "It's not what you think. Carl has been with me for ages. I trust him implicitly."

"Charlie said you told the police?" Jack asked.

"I told them I was robbed. They think I am still trying to be sure what was stolen. In fact, it was nothing but the letters. If the press found out what was in those letters, it would be in every paper in the country."

The kind of publicity that you crave, Jack thought. He tried to phrase it more diplomatically. "Your name has been linked with several men—that's easy to understand. Would it be that terrible if the press reported this?"

She sought the right words. "One of the letters contained other information that could be—well—misunderstood."

Jack had no idea what that could mean. He waited for her to elaborate but she did not. Instead, she asked, "Tell me, Jack, is there anything you can do?" She leaned forward, pleading but not suppliant.

"I'll do what I can." The words were out before Jack realized it.

She gave him a wan smile and reached into her handbag. "There's a hundred dollars in there," she said, handing him an envelope. "If you are able to get the letters back or get news of Carl, I'll give you the other four hundred. Does that sound fair?"

She took Jack's stunned silence for agreement. He tried to gather his thoughts. "When Carl went to make the exchange of the letters for the money, where was he going?"

She reached into her handbag again. "Yes, I brought the note that was left at the hotel."

It was crudely printed and read, "BE BEHIND BELLINI'S FISH BAR 11 THURSDAY NIGHT WITH THE MONEY."

Jack was beginning to regret letting his admiration for this beautiful woman get him into this. The money she was offering him was a lure—more than he was making in a year, even if he sold everything he wrote. How could he go about this though?

It was a long shot but he tried it. "Did Carl wear a uniform?"

"Yes, he did."

"Could you describe the jacket?"

"Of course, I picked it out for him . . ." Jack held his breath. "It was black with wide, black leather lapels and leather around the cuffs and the pockets."

"The buttons?" asked Jack.

"They were black." She leaned forward eagerly. "Have you seen him?"

Jack shook his head. "Have you reported Carl missing?"

Jack wondered why she hesitated. "No," she said, "I have been hoping . . . but I suppose I must now."

It was the only idea Jack had. What could he do now?

She seemed to be reading his thoughts. "I know it's a difficult task and I do appreciate your trying to assist me." Her eyes softened, the sophistication was gone and she was a helpless woman. Or was she perhaps that good an actress? That question was promptly dismissed from Jack's mind.

"I'll do all I can," he promised.

There was so little to work on, Jack thought as he went on his rounds of the bars and the music halls. The entertainers were a popular subject of conversation and especially the big stars like Lillie Langtry. Jack chatted with bartenders, owners, waitresses, bouncers, singers, and dancers but without learning anything useful. At the Midway Plaisance, one of the leading music halls on the Barbary Coast, he was able to talk to Flo before the next show started.

A source of knowledge concerning many celebrities, Flo had been a celebrity herself a few years ago. At the Columbian Exhibition in St. Louis, she became a star overnight as "Little Egypt" and her "hoochy-coochy" dance was a worldwide sensation. A very level-headed girl, she decided that fame was ephemeral, gave up performing, and became a teacher of dancing. She was currently rehearsing the girls of the chorus at the Midway Plaisance for a new presentation.

Flo was barely medium height and with an exquisite figure. She moved lithely and with a sensuous grace that was completely natural. Her face had a serene beauty that contrasted with the fiery dance that had made her famous. She was a great fan of "the Jersey Lily."

"She's here to discuss a new show," Flo told Jack. She was intrigued when he gave her an account of his job. He knew she was discreet but nevertheless made the account abbreviated.

"Yes," she said, "a millionaire in San Francisco is said to have been one of her many lovers but no one knows who he is."

"It probably doesn't matter," Jack said. "I don't see how it would help." He pondered. "Still, I wonder . . ."

"I do remember that when she came into town the other day, she came on a private train."

"She does that a lot, I suppose," Jack said.

"She has a private coach," Flo corrected him. "They usually hitch it onto a train."

"But this was a private train?"

"Yes." Flo's big dark eyes studied him. "Does that help?"

Jack walked to Market Street, crossed, and went down Fourth Street. It was late in the evening but trains ran at all hours into the busy San Francisco depot. A friend from Jack's days at the University of California in Berkeley worked in the ticket office and had just arrived for the night shift. Jack took him aside.

"Nate, what do you know about the private train that brought Lillie Langtry into town a few days ago?"

Nate was shock-haired and with a permanent friendly grin. He mistook the point of Jack's question.

"Boy, wasn't she something? The Berkshire 2-8-4—it's the first one Baldwin built! She must do sixty miles an hour! Probably kept it up all the way from Denver too! Some beauty, eh?"

Jack grinned. Nate's enthusiasm about locomotives meant that he would not be asking about Jack's interest in the Jersey Lily. "She certainly is," he agreed. "Came from Denver, did she?"

"You saw her?" asked Nate.

"I certainly did," said Jack, not finding it necessary to correct Nate's misapprehension.

"That railroad car too! That's Mr. Pullman's latest! They call it the 'Arlington.' Folks say it's the most luxurious Pullman car ever built."

"I didn't see that," Jack admitted. "Was there a name on it?"

"No," Nate replied, "but it's the only one they've built so far and only the Rio Grande-Western Pacific Railroad has it."

Jack found that surprising. Most of the trains coming in and out of the San Francisco Depot belonged to the Central Pacific or the Union Pacific. They were owned by the Big Three—Charles Crocker Junior, Leland Stanford, and Collis P. Huntington. The Rio Grande-Western Pacific was a common name but had less track in California.

"Do you have a U.S. Railroad Directory?" Jack asked.

Nate looked puzzled but pointed a finger. "On that shelf."

Jack quickly found what he was looking for. Judson Fairburn was the sole owner of the Rio Grande-Western Pacific.

Jack and Nate got into a chat about mutual friends from college days, Jack keeping the subject in that realm. He thanked his friend and went out through the main concourse of the huge station. Posters along one wall caught his eye. One showed a beauty with reddish-gold hair and Jack went to take a closer look. The Jersey Lily was coming to San Francisco and opening soon at the Midway Plaisance. "Direct from her huge success in Denver," the poster added.

The next morning saw Jack London back in the Klondike, lugging a hundred-pound pack over the Chilkoot Pass in temperatures well below zero and with a blizzard blowing like a thousand slashing knives.

He was partway into another story about his experiences searching for gold in the icy wastes when there came a banging on the door. It was a uniformed policeman and behind him, a horse snorted and stamped, impatient to be pulling the wagon back to where his ration of hay was waiting.

"They want to see you at the station," said the man and they set off at a fast trot.

Their destination was the Grant Street Station again where Sergeant O'Halloran greeted him impassively. "You were here—you and your pal—found that blue jacket floating in the bay. Said you saw a body."

Jack nodded.

"Come this way."

They went through rooms with drunks, muggers, pickpockets, and thieves protesting their innocence and other rooms with complaining citizens, many nursing physical grievances. The last room was a small office where Jack recognized Police Captain Regan. They had had some contact when Jack was a law enforcement officer with the Fish Patrol.

Regan took Jack into the morgue, reeking of lye and chilly as the grave. Bodies lay on wooden trestles and Regan went to one and pulled off the rough gray blanket.

"Seen him before?"

The man had been in the water some days. Jack shook his

head, still looking at the body. "I can't say. Might be but we only got a glimpse."

Regan asked Jack the details of seeing the body. He was mainly interested in exactly where they had found it and Jack described it as well as he could.

"Sounds as if he went into the bay from somewhere along the Embarcadero, doesn't it?" asked Jack.

Captain Regan was a big, beefy, red-faced Irishman and less corruptible than most on the force. He nodded. "Tide's that way and the timing's about right if he went in the previous night."

"Any idea who he is?"

"No. Nobody's claimed him. Not a miner or a dockworker, judging by his hands. No money in his pockets though," Regan went on. "Must have been rolled."

It was a familiar story on the Barbary Coast. Captain Regan asked a few more questions and let Jack leave.

As Jack was about to go out of the door, O'Halloran beckoned to a young woman standing waiting with another uniformed man.

She was pretty, fair hair cut shorter than was usual, and with a face that was almost aristocratic. She went to O'Halloran and they headed in the direction of the morgue. Jack watched her as she followed the sergeant. Her walk was stately and measured, she held her head high as if oblivious to the squalor and decadence around her.

Jack waited outside. It was not long—he had guessed that she was not likely to be in there a second longer than necessary. She came out and looked up Grant Street, toward Union Street where there would be a cab. He approached her.

"Excuse me—I saw you in there. The body was no one I know. I hope that you didn't get bad news."

She looked at him as if trying to decide whether to speak to him or not. Her eyes were light brown, he saw, a soft shade, soft and gentle. Her voice had an edge to it though when she finally answered.

"It was not the person I was looking for."

"Then there's always hope," said Jack.

She nodded, hesitant. Then she said, "I'm looking for my brother. He disappeared several days ago."

"What's his name?" asked Jack.

She shook her head quickly. Her glance had taken in his sailor's sweater, his seamen's pants and shoes. "You wouldn't know him."

"I know a lot of people," said Jack with his most winning smile. "Lived here all my life."

"He has very blond hair, light gray eyes, a fair complexion. He's an athlete and looks like one, about your height but slimmer."

"Doesn't sound familiar," Jack admitted. "I'll keep an eye open for him though."

She gave him a nod and a slight smile, turned and walked away with that patrician walk. When she had gone, Jack went back inside the station. O'Halloran was not in sight but another sergeant at the desk called out to him.

"You was just in here, wasn't you? Looking at that stiff? You and that young lady."

"That's right," Jack said. "Shame about her brother. You must be looking all over the state for him."

"She told you?" The sergeant sounded surprised.

"She's really worried about him," Jack said.

"Well, they're trying to keep it quiet. Waiting for the ransom note."

Jack nodded knowingly. "They can pay it anyway—all their money," he said, watching the sergeant closely. He was rewarded with a nod of agreement.

He waited for the sergeant to be distracted so that he could get a glimpse of the pad on his desk with the names and addresses of visitors to the morgue. Someone called a question and Jack's chance came as the sergeant's head turned. The first name was Laura but he could not see the last. The address was plain though.

It was "Octavia Street."

The most exclusive stretch of the exclusive Nob Hill. So exclusive, the mansions had no numbers.

He was accumulating some information, Jack admitted to himself. The trouble was that in his initial ignorance, desperate to make some progress, he had followed a lot of leads. Did any of them make sense?

He had started with Lillie Langtry's letters from a millionaire admirer that had led to an attempted payoff and the disappearance of the money and the driver, Carl. There was the find, by Jack and Scratch, of a uniformed body floating in the bay. Was it the body of Carl, the driver-bodyguard? Now, a kidnapping of a millionaire's son was added to the other mysteries. Were they connected? They did not have to be but Jack did not believe in coincidences.

He resumed his writing, pausing to walk around his room from time to time and mull over the tangle of puzzles. He ate some bread and cheese late in the afternoon. There was no point in eating much during the day as all the places he frequented in the evenings had huge bowls of food on the bar. They had shrimp, oysters, clams—as much as you could eat and all free. Naturally, everything was heavily salted to encourage more drinking.

On his way to the Barbary Coast, he stopped at the Oakland Public Library. The head librarian, Ina Coolbrith, had been a friend for a long time and she took him immediately to a city directory that told him who owned the mansion on Octavia Street, next to the home of Claus Spreckels, the sugar millionaire.

It was Judson Fairburn, the president and owner of the Rio Grande-Western Pacific Railroad.

Jack's first stop was the Eureka, an enormous barnlike structure that combined many of the features of the music hall and the dance saloon. Its girls were exceptionally pretty and many noted artistes appeared in its shows. He chatted with bartenders and waitresses but picked up no gossip that was of any use. He went on to the Rosebud, then the Arizona and even to a couple of the "blind pigs," the unlicensed bars of which the Barbary Coast had over two thousand.

The Lady Jane was his next stop. It had been a bar with a murderous reputation but two Italian brothers had bought it and put in a stage and turned it into a music hall. So far, it had a fair record but skeptics said, "Wait and see." Until something happened to justify their pessimism, the shows were good, the girls shapely and uninhibited, and the drinks not too expensive and only slightly watered.

Jack leaned on the bar, sipped his beer, and examined the crowd. A few faro games were going and a bunch of cowboys were in a boisterous poker game. Several Easterners, easily distinguished by their clothes, had been playing a poker game of their own, a cloud of cigar smoke hovering over their table. Now they were joined by a sleepy-looking local, known to Jack as an expert cardsharp.

A piano, a violin, and a trumpet were just making themselves heard over the din of voices. They increased their volume at the expense of tunefulness and as heads turned, the girls came out onto the stage.

The tune was "My Wild Irish Rose," the popular hit by Chauncey Olcott, the former black-faced minstrel. The girls wore costumes that looked to be a number of bright green shamrocks fastened together in a flimsy manner that suggested their number would be steadily reduced as the dance went on.

All the girls were pretty and passable dancers. One in particular caught Jack's eye. She was fair-haired with a face of unusually classical features . . . Jack put his stein of beer on the bar and turned fully to get a better look. It couldn't be— but he watched and had no doubt. It was the girl he had seen at the Grant Street police station, viewing the bodies in the morgue.

The music grew louder and more insistent, the dance more active. When the floor of the stage was covered in shamrocks, the girls became aware of their near-naked condition. They looked shocked, pouted provocatively, and shrugged helplessness. As they ran off the stage to tremendous applause, the remaining shamrocks fluttered away.

The roaring of the crowd for their return was finally rewarded and they wore fresh, though equally precarious, shamrock outfits. Jack waited for their next return—when they would mingle with the audience.

He watched the fair-haired girl talk to a man here and there, laughingly refusing an offer. When she was a few yards away, he pushed through the crowd to face her. Jack smiled at her involuntary start.

"Does your father know you dance here?" he asked, widening his smile.

She turned away angrily, then stopped.

"It's none of your business," she said sharply.

"It is if it involves your brother," Jack said.

"Do you know where he is?" she asked and her concern seemed genuine.

"What do the Pinkertons say?"

She looked at him and her soft brown eyes were harder now. "How do you know the Pinks are involved?"

Kidnapping was not commonplace but there was an occasional case. Jack knew that when it was a child of wealthy parents, they would bribe the police to stay out of it and then they would call in the Pinkerton Detective Agency that operated more forcefully and effectively than the police.

"I know a lot more than you think," said Jack. He hoped she would believe that and then he could really learn something.

"Who are you?" She was still suspicious.

"Jack London."

She shook her head, the name presumably meaning nothing. "Why are you involved?"

"I have been hired." Jack liked to stay as close to the truth as possible.

"Who hired you?"

"I can't tell you that."

"Hired to do what?"

"Can't tell you that either."

Her eyes flashed and he thought she was about to unleash a strong retort but she clamped her lips firmly.

"You tell me something," Jack suggested. "It might help in finding your brother. Why were you at the morgue?"

She hesitated and then said, "They let me know every time a body is found. One of them might be his. They showed me the jacket. Since then I have been expecting—" She broke off and looked away.

"The blue jacket with the silver buttons."

She nodded.

"You think the uniform is his but the body is not."

"That's right."

He asked her a few more questions but she gave only in-
direct answers. She asked Jack a question or two, mainly trying to find out who had hired him, and he was equally
evasive.

"How can I get in touch with you if there's some news?"
she asked finally.

"I'll be able to find you here," said Jack easily and slid
through the crowd to the door.

It was too late to go visiting on Nob Hill but by nine o'-
clock next morning, Jack was at Solly Blum's shop on
Philadelphia Street. Solly had been a tailor here for forty
years and Jack knew his son. He talked with Solly, left, and
headed for the ferry and Nob Hill.

An hour later, Jack was ringing the ornate brass bell in
front of the house on Octavia Street. The huge Moorish-style
door, studded with wrought-iron emblems as big as a hand
and surrounded by an elaborate stone archway that looked a
thousand years old, was opened by an elderly man in a smart
uniform and with a forbidding countenance.

No, Mr. Fairburn did not see anyone without an appointment, he announced in ringing tones but Jack was not to be
put off.

"This concerns the welfare of his son," he told the butler.
"It is very urgent. I must see him at once."

Jack's youthful appearance was against him and so were
his clothes but his compelling manner got him inside the door.
He waited in a massive room with priceless carpets on the
floor, centuries-old, golden-threaded tapestries on the walls,
and furniture that looked like it belonged in a museum. Glass-
fronted cabinets held china and porcelain objects and
Japanese screens stood beneath a sparkling glass chandelier.
Through the open door, he could see a wide stairway in onyx
and white marble.

He waited a few moments, then the butler came back and
conducted him to an adjacent room, walls lined with books
and mellow gas lamps casting a dim yellow glow on several
armchairs.

In one of them sat Judson Fairburn, distinguished and
white-haired, trim despite his age, bushy eyebrows over sharp

eyes that focused on Jack as he entered. The millionaire motioned him to a chair and before Jack had occupied it, barked in a commanding voice, "What can you tell me about Ronald?"

"Have you received a ransom note yet?"

The abrupt approach might have taken some men aback but Judson Fairburn was not one of them.

"I might tell the Pinkertons about that," he snapped, "but I won't tell the police and I won't tell you. Who are you?"

Jack told him but the name clearly meant no more to him than it had to his daughter.

"Why are you meddling?" barked Fairburn.

"I have been hired," Jack said. He considered mentioning Lillie Langtry but decided against it. As the writer of the letters to Lillie, Fairburn might not agree with her action in hiring Jack.

Fairburn tried to pry information out of Jack but having made up his mind, Jack refused to change it. On the table beside the railroad millionaire were several photographs. All were of a good-looking, fresh-faced young man with a dashing smile and blond hair. He was on a boat, on a horse, at a party, with a polo stick, on skis—over a dozen of them, all in silver frames.

"So you have received no communication at all?" Jack asked and the answer was a brief headshake.

"Doesn't anyone at the school know anything?" Jack wanted to know.

"School?" Fairburn's tone held alarm.

"The Piedmont Military Academy."

"No, he—no," Fairburn grunted. He was clearly surprised at Jack's knowledge.

"Your daughter has no ideas? About his friends, acquaintances, anyone?"

It was the first break in the iron facade. "Daughter! I have no daughter."

Jack stared, bewildered. The other took it for doubt.

"Dammit, London, or whatever your name is! Wouldn't I know if I had a daughter? I have only the one son. And he's a good boy—he was only trying to help me."

"To get back the letters?"

"Get out of here! I don't intend to answer any more questions!"

Instead of heading back to the ferry, Jack took a bus in the other direction, toward adjoining Piedmont. As he rode, he was trying to sort out the facts buzzing through his head.

He had thought it strange that a millionaire's daughter would be dancing in the Lady Jane. This must explain it. But if she wasn't Fairburn's daughter, who was she? It seemed clearer than ever that a connection existed between the stolen love letters and the kidnapping—but what could it be?

The tailor, Solly Blum, had instantly recognized the uniform from Jack's description of the jacket. It was that worn by cadets at the Piedmont Military Academy. Most of them were ne'er-do-wells who were sent there to keep them out of trouble. Only the richest families could afford it.

The academy was a smart, white-painted group of buildings with a flag flying from the high flagstaff by the door. A man of about thirty with close-cropped hair said the major was busy and could he help? He was the adjutant, he explained.

As soon as Jack mentioned the Fairburn name, the face of the adjutant, Morland, tightened. Ronald Fairburn was a cadet there, he admitted. No, he was not there at the moment. He had been given a few days leave to take care of some family business.

"I hear he is one of your top cadets," Jack said lightly.

A muscle twitched in the other's face. "Just what is your business with him?" he wanted to know.

The muscle twitch had given Jack his clue. "Oh, nothing serious. Just a matter of a little money." The only son of a rich man, in a military academy rather than a university . . . it was very probable that he had run up debts around town.

Adjutant Morland inclined his head. Jack's guess had been correct—it was not an unfamiliar story to him. But though Jack pressed him, he was not able to learn any more. Nor would the adjutant allow him to talk to any of the other cadets. Jack left, still pondering the puzzle.

He spent the rest of the day writing, imagining himself back in the icy hell of the Yukon, hands and feet numb with cold, the ceaseless pounding of the wind enough to drive a man crazy.

About nine o'clock, he set out on his rounds of the Barbary Coast bars. He visited a number of them, nursing a beer in each one, not usually finishing it for he wanted to be fully sober after midnight.

It was, in fact, past one-thirty when he watched the girls take their final bow at the Lady Jane. He slipped out and waited in the shadows near the back entrance. After a while, the girls came out. They did so in groups for the Barbary Coast was not safe at night even in twos or threes.

The fair-haired girl who had claimed to be Ronald Fairburn's sister was in the second group. Jack followed them, assuming that they would head for the cable car stop on Union Street. He was right and despite the hour the car was crowded. The girls all managed to get on and Jack squeezed onto the rear platform, which was usually filled in defiance of the sign prohibiting riding there.

The girl got off at Panton Street, in a dark neighborhood, and Jack jumped off too, keeping the cable car between them until it had gone. He followed her from across the street. She went only one block, then disappeared. There was only one entrance she could have used—an old house that appeared to be shuttered and empty. Jack crossed the street.

A side door in a narrow alley seemed flimsy and as Jack put his shoulder against it, it opened and he went in. All was darkness but there was a smell of stale food. The rooms on the ground floor were empty and Jack took a flight of rickety stairs up to the next floor. He thought he could hear sounds inside. He tried the door and opened it a few inches.

A large chair with a high back and wide wooden arms stood in the middle of the room that was illuminated by a kerosene lamp on a wall. In the chair was the young man of the photographs, Ronald Fairburn. His arms and legs were roped to the chair. He was half in profile from the door and did not see Jack, who sidled in and along the wall.

Jack stopped as he heard sounds from across the room where a door opened into a small kitchen. Jack smelled a wood-burning stove and could hear a clatter of pans. He took cautious steps along the wall and stepped out in front of Fairburn. The young man's eyes widened. Jack motioned him to silence and walked quietly toward the kitchen.

As he did so, a fair-haired, attractive girl came out. It was the Laura he had seen at the morgue. She did not seem surprised to see him and Jack had a nasty feeling that he had been expected to follow her. "What do you want here?" she demanded.

"I wanted to ask you about your brother," said Jack lightly. "Is this a friend of his you have tied up here?"

Perplexed expressions were flitting across her face. Her eyes moved past Jack and she frowned. Jack turned—to find himself looking into the muzzle of a Colt revolver.

The blond-haired young man had an unpleasant smile on his face. Jack looked at the floor. The ropes lay where they had been thrown—they had not been tied at all.

"You're a nosy fellow, aren't you?" sneered Ronald Fairburn.

Jack's brain was buzzing, putting two and two together, but he realized that the answer wouldn't help him if the nasty smile and the revolver together made an even bigger total.

"Your father is worried about you," Jack said, trying to keep the situation calm.

"More worried about his precious love letters," Fairburn said.

"Love letters!" Laura said derisively. "That's what he should have kept writing. He was a fool to tell Lillie Langtry on paper that she should buy Central Pacific stock because his own railroad was going to withdraw from the San Jose contract."

"Mercenary, our Lillie," said Fairburn. "She should stick to the stage, she can make enough money there." He waved the gun at Jack. "Now what are we going to do with you?"

"I hope you're not going to kill me like you did Carl." Jack tried to keep his tone level.

The girl's head jerked. "We haven't killed anybody. Ronald gave Carl money and he's gone to St. Louis to spend it."

"Is that what Ronald told you? My guess is that Ronald drugged Carl and put his jacket on him before he dropped him in the bay," Jack said. "Carl struggled his way out of the jacket, ripping off the buttons. With Ronald believed to be dead, he could disappear with the money and you." Jack's tone was derisive.

"Me—dead?" Ronald sneered. "Yes, just for a while—but I sent Laura to the morgue every day to find out if the Langtry woman had been there and identified Carl. Sooner or later, he would be and then he would be considered guilty—the police like it convenient. Suspecting me dead was all I wanted—I didn't want to take a chance that the body had been identified as mine."

Jack nodded. "You wanted to have it both ways, didn't you? The money now, and Carl guilty when you had spent all the cash. You could forget Laura and go back to father. He'd believe anything you said. Had you worked that out too—'lost your memory'? You could make sure you'd get your inheritance that way."

Laura was still staring aghast at Ronald. "Tell me you didn't kill Carl—you said—"

"That's enough!" Fairburn snarled. "Let's you and I take a walk." He glared at Jack and waved the gun toward the door.

"You'll need these," Jack said and picked up the ropes. Always do the unexpected when the other fellow has a weapon and you don't—that had been the advice from Swede Larsen, his seal-hunting shipmate on the *Sophia Sutherland*, and it had already saved his life on more than one occasion.

"Ronnie, no!" the girl protested. "You said no one would get hurt!"

"You tried to get Carl in on your scheme, didn't you?" Jack was putting together all the pieces. "He had served time on a chain gang—"

"How could you know that?" the girl asked.

"I saw the fetter marks on the wrists of that body in the morgue. That's why he liked to wear a long-sleeved jacket. But you didn't want him to be recognized and you switched jackets with him. I suppose you threatened or bribed him to steal those letters. Then you persuaded your father to let you be the go-between and buy them back. You must really have needed the money."

Jack was under full sail now and overrode the other's blustering attempt to interrupt him. "I would guess that you'd been thrown out of the academy and told your father that you wanted to make amends by helping him get the letters back. All this kidnap story was sheer invention, just a diversion."

"All we wanted was enough money to get away, be together," the girl blurted out.

"Shut up!" Fairburn blazed at her. "Can't you see he doesn't know anything, he's just—"

For a couple of seconds, his gaze was directed at the girl. Jack took his chance and flung the ropes in his face. The gun blazed but the bullet crashed into the ceiling, then Jack had grasped his wrist and twisted until the weapon fell to the floor.

At the military academy, Fairburn had evidently had some boxing lessons. His left hand came up in a vicious jab to Jack's stomach. Jack gasped as he fell away but he managed to half roll so as to be close to the gun on the floor. As he fumbled around for it, Fairburn raced to the door and was gone.

Jack picked up the gun. The girl let out a cry but Jack shouted, "I'm not going to use it on him. Stay here."

He went out in pursuit. There was no moon and it was very dark. Jack could hear running footsteps and went in that direction. The chase took him into the dock area. Jack stopped for breath. It was quiet, then Jack heard his quarry ahead.

"Fairburn—be careful!" Jack yelled. "It's dangerous at night! Ropes everywhere!"

There was one around and he came to a dock where a large freighter was tied up. A distant lamp shed a dim radiance and Jack could see a vague moving figure. He started in that direction as a yell split the night air.

Jack raced to the scene but it was too late. A splash was all he heard, and he reached the dockside and looked down where a gap of a couple of feet yawned away into the blackness of the water below. Jack hurried to and fro, trying to find some trace of a body floating in the water, but he could see nothing.

When Jack got back to the house, the girl was gone. Jack went through the room. It was bare and he found nothing, but looking at the floorboards, he noted one corner where a board protruded. He levered it up with the pistol barrel, reached in, and pulled out a dozen letters tied with ribbon.

The next evening, a delighted Lillie Langtry counted out fifty-dollar bills, eight of them, as soon as she had glanced through the letters.

"I wouldn't blame you a bit if you had read them," she told Jack. "All I ask is that you—"

"Don't worry," said Jack. "I didn't."

He thought she was about to peel off two more bills, but good businesswoman that she was, she rewarded him with a kiss instead.

"Now tell me all about it," she commanded.

Her beautiful eyes widened as he did so. Jack thought he saw a tear as he told of Ronald Fairburn's death in the bay.

"I talked to his father this morning," Jack told her in measured tones. "I told him how the thieves who took the letters evidently refused to hand them over to Ronald Fairburn and decided they could make more money by holding him and demanding money for his ransom."

"So the thieves escaped?"

"Yes. It was very unfortunate that Ronald Fairburn fell into the water while running away from them."

"And they had already killed poor Carl."

"Yes. They wanted him to help them and he refused."

She looked away, then turned to Jack. "Carl had a prison record, you know."

Jack managed a look of surprise but said nothing.

Later, as he told Flo of the hectic events, she eyed him shrewdly.

"Lillie Langtry, then Judson Fairburn, and, I suppose, the police—how do you manage to keep all your stories straight? Makes me wonder about the stories you tell me."

"Flo!" he protested. "I—"

She smiled. "Oh, I forgot. You're a writer. It must come in handy sometimes!"

THE JUNGLE

A Willie Cuesta Mystery Story

John Lantigua

Edgar-nominated author John Lantigua introduced private eye Willie Cuesta in *Player's Vendetta*, set in Miami's Little Havana. He returned in *The Ultimate Havana*.

Willie Cuesta drove over the Intracoastal Waterway and entered Palm Beach at about 10:00 A.M. that Tuesday morning. He had made it from Miami in a little more than an hour and a half. But, of course, there was no way to measure, in either miles or minutes, the distance between his blue-collar neighborhood of Little Havana and this posh playground of America's aristocracy—home to the Vanderbilts, the Kennedys, the Pulitzers, and the Posts.

It was his friend Alice Collins, riding shotgun, who put it into words.

"Make sure you don't hit anybody in this town, Willie," she said from behind her sunglasses. "The locals here have lawyers who eat human flesh."

"I'll do my best," Willie assured her.

Willie followed the directions he had received from his old police colleague, Arnie Corcoran. They took him onto Worth Avenue, the main drag, which was no commonplace shopping strip. It featured Saks and Chanel, Ungaro and Armani, lots of galleries, and a Gucci instead of a Gap.

Alice's eyebrows arched. "It's Worth Avenue, but I bet it used to be Net Worth Avenue. They shortened it."

They turned and traveled along the oceanfront, but Willie wasn't sure where he was going. So they stopped and talked to a young man dressed in white linen, just getting out of a lemon-colored Lamborghini. They asked him how to get to the Breakers Hotel, where they were supposed to breakfast with Corcoran.

The man pointed up the road in the direction they were going.

"You go to the estate on the corner that used to belong to Estee Lauder. You turn left, go the length of a good three-wood shot, hang a right at that street and you'll see the twin towers." They thanked him, took the dogleg he described, and found the place.

The Breakers was a legendary hotel, hard on the water and also hard on the wallet. They valeted the car in the porte cochere and entered a lobby that looked something like the Palace at Versailles. Lots of columns, tapestries, mythological figures painted on the arched ceiling, and large chandeliers out of the Middle Ages. Willie offered Alice his arm and she took it regally, accepting her chance to play Marie Antoinette—in sunglasses.

They found Arnie Corcoran in a circular dining room topped with a leaded glass cupola. Arnie was a former patrol lieutenant in Miami who had taken the job of assistant chief in Palm Beach. He was a tall, sandy-haired, red-faced guy, in a summer suit, bright pink shirt, and no tie. They ordered breakfast and Arnie addressed the issue at hand.

"It's like I told you on the phone, Willie. We have an extremely old and wealthy man, one of our leading citizens, who has received anonymous messages that his life is in danger. The messages, left on an answering machine, are in Spanish."

"But this gentleman isn't Latino," Willie said.

"No, but his family made its fortune in Latin America. They were officers and principal stockholders in a firm called the Central American Fruit Company, based in Guatemala. Very big banana importers. He worked down there part of the time, running things. His name is Harold Usser."

"He was the big banana."

"Exactly. He said his Spanish was never great because he had managers to actually convey his orders and oversee the native workers, but he understood enough about the messages to comprehend that someone wanted to kill him. The messages are still on the tape. They mention his family and supposedly certain crimes they committed down there."

Willie frowned. "What crimes?"

Arnie shook his head. "Usser insists he doesn't know what the messages mean."

"Does he have any idea who might have left them?"

"No."

"What kind of security does he have?"

"A gardener lives on the property and doubles as a security guard. Usser also has a houseman, a cook who's married to the gardener, and a maid. All of them live on the premises."

"Sounds like a big spread."

"You'll see. Anyway, his niece, who lives nearby, feels he's not safe no matter how many servants surround him. She says these threats are the kind that political terrorists in Central America make, maybe because the family took all its money from down there. I don't have anybody on my staff who has ever handled this kind of stuff. But you have, Willie."

Willie shrugged in acknowledgment. Before becoming a private investigator, Willie had worked for years in the Intelligence Unit of the Miami Police Department. He and his colleagues tracked all the political organizations in Miami— Cuban commandos, Central American freedom fighters, Colombian guerrillas, Haitian patriots, Israelis, Bosnians, etc. The unit also helped guard visiting diplomats and other dignitaries. It was a busy beat.

Arnie sipped his coffee. "The hotel manager here has very generously given the department use of a double room for the rest of the week, plus access to the health club, golf course, tennis courts, sauna, etc. You look into the case, Willie, and tell me what you can, and then you can wile away the rest of the week with Ms. Collins here, on the house."

Willie had a couple of questions, but Alice didn't give him a chance to ask them. She beamed at Arnie. "In the name of Willie Cuesta, I'd like to accept the assignment."

A half hour later they had checked in, Alice had been deposited happily at the pool and Willie and Arnie were on their way to the Usser mansion. They followed the oceanfront road south and as they did the mansions seemed to swell. Behind the high walls and the wrought-iron gates guarded by stone lions, Willie saw palaces in different designs—Mediterranean, Spanish Colonial, and some in a style that could only be called Classical Gaudy. Arnie noticed Willie's wide-eyed gaze.

"A lot of these were built before there was an income tax. They had some extra change to spend."

"So I noticed."

A minute later they pulled up to a pair of those tall gates. A gold plaque embedded in the wall announced that this particular bungalow was called LA SELVA. In Spanish that meant "The Jungle." The white stucco wall was about twelve feet high and vines crawled over it from the other side.

Arnie spoke into an intercom and the gates swung open automatically. A long, winding stone drive, at least a quarter mile long, led them through a lush tropical garden, a few acres across, which explained the name on the plaque. There had to be a hundred varieties of palm trees in there, not to mention banyan trees, flamboyans, air plants, and several peacocks strutting about.

The road emerged from the trees and became a driveway that swept up to the front door of a two-story, Spanish Colonial fortress. It was about a block long, complete with bell tower. The roof was red-tiled, the walls white stucco, the railings and window grilles black wrought iron. All that architecture seemed to be held together by leafy green vines that had almost consumed the construction. The jungle indeed.

They were met at the marble front stairs by a short, stocky, serious Latin man about forty, dressed in a camouflage shirt and cap, with a rake in his hand and a pistol on his hip. He introduced himself as Juan, the gardener and security guard.

Then the houseman appeared at the door. His name was Carlos, a slender and slightly older man with salt and pepper hair, who wore a crisp white shirt, and pants and bow tie that were both black. He led them into a dark foyer as big as the lobbies of some hotels; then through a high-ceilinged drawing room large enough for a national dance contest and so dank it felt as if a torrential rain would fall inside at any moment; and finally into a cluttered study that smelled of books rotting from humidity. Each room was crowded with pre-Columbian ceramics, old paintings, and studded Spanish Colonial furniture, so that you might have been in a minor and badly lighted museum south of the border. In between those artifacts stood potted banana plants, lots of them, maybe to remind visitors where the money had come from to buy everything.

The man they had come to see also resembled a museum piece. Harold Usser sat in a high-backed red chair and a beam of light fell through the arched window right on him, although he looked exactly like the physical type who shouldn't be in the sun. He was a heavyset, red-faced man, with a bald dome, who had to be at least eighty years old. It looked as if he were dressed to match the banana plants, in a green silk robe and green slippers. His expression was disgruntled, maybe because of what he was seeing on a nearby television screen, where stock prices crawled by. His yellowed teeth were bared in a growl. A cigar burned in an ashtray next to him, clouding the room.

Near him stood a slender, middle-aged woman, expensively dressed, who Willie figured had to be the niece. He was right. Her name was Nadine Usser.

After introductions were made, Ms. Usser simply pushed the message button on the answering machine next to her uncle. A man's voice was heard, speaking somber Spanish.

"This is a warning that Senor Harold Usser has very few days left to live. The crimes committed by him and his family in the past will be the cause of his death. His sins have finally caught up with him."

That message ended and then another came on, the same voice, but recorded several days later, according to the dates given by the machine. It was basically the same warning, but it ended differently.

"Now you are even closer to your undoing, Senor Usser. The spirits of the past will put you in your grave soon. Very soon! You know your crimes and you know why you will die." That was it.

Arnie asked to hear them again. Willie listened as he glanced around the room. The walls were decorated with old, framed photographs, some of them sepia tint, most of them taken in the tropics, particularly on banana plantations. They depicted lush stands of banana plants; a few large, white-faced men, some in sun helmets; and lots of small, dark local workers. Other photos depicted fancy social occasions where the white people were dressed more formally and the local workers, dressed in white, helped serve the food and refreshments. Those workers all had the same dazzled look on their faces that peasants seemed to get before cameras—like deer caught in the headlights.

The messages finished playing and Willie sat down before the old man.

"Mr. Usser, you've said before that you don't know what these messages mean—the reference to crimes. Is that still true?"

The old man fixed him with rheumy eyes and that bitter expression, as if he'd just bitten into an unripe banana. He spoke loudly, the way people do who don't hear well.

"I said I didn't," he shouted in a gravelly voice and turned back to the television.

His voice indicated he had smoked too many cigars, his belly reflected too many bananas, and his face was fissured not only with time, but with rum and maybe other drink. Mr. Usser had not only been a producer of bananas, but a consumer of "the good life." Although it appeared he didn't have much good life left. He looked like a very unhealthy man.

"And you have no idea who issued these warnings?"

The old man erupted then. "I just told you, didn't I! Do what you're paid for and leave me alone! All of you, get away from me! Get away from me now!" He waved his hand irritatedly, as if to strike at Willie, and turned back to the stock ticker on the television screen, as if it were his own heart line on a hospital monitor.

The niece rolled her eyes and then she, Arnie, and Willie left Harold Usser to keep track of his largesse. They went into the drawing room and Nadine Usser apologized.

"Excuse my uncle. He doesn't sleep well. He's been under the weather."

Willie suspected that Harold Usser's climate had always been somewhat unpleasant.

"I take it you also have no idea what those messages mean," Willie said.

She shrugged. "For years I've heard what everyone in my family has heard. That the company always paid off politicians down there, that we controlled a corner of Guatemala, that if the family had trouble, labor trouble, it just hired the army to go in and take care of it. I've heard that people were killed in those disputes. Now some say those were crimes the company committed. My uncle insists it was a jungle and that's the way business was done back then in the jungle. He says he has committed no crimes. Period."

As the niece spoke, Willie noticed a maid in a black uniform dusting a table just outside the room, her back to them. He nodded in her direction.

"I've seen three of your servants and noticed they're all Latin. I imagine they all speak Spanish."

She nodded. "All the servants are from Guatemala. My uncle has always had people from there working for him."

"Do you think any of them might know who's behind these threats?"

She shook her head. "I can't imagine it. These are good people, Mr. Cuesta, not terrorists. And they've all been with him for a while. The truth is my uncle can be unpleasant, as you've seen, and he has had trouble keeping servants. But this group has been very steady, very loyal. In fact, lately one or more of them has been staying up at night to make sure he is safe."

The maid was still dusting that same small table just outside the door. She was within earshot and had been for a while. Of course, servants would always be curious about strangers in the house, such as Willie. He turned back to the niece.

"Does this house have room for a guest?"

"Of course."

"Then I think I'll spend the night."

Arrangements were made. Arnie went back to the hotel to pick up Willie's toiletries and a change of clothes and Willie called Alice. She had just come in from the sauna.

"A lot of ladies only in towels, Willie. You would have liked it. I've been invited to play croquet on the back lawn later and drink martinis. We'll miss you." Willie told her it was good that at least someone was enjoying *his* vacation and that he would see her the next day. He hung up then and headed outside.

First, he wandered into the extensive garden, drifting

around, then examining some orchids, until he felt eyes on him. It was Juan, the somber gardener, watching him through the vegetation. He was replanting a small palm next to a fern-lined pond when Willie approached. Willie spoke to him in Spanish, complimented him on his green thumb, and they exchanged pleasantries.

"How long have you worked here?" Willie asked finally.

"Two years now, senor," he said, still working his shovel.

"I understand your wife is the cook."

"That's right, senor. Her name is Naomi."

"Did you come to work here together?"

"First I came and then my wife, after the other cook left."

"I understand quite a few servants have left over the years."

Juan shrugged and plunged the shovel into the rich earth. "I don't know about that, senor."

"And how was it you found these jobs? You just got lucky?"

Juan glanced at him from under the brim of his camouflage cap as if he were peeking at him from behind a bush. He was a watchful, wary fellow, which maybe was fitting since he was the security guard. "No, we came because I knew Carlos, the houseman. He helped get us the jobs."

"So Carlos has been here some time."

"Yes, senor."

"Is he the one who has been here the longest?"

Juan nodded. "Yes, sir."

He seemed increasingly uncomfortable at the questions and now he put down his shovel.

"Excuse me, but I need to bring more soil." He turned and disappeared into the dense foliage.

Willie waited a few minutes for him, but Juan didn't return. The soil must have been far away. Willie then found his way back to the house and went looking for a glass of water to fend off the afternoon heat. He found it in the kitchen, a dusky, high-ceilinged cavern full of ovens and cupboards, at the rear of the house, where he also found Juan's wife, Naomi.

A small, dark woman of about forty, she had a stocky build like Juan. But unlike her husband, she was friendly and smiling. She wore a long apron with black and white cows imprinted on it.

Willie gulped his water. "Do you like working here, Naomi?"

She nodded enthusiastically. "Oh, yes, senor. I like it here very much. It is a very beautiful place."

"But I understand that Mr. Usser is sometimes difficult, unkind. That he has driven many servants out of here over the years."

As Willie might have expected, the woman didn't want to discuss the disposition of her employer. One could lose his or her job that way. She simply shrugged and smiled enigmatically.

"I guess you and the other servants who work here now are just more understanding than the others were," Willie said.

She nodded. "Maybe, senor."

"I'm told you and your husband came to work here at about the same time. Did you come directly from Guatemala?"

"Oh, no, senor. First we worked in the sugar cane fields near here. Then *Don* Harold—Senor Usser—he hired us."

"I see."

The western side of Palm Beach County was dedicated to agriculture, much of it owned by sugar companies. The work was hot and backbreaking and was performed almost exclusively by Latin and Caribbean immigrant cane cutters. The arrangement made for radically different populations from one side of the county to the other. The cane cutters on the west and the Social Register types in the east, right on the ocean. Willie imagined that it also made for a handy supply of servants who would be more than willing to move across the county and live in mansions.

Willie sipped his water. "I understand that Carlos, the houseman, helped you find this work. Did you know him from the cane fields?"

Naomi nodded and the smile remained in place, but behind her eyes Willie suddenly saw the same wariness he had seen in her husband. He sensed someone behind him and when he turned he found Juan standing in the doorway watching them. He didn't have his rake, but his gun was still on his hip. Naomi reached for her coin purse.

"Juan has to take me to the store now, senor. I need to buy shrimp for dinner. *Don* Harold he only wants it fresh." They excused themselves and hurried out about as fast as they could go.

Willie drained his water and went looking for Carlos, the houseman. But he didn't find him. Harold Usser was napping in that same red chair and apparently Carlos had snuck out.

But Willie did find the maid, the same one he had seen earlier in a black uniform. She was cleaning the guest room, or at least she was pretending to, when Willie went to freshen up. When he walked in she was looking into the closet where his clothes hung.

As he opened the door, she whirled around as if she'd been caught at something. Earlier, Willie had only seen her from behind. Now he saw that she was an older woman, about sixty. Her skin was extremely creased by age and by the sun and across her right cheek was a scar, light pink amid the dark lines, where she had once been badly cut.

"Were you looking for something?"

"I was just making sure your clothes were hung up correctly, senor."

She closed the closet door and they introduced themselves. Her name was Beatrice. Willie encouraged her to finish her dusting and sat down on the edge of the bed.

"How long have you been here, Beatrice?"

"About three years, senor."

She didn't look at him as she dusted. Maybe it was out of Latin deference. Maybe she was shy, or maybe it was behavior that came with that scar.

Willie watched her work. "So you've been here a bit longer than Juan and Naomi."

"That's right, senor."

"Did Carlos, the houseman, also help you get this job?"

She passed her dust cloth over the dresser, which already looked clean.

"Yes, senor. Carlos helped all of us. He's a good man."

Willie was afraid she would skip out on him as the other two had, so he got right down to the nitty-gritty.

"Do you know anyone who might have reason to threaten Senor Usser? You must have heard about the phone calls."

She was shaking her head before he concluded the question. "I don't know anyone who would want to hurt *Don* Harold."

"Even though *Don* Harold is sometimes a very unpleasant person?"

"I don't know what you mean, senor."

"You must have heard the accusations against him and his family. You're from Guatemala, aren't you? His was a very well known company down there."

"I know nothing of such things, senor. I'm just a simple servant."

She made for the door then. Willie stood up and blocked her way. For several moments they stood in silence just inches apart. He wanted to ask her how she had gotten the scar on her face, but he couldn't bring himself to do it.

"What is it, senor?" she asked him.

"I understand that the servants have been staying up at night guarding Senor Usser. Is that right?"

"Yes, Carlos and Juan have done that."

"I guess you're all very worried about him."

Willie looked into her eyes and she hesitated before she spoke. "Yes, that's true. We are very worried," she said. "Is that all, senor?"

Willie nodded. "Yes, that's all." He stepped out of her way. She turned the scar away from him and hurried down the hall.

Dinner was served promptly at eight o'clock in the formal dining room. The only two people at the table were Harold Usser, who sat at the head, and Willie, right next to him. The table had to be twenty feet long, and was covered in a bright white linen tablecloth, held in place by antique silver candlesticks that looked Mexican in design.

Carlos was the principal dinner servant. Willie hadn't seen him all afternoon, until he came to the table wearing a short, white waistcoat and carrying the wine.

Usser and Willie ate in almost total silence. Willie tried a few conversational gambits, but the old man didn't respond. He ate very little, grumbled about the food, and tired before the last course was served. He was helped into a wheelchair and was taken up in the elevator to the second-floor bedrooms

to retire for the evening. Willie ate his dessert alone—
carmelized bananas with vanilla ice cream. They were delicious.

Right after dinner it got dark. Night fell over the sea and
the shaded grounds like a shroud. Willie smoked a cigar on
the patio facing the ocean and watched the last daylight disappear. Then he went looking for the servants, figuring to ask
a few more questions, or at least have someone to talk to.

But he couldn't find any of them. First he tried the kitchen,
but Naomi had decamped and no one else was there. Then he
roamed the gloomy house, first floor and second. Old man
Usser was asleep in a four-poster bed in the master bedroom.
But no one else was to be found.

The servants' quarters were in a separate structure across
the driveway from the main house. That building was also finished in white stucco and consisted of a central corridor with
four rooms leading off it, two on each side, like a dormitory.
The hallway was decorated with more old photographs of the
banana plantations in Guatemala, maybe to make the servants
feel at home. Willie knocked on each door, but received no
reply. The place was abandoned.

The garage stood right next to that building and it appeared
all the vehicles were there, including a relatively new Rolls-
Royce, a vintage Rolls, and a pickup truck for the servants.

The only place left to look was in that sprawling garden, or
the Jungle as it was called. Willie began to walk the trails that
wound through the vegetation. There was a moon and it provided him with just enough light to navigate the narrow paths.
The night insects made quite a racket. The garden was as
dense as a jungle and Willie wondered what other kinds of
creatures—snakes, in particular—might also be found there.
But he kept going.

Then he heard voices. Quietly, he made the last bend in the
trail and saw the servants, all four of them, plus a fifth man
who was younger and wore a full beard. He was dressed in
black.

They all stood in the shadow of the outer wall of the estate
and next to an open wrought-iron door that said SERVANTS EN-
TRANCE. Over the door burned a lightbulb that illuminated

them. As Willie approached, the fifth person, the bearded one, was speaking excitedly. Willie heard only a few words.

"... *que le matemos*." That we kill him!

Carlos answered him excitedly, but Willie didn't hear what he said.

Then, suddenly, they all saw him. As Willie stepped into the light of the bulb, the bearded man bolted through the open gate. Willie tried to get to him, but both Carlos and Juan clogged the doorway and Willie couldn't grab him. By the time Willie squeezed through them, the bearded man had run down the road and he soon disappeared into the darkness.

Willie turned and confronted them all.

"Who was that guy?"

It was Carlos, still in his white waistcoat, who answered.

"He's a young man who used to work here as a chauffeur. He came by just to say hello."

"What's his name?"

"Ramón."

"And why did he run away?"

Carlos shrugged. "Because he isn't supposed to be here. Those are the rules that Senor Usser made for former employees. But Ramón just came for a harmless visit."

Willie's eyes narrowed into a squint.

"Harmless? That's why he was recommending that you kill Harold Usser?"

Carlos feigned surprise. "No, senor. He did not say that. He wasn't speaking of Senor Usser at all."

"I heard it."

Carlos shook his head, his intelligent eyes delving Willie's face. "You misunderstood, senor. You see we have a cat that has come on the property and tried to kill the peacocks. He was speaking of that. No one here would ever think of killing *Don* Harold. That's preposterous."

He glanced at the others and they all shook their heads. Willie wasn't believing any of it.

"There's something going on here and you people know what it is."

Carlos closed the gate, secured a padlock, and turned to Willie. "We don't know what you're speaking of, Senor

Cuesta. Believe me, none of us wants to see Senor Usser hurt. Now, it's late. We need to rest."

Before Willie could say anything else, the servants all headed back toward the house. They disappeared into their quarters. Willie watched them go and then hurried into the house.

He decided right then not to take any chances. He went up the stairs to the master bedroom, entered quietly, and found old man Usser asleep. He was breathing shallowly, but breathing nonetheless. Willie plopped down in an armchair in the corner and lighted the lamp there. He kicked off his shoes and reached into a bookcase next to the lamp for an old mystery novel. Harold Usser wasn't going to die on Willie's watch, even if it meant staying up all night.

Over the next several hours he heard all kinds of noises. Usser issued a couple of weak cries, as if he were having nightmares. Other noises came from the sea, but lots of them came from that old creaking mansion. At one point he was sure he heard voices outside the window. He had his gun on his hip when he looked out. He thought he had heard a voice speaking urgently, like the young bearded man had earlier. But he saw nothing. Maybe he imagined it. Maybe it was the winds off the sea, whispering through the house. Whatever those noises were, they didn't come any closer. Not then and not all night.

It was just after dawn, 6:30 A.M., when Beatrice, in uniform, opened the door and entered to attend to the old man. She was surprised to find Willie there. Then she looked down at Harold Usser. The old man's mouth was open and his eyes were closed. She bent down close, as if to wake him, and Willie saw concern cross her face. She reached out, put her hand on Usser's cheek, and pulled it away as if she had been burned. She whirled toward Willie.

"He's dead!"

Willie jumped from the chair. He took Usser's limp wrist, but found no pulse. He too touched the old man's cheek and found it as chilly as marble. Usser had been dead for hours.

Willie stared at the only door. He hadn't fallen asleep. No one had come through it. He was sure. Usser and he had been served from the same wine bottle and same serving dishes the night before, so he couldn't have been poisoned at dinner.

Usser's doctor was called right away and then his niece. Willie left a message at the station for Arnie, asking him to come. The servants were all clustered in the hallway when the doctor arrived.

He did a quick examination of the corpse and said it appeared that Usser had died of natural causes. "He was dying for a long time. He ate too much, drank too much, and screamed too much." But he said an autopsy would be performed nonetheless because of the recent death threats.

Willie left them all gathered in the room and the hallway and walked outside. Looking over his shoulder, he made sure no one was watching and entered the servants' quarters. He opened the first door and slipped in, closing the door behind him. He saw right away that it was Carlos's room. An old, framed, black and white photo sat on a night table. It was of a man who looked much like Carlos, with his arm around a young boy of about five. It looked like it had been taken in Guatemala, maybe fifty years before.

Willie opened the one small closet, found nothing of interest, then inspected the dresser. In the bottom drawer, under some clothes, he found Carlos's immigration papers. His last name was Castillo and he was fifty-five years old.

Willie also found a bound sheath of old, yellowed newspaper clippings, in Spanish from the 1950s. The headlines spoke of turmoil—demonstrations, land disputes, army offensives, battles, people killed. They were the events Usser's niece had spoken of. The name of Usser's company appeared many times and even a photo of Usser, as a much younger, healthier, and flint-eyed businessman. He had been the most powerful man in one corner of that small country.

The last clipping carried the headline "LABOR ORGANIZER ASSASSINATED!" A photo depicted a lifeless body lying faceup on a muddy rural street. The dead man was named Carlos Castillo. Willie looked at the photo in the paper and the one on the dresser. It was the same man.

Willie was still studying the clipping when the door opened behind him. It was Carlos. He looked at Willie, at the clippings, and back at Willie. His face was flush with both surprise and fear.

Willie held up the last clipping. "This was your father, wasn't it?"

Carlos nodded cautiously, but said nothing.

"He was a union organizer who went against the banana company, Usser's company, and they killed him. That's what these clippings say."

Carlos nodded. "And those clippings are correct."

The other three servants had appeared in the doorway behind him. They entered and closed the door.

"And the rest of you?" Willie asked.

Carlos answered. "Juan and Naomi, their families both had their land taken away from them by Usser. Their parents were forced to work the rest of their lives on the plantations and they all died young."

"And Beatrice?"

"Beatrice was the most beautiful girl on the plantation until she said no to one of Usser's managers, then he cut her with a machete. She went and showed Usser, but he did nothing, because the manager was a favorite of his. He produced a lot of bananas. There was no recourse. Usser was a law unto himself in that part of the jungle. He was an evil man."

"And you all wanted revenge?"

Carlos nodded solemnly. "Wouldn't you?"

Willie said nothing and Carlos continued. "We worked this out over several years, waiting for openings, arranging who would take the jobs, making sure that everyone who worked for the old man thought the same way. That we were all from that same corner of our country, all had suffered at his hands, and we all wanted him dead."

"And Ramón, the young chauffeur?"

"Him too."

"So why didn't you kill Usser, like Ramón wanted last night?"

"Because we saw that Usser was dying of his own evil. Not just of old age. He never knew that I was the son of a man he had ordered to be killed, but in these last years he would tell me that I reminded him of someone, of a man who had been killed. To Beatrice he used to say that she reminded him of a girl he had once known in Guatemala. Juan and Naomi made him remember all the people whose land he had stolen and who he enslaved. He was haunted by all those faces. Hardly anyone came here to see him because he was such a terrible old man. We were the only ones who surrounded him and we gave him nightmares. If he didn't speak about those old days himself, then we would ask him, remind him of those who had died. He was dying of those nightmares, stewing in his own juices, because our faces forced him to remember his own savagery."

"But Ramón wanted to kill him."

"Yes, Ramón also comes from a poor plantation family from our part of the country. He wanted to poison Usser, shoot him, anything. He had young angry friends who wanted to help him. But we told them no. In fact, we kept Ramón from killing Usser."

Willie frowned. "What do you mean?"

"Exactly what I said. We not only didn't kill Harold Usser, Mr. Cuesta. We saved his life. You yourself heard it last night. And that's why we kept watch these nights. But we did so only so that Usser would die from the nightmares of his own making. That was justice enough."

"So when the autopsy comes back, it won't say he was slowly poisoned, or any other act of murder."

Carlos shook his head. "All the autopsy will say is that an old man—a bad old man—died of his own bad habits, his own evil."

Willie looked at the clippings in his hand again, considered what had just been told, and then finally put them down. He glanced at the servants and left that room, knowing he would never say a word to anyone. What was there to say?

Then he went back to the guest room, packed his things, and got out of that tropical haunted house as quickly as he could. Alice was waiting next to the pool.

THE LOCH NESS MYSTERY

A John Darnell Mystery Story

Sam McCarver

Sam McCarver is the author of three novels featuring Professor John Darnell, the world's first and only "paranormal detective," who debunks reported supernatural events. John Darnell and his wife, Penny, have appeared in *The Case of Cabin 13*, *The Case of Compartment 7*, and *The Case of the 2nd Séance*. Look for *The Case of the 5th Victim*, coming soon.

Scottish Highlands, June 1917

Professor John Darnell stared at the dark, grim silhouette of Drumnadrochit Inn in the fading light of the cloudy sky, then glanced sidelong at his wife, Penny, next to him in the horse-carriage seat. Her look told him without words what she thought—*"Another strange vacation."*

Penny Darnell shivered. "Your Inn looks a bit spooky, doesn't it?"

Darnell summoned a smile. "It'll be better once we're inside by a cozy fire, enjoying a hot meal. I know—when I try too hard to combine a vacation with a case . . ." He sighed, and gave up on trying to soften it.

Penny smiled. "At least we're together, John. We're out of London and I'm seeing Scotland at last. We'll enjoy it."

The clop of the horse's hooves on the dry road echoed against the hills abutting the lake as they approached the Inn. Darnell shook his head. Penny was right—it looked no better up close. The weathered wood of the two-story structure had darkened over the years to black. Two large chimneys emitted smoke into the sky. Broad picture windows facing the water seemed to glare out at the lake like wide, square eyes, as if watching for something mysterious to appear. Darnell also gazed at the lake, its shimmering water catching the last faint rays of the sun, partially obscured by haze, as it set beyond distant hills bordering the lake on the far side.

Darnell recognized the red-haired, somber-faced man standing at the entrance of the Inn, waving a hand at them as the carriage eased up the slight incline to the front of the building on the rise of ground. Sandy MacDougall, as he promised, had waited there for them. With their delays, arriving over two hours late, Darnell felt the *London Times* reporter no doubt would have had his fill of ale by now.

"John—and Mrs. Darnell—I'm glad you're here." MacDougall reached up a hand to help Penny down from the carriage. The carriage driver jumped down and quickly took bags from the back of the vehicle into the Inn.

Darnell shook MacDougall's outstretched hand. "You should have warned us—General Wade's Road isn't much better than a wide dirt path."

MacDougall nodded. "It's just an old military supply road, but for us natives of the area, it has a certain charm and nostalgia. I'm sure they'll build a better one someday." He smiled at Penny. "But come inside where it's warmer—and we'll talk." As they walked up the path to the porch and reached the doorway, he looked at Darnell. "Did you, ah . . . tell Mrs. Darnell about my telegram?"

Penny's musical laughter resounded in the entryway of the Inn as MacDougall opened the door and they stepped inside. "John tells me everything—*his* way. He put it, '*A working vacation in a quaint old inn by a lake.*' Well, it' s quaint."

"But the rest of it—" MacDougall glanced at Darnell and saw his frown. He quickly added, "Oh . . . of course, we'll talk at dinner. Let's get you into your room first."

The Inn guests, congregated in chairs and sofas about the sitting room, looked up from their books and conversations at the striking woman with long auburn hair and violet eyes and her tall, lithe husband. The locals whispered among themselves, eyeing the newcomers as they crossed the lobby to the front desk.

MacDougall said to the desk clerk, "Fergus, these are Professor and Mrs. Darnell."

The gray-haired, slender man squinted over his glasses at

them. "Saved the best room for you, ma'am. Direct view of the lake. Pretty sight, in the morning, sun twinklin' on the water."

"I'm sure it is." Penny smiled, then looked about the room.

Darnell knew she was absorbing the Inn's atmosphere—lined mahogany bookshelves, paintings of the lake and hills—probably questioning what she'd do while he did his work. He wondered, should he have combined this trip with a vacation? He noticed a number of recent signatures on the register. "Busy period?"

The clerk frowned. "Oh, no, sir, I did na' really expect this business. But with everything's that happened . . ."

MacDougall said quickly, "I'll walk you up to your room. Mine's on the same floor—the second. Best views there."

In their room, Darnell took Penny in an embrace and kissed her warmly. "We're alone"—he smiled—"and on vacation. Let's enjoy our 'quaint inn,' shall we?"

A half hour later, after refreshing themselves in their private bathroom after the long road trip from the train station, and slipping into a change of clothes, Darnell and Penny walked down the hall to MacDougall's room and rapped on his door.

When MacDougall swung his door open, Darnell said, "We're ready for dinner and a bit of sherry, Sandy."

Dark had settled in, giving the lake an ominous look by the time they took seats at an alcove table by a window facing the water. A nearby fireplace warmed the area. The waiter poured sherry for Darnell and MacDougall and hot tea for Penny.

Darnell glanced about the room. What appeared to be local gentry occupied a few tables, but none near them, and it was clear the dinner hour would start later.

Penny teasingly glared at the two men. "Now I'm ready to hear what Sandy called *'the rest.'* What else was in that telegram?"

MacDougall took a large sip of his sherry and looked at her with serious eyes. "As I said, I'm a native of the Highlands. I was born about twelve miles south of here in a small village, Invermoriston. My mother still lives there, and I visit her at least once a year. But I like to stay here in the Inn."

"I'm sure it's the best accommodation in the area," Darnell said with a wry smile.

MacDougall let the remark pass without comment as he removed an envelope from his inside coat pocket. He held it close to his chest with both hands, as if protectively, and looked at Penny.

"When I telegraphed John," he said, "I had to be vague because of prying eyes. People, even telegraphers, are curious. We're an odd lot here . . . we thrive on strange superstitions, stories, and legends. Old-timers speak of a curse over this lake. At night, when the wind is blowing across the lake in winter they talk around their fireplaces of black magic and secret rituals."

Penny studied MacDougall. When he paused, she looked at him with eyes twinkling. "Very mysterious and macabre, Sandy. But for a reporter, you take a long time to make your point."

A waiter came and took their orders. When the man had disappeared into the kitchen, MacDougall continued in a low voice. "This time . . . well, I found more than I expected, even in these Highlands. Something that disturbed me, Mrs. Darnell."

"Please call me Penny. I'm sure after several days here we'll be well acquainted."

MacDougall nodded. "My telegram to John said what I found here might fall into his sphere of knowledge as a paranormal-events investigator. He's the only one, isn't he? I had to bring him into it. My idea was, he could investigate, and I'd write the exclusive story for the *Times*." He handed the envelope to Darnell. "Look at this, John, and show it to Mrs. . . . I mean . . . to Penny. And hold your breath."

Darnell slipped a photograph out of the envelope and held it so both he and Penny could see it. Penny said, "Oh!"

Darnell's eyes widened. "You don't mean . . . ?" He studied MacDougall's face. "Is this serious?"

"A guest of the Inn said he saw something out on the bay at Urquhart Castle and snapped the picture. When he showed me the print, I paid him a good sum to have another copy made for me and telegraphed you. John, the phenomenon in the photo has been seen by locals only rarely. Sometimes it's years from one sighting to another. And as far as I know, it's never been captured in a photograph. I think this is the first time."

Darnell scowled. "You're saying this is Nessie?"

"Nessie?" Penny looked at Darnell. "That's supposed to be a sea serpent, isn't it, John? What do they call it?"

"The Loch Ness monster," MacDougall said. He gestured at the photograph. "Notice the long trunk, the hump in the body, the V-shaped trail in the water behind it as it swims away. It's a classic photo, just like people have described it. And the first one." His eyes glistened. "Wait'll my editor sees this!"

Darnell studied the photograph. "But, Sandy, although the object seems to be quite a distance away, it might be a smaller beast, close-up. A large otter, or an eel. Easily explained."

Sandy MacDougall's tone became testy. "That's no otter, John. It's no eel. It's Nessie. If you'd lived around here like I have . . ."

Darnell assessed the grim humor of the situation. He gave MacDougall a twisted smile. "Is that the avid newspaper reporter speaking, wanting an exclusive story? Or is it a superstitious native, loyal to the local legends?"

"Maybe a bit of both." MacDougall returned the look with steady eyes. "But I do think it's genuine." He turned to Penny. "What do you think?"

"Well . . . I've heard the tales as a child, but never thought it was real." Penny peered at the photograph. "The picture isn't very clear. Seems to be either late in the day or overcast."

"It's always cloudy here, in late afternoon." MacDougall frowned. "This is about as good a picture as anyone could expect to get."

Darnell sat back and sipped his sherry, looking over the rim of the glass at the reporter. "We traveled six hundred miles just to see a photograph?"

MacDougall's expression darkened as he shook his head. "I'm afraid there's more, John. I wanted to get your reaction to this photograph first. After I bought my copy of it, the man who took it—well, he died in his room that same night. The maid found him an hour after he was last seen alive at the desk, talking with Fergus."

"How did he die?"

"Heart attack, they said at first, unofficially. That was almost a week ago. But I hear the medical examiner's still working on it, and hasn't issued his report. I think there's more to it than a heart case."

"Why do you doubt it?"

"John, I talked with the constable who inspected the body and the man's room. I learned some things from him. The man's copy of this photo, all his photos, his negatives, even his camera, were gone." He scowled. "I think the man was murdered."

The next morning after breakfast, Darnell, MacDougall, and Penny—who insisted on going along with the men—sat in the horse-drawn carriage MacDougall had hired, along with its driver. The carriage trundled bumpily along General Wade's Road toward the small village of Drumnadrochit, where, after talks over sherry the night before, Darnell decided the answer to the mystery most likely would be found.

Darnell turned to MacDougall in the backseat. "I want to talk to the chemist who developed the photos—and the constable."

"The chemist . . . ?" Penny said. "Oh, yes, the druggist."

MacDougall smiled at Penny. "I know them both. I know all these people. Most have lived here all their lives. One you'll have to meet, John, is Old Doc Angus Baird."

"Your emphasis was on 'old.' How old would that be?"

"Old enough to know about all the sightings of Nessie in the past seventy years around here, the ones on land, the others on the water. He's like a patriarch of the village—outlived two wives after producing eleven children between the two women. Eight of his children and their families live all up and down this road on the lake."

"And he'll do what, for us?"

"For *you*. Tell you about the sightings. Maybe persuade you they happened. Doc Baird saw the 'beastie' himself

once, he says, when he was just a lad. Nessie is his obses-
sion."

Penny turned toward MacDougall. "How long have these
sightings been going on?"

"You and John may not believe this—but St. Columba
saw a beast in the year 565. And he wasn't the first. Before
his experience was recorded, the Vikings spotted them in the
lochs. They called them 'water horses.' Maybe you two can
separate the fact from the folklore. I can't. No one around
here can."

Darnell frowned. "And in recent years . . . ?"

MacDougall stared out at the lake. "I'll let old Doc Baird
tell you all that. He'll make a believer of you."

"This chemist shop," MacDougall said, "is the one place
in the village you can get prescriptions filled and photographs developed. The chemist does them in his own dark
room."

Darnell studied a hand-lettered sign on a counter reading,
"Photographs Developed. Next Day."

"It's his hobby," MacDougall said. "He's quite expert."

"I'll bet someday this could be a tourist stop," Penny said.

MacDougall nodded. "That's what some people here are
afraid of." He lowered his voice as the proprietor approached. "But not Campbell. He'd welcome it."

The store owner stepped over to the three and spoke in a
thick accent. "Hello, Mac. How can I help you?"

"Evan, this is Professor Darnell, and Mrs. Darnell . . .
Evan Campbell. If you want a bromide or a salve, he's the
man to see. Evan, Professor Darnell would like to ask some
questions about the photos you developed for the, ah, deceased tourist."

The chemist looked quizzically from one to the other.
"Yes? Of course, I remember the man. Yes, he had photos developed. I heard the unfortunate news later." He shuddered.

Darnell took up the questioning. "Did you study his film?
I'm wondering whether the negatives could have been faked.
Did you look at the prints closely?"

Campbell's head shook decisively from one side to the
other. "The film was normal. I did na' look at the photos. I

consider them private. Of course, if they complain of quality, I'll look them over. No, he left the roll while he shopped and I processed them, before lunch." He motioned toward the back of the store. "He came back, took them. Then he returned that afternoon."

MacDougall said aside, to Darnell, "I came with him."

"Another set, he wanted," Campbell said, glancing at MacDougall, "and they both waited for them. I did na' look at the photos then, either—they seemed in a wee bit of a hurry."

"Thank you," Darnell said. "By the way . . . have you developed any unusual photos here, over the years?"

Campbell shook his head again with vigor. "No. But I've been here only sixteen years." He smiled. "They call me a newcomer. I, ah, have heard some stories from people passing through, saying they wished they'd had their cameras with them."

"And you—have you seen anything peculiar around the loch?"

The head wagged. "Mostly I see the inside of this store and my rooms upstairs. I don't put stock in fairy stories, loch monsters, and such like, if you mean that. But if our visitors, the few we get, ask about them—well, it's good for business."

Leaving the store, Penny asked, "When you were here, Sandy, did the tourist give you all twelve pictures?"

"No, just the one I was interested in, the copy of the one he showed me in the Inn's pub." He tapped his inside coat pocket, looking up and down the street. "The one of Nessie."

Old Doc Angus Baird fitted his nickname of "Old," Darnell thought, more than anyone he'd met. A shock of snow-white hair topped his head and matched his robust growth of mustache and the equally white whiskers that extended six inches below his chin. The man sat on the front porch of his house in a chair that rocked back and forth with the rhythm of his tapping right foot.

"Young Sandy," he rasped in a heavy accent, "will ye no come up on the porch where I can see you? What ails ye, lad?"

As they approached, MacDougall explained, "They also called my father Sandy—same red hair, you know. I was known as young Sandy. When I was growing up, Doc Baird was our doctor."

"I was everybody's doctor," Baird said. "Only one in the village. And I'm still doctorin'—for those as need it, helpin' the new man when he's busy. In winter, most everybody gets sick from the damp and cold." He squinted at MacDougall's face. "You're not looking any too well. What's worrying you, lad?"

"Nothing, nothing. But I want you to tell my friend, Professor Darnell, about all the sightings you know of—in your lifetime."

"Nessie?"

"Yes."

"Making a study of it?" Baird looked at Darnell.

"You might say that."

"Well . . . eighty-one years is a fair time, do you know. But I've told the stories many times—I guess I remember them."

MacDougall leaned closer to Darnell's ear. "I'll interpret if his accent's too thick."

Angus Baird went on. "I was, oh, eleven or twelve, when I saw her—Nessie. My older brother—he's gone now—he and I were walking down the General's Road after fishing. Happened to look out at the lake and there she was, just like my own dad told me. The long neck, sort of like a—what's that word, lad?"

"Dinosaur."

"Yes, dinosaur. It swam away while we watched. Bashful kind of beastie. No one believed us, of course, except my dad, bless him. Said he'd seen it himself. And he believed in all those things, the curse, the witches. Used to tell us stories . . ." He suddenly lapsed into a protracted coughing spell.

MacDougall bent over him. "Is this talking bothering you?"

Baird waved a hand. "No, no. So you wanted to know about the others? Well . . . none after I saw her until the seventies. Some children saw it on the north shore. Then old Ed

Bright saw it on the land. It slipped right into the water and swam away. In the eighties, let's see . . . two saw it out on the water. Then in the nineties people saw it on land or in the water two more times. And two more sightings a few years later. Then again about five years ago, right down by the bay, MacGruer saw it. Was that nine, lad? It's eleven in all, including my dad's and mine, in my lifetime. It's a long time between sightings of the old girl, sometimes, but I say, Nessie's a bit shy."

MacDougall smiled. "They call the monster 'she.' "

"Interesting." Darnell kept a serious face, despite his natural instinct to challenge the doctor's accounts. Still, the earnestness of the man's stories left him with a queasy feeling about the mythical beast. "And the descriptions of it— or her?"

"Always the long neck," Baird said. "Two humps, sometimes three, almost like a camel, but sort of like a horse. Always slipping into the water, or swimming away, fast, with its four flippers. It don't happen often, but everyone who sees it tells it the same, and when you see it, you remember it all your life."

Angus Baird studied the three people before him with a light gradually dawning in his eyes. He glared at Mac-Dougall. "You're not saying Nessie's back, are you? Is that what you're telling me, lad?"

"No, I'm not saying that, Doc."

"If she's back, I want to know it. And I want to know everything about it."

"Of course."

"Add it to my stories, you know. For my kids."

They took their leave after copious thanks, and Mac-Dougall led the way back to the carriage. "The kids he spoke of are his great-grandchildren, about twenty of them. They visit him on his birthday every year and he tells them stories about fairies, and witches, and curses. And, as you can imagine, about Nessie."

Their driver took them back into the village. They passed slowly through the town square.

"You mentioned dinosaur," Penny said to MacDougall. "Is there a connection?"

He nodded. "A plesiosaur. Plesiosaurus to be exact. The beast that people have seen—well, that they said they saw—resembles it, particularly its very long neck and rounded body."

Darnell interrupted, pointing at a sign in a store window. "Look, Sandy—that sign says there's a town meeting at one. It's almost one now."

"Do you want to go to it?"

"By all means."

MacDougall told the driver, "Take us to the church." To Penny and Darnell he said, "Meetings of the villagers are always held there. It's the largest meeting room in town."

As they arrived at the church and approached the oversized front double doors, Darnell glanced about at the villagers streaming into the church. Common folk, some in trades, a fisherman or two, housewives, some carrying small children. He recognized the chemist. Inside, stage center on an elevated platform in front of the pews, stood a young man conversing with an older one wearing a black frock. Seats filled up quickly with people. Darnell gestured toward three seats at the rear and Penny, MacDougall, and he took them. Darnell studied the two men on the platform, curious about the meeting.

In a moment, the younger of the two men rapped on the minister's podium with a gavel and said, "Come to order, if you please."

"Mayor Bruce Donnell," MacDougall whispered. "Full of vinegar. The other's Vicar Murdoch. Been here forever."

"Come to order," the words came again, and the crowd slowly quieted down. "As you know . . . as you know," the mayor repeated, seeking their attention, "we have had a tragedy at the Inn. A man"—he waited for quiet—"a man, a young tourist died. I realize rumors abound, but you should understand the man had a heart attack, that's all we know at this time. Don't believe any reports to the contrary."

Voices rumbled in the audience as villagers turned to one another and commented. The voices rose, until the vicar stepped over to the podium next to the mayor and held up a hand. When the noise abated, he said, in a strident voice, "It was evil! Evil is rising up again in Drumnadrochit. And it's only the beginning. Do you no ken those reports of things on the water over the years? How each time they drew people to the town? People! People prying, cluttering, destroying, trampling. And now this death. We can't let that happen again. We must protect our village."

The mayor stepped in front of the vicar's place at the podium. "There's no evidence of new reports of the water beast, but if there were, that would not hurt this town. With all due respect, Vicar"—he glanced at the frocked man— "Drumnadrochit could use the money from visitors, even God knows that. A death, yes. But no proof it's related to any new sightings. So I urge calm, and let those of us in authority deal with this."

The constable and town doctor came to the podium at the mayor's beckoning. Each briefly confirmed the mayor's words.

Vicar Murdoch spoke out following the last words of the two. "More will come out about this death. I warn you. This is the devil's work."

The crowd left the church engaged in conversations, some muted, some vociferous. Darnell took Penny and Mac-Dougall aside out of the flow of people. "I have to talk with those two, the constable and doctor. I saw them leaving. What can you do, Sandy?"

MacDougall looked about the room. "Let the crowd dissipate. I'll take you to the courthouse. They'll both be there. If we can get them alone, we may get more truth than we got here."

Penny said, "Truth about the photograph?"

Darnell nodded. "About the photograph. And the death."

John Darnell could see the courthouse clearly ranked as the second-largest edifice in the small town. As they walked through the hallway he read brass plates on the doors— MAYOR BRUCE DONNELL . . . MEDICAL EXAMINER . . . CONSTA-BLE. At the back of the building a door bore a sign stating simply, JAIL.

MacDougall stopped at the constable's office and rapped

on it twice. He heard the word "Come," and entered, followed by Darnell and Penny.

A lanky, semibald man wearing thick glasses looked up from his desk and squinted at MacDougall and the others. "Mac?"

MacDougall nodded in greeting at the constable. "This is Professor Darnell, Ross, and his wife. Constable Ross Lachlan. Ross, the professor would like a few minutes of your time."

"Questions? For one of your articles, Sandy?"

Darnell stepped forward, closer to the man's desk. "It's about the tourist, the one with the, ah, heart attack."

"Can't add much to that. What do you want to know?" He frowned, looking first at MacDougall, then Darnell. "And why?"

"I make a study of mysterious happenings," Darnell said. "At the town meeting you indicated the death was natural, and not connected with any sighting of your local legend."

"Correct."

"But the medical examiner's report isn't final yet. Are you sure of all that?"

The constable nodded. "As sure as we can be. The M.E. sent some things out for testing. Due back by tonight."

"The man's camera and photos were missing."

The constable smoothed back his sparse hair. "Can't explain that. Might have been a valuable camera. Maybe he startled a burglar when he returned to his room. The thief might have scared the man to death, with his weak heart and such."

"If that's all, then why send anything away for tests?"

"Muir, our town doctor—serves as medical examiner when we need one—wanted to be sure." He snorted. "Suspicious type."

"Is he in?"

"I don't follow him around. Look in his office."

They found Medical Examiner Muir in his office. Darnell asked his same questions.

Muir said, "Why do tests? Because some years ago I saw the body of a man who died ingesting arsenic. This dead man—Lester Ramsey—had the same jaundiced skin. The desk clerk said the man was alive an hour before they found him, and arsenic acts fast. I don't have good equipment here, so I sent it up to Inverness."

A knock came on his door, and it opened to reveal a man holding a brown envelope. He handed it to Muir and left the room, closing the door behind him.

"This is it." Muir ripped open the envelope, pulled out a single sheet, and studied it with a dour expression. He looked up at them. "No harm in telling you. Word gets around, and it'll be known soon enough in this village. The test was positive. Arsenic."

That evening, John Darnell looked at Penny in the seat next to him at their table in the Drumnadrochit Inn dining room. He frowned and sipped his wine. "Something missing in all this."

Penny nodded. "Yes, common sense. There's no Loch Ness monster. I'm surprised you give any credence to those stories."

Darnell's head shook back and forth. "I don't, Penny. I listen to the stories and opinions people express on that subject and on the death not as facts, but as reflections of what locals are thinking, and how it might affect their actions."

"The professor part of you is coming out. You're drawing on your teaching of philosophy and psychology."

"Exactly. I'm trying to explore the thought processes of these locals, study their psyches. And something's missing."

"And what is that?

"A motive for the murder."

She frowned. "Well, perhaps theft, as the constable said. But not the camera. Maybe the photographs. Someone wanted to sell the sensational photo of whatever it was to some newspaper."

Darnell shook his head again. "Possible. But then whoever sold the photo would have to allow his name to be connected with the photo. That would be like a confession on the front page."

Their waiter filled their water glasses and asked, "Would you like to order, now?"

Darnell said, "No, we'll wait a bit for our companion—oh, here he comes."

Sandy MacDougall took a seat at the table saying, "I'm sorry. My mother loves to talk, and I couldn't get away."

They glanced over the menu and ordered. The waiter quickly brought salads, and they conversed as they ate.

Darnell went on, "We need a motive, Sandy. Of course, it may become apparent if we identify the other two ingredients of murder—the means and opportunity."

"We know the means," MacDougall said. "Poison."

"But from what source? The chemist's shop? Your friend there, Evan Campbell, would have ready access to arsenic."

"As would anyone with a supply to kill garden pests. Like my mother. She's vicious when it comes to bugs on her flowers."

"And opportunity? Who was at the Inn that night?"

MacDougall nodded. "We'll talk with the desk clerk."

"Someone may have entered the man's room," Penny said. "Maybe a maid would have noticed him—or her?"

"*Her?*" Darnell smiled at the word. "You mean, women tend to murder with poison?" As he said it, he looked up to see a woman approaching them from across the room.

Reaching their table, she addressed MacDougall. "Hello, Sandy." She turned to Darnell and Penny. "I'm Erica Gilbert, half owner of the Inn. May I join you for a moment?"

"Of course." Darnell and Penny said the words in unison and smiled at each other.

The woman took the vacant chair. "You're investigating the death of Mr. Ramsey."

Sandy replied for them. "Yes, Erica. We believe it was a murder."

"I have to think about protecting the Inn's reputation."

Darnell returned her gaze as she looked at him. "The best way to do that is to help us."

"Anything."

"The night he was killed, who came here from the village? Any unexpected visitors? Anyone other than Inn guests, of course, and the constable and medical examiner afterward."

"That's hard to say. You can enter the Inn from three different doors. Anyone could slip in and out unnoticed." She bit her lip. "But—well, I'll tell you what I do know. Mayor Donnell came here with Grant MacLeod about five that night."

Sandy said, "MacLeod's the village banker."

"They met with an out-of-town visitor."

"Business?" Darnell studied her.

"Something to do with money, I expect. They spent most of their time in the pub."

"No one else?"

"The chemist delivered a prescription to an elderly woman. He said he was on his way home, and happy to drop it off."

"That occurred before Ramsey's body was discovered?"

"An hour before. Evan was gone before we found the body."

"Anyone else?"

She frowned. "Oh, yes, the vicar stopped in to see an old friend passing through, just here for the night." At that point, seeing a signal from a waiter across the room, Erica Gilbert excused herself. "I'll be in my office if you need me."

As she left, the waiter brought their entrees and attended to their other table needs. The three ate quietly for a few moments.

MacDougall asked Darnell, "Did Miss Gilbert's information help?"

"Maybe." Darnell pursed his lips. "Let me run over the facts, and throw in an opinion or two. You two can tell me what you think."

When MacDougall and Penny nodded, Darnell gathered his thoughts. He knew he'd be trying to persuade himself as much as them of his logic, realized saying the words aloud was necessary to test his own convictions. He smiled, thinking, Sherlock Holmes would do no less.

He spoke in a methodical, thoughtful voice. "Let's consider the situation objectively . . . there seems to be two leaders who represent the factions in the village. The mayor and vicar jointly conducted the town meeting. They have opposing views. The mayor likes the notoriety of the lake creature, plays down the death of the tourist. The vicar, on the other hand, warns of evil from both sources. Of course, Dr. Baird, the chemist, the constable, the medical examiner, in fact all the locals—all have one thing in common with the mayor and vicar."

Penny smiled. "All right, John—don't be so dramatic."

He returned her gaze cheerfully. "No secret, that. It's the preoccupation with the monster legend. The one thing both uniting and dividing the town. Some love Nessie, some hate her."

Sandy MacDougall frowned. "And the impact of that?"

"Motives. Motives for murder." Darnell paused. "While you were visiting your mother this afternoon, Sandy, I decided to set some wheels in motion." He looked from Mac-Dougall to Penny. "I sent around messages to several people."

"Messages?" Penny repeated, her brow wrinkling. "I'm sure you'll explain that too, eventually."

"I think we'll have two or three puzzled or even annoyed locals, and perhaps one a bit more disturbed than that. The messages went to your chemist—Evan Campbell, to Mayor Donnell, to Vicar Murdoch, and to Erica Gilbert."

"The same message?" MacDougall ran a hand through his tangled hair.

The waiter brought coffee. When he left, Darnell went on. "I tailored each one, after speaking to the constable . . ."

Penny glared accusingly. "That's why you went to town."

Darnell brushed past the comment. "My note to Campbell suggested his ready access to arsenic called for investigation. My note to the mayor referred to his comments about needing tourist growth and money in Drumnadrochit. The note to Erica Gilbert pointed out that the tourist's death and the report of the monster sighting had increased the business of the Inn, might make it a tourist stop here. And my note to the vicar . . ."

"I hope it didn't give the old codger a heart attack," Mac-Dougall inserted.

". . . suggested he seemed very zealous to keep any information on Nessie from circulating to the outside world."

"Motives, then," Penny said. "Back to that."

"It's all we have. As you said, Sandy, these four all had

means. And as to opportunity, well, this Inn seemed to be as popular a place to visit that night as Paddington Station."

MacDougall said, "What now?"

"You and I visit each of the four, accompanied by the constable, as I arranged, and see what happens." He turned to Penny. "This time, you should stay here. There could be danger."

She shook her head vigorously. "Not on your life, John Darnell. I'll stay in the background—but I'm going along."

He sighed. "All right. Then let's finish our coffee—here comes the constable now."

Constable Lachlan and his entourage crossed the lobby of the Inn to the office of the owner and manager, Erica Gilbert. She rose from her chair as they entered. "What . . . ? Ross?"

"A few questions, if you please," he answered. "Anything you'd care to admit? We know how the man died, Erica."

"Admit? If you're trying to blame this Inn . . . that reminds me, I found a strange note on my desk just now. Asking about the Inn's business."

"It seems to be booming," Lachlan said.

"Maybe temporarily. But I don't want my Inn's reputation built on the death of a guest."

"And the monster? The photograph?" MacDougall asked. "People would flock to see that."

"What photograph? You're not making sense." She looked from MacDougall to Darnell.

The constable began mumbling some excuses and quickly untangled himself from the situation. The four left the office and walked out to his motorcar.

"She knows nothing," Darnell said. "That's quite clear."

Lachlan said, "My car isn't much, and neither are these roads, but we'll get into town faster than in a horse cart." He helped Penny into the back seat as Darnell joined her, and MacDougall took the front seat. In a short time, he was pulling up to the front of the shop of the chemist, who lived upstairs, above the shop. Evan Campbell answered the door after spirited knocking by the constable.

"Sandy—Ross. What is it? It's past eight o'clock."

Lachlan removed his hat. "Sorry, Evan. May we come in for a few minutes?"

The four entered the shop, and Campbell locked the door behind them. "I've been closed for two hours."

"The arsenic—" Lachlan began.

"One of you sent that damn note, didn't you? You think I killed that poor man, just because I have arsenic here? Why would I do that?"

Darnell said, "You told us today you would like more tourist business. You developed the film, prepared the photographs. You put a doctored print in the package, didn't you—substituting that phony monster photo for whatever the tourist's film actually showed? Then on a pretext you could have gone to his hotel and given him something to imbibe with arsenic in it."

"You knew about the photo?" The chemist sat on a stool and wiped his forehead. "I thought you suspected something, with all those questions. Yes, he said he'd filmed something peculiar. It looked like an otter to me, but it was my chance to substitute a photo I'd shot earlier of a wooden model I carved. He'd never know the difference, and word would get out to the world." He looked up. "But I didn't kill him! I swear it!"

Darnell glared at him. "Don't you realize your faked photo was the very cause of his death?"

The dazed chemist mumbled the words again. "I didn't kill him." He shook his head. "It was just a little hoax."

They left him sitting on his stool and drove the short distance to the City Hall. "The mayor said he'd be working here tonight," Constable Lachlan said.

They walked down the corridor to the office bearing the brass plate MAYOR BRUCE DONNELL, and the constable rapped on the door. No sound came from within. "Should be here," the constable said. He rapped again. He tried the doorknob, and the door swung open wide, easily. The four looked into the room.

Penny gasped. "He's dead!"

Mayor Bruce Donnell lay slumped over his desk, his head down, eyes staring to one side. A large circle of blood surrounded his head on the desktop.

"Stay out here, Penny," Darnell said.

The three men stepped over to the body and Constable Lachlan made a quick examination. "Yes, he's gone." He studied the wound on the mayor's head. "Bludgeoned, I'd say. Some large heavy object."

As they looked about the room, their gazes uniformly fell on the brass statue on the bookcase behind the desk. Without touching it, Lachlan peered at a stain on the statue. "Blood."

Darnell said, "We have to go quickly, to our last stop."

Lachlan nodded and straightened up. "I'll have my deputy come in here to take charge of the scene. I'll go over it later." He hurried back to the jail and returned with a youngish man in a tan uniform. He instructed him to touch nothing, to remain there on guard, and the four hurried back out onto the street and climbed into Lachlan's car.

"The church, fast," Darnell said. "I hope we're not too late."

At the church, Darnell jumped out of the car and ran to the front double doors as the others followed. He pulled the doors open and burst into the church. A door at the side of the front of the auditorium stood open. "Where does that lead to?" he demanded of the constable.

"The bell tower."

"Quick." Darnell ran to the doorway and up the stairs followed by Constable Lachlan and MacDougall.

The unrecognizable voice of Vicar Murdoch cried out in warning. "Stop!" The vicar held up a hand. "Don't come any nearer." He stood near the wood railing of the parapet, his dark outline showing starkly in the moonlight against the night sky.

Darnell urged, "Come down, Vicar. Talk with us."

"Never! I can't go to prison. I won't."

Darnell heard the desperateness in the vicar's voice. He needed time, and inched forward. "Why did you do it? To protect your village?"

"Yes, from the monsters."

"You mean, the Loch Ness monsters?"

"No, the tourists. They'd ruin Drumnadrochit, make it into something it should never be."

"You poisoned the man." Darnell continued moving forward slowly as he talked, and saw that the constable was doing the same. "And somehow the mayor knew this."

"He saw me buy the chocolates I gave to Ramsey as a welcome gift, the ones they tested for arsenic. Donnell was going to have me arrested." The vicar made a move and stepped up determinedly on the railing. "It's better this way."

Darnell and MacDougall rushed forward. Darnell tried to catch the sleeve of the vicar's frock but it slipped through his fingers as the man jumped. They heard the sound of the body crumple as it hit the ground, and looked down at it.

John Darnell shook his head. "Two murders, and now this. And what caused them? A legend. Greed. A faked photograph. The vicar's obsessive fear his precious town would be destroyed. Three violent deaths from such strange, fateful coincidences."

MacDougall scowled. "It's the village curse."

The next morning Sandy MacDougall stood at the side of the horse carriage after helping Darnell load the suitcases on the back. Penny sat in the carriage, waiting for their departure.

Darnell shook the reporter's hand, saying, "Your Old Doc Angus Baird won't have another Nessie tale to tell this time."

MacDougall grimaced. "No, but now Doc's got two murders and a suicide to add to his stories. Everyone in the village does."

"And so do you, Sandy. I can visualize the front-page story on the *Times* already. *'Personal account by intrepid reporter.'*"

"It's not the one I wanted to write." He shook his head. "But I'll telegraph it, and stay on awhile with my mother. I'll look you up in London next week, John."

Darnell stared out at the waters of Loch Ness. "You know, Sandy, the way this tragedy played out could be a prelude to the future. More and more sightings, eventually a photograph that really appears authentic, swarms of tourists descending upon the town every summer, the nature of Drumnadrochit completely changing over the coming years. Very much like the unfortunate vicar predicted."

"I'm afraid you're right."

Darnell climbed aboard the carriage and turned to Penny as the horse clip-clopped down General Wade's Road. "I'm sorry about our vacation. It was a bit spoiled for you."

Penny Darnell shook her head. "Nonsense, John. Anyway, we're just getting started. On our way back to London, you promised we'd spend some time in the fine shops of Glasgow, and stop at Edinburgh. I want to take home some good memories of our summer vacation in Scotland."

He smiled. "With some souvenirs, I'm sure. And . . . ?"

"Take me to Urquhart Castle, by the bay, John. It's on our way. I want to gaze out at Loch Ness from the castle ruins." She smiled. "Maybe I'll see some mysterious beast skimming along on top of the water." She took John Darnell's hand in hers. "If not, we'll have a last, peaceful look at beautiful Loch Ness."

Behind them, in front of the Inn, Sandy MacDougall stood watching them leave. As the carriage edged its way down to the road, the reporter sighed, pulled a small, glistening sheet from his coat pocket, took a last look at it, and tore it into small bits. A gust of wind caught the pieces and swirled them in eddies into the air.

One by one the bits of paper fluttered down onto the loch, and the torn pieces of the photograph of what some thought could have been the loch's legendary monster—a photograph that ironically led to the deaths of three men—now floated on the loch's surface, now glistened briefly in the sunlight, now slowly sank into the murky depths of Loch Ness.

PORRIDGE AND BESS
A Pennsylvania Dutch Mystery Story

Tamar Myers

•

Tamar Myers is the author of nine Pennsylvania Dutch
mysteries, including *The Crepes of Wrath*, *The Hand That
Rocks the Ladle*, and *Too Many Crooks Spoil the Broth*.
Her upcoming title is *Gruel and Unusual Punishment*.
This story marks Magdalena Yoder's first vacation.

"The last thing Monty saw was the horse's rump. And that's
putting it politely."

Investigator Brown raised a shapely eyebrow. "How do you
know that's the last thing he saw?"

I smiled pleasantly. The detective was a woman about my
own age—forty-six. I like to see women succeed in what is
still a male-dominated world, and I was determined to give this
woman as many breaks as possible.

"Because I was sitting right there. Not on the horse's patooty, mind you—although I have sat on a few in my day. I'm
a farm girl, you know."

Investigator Brown returned my smile, but I could tell that
her patience was wearing thin. I was the last of the six suspects
to be interviewed, and apparently the previous five had not
been as cooperative.

"Please, Miss Yoder," she said. "Do you mind if we stick to
the relevant details?"

"Not at all, but I've done a little investigative work of my
own. Nothing official, or anything, but still, I'm pretty good.
Take that time I found Sarah Weaver, dead, in a barrel of pickled sauerkraut. Well—"

She cleared her throat. "Miss Yoder."

"All right!" I wailed. "But you don't want me glossing over
some detail that might just turn out to be important, do you? I
mean, if I didn't happen to mention that Sarah had been in that

barrel for twenty years, you might conclude that her killer's trail might be fresh. Which it wasn't, of course. Still, I managed to catch him, and all because I have a knack for observing things other people miss."

She sighed. "Okay, tell me everything about Monty and the horse's rump. Start wherever you want."

I propped my aching feet up on the detective's desk, took a swig of the warm soda left in my bottle, and plunged into my story. Needless to say, the good detective tried to interrupt a million times, but I have not included those interruptions in my story. Neither have I omitted anything of importance.

You be the judge.

My full name is Magdalena Portulacca Yoder. I own the PennDutch Inn—one of this country's finest full-board establishments—up in Hernia, Pennsylvania. And no, Hernia is nowhere near Intercourse, which is all the way over on the other side of the state.

I am a Mennonite, as you may probably have guessed by my white prayer cap, but I am not Amish. I have Amish ancestors, however—not all Mennonites do—and since my people are so intermarried, I am, in fact, my own cousin. If I'm in the mood for a family picnic, all I need to do is to make a sandwich.

At any rate, the trip to Charleston was my very first vacation. I've always loved history, and South Carolina is jam-packed with it, Charleston in particular. Besides, it's an incredibly beautiful city with three-hundred-year-old buildings, cobblestone streets, lots of palm trees, and of course water. Before I read the brochures I had no earthly idea that Charleston is where the Ashely and Cooper Rivers come together to form the Atlantic Ocean.

I arrived just last night, but the first thing I did this morning was hustle my bustle over to the Visitor Center on Meeting Street. Frankly, I was a bit overwhelmed by all the possible tours, and even if this dreadful thing with Monty hadn't happened, I'm not sure I chose the right one. It was frightfully expensive—costing easily twice as much as any of the other tours, but you see, True Grits Tours just happened to have an opening on their Lunch & Learn midday excursion. According to my guidebook, this was one of the most desirable things to do in the city. These tours are normally booked months in advance, but there had been a last-minute cancellation. Not half the fool I appear to be, I signed up.

My instructions were to meet up with the group at precisely noon at the True Grits restaurant across the street from the Old Slave Mart where, incidentally, slaves were never sold, but went to shop for their masters. Anyway, I found the restaurant without any trouble, and as soon as I arrived, I was shown to a large table in a private room off the back.

Monty was already there, standing with his back to the table. When he turned, I was surprised to see the True Grits crest on his shirt. Because, as you know, he was a short little thing in tight blue jeans, and he had those bowed legs, and that shaved head with the dragon tattooed on the back. Oh, and that horrible scraggly beard. Why don't men just shave it off if they can't grow a proper one? And that earring! Wearing a cross for an earring—especially on a man—is sacrilegious if you ask me. Anyway, he heard me come in and sidled over.

"Well, well, who have we here?" he practically shouted. That's when I noticed his tongue was pierced.

"We have Magdalena Yoder, and we have you. As to your identity, I haven't a clue."

"What did you say?"

I repeated myself.

"Ha, a poet!"

"Not hardly, dear. I was hoping you'd introduce yourself."

"Monty Kravitz. I'm your guide." He began circling me like a hungry wolf, or a venomous viper. Take your pick. "My, my, you're a tall one. How tall are you?"

I gasped. "Don't be rude."

"No, really, how tall are you?"

I glared at the little man. I'm five feet ten, which doesn't exactly make me a giantess, but it was none of his business.

"A whole lot taller than you, dear," I said through gritted teeth.

"Ha, a live one!"

"You bet your bippy."

My glares generally set people straight, but Monty seemed

immune. "What's with the funny hat?" he asked in that loud voice.

I know, I should have seen that as an opportunity to share a little about my faith, but I was too vexed for that. Instead I prayed that the Good Lord would keep my mouth shut, like He did those of the lions when Daniel was thrown into their den. My prayers must have been answered, because seconds later Chuck and Irene Bibbson entered the room.

Monty grimaced. "Well, look at the hayseeds," he said.

"I beg your pardon?"

"Hicks," he said in what was supposed to be a whisper, but might well have wakened the dead two counties over.

I knew Irene Bibbson heard him, because her face turned the color of pickled eggs. I felt sorry for the woman. It was bad enough she was on the plain side, but the poor gal didn't have a clue as how to dress. I'm not saying that I'm a fashion plate either, but if my hair was gray I wouldn't chop it off myself in a crude bob and push it back from my temples with tortoise-shell barrettes. At the very least, I would clean my glasses occasionally. I wasn't sure at first if it was Irene behind those opaque circles, or Little Orphan Annie.

Chuck Bibbson was a giant of a man with flat, sunburned features and faded blue eyes. Despite the fact that it was ninety-four degrees outside, he was wearing heavy work pants and a blue broadcloth shirt. He had the smell of fresh earth about him, and I knew instinctively he was a farmer. Well, a retired farmer at any rate.

If Chuck heard Monty's rude comment, he didn't let on. He shook the tour guide's hand and then took mine in his enormous paws. Quite frankly, those oversized mitts of his felt like pineapples.

"Pleased to meet you," he said in a broad accent that I guessed to be from one of those square states. Iowa maybe. Turns out I was right.

"Pleased to meet *you*," I said.

"And this is Mother," he said, indicating Irene.

"Get out of town!" I cried. "You don't look much older than your son. Ten, fifteen years at the most!"

"I'm his wife," she said, on the verge of tears.

Of course I felt lower than the muck on Miller's pond back

home in Hernia. I should have known better. Lots of couples in their age bracket do that "mother" and "father" thing. Fortunately that's when Pepper Saltsman waltzed into the room. All four of us turned and stared.

Pepper had energy and style. I think it was the straw hat with the scarlet hibiscus tucked into the band that first caught my attention. Of course she's at least ten years older than I, and I wasn't fooled by that blue-black hair. Still, everything about her was elegant. She was wearing a gauzy dress that reached to her ankles—well, you know all about that. And the fresh-water pearl necklace with the cameo locket.

"Are you from Charleston?" I asked Pepper, when I heard her charming accent.

"No, I'm from Meridian, Mississippi," she said and laid a cool hand on my arm.

"Ah, the state capital. I bet it's lovely too."

"Oh, it is."

We bonded immediately. Some people you like right off the bat, and Pepper was one of them. But don't get me wrong, I'm not a snob. I tried to include Irene in our conversation, but the woman was shy. I've known milkweed pods that were more forthcoming.

I guess it was a relief for all of us when Todd and Betsy Duncan breezed into the room. I know Monty had to be happy, especially if he was expecting any tips. The Duncans, I knew just from reading the *Hernia Herald,* were filthy rich. Todd was, after all, the inventor of the electric toothpaste tube squeezer.

Both Duncans were as brown as acorns. And those weren't farmer's tans they were sporting either, but the sun-damaged skin of the idle rich. Against that dark background their capped teeth dazzled like miniature snowdrifts.

Todd's hair was dyed with that one-color-suits-all stuff men fool themselves with, but his silk shirt was unbuttoned nearly to the waist, revealing hair every bit as gray as Irene's. In the right hands, the gold chain he wore around his neck would keep Social Security afloat to the end of this century.

Betsy Duncan wasn't fooling anyone either. Her hair was an impossible shade of blond, and although she was a good twenty years younger than her husband, parts of her were much younger than that. Cantaloupes don't normally grow on bean poles, if you get my drift. As for her buttocks—well, something that's been sat on for even just twenty years is not going to stay that firm without a surgeon's help.

Although Betsy's body may have come as a kit, her wardrobe was definitely old school rich. That is to say, she wore linen. Just why it is the wealthy like to walk around wrinkled is beyond me. I mean, if the Good Lord would have wanted us to look like that, he would have made us all Chinese Shar-pei dogs. (At that point the investigator interrupted with exceptional vigorousness, and I was forced to get on with my tale.)

It was no surprise to me then to see Monty greet the Duncans like long-lost relatives. It was a surprise, however, to watch Monty greet Todd with his right hand, while his left hand inexplicably found its way within close proximity to Betsy's buttocks.

"Don't even think about it," Betsy said out of the side of her mouth.

Of course Monty didn't hear her. The hand hovered precariously near her, until, finally she slapped it away. It was a playful gesture, but I could tell she was annoyed.

Her husband Todd seemed oblivious to the whole thing. He was too busy describing to Monty the thirty-foot yacht the Duncans had sailed into Charleston Harbor.

With one ear—and I have exceptional hearing, by the way—directed toward the yacht conversation, I conversed with Pepper Saltsman and the farm couple. Although the four of us were obviously well off financially, we felt like poor cousins compared to the Duncans. We certainly didn't rate our guide's attention after that golden couple walked in.

"Well then," Monty finally said to the rest of us, "it's time for lunch." He pointed to the table that, incidentally, was round. It was attractively set with real cloth napkins in seafoam-green, and there was a conch shell centerpiece spilling daisies in a fan.

We must have all been famished because we seated ourselves quickly, I between the perky Pepper and the two-tuned Todd. This was not acceptable to Monty.

"You're going to have to move," he said to me. His tone was rude, or I might have been more cooperative.

"Why?"

"Because this is my tour and I make the assignments."

"But I'm paying the king's ransom to take this tour. There's an empty seat between Chuck and Betsy. You can sit there."

"I don't want to sit there. This is my seat."

I sighed. Moving for the sake of peace would have been the Christian thing to do, but I'd already taken off my shoes. My footwear has a tendency to migrate, and already one of my size eleven clodhoppers was out of reach. If I moved I was either going to have to crawl under the table, or parade around the table in one stocking foot.

"Hey, I tell you what, young fellow," Chuck said in that wonderfully flat voice. "I've got me an idea. Why don't you come sit here between Mother and me."

I could see Irene cringe. Personally I couldn't blame the woman. Owning an inn, as I do, I frequently come into contact with less than savory characters. But a farm wife like Irene—well, just the prospect of sitting next to someone like Monty had to be traumatic.

"Okay, I'll move," I said, and fished one last time for my wayward shoe. Unfortunately, I did not find it. I did, however, find Pepper's shin. I shall forever be grateful that the woman didn't let on. I muttered my apologies and plodded, one shoe off, and one shoe on, to my new seat.

And just in time too, because a team of waitresses in shamefully immodest attire entered the room, bearing huge trays containing our lunch. As they set the steaming plates before us, our faces in turn registered first surprise, then dismay. Only the perky Pepper appeared unperturbed by the plate in front of her.

Chuck was the first to speak. "Excuse me," he said, and very politely I might add, "there must me some mistake. This here is porridge. The brochure said we'd be getting lunch."

Monty seemed to find that very funny. First he brayed like a donkey in heat, and then cackled like a hen that had just laid an egg. "It isn't porridge," he finally sputtered.

"So it isn't porridge, but cream of wheat," I said, sticking up for simple Chuck. "It's still breakfast food. Big diff."

Monty slapped his skinny thighs. "It isn't cream of wheat either. It's grits. Shrimp and grits."

I stared at my plate. I'm a big fan of seafood—tuna casserole is a favorite of mine—but serving shrimp in gravy atop something that looked for all the world like hot cereal, well, was it any wonder the South lost the war?

"Go ahead," Pepper urged. "Try it. I think you'll be pleasantly surprised."

"You've had this before?"

"Oh, yes it's quite popular in Mississippi." She took a big bite of her lunch and smiled approvingly.

Todd turned to his wife Betsy. "We've had shrimp and grits before, haven't we?"

She nodded. "New Orleans, I think. Yes, I remember now. That charming little place in the French Quarter—you know the one we almost bought."

The Duncans, I remembered from the article, hailed from one of the northeastern states. They had Barbara Walters accents to go with their designer clothes. No doubt they'd even eaten escargot. Shrimp on porridge was no big deal for them.

It was for me, however. That first bite made its trip mouthward a good ten times before I had the nerve to taste the stuff. Frankly, it wasn't too bad. But just so as not to give Monty satisfaction, I ate slowly.

Not that Monty noticed. He had somehow persuaded bottle-blond Betsy and two-toned Todd to switch places. With perky Pepper on one side, and bouncing Betsy on the other, Monty was oblivious to the rest of us.

"So, do you travel much?" I asked Chuck. Small talk has never been my forte.

"No, ma'am. This is Irene's and my first trip out of Garden Grove since—well, since we went to the state fair in Des Moines back in 1972. Mother, you remember that trip?"

Irene nodded.

"Mother, tell this nice lady what took us all the way to Des Moines."

Irene blushed and stirred her grits. She hadn't eaten a single shrimp.

"Mother's kind of shy," he said. "But it's really a humdinger of a story."

I tapped on my water glass with my knife. "Hey, everyone," I said helpfully. "Listen up. Mother—I mean, Irene—is going to tell us all about the Iowa state fair of 1972."

"Spare me," Monty moaned. Then quite unexpectedly, he let out a yelp. He sounded just like a puppy will if you step on its tail—not that I do much of that, mind you, but you know what I mean.

I glared at the rude man. "Please, Irene, proceed."

"Well, we have our farm you see, and then we have our vegetable garden. That's my job. Some years I grow a little bit of everything, but others—"

"The point," Monty said. "Get to the point."

Irene whimpered before finding her speaking voice. "It was a rutabaga," she said, staring down at the mess on her plate. "A ten-pound rutabaga."

"My that's exceptionally large," I said and clapped enthusiastically.

But Irene was shaking her head. "Oh, that wasn't the largest rutabaga there. But it was the only one that looked like Richard Nixon."

"You're kidding, right?" Monty said.

"But she's not," Chuck said. He was beaming with pride. "It looked exactly like the president. Of course it didn't win a prize, but it was on display all week. Heck, it did more that. It made the papers. I heard that the AP picked it up, so some of you might even have seen it."

"Yeah," Monty said. "I remember now. I lined my bird cage with that section."

I wanted to slap the boy. Five hundred years of Mennonite and Amish ancestors are all that prevented me from circumventing the table and doing just that.

"For shame," I said. "I'm going to report your rude behavior to the owner of this tour company."

Monty grinned. "Go ahead. The owner is my daddy."

"Then he'll set you straight," I humped.

Monty twirled his earring with a dirty finger. "Daddy's recovering from a quadruple bypass. I've been in charge of things for two weeks." He ran pierced tongue over yellow teeth. "Hell, do you really think I'd be here, leading this crappy little tour, if I had a choice?"

Our collective gasps depleted the small room of its oxygen. Fortunately the door opened just then and a waitress poked her head in the room. The fresh air that flowed in around her was a blessed relief.

"Mr. Kravitz," the young woman said, "I'm sorry to interrupt, but you're needed in the kitchen."

Monty glared at her. "Tell the cook to handle his own problems."

The waitress blinked. "I'm afraid the cook is the problem. He just quit."

"Damn!" Monty threw his napkin down like a child and stomped out of the room, slamming the door behind him.

For at least a minute we all sat mute, too stunned to speak—well, the rest were at any rate. I took advantage of the moment to slide under the table and retrieve my shoe. When I emerged triumphantly, it was bedlam, with everyone, including the mousy Irene, having their say. I had no choice but to tap on my water glass again.

"Ladies and gentlemen," I said sternly, "we need to quit acting like children. I propose we simply all get up and leave."

Chuck's sunburned features paled. "But the money. This was our first vacation. Mother and I spent a fortune to get here, and this tour was recommended as the best. Why, it alone cost as much as the new heifer I bought last week."

"We'll make him give our money back," Todd said. "I've got lawyers."

"That man groped me under the table," Betsy said calmly. "I had to stab him with my fork."

Chuck nodded. "So that explains the dog noises. I thought maybe the boy was on drugs."

"We don't know that he's not," I said. "He certainly fits the profile."

"I'll sue the bastard," Todd said. He didn't sound at all surprised by his wife's revelation. Perhaps Betsy was groped on a regular basis.

Pepper leaned over Monty's plate and whispered something to Betsy. As she talked she fiddled nervously with the pendant that dangled from her pearl necklace. At last she straightened.

"First," she said, "allow me to apologize on behalf of

Southerners everywhere. We don't normally act like this. The boy is an exception, I assure you. In fact, I'd be willing to bet there's a Yankee somewhere in his woodpile."

We all laughed good-naturedly. Truth be told, I thought Monty had a Pittsburgh accent.

Pepper smiled. "But," she continued, "as disgusting as his behavior is, I urge y'all not to abandon the tour."

"There are other tours," growled Todd. "I'll be glad to pay for them if money is an issue."

"That's very generous of you, Mr. Duncan, but it's the principle of the thing. I mean, we paid for this tour, so we should get our money's worth."

Irene chased a stray gray lock with a cheap barrette. "Even if he's mean?"

"*Because* he's so mean. I say we ask for seconds of this delicious shrimp and grits, even if we're no longer hungry. I say that once we're on the actual tour we ask as many questions as possible. Make real pests of ourselves. Then, after we've worn him to a frazzle, that's when we ask for our money back."

We stared at her, and then one by one our smiles clicked on, as if someone was flipping a panel of switches.

Monty returned to an orderly group. I don't think he noticed at first, because he was too busy wolfing down his own lunch. When he finally looked up, our smiles were in place.

"We'd like some more please," I said.

He glanced around the table. "All of you?"

I held out my plate. "It's delicious. This porridge—I mean grits—is really something. I simply must have the recipe."

"We don't share our recipe," Monty growled. However, he reluctantly got up and secured a waitress to serve us. The cook, thankfully, had been talked into staying through the noon shift.

We all ate seconds. Some of us ate thirds. Even Irene had a second helping, although she confessed to me later that she'd passed half the shrimp to her husband's plate. The other half ended up in her vinyl pocketbook.

Of course it annoyed Monty to see us eat so much. He was visibly relieved when we finally all agreed it was time to crawl aboard his horse-drawn carriage. Perhaps he thought we would fall into a gluttony-induced stupor and sleep through his spiel. Boy, was he wrong.

We clambered aboard the carriage with more questions than a pack of six-year-olds. Did it have brakes? What was insurance like on a contraption like that? Was the fringe around the top just for show? What was the horse's name? How old was the horse? What was that funny diaper thing hanging off the horse's patooty? This last question, incidentally, came from Irene, who had become emboldened by our plan. A farm woman—but not a Mennonite—Irene used a more graphic term.

Monty tried to evade our questions, but we persisted until he answered. Yes, the damn thing had brakes, insurance was hideously high, the animal's name was Bess, and she was sixteen years old. The fringe was basically for show, although there was some evidence that its swinging motion helped keep flies away. As for that funny diaper bag, the city required it. Of course Bess didn't always hit her bag, which served the persnickety residents of the historic district right.

The poor boy had a seating plan all worked out, which we blithely ignored. I decided to sit right behind Monty because I know a little something about horses—just in case something went wrong. Not that I was anticipating anything, mind you. Anyway, Pepper sat next to me, behind us were the Bibbsons, and Todd and Betsy brought up the rear.

Our route led us down East Bay Street, which was fairly heavily trafficked. Every now and then Monty would pull Bess over to allow motorized traffic to pass, or to elaborate on a particular house. Sometimes the owners would be standing in their yards, or sitting on their porches, and you could tell they weren't happy with all the attention. Especially since not everything Monty said was true. Or flattering for that matter.

"See that shabby gray house there on your left?" he asked. "See the double flight of steps going up to the porch? The one on the left is called the Gentleman's Stairs. Ladies used the one on the right. You see back then it wasn't considered proper for a man to see a woman's ankles—"

"Or to pinch them either, I bet," Betsy said.

We all laughed, Betsy as loud as the rest of us.

Monty reddened. "Now, see that house over there? That's

what we call a single Charleston style house. It is only one room wide, to allow breezes to pass through the house. Notice that there is a porch—a piazza, the locals call it—along one side. If you look carefully you'll see a door that opens onto the porch. This is really the main entrance to the house. What appears to be the front door up here by the street is really more of a gate. Can anyone guess why that is?"

Pepper raised her hand. "I took a bus tour yesterday," she whispered to me.

Monty nodded at Pepper. "Okay, the little lady from Mississippi thinks she knows."

Pepper stood long enough to bow, and we all clapped. The act of bowing made Pepper's hat slip, which in turn messed up her beautiful blue-black hair. She turned away to straighten things before giving us her explanation.

"The door up here by the street gives the piazza privacy," she said. "The locals probably like to sit on their porches without being observed."

Monty frowned. "Well, you're half right. The truth is Charlestonians tend to be snooty, and this fake front door allows them to observe visitors without being seen. If they are invited guests, or at least desirable, they make it past the fake front door."

"Why that doesn't make a lick of sense," I said. "I have only one front door back at home and I don't open it to just anybody. I don't think it has anything to do with snootiness, but privacy, like Pepper said."

There was a chorus of "that's rights" and Monty glared at me. "Y'all aren't from around here," he said in his Pittsburgh accent. "Y'all don't know, so maybe y'all should keep your big mouths shut."

I snorted indignantly. "Well, I do know that y'all is the plural of you, and if you were just now speaking to only me, your usage was incorrect."

That did it. That hiked Monty's hackles. But instead of lapsing into shamed silence, he proceeded to relate everything he'd ever memorized about the city of Charleston. He told us how it all used to be swamps and that even now it sits only a few feet above sea level. He pointed out the earthquake bolts in the walls. He showed us Cabbage Row and the Heyward Washington House where DuBose Heyward lived.

At one point he got so hoarse that poor Irene, feeling sorry for the banty-legged man, offered him a mint. Thank heavens that shut him up for a few minutes.

He pulled old Bess over to the side of road—I think we were on Church Street by then, and sat sucking his mint. Mercifully, we were in the shade of a spreading live oak tree. However, this respite from Monty's spiel wasn't as pleasant as you might think. This particular spot seemed to be a favorite of the carriage-drivers, and there was an abundance of road apples lying about. Monty had been right about the horses not always hitting their bags.

Frankly, I didn't mind the smell. In fact, it made me rather homesick. Too bad the others didn't feel the same way. Even the Bibbsons held their noses. Apparently horses aren't much in demand by wheat farmers.

I'm sure Monty enjoyed their discomfort. I wouldn't be surprised to learn he'd planned to stop there anyway. Maybe he did that to all his so-called guests, just to get back at his father for making him work.

At any rate, the foul odors apparently made some folks delirious. "Go home, Betsy," I heard Pepper say at one point.

At first I thought she was speaking to Mrs. Duncan, then realized she was addressing a pint-sized pooch that was sniffing around the wheel on her side of the carriage. The minuscule mutt eventually obeyed.

In the meantime, the real Betsy was gasping dramatically through a silk handkerchief she'd tied around her mouth, her husband was railing about a possible lawsuit if his sinuses didn't recover, and both Bibbsons were sucking on mints like there was no tomorrow.

Finally, after extracting his vengeance, Monty gave old Bess a gentle slap with the reins and we headed back to True Grits restaurant across from the Old Slave Mart. Oh, don't get me wrong, our guide wasn't done with his spiel. It's just that some of the fire seemed to have gone out of him.

Then, just after we'd turned the corner of South Market and Church—I remember seeing those signs—Monty collapsed. Like I said, he toppled face forward into Bess's patooty.

* * *

"That was all very interesting, Miss Yoder." Investigator Brown gave me a lukewarm smile. "You may go now."

"But don't you want to know who killed Monty Kravitz?"

She blinked. "Are you saying you know?"

"Of course, dear. Like I said before, I've done a bit of detecting in my day."

"Yes, but unofficially, right?" She made a brief note on a small pad of paper.

"That's right. It doesn't take a genius, however, to figure this one out—oh, not that you're not a genius. For all I know you're even smarter than that Marilyn woman who writes a column for *Parade* magazine. Of course, even she has her limitations. I once wrote and asked—"

"Miss Yoder, *please*."

"Okay, okay. It was that nice Pepper Saltsman who killed Monty."

Investigator Brown all but rolled her eyes. "Oh, really?"

"But it was. She's not from Mississippi, you know. I goofed when I said that Meridian was the capital. It's not, of course. Jackson is. I really do know better. I was the only student in Miss Lehman's third-grade class to get all fifty states and their capitals right. Dorothy Ediger came in second, but she only got—"

"Miss Yoder, I think you may be on to something, so would you please continue making your case."

I smiled benevolently. "Of course, dear. So, as I was about to say, Pepper—if that's even her real name—doesn't have black hair either. When her hat slipped, so did her wig. Her real hair is every bit as gray as Irene's.

"But what really tipped me off was that dinky dog. At first I thought Pepper was calling it Betsy, but then it struck me that just maybe she was saying Bitsy. After all, the thing was hardly bigger than a rat. Bitsy may well have been its name. But if that was the case, how did Pepper know?

"Well, I'll tell you. Pepper knew because the house in front of which Monty parked the carriage—the spot with all the road apples on the street—that was Pepper's house. I'm telling you, that ugly little dog was either hers, or it belonged to a neighbor. It listened to her, didn't it?"

Investigator Brown shook her well-coiffed head. "Are you trying to tell me that finding horse dung in your driveway is sufficient motive for murder?"

I nodded sagely. "I might find it a pleasant enough odor, but most people don't. Imagine having to put up with horses parking their patooties in front of your house every day. Not to mention throngs of tourists looking in your windows, trampling through your garden, and even knocking on your door. My point is, Pepper simply got fed up with these impositions and snapped."

She closed one eye. "How did you know that our tourists sometimes behave like that?"

"Because that's exactly what I'd be doing right now, if I hadn't been detained for questioning."

She actually smiled. "Good answer. I've always liked an honest person. But okay, let's say, just for the sake of argument, that Pepper Saltsman killed Monty Kravitz. How did she do it? And when?"

"She poisoned his porridge."

"Oh?"

"Grits, I believe you call it here. Anyway, Monty had to leave the private dining room at one point because the cook had threatened to quit. That's when Pepper saw her opportunity—although Heaven knows, she might well have bribed the cook to quit. At any rate, she leaned over Monty's plate and dispensed a slow-acting substance from that little locket she's wearing on those freshwater pearls. Some kind of deadly poison. I'm sure if you check the locket, you'll find the residue."

Investigator Brown circled something on her notepad. "Hmm. Well, we'll just have to see about that."

I stayed on in charming Charleston for two more weeks. I am ashamed to confess that I peeped in my share of windows, trampled a few gardens, and even knocked on a few doors. None of the doors were opened to me, and I paid for my sins by slipping on one particularly fresh road apple and spraining my back.

But when I left Charleston it was by rental truck, not plane, and I was towing a horse trailer. Monty's father, grateful that I'd solved his son's murder, had given me Bess. The senior

Kravitz had decided to throw in the towel on his Lunch and Learn tours, although he was keeping True Grits. The city was getting just too clogged with tours, and anyway, it was time for old Bess to retire.

However, Bess wasn't the only gift I took north with me. Investigator Brown was also grateful, and while her recipe for shrimp and grits isn't nearly as good as the stuff served by True Grits, it is worth a try.

Investigator Brown's Shrimp 'n' Grits

    1½ cups peeled raw shrimp
    juice of ½ lemon
    salt and cayenne pepper to taste
    1 cup chicken or vegetable broth (canned will do)
    2 tablespoons flour
    1 tablespoon ketchup
    1 teaspoon Worcestershire sauce
    1 small onion finely chopped
    2 teaspoons chopped green pepper
    3 tablespoons bacon grease

Season raw shrimp with lemon juice, salt, and pepper and set aside. Add broth to flour in small bowl, a few drops at a time, stirring constantly until smooth paste is formed. Continue to stir in remaining broth, ketchup, and Worcestershire sauce and set aside.

Sauté onion and chopped bell pepper in bacon grease until onion begins to turn translucent. Add shrimp and cook two more minutes.

Slowly add flour mixture until desired amount and consistency of sauce is reached.

Immediately serve over grits that have been cooked according to package directions.

MISSING, PRESUMED . . .

An Alaskan Mystery Story

Dana Stabenow

Dana Stabenow is the Edgar award–winning author of three novels featuring Liam Campbell, *Fire and Ice*, *So Sure of Death*, and *Nothing Gold Can Stay*. In this story, Dana uses her favorite setting, the Alaskan Bush.

One

> **Sec. 09.55.020. Petition and inquiry.** If a petition is presented by an interested person to a district judge or magistrate alleging that a designated person has disappeared and after diligent search cannot be found, and if it appears to the satisfaction of the judge or magistrate that the circumstances surrounding the disappearance afford reasonable grounds for the belief that the person has suffered death from accidental or other violent means, the judge or magistrate shall summon and impanel a jury of six qualified persons to inquire into the facts surrounding and the presumption to be raised from the disappearance. If no one submits a petition within 40 days, a judge or magistrate may submit the petition from personal knowledge of the case.
>
> —Alaska Statutes, Code of Civil Procedure

Eli Sylvester Horrell, fisher, husband, father, went overboard halfway between Dutch Harbor and the Pribilof Islands. Weather conditions that day in January included fifteen-knot winds and twelve-foot swells. The crew of the *Jeri A.* had seen Horrell go in. In spite of an intensive search by the United States Coast Guard, the *Jeri A.*, and three other crabbers, his body had not been recovered.

Now it was June. Horrell's widow, two sons, and one daughter were seated in the front row. The widow, daughter, and youngest son were weeping. The oldest son stared at nothing, white-faced and without expression.

Magistrate Linda Louise Billington, known to friends, defendants, and bar patrons as Bill, was new to the state, new to the town of Newenham, and new to her job. The hearing had come less than six months into her first term of office. It was a balmy spring day, sixty-three degrees with sunny skies and a light breeze. The last of the snow had melted, the last of the mud had dried and the birch and the diamond willow and the alder all showed tiny leaves of a bright, vivid green. She wanted to be outside, catching her first monster king salmon, or climbing her first Alaskan mountain, or taking her first ride in a float plane with a real bush pilot, or even slapping away her first horde of the infamous Alaskan mosquitoes. She looked around the cramped, windowless courtroom lodged in a forgotten corner of the prefabricated building that served as the seat of the third judicial district of the state of Alaska, and thought, How I Spent My Summer Vacation.

In the six months since she had been sworn in she had stumbled through her first arrest warrants, fumbled through her first search warrants, and muddled through her first arraignments. She had figured out how to set bail, and how high. She had issued half a dozen restraining orders, and had taken emergency action in one case of child abuse that still gave her nightmares. She had tried, convicted, and sentenced no less than sixteen drunk drivers. She had tried and convicted one fisher of fishing without a permit, a second for fishing past the end of the period, a third for harvesting female opilio, a fourth for harvesting undersized kings, and a fifth for fishing outside the district to which his permit restricted him. She had learned to discount most excuses offered by fishers, because if all the engines alleged to have broken down in her courtroom really had, half the Bering Sea fishing fleet would be in dry dock.

She was beginning to build a reputation. The night before in the bar she'd heard one fisher mumble at her approach, "Gawd, here she comes, Hanging Bill." No compliment in her life had ever tasted so sweet.

This, however, was her first presumptive death hearing.

Sudden, violent death was no stranger to Alaska, especially the Bush. Pilots wrecked planes. Hikers disappeared into national parks. Climbers fell down mountains. Snow machiners started avalanches. Cross-country skiers fell into glaciers.

And, as in this case, fishers fell overboard. Alaska had thirty-six thousand miles of shoreline. Much of its living was made on the water.

Many of its missing people were lost on that water.

When it became obvious that the missing was dead, a presumptive death hearing was held to engage the machinery of the state to issue a death certificate.

The two-by-four folding table that stood in for a judicial bench was stacked with the necessary tools as specified by the Magistrate Correspondence Course: the case file, the list of witnesses, no exhibit list as there were no exhibits, her jury instructions, a log sheet, a blank verdict form, paper and pencils, and a box of Kleenex. There was a copy of the Presumptive Death Hearing Script, extracted from the correspondence course binder, held between her knees and the bottom of the table in case she forgot what she was doing midway through the process. She'd already checked the tape recorder twice; she checked it a third time on the principle that it was a mistake to allow any mechanical object to realize its own importance. Hattie Bishop had been sworn in as bailiff. The jury was impaneled. The witnesses were waiting.

One of the fluorescent lights flickered overhead behind a plastic lens yellowed and cracked with age. Her back brushed against the standards bearing the American and Alaskan flags. Metal chair legs scraped the floor when someone shifted his weight, somebody else coughed. The second hand on the plain white face of the clock over the door clicked loudly up to twelve: 9:00 A.M.

She cleared her throat and restarted the tape recorder. "We are again on record. This is the district court for the state of Alaska at Newenham, Alaska, Magistrate L. L. Billington presiding." She noted the date and the time, the name of the deceased, and the case number. "Ladies and gentlemen of the jury, Eli Sylvester Horrell, deckhand on the fishing vessel *Jeri A.*, went into the Bering Sea somewhere between Dutch

Harbor and St. Paul the night of January 12 of this year. His body has not been recovered. It is your duty to decide if sufficient evidence is available to presume that he is dead."

She paused, and peeked at the papers in her lap. When she looked up again the sixth juror was staring at her, as he had been staring at her pretty much unblinkingly since she had sworn in the panel. She straightened in her chair and frowned at him to dispel the notion that she'd been caught cheating. "The standard of proof is probable cause, which means you must find it to be more reasonable than not"—she underlined those last four words with her voice—"that Mr. Horrell is dead."

Mrs. Horrell gave a gasping sob. Bill held out the box of Kleenex. Mrs. Horrell took one with a damp and grateful look.

"You may ask questions of the witnesses; indicate that you wish to do so by raising your hand after the witness has finished testifying. You may take notes." She gestured at the pads and pencils. "Once all the witnesses have testified, you will retire to deliberate your verdict. That verdict must be unanimous; that is, all six of you must agree on the verdict." She paused. "Are there any questions?"

There weren't. Hiding her relief, she said, "Very well. The court now calls its first witness, Alaska State Trooper Daniel Reynoldson, to the stand." Trooper Reynoldson, whose uniform had seen better days, stood up and came forward, hat under his arm. "Raise your right hand. Do you solemnly swear or affirm that the testimony you will give in the case now before this court will be the truth, the whole truth, and nothing but the truth?"

Trooper Reynoldson's voice was thin and reedy, unexpectedly so coming from such a large, barrel-chested man. "I do."

"Please be seated." Reynoldson sat and straightened his spine as if to counterweight the bulging belly sitting in his lap. "State your full name, your mailing address, and your occupation." He did so, declared he had no relationship to the deceased, and told the jury what he knew about the circumstances of Horrell's disappearance, which wasn't much. When the *Jeri A.* had docked, Captain Quinn had called the trooper post. Reynoldson had been catching that day and he had responded to the call, taking Quinn's statement, talking to the other three deckhands, and talking to the family about the deceased's state of mind (code for whether he was suicidal; he wasn't).

"Thank you, Trooper Reynoldson. Does the jury have any questions for this witness?"

They hadn't. Bill called Captain Enrique Quinn to the stand. Captain Quinn, a tall, wiry man in his mid-forties with elegant Latino features and nervous hands, took the oath and described the night (dark, temperature and barometer both dropping, twelve-foot swells, wind blowing out of the northwest and creating spray that turned instantly to ice), the crew's activities (hot on the crab, pulling one pot after another, the hold half full and less than twelve hours left in the fishing period), and his last sight of Horrell. "We were moving from one string to another when we started to ice up. Eli got a bat out of—"

"Excuse me," Bill said, "a what?"

"A baseball bat."

She was new to the place and the job, so she was careful to keep the incredulity out of her voice. "You use a baseball bat to fish for crab?"

Everyone looked tolerant, even the jury. "We use them to break ice off when the deck starts icing over." When she continued to look blank, he added helpfully, "If we don't, the weight of the ice might pull the boat over, make it turn turtle." He paused. When she didn't say anything, he added, "So then we'd be in the water and—"

"Thank you, Captain Quinn, I've got the picture," Bill said, and wondered how long it was going to take her to learn everything she needed to know about the fishing business. She wasn't sure but she thought the sixth juror winked at her.

"Mick, Joe, and Harlen"—Quinn nodded at the three scruffy young men sitting at the back of the room—"baited pots while Eli beat ice."

"What happened then?"

"He slipped," Quinn said. His voice was suddenly weary, his face drawn. "He just—he slipped. He skidded right across the deck, came up hard against the gunnel, and somersaulted right over the side." He ran a hand through thick black hair. "It all happened so fast, I—"

He stopped, and into the silence that followed Bill prompted, "What did you do?"

"I stopped the engines, tripped the beacon, took a bearing, yelled 'Man overboard' on the loudspeaker." Quinn's voice dropped.

"Captain Quinn," Bill said, gently but firmly, "I'm going to have to ask you to speak up."

"I'm sorry," he said. His voice deepened, his words becoming more clipped. "I stopped the engines, marked our location, triggered the emergency locator beacon, yelled 'Man overboard' on the loudspeaker. We already had all the deck lights on. Everybody ran back to the stern, we heaved life rings and a raft over the side, hollered Eli's name. There was no answer." A pause. "I called the Coast Guard"—he nodded again, this time toward a trim young man in a crisp blue uniform—"and told them what happened. We sat there until dawn, about nine, nine-thirty, I guess. Some other boats showed up to help look, the *Sandy C.*, the *Rhonda S.*, and"— he thought—"oh, yeah, the *Dixie G.* Search and Rescue showed up about then, too. They couldn't find him either." His voice dropped again. "We looked for two days. There was—he was just—gone."

"And then?"

"And then we went back to Dutch. The period was over, the quota was met, we couldn't do any more fishing."

"Thank you. Does the jury have any questions they would like to ask this witness?"

One man, portly, grizzled, raised his hand. "Was Horrell wearing a survival suit?"

Quinn shook his head. "No."

"Were any of your crew?"

"No."

"Do you have survival suits on board?"

"Yes."

"Enough for everyone?"

Quinn's expression hardened. "Yes."

"Where?"

Quinn bit the words off. "In the portside galley locker."

"Everybody know where they are?"

"Yes."

"Everybody know how to put them on?"

"I run a survival suit drill the day before the season starts. I always do."

"Then why wasn't Horrell wearing one?"

"You know damn well why, Warren," Quinn snapped. "They're too bulky to work in."

This was what came of holding a jury trial in a town small enough for everyone to know everyone else. "Gentlemen," Bill said.

"I'm done, Your Honor," the juror said, sitting back in his chair with the air of a righteous pigeon.

One at a time, Bill called Horrell's fellow deckhands to the stand. One by one, they corroborated Quinn's testimony. As the third left the stand, the Horrell daughter buried her face in her mother's shoulder.

Bill consulted the witness list. "Lieutenant Commander Richard Klessens?"

The man in the blue uniform came forward to take the oath. He had round pink cheeks and wide-spaced round blue eyes. He didn't look old enough to drive a car, let alone a helicopter, but a pilot he was. In command of the Search and Rescue helicopter that had flown to the scene of Horrell's disappearance, he testified that they had spent the daylight hours of the better part of two days searching for Horrell's body. They had spotted two of the *Jeri A.*'s life rings, an empty plastic bottle of Coke, and a homemade buoy made of a Clorox bottle painted fluorescent orange, but no Eli Horrell.

Next up was paramedic Joe Gould, a thin, intense young man with the fanatical look of a medieval martyr. He spoke in a laconic monotone that negated the impact of what he had to say. Two minutes was his estimate of how long Horrell would have had in the Bering Sea in January without a survival suit or a raft. "After that, hypothermia sets in, the victim becomes disoriented, can't tell which way is up, loses consciousness, and drowns." It was Joe Gould's educated opinion that Eli Sylvester Horrell was dead a minimum of twenty-two minutes after he went into the water. At that point the youngest Horrell son left the courtroom at a run. Mrs. Horrell looked at the older son and he followed his brother.

Gould was the last name on the witness list. The clock showed twenty minutes after ten. Bill felt as if it ought to be much, much later. "Ladies and gentlemen of the jury, you have heard the testimony of the witnesses in this case. Do you have any questions?" She was beginning to feel restive beneath the steady gaze of the sixth juror, who hadn't looked away from her once during the testimony of the witnesses. She consulted the jury list. "Mr.—Alakuyak?" She stumbled a little over the name.

His gaze unwavering, showing no shame at being caught staring and no perceptible alarm at being confronted, he said, "Nope. No questions."

Ruffled but determined to retain at least the facade of impervious judicial calm, she said, "Anyone else?" No one else. "Very well. You may retire to the jury room"—a glorified reference to the conference room reached through the door in the wall on her left, which was even smaller and dingier than her courtroom, not to mention less well furnished—"to deliberate your verdict. Court is in recess."

She waited until the jury had filed out. To Mrs. Horrell she said, "I don't think they'll be long, ma'am. Why don't you take a break, get yourself a drink of water, stretch your legs?" She nodded at the daughter. "There are pop and snack machines down the hall to the left."

Mrs. Horrell managed a smile. "Thank you." She and her daughter waited for Bill to rise and then stood and shuffled out, heads together, arms around each other, moving like two old women. The paramedic had already left, as had Horrell's three crewmates, immediately following their testimony. Trooper Reynoldson, Commander Klessens, and Enrique Quinn sat where they were, Reynoldson and Klessens conversing in low tones, Quinn staring at the floor over folded arms. His face was pale beneath its outdoor tan and there were shadows beneath his eyes. Bill paused in front of him. "Are you all right, Captain Quinn?"

He started, and stared up at her. "What?"

"Are you all right? Do you feel ill?"

"Oh. No. No." He sighed. "This is the first time I've lost

a member of my crew. I keep thinking there was something I could have done."

"Was there?"

He looked startled again by her blunt question. "No," he said quickly. "No. There wasn't."

"Well, then?"

The lines of his face eased a little. She turned to walk away, and to her back he said, "Your Honor?"

She looked over her shoulder.

"Thanks."

Bill retired to her chambers, another tiny, airless room with just enough space for a desk, a chair, and a filing cabinet, and busied herself with paperwork.

When she looked up again, it was ten to twelve. She frowned, and rose to open the door.

The widow and her children were back. Reynoldson was gone; Klessens looked impatient. Enrique Quinn was now sitting next to Mrs. Horrell, patting her shoulder with a kind of helpless awkwardness as she wept silently into a Kleenex. The kids looked miserable, but they were also young enough to begin to be bored, and restless with it.

In the chair next to the door into the jurors' room, Hattie Bishop dozed, her head against the wall, her mouth slightly open, a soft snore issuing forth. Bill let her own door close with a loud thud and when she opened it again Hattie was sitting upright, blinking. "Bailiff," Bill said, beckoning. Hattie, looking sheepish, got to her feet and crossed the courtroom. Bill closed the door behind her.

"Any messages from the jury?"

"No," Hattie said, relieved that she wasn't going to be chewed out for sleeping on the job. "No, Your Honor," she added hastily.

"Hmm." Bill pursed her lips and tapped her foot. "Go knock on their door, ask them if there is any testimony they would like to review, or if I can help them in any other way."

She waited. The jury probably wanted lunch on the state, and were drawing out their deliberations to include the noon hour. Not in my courtroom, she thought.

The door opened and Hattie looked in, bright-eyed and bursting with news.

"Well?" Bill said.

"They say they're deadlocked, Your Honor!"

Bill stared for long enough to make Hattie fidget. "They say they are what?"

"Deadlocked!" Hattie repeated in the same thrilled accents. This was better than Court TV off the satellite.

Bill's lips thinned. "Call them into the courtroom. Now."

The jury filed back in and took their seats. Bill looked at the portly juror. "Is there a problem, Mr. Foreman?" Her tone indicated that it would be better for them all if there wasn't.

The portly juror—what the hell was his name? She consulted the jury list. Warren Ollestad. Mr. Ollestad shifted uncomfortably in his chair.

"Well?" she demanded.

Ollestad cast a fleeting look at his fellow jurors. "I'm afraid so, Your Honor."

Bill felt rather than saw new tears forming in Mrs. Horrell's eyes. "Explain," she snapped.

"Well, we seem to be deadlocked."

"Really," Bill said. "How extremely interesting. Deadlocked on what, precisely?"

"Well—" Ollestad floundered for a moment. "Five of us are willing to sign the verdict. The sixth isn't."

Bill looked down the row of jurors with a sense of fatalism. Yes, the sixth juror was still staring at her, that dark, intense, irritatingly knowing stare. She'd never seen him in her life before this day; what right did he have to that look of possession, that air of knowledge? "Mr. Alakuyak—"

"That's Ah-LAH-coo-YAK," he said.

"Mr. Alakuyak, what's your problem?"

"I don't have a problem, Your Honor."

She resisted the impulse to glare. "Then why can't you join the other jurors in a reasonable presumption of Mr. Horrell's death?"

"It's not his death I can't agree to," Alakuyak said, "it's the manner of it."

"What?" gasped Mrs. Horrell.

"What the hell?" Captain Quinn said.

"Your Honor," Klessens said in protest.

Bill waved them all to silence. " 'The manner of it?' Mr.

Alakuyak, four people saw him go over the side of the *Jeri A.* in high winds and heavy seas halfway between Dutch Harbor and St. Paul Island. An extensive search by four boats and one helicopter failed to locate him, alive or dead."

"I know that. My voices tell me something different."

Bill stared. "Voices?"

"Yes."

"What voices?"

"The voices that talk to me."

"You hear voices?"

"Yes."

The silence that followed didn't seem to weigh on the sixth juror as much as it did on everyone else. "You mean like Joan of Arc?" Bill said at last.

He grinned. The jolt of that grin nearly knocked her out of her chair.

"What the hell is going on here?" Quinn said, starting to his feet. "Who is this nutcase—"

"Sit down, Captain Quinn," Bill said sternly, recalled to her office and her sworn duty. He sat.

"Your Honor—" One of the two women on the jury spoke up, a young woman with the Tatar features of the upriver Yupik. Her voice was so soft as to be barely audible.

"Yes"—Bill consulted the jury list—"Ms. Nickolai."

"If Uncle's voices say there is something wrong, then there is something wrong," Mary Nickolai said, still in that same soft voice.

Ollestad said warningly, "Mary—"

"Warren," she said, still in that soft voice, "I let you talk me into agreeing in the jury room, but maybe we should listen to Uncle."

Moses Alakuyak kept that steady, watchful, aware gaze on the magistrate, and said nothing more.

For her part, Bill felt things were getting out of control. She didn't like it. She did what she always did when things got out of control, when she'd suffered her third miscarriage, when her husband had been laid off at Boeing, when he had hit her. She went on the attack.

She leaned forward, pressing her hands flat against the table in front of her, and fixing the sixth juror with an unyielding stare. "Mr. Alakuyak, do you have any evidence to support your feelings?"

"They aren't feelings, they're voices."

This time she didn't resist and did glare. "Then do these voices have a shred of hard evidence to back up what they have told you?"

He was silent. Mrs. Horrell was sobbing, the children looked miserable, Quinn furious. Klessens looked like he was struggling not to burst out laughing. "Mr. Alakuyak, this proceeding is solely to determine the fact of Eli Sylvester Horrell's death. Do you have any reason to believe he is still alive?" When he remained silent, she repeated, "Do you?"

"No."

"Do you have any reason to doubt the evidence given by the paramedic who testified before you this morning? Do you think that Mr. Horrell could have survived in the conditions in which he went overboard?" Again he was silent, and in spite of her determination to remain calm and in control Bill could hear her voice rising. "Do you, Mr. Alakuyak?"

"No."

"Do you have any reason to believe that the three deckhands and the captain of the *Jeri A.* were mistaken in their separate eyewitness accounts of Mr. Horrell's disappearance?"

"No."

"Do you have any evidence to offer that the United States Coast Guard was negligent in its search for a survivor?"

"No."

"You have no doubt, then, that Eli Horrell is dead."

Alakuyak ran a hand through a thick mane of already rumpled dark hair. "No."

Bill sat and folded her hands on the table, shoulders square, severely erect. "As I explained to you in my instructions to the jury before the hearing, Mr. Alakuyak, and may I remind you that when I asked, you had no questions about them, this jury has only to determine the fact of death, not the cause or the manner of death. The fact of death. In other words," she said, leaning forward again and for a moment forgetting who else was in the room, "I don't care if your little voices told you that Scotty beamed Mr. Horrell onto the bridge of the *Enterprise* two seconds after he went into the water. The preponderance of the evidence, evidence which you have just admitted you accept, leads us to presume Mr. Horrell's death."

The younger Horrell son was out of the room for the second time, and Bill was recalled to the grieving family's presence. "Do you understand, Mr. Alakuyak?"

"Yes, Your Honor," he said.

"Good," she snapped. "Then get in that jury room and bring me back a verdict form with six signatures at the bottom."

"Yes, ma'am," he said.

And then he did something very odd. He smiled at her, a smile one part rueful, one part apologetic, another part something she couldn't identify but that seemed familiar to her, as if she'd seen it in her own mirror. For a split second she wondered where they had met before, and reassured herself that they hadn't. Of course they hadn't. She would have remembered that smile.

Two

Sec. 25.24.050. Grounds for divorce. A divorce may be granted for any of the following grounds: . . . (2) adultery; (3) conviction of a felony; 4) willful desertion for a period of one year; (5) either (A) cruel and inhuman treatment calculated to impair health or endanger life; (B) personal indignities rendering life burdensome; or (C) incompatibility of temperament . . .
— Alaska Statutes, Marital and Domestic Relations

He aimed it at her again that evening from the open door of her office at Bill's Bar and Grill. "Hey, girl."

She sat back in her chair. "Mr. Alakuyak." She overlooked the familiarity of his address as she had laid off her judicial robes for the more casual dress of the owner and proprietor of the best bar in Newenham. There were only two, so the competition wasn't fierce.

"Try Moses," he suggested. "Easier to pronounce."

He stood about five-seven, not much taller than she was,

weight about one-sixty, she thought, most of it muscle and bone. Gray eyes narrowed between Yupik folds, something she saw in many of Newenham's polyglot faces, dark hair graying at the temples. She thought he was older than she was, but she couldn't tell by how much. He was dressed in frayed and faded jeans, a blue plaid wool shirt worn at the elbows, and Sorel boots, pretty much the standard uniform for a Bristol Bay fisher.

In turn, he took his time surveying the long swath of silver hair combed straight back from her brow to fall softly around her shoulders, the full breasts barely contained by a powder-blue T-shirt with "Bourbon Street" scrawled in sparkling pale green letters across the chest, the narrow waist nipped in by a wide leather belt. He made no effort to hide his admiration; he even craned his neck for a better view of her skintight front button Levi's. "I'm going to find that black tent you were wearing this morning and burn it."

She found herself doing something she hadn't done in years, something she had thought that at fifty-three she was no longer capable of doing at all. She blushed.

He grinned. His was an angel's grin, but only if the angel's name was Lucifer. "Buy me a beer?"

Three

Sec. 25.05.0301. Form of solemnization. In the solemnization of marriage no particular form is required except that the parties shall assent or declare in the presence of each other and the person solemnizing the marriage and in the presence of at least two competent witnesses that they take each other to be husband and wife. A competent witness for this purpose is a person of sound mind capable of understanding the seriousness of the ceremony. At the time of the ceremony, the person solemnizing the marriage shall complete the certification on the original marriage certificate. The person solemnizing the marriage and the two attending witnesses shall sign the original marriage certificate and the necessary copies.

—Alaska Statutes, Alaska Marriage Code

The couple had elected to take the traditional vows, Bill noticed as she looked at the ceremony clipped to the back of the marriage license. Short and sweet, no invocations to the goddess, no praising of Allah, no chanting for Buddha. Good. "Send them in," she told Hattie, who a year into Bill's term of office had proved to be her most reliable bailiff, and who needed the extra money to supplement her Social Security pension anyway. So Hattie dozed off while the jury deliberated behind the door at her back, so what? She could be passing them newspapers with stories about the case being heard on the front page, something that had happened during a recent trial in Fairbanks. Everything was relative.

Bill waited as Hattie left the courtroom. It was the end of the day, a long, cold dark day the January following Eli Horrell's death. The luck of the draw hadn't tossed many wedding ceremonies her way; she was glad to go home on a note of optimism. She believed in marriage as long as she wasn't the one saying "I do."

And Moses returned from Anchorage this afternoon. She smiled as she thought back to the day in this very court when they had first met, when for a terrifying moment she had thought she was going to have to find out if a simple magistrate had the authority to issue a directed verdict or even declare a mistrial, all because of this half Anglo, half Yupik hearer of voices.

He'd moved into her small home on the bluff of the Nushugak River a month after that day. The only times they had been apart since was when he went to fish camp in August and this last trip to Anchorage to see the dentist at the military hospital on Elmendorf Air Force Base. He'd been gone four days. It wasn't his fault that it felt like four months.

The door opened and she looked up.

She didn't recognize them at first, as Mrs. Horrell wasn't crying and Captain Quinn wasn't looking ill or angry.

"Your Honor?" Hattie said, and Bill realized that it was the second time Hattie had said it.

"I'm sorry, what?"

Hattie looked at her, puzzled. "These are the folks who

want to get married." Ever helpful at pointing out the obvious, she nodded at the license on the table.

Bill looked down and read the license for the first time. Enrique Quinn and Cynthia Horrell. She had not known Cynthia Horrell's first name before this. She didn't recognize the names or the faces of the two witnesses, although the best man gave off a strong aroma of beer and the maid of honor was flushed and giggly. It seemed the wedding party had begun without benefit of ceremony.

"Your Honor?"

She looked up again. "I'm sorry?"

"All you all right?"

Bill pulled herself together. "Of course. I'm fine—I'm just—I'm fine." She wondered if she should say she was pleased to see them again, and decided against it. She forced her mouth into what she hoped was an acceptable smile. "You have asked for the traditional vows, I see. Would you like me to lead you in them?"

"No, Your Honor, we've got them memorized," Cynthia Horrell said, blushing.

"Then please begin."

They faced each other. "I, Enrique, take you, Cynthia, to be my lawfully wedded wife, to have and to hold from this day forward, for better, for worse, for richer, for poorer, in sickness and in health, to love and to cherish; and I promise to be faithful to you so long as we both shall live." He didn't stumble once or miss a single word.

Bill nodded at the bride. She peeped up from beneath her eyelashes with a flirtatious look better suited to a fifteen-year-old and said in a voice that was almost indecent in its triumph, "I, Cynthia, take you, Enrique, to be my lawfully wedded husband, to have and to hold from this day forward, for better, for worse, for richer, for poorer, in sickness and in health, to love and to cherish; and I promise to be faithful to you so long as we both shall live." She, too, was letter perfect.

They exchanged rings and turned to Bill with expectant faces. In a voice she did not recognize as her own she said, "By the authority vested in me by the State of Alaska, I pronounce you husband and wife."

Four

> **Sec. 11.41.110. Murder in the second degree.** (a) A person
> commits the crime of murder in the second degree if . . . (2)
> the person knowingly engages in conduct that results in the
> death of another person under circumstances manifesting an
> extreme indifference to the value of human life . . .
>
> —Alaska Statutes, Code of Criminal Law

"Was it one or both of them?"

"Who took out the life insurance policy?"

"She did."

"Who was it through?"

Bill sighed and rolled over to snuggle her head into
Moses's shoulder. "The same people who insure the *Jeri A.*"

"Quinn's boat."

"Yes."

"How much was the payout?"

"A million five."

He whistled through his teeth. "Definitely for richer. You
can split a million five five ways without anybody feeling
shortchanged." He thought. "Given that Alaskan fishers are
virtually uninsurable because of their high percentage of violent death, the premiums must have been astronomical."

"Not as high as the payout. And they only had to pay a
year's worth."

"Yeah. How did Reynoldson find out?"

"Somebody owed him a favor who called somebody else.
Moses?"

"What?"

"I'm sorry."

He was silent. She waited, listening to the slow, strong
beat of his heart. "No," he said. "You were right. It was fact
of death you were looking for, not cause or manner. In law,
you were absolutely right to ignore anything I said. And you
didn't know me, then." She could hear the smile in his voice.
"Can't say that's the case now, can you, girl?"

She sighed again. "Doesn't make me feel any better." Another silence. "How did he do it?"

Moses snorted. "Dying on a crabber is easy, Bill, it's stay-

ing alive that's hard. He probably watched, waited for just
the right moment. The story they all told was probably
mostly true, they were icing up, Horrell was using the bat, the
rest of the crew was pulling and baiting pots. All Quinn had
to do was wait until just the right moment to jerk the bow
around crossways of the swell. The hull would thump down
and the boat would roll and Horrell would lose his balance
and go over. It happens often enough when it really is an accident. It would be easy to make it happen. Make it murder."

She flinched. "I suppose that is what it is. Murder."

"You can't prove it."

"That's what Reynoldson said. What about the rest of the
crew?"

"They might suspect something, you mean? Well, so they
might, especially now that the boss has married the beneficiary. Suspecting is different than knowing, though, and like
I said, even split five ways, there's enough to go around with
a million five."

"You think they were in on it?"

He shrugged. "The *Jeri A.* is one of the high boats in the
Bering. Pulls a lot of pots, catches a lot of crab, makes a
lot of money, pays a high crew share. They're not going to
risk losing that by accusing their captain of premeditated
murder."

She thought of Mrs. Horrell's endless tears, which in
hindsight looked more like tears of guilt than tears of sorrow.
Quinn's queasiness now looked like fear of discovery and
punishment. She raged again at the thought that she had actually consoled him over the loss of a crewman. She felt furious and frustrated and impotent. She didn't like it. "What
do the voices say now, Moses?"

He pushed her over on her back and slipped between her
legs. "They're not talking, babe," he said, eyes gleaming
down at her as he settled himself into her embrace. "They
know enough to leave me alone at times like these."

"And when you've got a skinful of beer."

"And when I've got a skinful of beer," he agreed. "They
show that much mercy." He kissed her, and it was long and
slow and sweet. He raised his head to look at her. "Leave it
go," he said. He grinned, the grin that said one day he would

be either beatified or burned at the stake, or both, and kissed her again.

She let herself drift with the now familiar current of pleasure and when she was left, spent and gasping in extravagant satisfaction upon the shore, she remembered Cynthia Horrell, now Quinn, and her flirtatious up-from-under look at her new husband in the courtroom that afternoon.

I'll be here a long time, she thought. And so will they. I'll watch, and I'll wait. Someday.

Moses pulled her close. "Leave it go, girl."

"Okay," she said.

He knew her so well after half a year that he didn't bother calling her on the lie.

Besides, it didn't matter. The Quinns would get their due. The voices had told him so, and they never lied.

CALL IT DEAD TIME
A Frank Pavlicek Mystery Story

Andy Straka

Andy Straka's police-detective-turned private eye, Frank Pavlicek, made his debut in *A Witness Above*. Frank's next case will be published next year.

When the fax went off, the one down the hall I shared with the travel agent and the two Russians, I paid it little mind. Just another cruise promo, I figured. Maybe one of those ciphers bearing specs for Slavic disk drives. The first Thursday in a Charlottesville August was sweltering, as usual, hot enough to spawn insta-sweat outside my window on Water Street where two men from the phone company worked a bucket truck against a pole and the five o'clock sun made shadows longer than the buildings. Across town the university slept its summer slumber. Traffic moved as if in a dream. Almost everybody with whom I did business—lawyers, insurers, spouses—was somewhere else on vacation. Call it dead time.

A persistent fly darted around my office, confident he owned the place. He could have it—in a matter of hours I would be joining the crowd at the beach, a rendezvous with a certain woman in mind. I had even taken an extra long lunch on a bench beneath one of the poplars lining the downtown mall in order to finish the final chapters of Mark Helprin's *Memoir from Antproof Case*. For the moment, however, I shuffled through a stack of bills on my desk to determine who, besides myself, was most in need of getting paid.

A door opened. The wall vibrated as someone clomped over to the fax. The part-time receptionist had already escaped for the day, but it didn't make any difference: secrets never lasted around here. There was a delay before I heard the sheet being ripped from the platen. Then the clomping continued to my half-open door.

"For you," a voice said.

It was a curious combination of foreign and acquired Dixie undertones, one of the Russians. He stood in the doorway, the curled paper lodged between his meaty fingers. An amiable fellow, big and broad-shouldered. His nose had long ago been surrendered to a roseacea that seemed to ripen further every time I saw him.

"Thank you," I said, and got up and took the sheet.

He didn't move.

"Business okay?" I tried not to sound too encouraging of discourse.

"Some days okay . . . Some days, not so okay."

I nodded. He still didn't move.

"Today?" I asked.

"Not so okay." He turned and left, his feet falling less loudly down the hall than before.

Returning to my chair, I uncurled the fax. The Russian was right. It was for me. "NEED YOUR HELP," the paper read. Signed, "TORONTO."

Help? Sure. But a fax? Smacked of something sinister— Toronto didn't even own a machine, as far as I knew.

Keen brain that I am, however, I picked up my regular line. Sinister evaporated. I waved through the window to the guys working the pole. The phone was as dead as the rest of the day.

The buck snorted at our approach, then disappeared, hooves crashing into the pitch-black woods. Probably curious, and who could blame him? For a moment he'd been caught in the glare from the lights Toronto had left burning, even out here in the middle of nowhere, around a perimeter of power cords and crime tape.

I should have expected that. My former NYPD partner is nothing if not anal-retentive. I had called him from home a couple hours before, worried about the start of my vacation. "Sorry about the timing," he said, and specified precisely where and when I should wait for him on the mountain fire road behind his battered Wrangler after a drive over the Blue Ridge, down I-81, and across I-64 into the Allegheny highlands. I had a bit of a hard time understanding all the reasons why, but loyalty is loyalty after all. I knew Jake Toronto would swim a river full of anacondas for me. So I had turned my truck westward from C'ville instead of heading for the Carolina coast. I had bided my time in the darkness while my engine plinked and popped to silence in the heat.

When he finally arrived, appearing like an apparition out of the darkness, his eyes held a cold glaze that told you something boiled just beneath the surface, something with which you would not wish to contend. It had taken twenty minutes of hard hiking to follow him back up the ridge. Another five to reach the spot where we'd surprised the deer.

"Let's get clear on this," I said. "You found the body and sent it down to a lab in Blacksburg for an autopsy?"

The three-sixteenth's Iroquois nodded. "Good people there at the vet school. You're here 'cause you're the big-picture guy," he said.

Right. My big picture now was that we'd reached a small clearing near the edge of what looked like a narrow plateau. The air was supercharged with a steamy veil. More tape and cords snaked everywhere through branches like some amateur's nightmare movie set. Small wire flags dotted the ground as if they were random daisies. Toward the back of the site, a portable generator, reeking of gasoline, managed to make just enough racket to drown out the tree frogs.

This was a crime scene. At least we were clear about that. Even though I had no idea where Commonwealth of Virginia statute stood when it came to private investigators looking into an incident such as this.

"Generator needs more gas," my friend said and moved to take care of it. He wasn't as lean as he'd been in his detective days, with a Roman nose, close-cropped black hair, and deep-set eyes. His narrow cheeks looked out of proportion to the rest of him.

"You said we're pushing fourteen hours since the kill?"

"Uh-huh . . . plus a front's moving down from Ohio. Be a monsoon out here before dawn."

"You got a line on where the shooter stood?"

"Not for sure yet . . . Was hoping you could walk it with me." He finished with the gas.

"What else do you know?"

"I think Jazzman was maybe perched in this maple when they shot him." Without looking, he pointed his thumb up and out toward the barely visible forest canopy overhead.

"How can you tell?"

"Found some droppings near the blood. He could've been in the air, but the perp would've been one hell of a shot."

A little explanation might be in order at this point.

Our victim in question was a peregrine falcon. A male called a tiercel, affectionately named Jazzman. He had belonged to Toronto who, from what I understood, had raised and trained him from a fledgling. Since we had left the force together years before under less than honorable circumstances, ex-detective Jake Toronto had gone through a metamorphosis of sorts. From street-wise Bronx native to naturalist and homesteader in Texas, then to Idaho, then Nebraska, then here. Along the way he had taken up falconry and spent a lot of time at it. He kept and trained two birds. Minus one now, that is.

How Toronto made a living these days was less clear. I knew he'd made some money in the market, knew he kept a stack of business cards that said he was a "security consultant," and that he disappeared occasionally, but not for long because of the birds. He lived like a monk in a house trailer on fifty acres of remote land.

Lightning flashed against distant clouds. "What kind of weapon you think was used?" I asked.

"The vets'll be able to tell us for sure, but from the wound, I'm pretty sure it was a .22."

"Might've been just a kid out shooting cans. Saw the big bird and he couldn't resist."

"Maybe." But his eyes said he didn't think so.

"We could be talking poachers . . . but they left the body. Doesn't fit." A mosquito dive-bombed my ear. I slapped at it.

Toronto nodded and sniffed the wind. He too had seen the lightning.

"Who owns this land? I remember coming up through here with you last year."

"A client," he said.

"Client, huh? Have you talked to this person about the bird yet?"

"Not yet, but I intend to. Wanted to get everything I could from up here first."

I looked around. "Soil and leaf samples gone to the lab too?"

"Uh-huh."

"Any tracks?"

"One. I made a moulage." He led me to the spot where a circle of flags marked the full print. It still glistened in the artificial light from the fixture he'd used. There was a can of hair spray next to a cardboard box that must have contained the cast.

"Looks like a hiking boot," I said.

He nodded again. "Frye. Not big. Size seven. Not deep either. Our trigger was not a heavyweight."

"That narrows it down to only a couple million or so . . . Was the bird's body intact? I mean, any pieces or parts missing?"

Toronto scratched at the stubble on his face. "If you're thinking rhino tusks here, forget it. There was a scandal back in the eighties. Operation Falcon. Feds caught a couple guys illegally exporting birds and tried to turn it into a sting op. But those were live birds . . ."

My watch said almost 11:00 P.M. A lot of sane people were fast asleep in their beds right now. A part of me wished I were there too. For his part, Toronto looked as though he were ready to go all night.

"So what now?" I said. I bent down to retie the laces of one of my own boots. Not Frye, army-navy generic. My prints would be larger than the shooter's, deeper too.

"I found another partial track about fifty feet into the woods." He pointed along the ridge.

"Okay," I said. "Why don't we see if we can reverse it? If the shooter used an automatic, maybe we'll get lucky and stumble upon some brass."

We made our way out of the light through the brush to the second footprint, also marked with a circle of flags. We began a sweep, walking in parallel about three paces apart. I swept my Coleman back and forth in front of me.

We had gone about twenty paces when Toronto said, "Got something."

I moved into his lane. He was examining another print, this, one a heel, and a broken sapling.

I caught a glint of something metallic in the corner of my eye. "Shine your light with mine over this way," I said and bent down to examine the object.

"It's a battery," Toronto said.

"You are a natural-born sleuth."

He ignored me, "Clean double A. Looks fresh."

"So our perp drops his Walkman in a hurry to split. Probably left us a nice fingerprint or two."

"Ummm," he said. He deftly picked up the object with a pair of tweezers, depositing it in a clean paper bag. "You know, usually a hawk gets killed and it's something stupid, like flying into a transformer. But losing Jazzy . . . this feels different somehow."

"Why's that?"

"J-man had a tail transmitter attached. I was tracking him, but I lost the signal. Bullet damaged the transmitter. Took me a while to find the body . . ."

"So?"

"These are the same kind of batteries I use in my receiver—even the same brand."

"You saying someone else was tracking your bird?"

"I'm saying batteries don't grow in the forest," he said.

We searched the rest of the area, but found nothing else.

"I think Joliker's away at a convention or some such. Atlanta's what his service said."

Affalachia County Sheriff Webster Daveys was speaking the next morning in the doorway to his office. A wiry, bespectacled man, whose pasty hair made him look more like an old preacher than a sheriff, he was talking about Latham Joliker, the local game warden. We were in the county office building in Leonardston, population nineteen hundred and twelve. My ex-wife and daughter lived around here too, but I wouldn't be seeing them this trip.

"Can't we get in touch with him?" Toronto asked.

"Looks to me there's nothin' either Mr. Joliker or my people could do that you and your buddy here ain't already thought of," the sheriff said. "The bird was an endangered species, you say?"

"Not exactly. Peregrines used to be endangered. They just came off the list."

"Too bad. Fish and wildlife people are hot after anyone messin' with an endangered animal . . . How long you been flyin' the thing?"

"Four years."

"How about you, Pavlicek?" The sheriff arched his eyebrows in my direction. "What's your involvement in all this? You ain't even showed me a license. Pee-I business must be a little slow."

Maybe my yellow flip-flops and *Elvis Lives with Me* T-shirt threw him off. "I'm supposed to be on vacation," I said.

He grunted. "You fellas really ex-homicide?"

"Yes," I said. "But . . ." I glanced at Toronto. Decked out himself in a flak jacket, Tony Lama boots, and mirror sunglasses that could have come straight out of a G. Gordon Liddy catalog, he shrugged.

"But what?" the sheriff asked.

"Let's just say I doubt the New York City Police Department would welcome us back with open arms."

He grunted again and looked at nothing.

"What about the missing receiver?" Toronto asked.

"You mean that electronic gizmo thing you showed me?"

"Right. I have another one just like it and it's missing." We had spent an hour that morning rummaging through his barn, which he never locked, looking for the second receiver.

"Just 'cause you found some battery out there in the woods don't mean somebody was out to kill your hawk." The sheriff worked his jaw as if he needed to spit. "But I suppose it could be. Had a couple old boys got into a dispute with the high school principal a while back. Kilt the family's dog, and no one's seen 'em since. Likely skipped the state . . . Someone upset with you, Mr. Toronto? Enough to pull a stunt like that?"

Toronto's voice dropped, betraying nothing. "Can't say for sure."

"Well, you'd best be givin' that some thought." He glanced

at his watch. "We'll check the battery for prints. I know I owe you, Toronto, but I can't do much more'n that right now. Got a meeting I'm supposed to be at and I'm already late."

In the truck on the way out of town, I said: "The sheriff owes you?"

Toronto shrugged. "He had a deputy thought he was the next Chuck Norris. I helped straighten the guy out."

"You've got somebody in mind for killing the peregrine, don't you?"

He nodded.

"Well, as your gratis hired investigator who's wasting a hundred bucks a day on a beach house right now, I'd certainly appreciate your sharing that information with me." It wasn't just the money. At the shore I planned to catch up with a woman I'd recently met named Marcia D'Angelo, an author and teacher who just so happened to be spending a month not too far up the Kitty Hawk beach from my own temporary digs.

"Take the next left." He pointed ahead to a narrow ribbon of paved road that I knew cut around the opposite side of the mountains from his own place. "We're going to talk to that client I was telling you about."

"He the one who's upset with you?"

"Not that I know of, but one of his ex-employees might still be. Mr. Clayton hired me to get rid of the joker about three months ago."

"Mr. Clayton . . . We're not talking the doctor here, are we?" Dr. Ricardo Clayton was a famous former physician on TV whose books on self-healing and nutrition had sold in the gazillions. I had heard he'd moved to the area a couple years before.

"One in the same."

"What did he do, the employee I mean?"

"Not he, she. The woman worked for him as a chef. Hot tempered, and not too bad to look at either. Clayton was afraid she might do something to his food."

"Why not just fire her then?" I asked.

"Tell you the truth, I think he was afraid of her."

"So he hired you to take the heat."

"My specialty."

We rode on in silence for a minute or two.

Then I said, "This what you do now, strong-arm people for a living?"

I felt his eyes on me. "Part of it," he said. "Pays the bills."

"Doesn't exactly fit, you know, the back-to-nature image."

"Uh-huh."

We were winding down a grade above a fast-flowing stream. The sky was bluer today, with cotton-ball clouds, and the air was less humid. The reprieve was only temporary, however. The weather people had predicted a return, by late afternoon, of the typical summer buildup of heat and moisture. Great day to be at the beach.

I steered into another curve. "So what are we hoping to learn from Dr. Clayton?"

"The chef didn't exactly leave me a forwarding address. I'll bet Clayton's sent her severance."

"How long ago was she fired?"

"Couple of months."

"She would have to be pretty peeved to take out your bird after all that time."

"Unless she's been planning it for a while . . . never should've let Jazzy get so far away from me, not this time of year anyway when we're not even hunting. We were only doing some lure training. Never thought he'd rake out on me like that."

"Good thing you had that locator thingamajig on him."

"Yeah, but if I'm right, the telemetry's what the shooter used to zero in on him too."

We both thought about that for a while.

"Jesting hidden behind gravity," I offered.

"Huh?"

"Nothing. Something I read once . . . Guy was talking about irony."

"Sure. Take the next right. Follow the fence line until you come to the dead end, then turn right again."

"This isn't the main entrance, is it?"

"No. That's about a half mile farther on. But it's where we go in. Don't worry. The security people know me."

We drove through a grove of birches along the fence line he described. When I made the turn I could see a guardhouse made of concrete and fieldstone. I pulled up to the gate and rolled down the window. A man dressed in black wearing a headset came out. His face bore a wary look.

That changed when he saw my passenger. "Oh, it's you, Mr. T."

"Hey, Mike," Toronto said. "Dr. Clayton home this morning?"

"Sure is. He and the Missus went out riding earlier, but they never go for long. Ought to be back up to the house by now."

"You mind announcing us then?"

"All right. Who's your friend?"

"Name's Pavlicek. Private investigator from Charlottesville."

The guard nodded, then wrote something on his clipboard.

"Have a nice day," he said. He turned a key in a console that opened the gate.

We drove through and found ourselves winding into forest again. The trees here were giant oak with pachysandra as ground cover.

"The main house is straight ahead," Toronto said. "We'll be coming into the employee parking lot behind the kitchen. The stables are around the other side. So are the tennis court, swimming pool, and sauna . . . You'll get to see the helipad though."

"No complete country manor should be without one," I said.

We broke over a rise and the house appeared. It was made of fieldstone like the guardhouse, with a slate roof and shutters painted a dark green. A stone terrace ran the length of the back of the structure, looking out on a lawn and a pond with a fountain.

A short man clad in tall boots approached as we pulled into the lot. His skin was tan. Black hair was beginning to gray around his temples. His mouth curved into a smile. He also had a royal air about him, one that only celebrity could bestow. I recognized him immediately as Ricardo Clayton.

Toronto and I exited the cab.

"Jake Toronto," Clayton said. "Come down from your lair?"

"We all have to sometime, I guess."

"How true." He clapped his hands as if delighted with his former employee, and they shook hands. Clayton then regarded me. "And who might your associate be? A private investigator, I understand."

"Dr. Clayton, this is Frank Pavlicek from Charlottesville."

"A pleasure to meet you, Mr. Pavlicek."

I shook hands with the doctor too. His grip was firm and confident, a practiced grip. He clasped my arm lightly with his opposite hand the way a politician might.

"Frank was my partner when I worked in New York," Toronto said.

"Ahhhh, I see . . . well what can I do for you gentlemen?"

"I came over to ask you a favor."

"A favor? Of course."

A woman emerged from the back of the house. She looked younger than Clayton, with unblemished skin and blond hair that swept down her back. As she came closer, however, small, telltale signs that the plastic surgeon's scalpel could not erase—tiny wrinkles around her eyes—revealed that she was probably about the same age as the doctor.

"Mr. Pavlicek," Dr. Clayton said. "I'd like you to meet Sylvia, my wife. Jake, I believe you two already know one another."

The woman came forward. Like her husband, she was clad in riding boots and skintight pants, except that they more favorably displayed her willowy figure. A green windbreaker with an orange and black patch on one sleeve was draped around her shoulders. She slipped to the doctor's side and he put his arm around her. Her eyes seemed to dissect me as I shook her hand.

"So you were saying?" Dr. Clayton looked at Toronto.

"Right. If you remember, I keep and raise falcons, birds of prey, and the like."

"Yes, of course. Beautiful animals. I gave you permission to hunt on our land. How has it been flying them on our mountain?"

"Great. Until yesterday morning, that is. Someone shot my peregrine falcon."

"Shot your bird on our land?" The doctor let go of his wife and folded his arms.

"I'm afraid so."

"What a shame," Mrs. Clayton said. "It must be a terrible loss for you." Her stare was fixed on Toronto. She had had so much surgery it was hard to read her face.

"The worst part is, I couldn't find any trace of him."

Now I looked at Toronto. This was one of the oldest detective tricks in the book. Give a suspect false information, something he would have to act on in some way. Was Clayton a suspect?

"No sign of the culprit either, I suppose," the doctor said.

"No. But I heard the shot just before I lost the telemetry signal. Frank and I will be going back up to the area tomorrow morning. If we can find the dead bird, we can come up with evidence that will point us to the shooter."

"Is there anything we can do to help?" Dr. Clayton asked.

The physician seemed sincere. In spite of his money and celebrity and all, I already sort of liked the man. I supposed the millions who bought his books and watched him on TV liked him for the same reason: we all bought image. I wasn't sure what Jake was up to yet, but I would find out soon enough.

"Your old chef, Maria Andros," Toronto said. He had told me about her earlier. "She hasn't come around here again, has she?"

"No. You don't mean . . . you don't think Maria was involved in this, do you?"

"I'm not exactly at the top of her dance card," Toronto said.

"I know, but—"

"Did you pay her severance?"

"Of course."

"And she's still in the area?"

"As far as I know. She's moved, but not that far away. I think she works at the Homestead in Hot Springs."

"You have her new address then."

"Yes I do. I have it in my study. Would you like me to get it for you?"

"Please."

"It'll only be a minute," he said. "Sylvia, maybe you could see if these gentlemen would like something to drink?"

"That's okay, Doc," Jake said. "We're fine."

"All right then." He disappeared into the house.

The mistress of the house regarded us with calm eyes. "I feel terrible about this," she said. "I can't imagine Maria doing such a thing."

"I hope she didn't," Jake said. "But she was pretty angry with me when she left your employ."

"Yes," Mrs. Clayton said. "But not that angry." She and Jake looked at one another for a few moments.

I shoved my hands in my pockets and leaned on the truck. "Did you know Maria Andros well, Mrs. Clayton?" I asked.

She tore her gaze from Jake. "Maria? Oh, not that well. She only worked here for a few months."

"How did you happen to hire her?"

"Ricardo sees to all the employees. I believe she was referred by an agency."

"I understand she is quite attractive."

"Well, I . . . I suppose she is. That is if you—"

The doctor was back. He handed Toronto a business card with the information written on the back. "You know, Jake," he said, "it occurs to me that if Ms. Andros was involved in any of this, she might be a threat to me or my family again. Do you think we need to reactivate our arrangement?"

"Not yet, sir," Jake said. "Why don't you let us talk with her first."

"All right. You've still got my cell phone number?"

Jake said he did. We said our good-byes and climbed back into our truck. The doctor slipped his arm around his wife again as they watched us drive away.

I waited until we had cleared the guardhouse before speaking. I found a nice shady area down the road a ways, pulled over, and hit the brakes.

"So what are we doing, playing Agatha Christie here?"

Toronto smiled. "You might say that."

"I didn't come all the way over here to waste my time."

"You're right. No reason to be jerking your chain."

"You're feeding a setup to Clayton and his wife. You think one of them wasted your bird?"

"Not exactly." He picked at his fingernails.

"Then what gives?"

He shifted in the seat. "You remember I told you this Maria had gotten into some difficulty with the Doctor and the Missus?"

"Right."

"Well, the specific difficulty had a lot more to do with the Doc than with his wife."

"Okay."

"He and the chef were having a fling."

So much for image. "Then why hire you?" I asked.

"Because he wanted to break it off and the chef didn't."

"Why didn't you tell me this before?"

"Because I've developed a sudden case of doubt regarding Dr. Celebrity. Wanted to see what you thought without prejudice."

"What I think is the guy could charm tax money out of a libertarian . . . So he brings you in to find a reason to fire the chef."

"Uh-huh. Plus maybe give the young lady a reason to forget about him."

"Part of your job was to woo her as well?"

He drummed his fingers on the dash.

"But I thought you said this Maria character hated you."

He shrugged. "Love. Hate. Two sides of the same coin."

"You sleep with this girl?"

He nodded.

"So you used her."

"If you want to call it that. Look, the man hired me to do a job."

"Some job," I said.

We were both silent for a minute. I had the a/c on and the windows up, so looking out from our shade on the bright Virginia landscape was almost like staring into one of those glassed-in exhibits at the zoo.

"Now that you've broken her heart," I said, "you think Clayton may have had second thoughts and gone back to whipping up some gourmet with the chef again?"

"Exactly."

"Likes the danger."

"Probably."

"And you're afraid he might tip off his lover if we tell him what we've already found."

"Uh-huh," he said.

"Guess there's only one way to find out," I said.

"Go see the girl."

"Right. But one more thing . . . might complicate matters."

"Yeah?"

"You notice that jacket draped around Mrs. Clayton?"

"Sure."

"How about that patch on the shoulder?"

"I saw it," he said. "Didn't know what it was though. You?"

I nodded. "That windbreaker belongs to a competitive marksman," I said.

Finding Maria Andros took a rolling forty-minute drive along the Jackson River into Bath County and the village of Hot Springs. Hot Springs is a resort town tucked into the mountains, famous for its mineral baths, around which stands the Homestead Resort, a brick and glass cathedral to fine old Virginia living, built around the turn of the century. There is a majestic ballroom and private bowling lanes for guests, a golf course and riding stables, and in the winter an outdoor ice skating rink and ski slope. There is even a falconry barn, Toronto informed me, where, for a fee, licensed falconers will take guests on educational "hawk walks."

At the chef's address we found a tidy frame house, with flower boxes in the windows, on the edge of the town near the stables. A blue Honda Accord was parked in the driveway. We stepped across the porch and rang the bell.

After maybe thirty seconds the door opened and there stood a striking young woman with dark, punk-cut hair. Her lips were full and glossy, her skin almost brown. Violet eyes matched a sleeveless shell over cutoff shorts that made the most of her long legs.

"I don't want to see you," she said to Toronto.

"This is important," he said. "I wouldn't bother you otherwise."

She stared at us, then stepped aside to let us in.

"Who's this?" she asked, meaning me.

"This is Frank Pavlicek. He's a private investigator and an old friend."

"A real private eye? Perfect." She rolled her eyes. "What, d'you two come to Gestapo me out of my new job too?"

"No," I said. "Mind if we sit down?"

"Why not?" She gestured toward a small living room. I took a rocking chair in the corner. Toronto sat on the large overstuffed sofa across from her. She crossed her legs; her toes were painted several different colors. "Forgive me for not offering high tea."

"I expect you get enough of that on the job," I said.

She said nothing.

"You have a beautiful place here."

"I like it," she said.

"Mind if we ask you a few questions?"

"I'm listening." She kept glancing over at Toronto.

"Did you know that Jake keeps falcons?"

"Those birds he hunts with. Sure."

"Where were you yesterday morning about nine o'clock?"

"Yesterday? Here, asleep in bed. I worked late the night before."

"Were you alone?"

She peeked at Toronto again, then turned and stared at me, expressionless. "Yes, I was alone."

"I lost Jazzy," Toronto said. "Think someone shot him."

Her eyes grew wide.

"Know anything about it?" I asked.

"Me?" She laughed. "You're kidding, right?"

"You were pretty upset with me last time I saw you," Toronto said. His monotone reminded me of how he used to question suspects in the Bronx, Had he felt something for this woman? It was impossible to tell.

She folded her arms. "Not enough to kill your stupid bird."

"I didn't say he was dead, Maria," Toronto said

"What?"

"I just said I thought someone shot Jazzy. Can't find any trace of him, in fact."

"Well, I . . . Hey listen, I'm not into any of your dumb games."

"Mr. Pavlicek and I will be going over that mountain first thing tomorrow morning," Jake said. "We'll find Jazzy's remains and you'd be amazed what kind of evidence killers leave behind."

"Go ahead. Knock yourselves out . . . Doesn't have anything to do with me."

"What about Dr. Clayton?"

Her eyes grew a little narrower. "What about him?"

"It happened on his land. We went by to visit him earlier, which is how I found out where you were."

"So."

"Talk to him lately?"

"No."

"You and he dancing a tango again?"

She snickered. "You've got balls, Toronto. After what you did . . ." She turned her head for a moment, brushing away a tear. "Why should I tell you anything about my life?"

Toronto seemed embarrassed. When she turned back to us, her eyes brimmed with tears. They were beautiful eyes. There was no getting around that.

"You wouldn't object to being fingerprinted though, would you, if the sheriff up in Leonardston asked?" I said.

"Why should I? Look, Jake, I didn't do anything to your friggin' bird, okay?" She stood, signaling an end to our interview. "I've answered your questions. Please leave now."

"All right," Toronto said.

We stood and moved toward the door. Maria followed. We were almost through it when she said, "Jake?"

He turned. "Yes?"

"I'm sorry about the peregrine."

"Sure."

I noticed a coat rack and a caddie for shoes beside the door. No falcon feathers. No Frye boots. No smoking guns.

* * *

The female goshawk was not even a year old, Toronto explained, and still in her immature plumage. He had named her Jersey.

She looked plenty mature to me, perched on the glove he had given me, her almost orange eyes fixed on mine. She had a rounded back and a bold white eyebrow, and was still mostly brown up top, although Toronto said this would eventually turn a bluish-gray. She wasn't heavy at first, but when she gripped the glove with her talons you knew it. Earlier, Toronto had taken me through a little album of photos he'd taken of Jazzman too. In life the peregrine falcon was magnificent: huge, dark eyes, steel-blue head, back, and wingtops, black and white stripes underneath.

"Won't be long," he said. "I'll have you out hawking yourself. It's a responsibility, you know. Federal license and everything."

I laughed. "Sure. Me in C'ville with a big bird. What am I supposed to do? Take the thing with me to work?"

"Hey. There's folks in big cities keep hawks."

I laughed again because the idea seemed go outrageous I could see myself doing it. "What time we leaving for the mountain?" I asked.

He took Jersey from me on his own glove and carried her back to her perch. "A little after eight. I want to be in position before dark."

"You really think someone'll show?"

He shrugged. "What else do we have? Daveys said Clayton's prints from the business card didn't match the ones on the battery."

"That would've been too easy," I said.

We had hijacked the sheriff again for a few minutes outside his office and explained our plan. In a word, he thought we were nuts. The fingerprint from the battery hadn't matched any in the FBI's criminal database up in Clarksburg—no surprise there. The only reason the lawman even entertained the idea of heading up a mountain in the dark with the two of us was his debt to Jake. But after tonight, he said, he considered it paid in full.

"You sure the chef and the doc and his wife are the only ones who could've stolen your other tracker?" I said.

"Not too many people know much about my business. The Claytons do because we're neighbors and I've worked for them."

"But they had no motive to kill Jazzy."

"Right."

"And Maria Andros knows you and has a motive, except—"

"Except, hotheaded as she is, she's no killer."

"You said it. I didn't."

"You think we're going in circles?" Toronto asked.

I gave it some thought. "There's something here I can't quite put my finger on, and that bothers me," I said. "Maybe we'll find out tonight. But maybe not."

"You wanna just head to the beach?"

"I'm hearing breakers in my daydreams. Anybody else, I'd already be gone. I'm afraid some hunter from Minnesota popped your poor falcon and hasn't given it a second thought since."

It was cooler later up on the ridge. The night was closing in fast, the bloodthirsty mosquitoes in full temper.

"You two got to be certifiable," the sheriff said as he helped us clean up the remnants of Jake's crime-scene investigation. His face was still beet-red and coated with sweat from the climb. We weren't expecting much, but we were well armed. Jake and I with our revolvers, the sheriff with his own plus a pump action shotgun. We concealed ourselves and settled in to wait.

A quarter moon rose slowly above the mist and after a while stood high over the clearing. By midnight I was almost ready to call it a night. The sheriff looked antsy—he'd already gone to relieve himself in the bushes more than once. Toronto, on the other hand, barely moved, and might've been asleep, except that his eyes were wide open and constantly scanning the dark.

I was just about to say something when headlights appeared for a moment down the mountain.

"Someone's on the fire road," Toronto said calmly.

"Shee-it," the sheriff said.

More lights became visible in the same spot, then vanished.

"Whoever it is has company," I said.

We waited.

Twenty minutes later, I spotted a pair of flashlights making their way up the ridge and pointed.

"I see them," Toronto whispered.

"Nobody comes up here in the dark like this unless they're up to no good. We'll wait until they reach the clearing, then take 'em into custody," the sheriff said.

"Don't you want to see what they're up to first?" I said under my breath.

He stared at me for a moment, then nodded his okay.

The sound of twigs snapping and boots pushing through leaves reached our ears. These people weren't worried about making a racket. A woman's laugh floated through the air, but it didn't sound genuine. It carried a hint of fear.

A few moments later the lights popped into view on the far side of the clearing. Two ghostly figures stepped into the pale moonlight. It was hard to tell for sure, but it appeared one held a rifle to the back of the other.

"Now, darling," a woman's voice said, "we're going to take a good look around and find that dead falcon before the Indian or his private eye lackey find it first. I only hope some bear hasn't made off with it. I know you'll cooperate, dearest. You've always been good before."

"I'm getting pretty sick of this shit, Sylvia." The new voice belonged to Maria Andros. "You said you had to meet me up here tonight. Just the two of us. What's with the gun?"

"It's just a little gun, pumpkin, just for safety," Mrs. Clayton said. "It's a fun game though, isn't it?"

"Not for me."

With my head and eyes I motioned to Toronto to move around to one side of the pair while I went to the other. The sheriff would take the middle. I crept around to position myself behind a pair of boulders. The two women were moving toward Toronto's position opposite me now, sweeping their lights back and forth.

"You're jealous of him, aren't you?" Maria said. "That's why you killed his bird."

"Jealous of who, Jake Toronto? What for? He was just being paid to get rid of you for Ricardo. Ricardo was the one who was jealous of you and me."

There were only the night sounds for several seconds.

Then: "I'm not sure I want to do this anymore, Sylvia . . ."

The figure with the rifle moved closer to Maria Andros, angling the barrel toward her head. "You're tired, darling. We'll talk this over." She began to stroke the younger woman's hair. "That falcon was such a beautiful wild thing, you know. Did I tell you it was spiraling upward when I finally found it? The wings weren't even moving. I think they ride the currents or something. It was really quite a shot."

"Ringing up." Toronto's voice punched through the darkness.

The women looked around, startled.

"When they rise like that," he said, "they ring."

The beam of Sheriff Daveys's flashlight illuminated the couple. "Hold it right there, ladies. Police!"

As if he'd been their shadow, Toronto seemed to materialize next to Mrs. Clayton and took hold of her arm and the rifle. Maria tried to turn from the light, but ran straight into me. She scratched my face, tried to bite my shoulder, and kicked at my ankles.

"It's okay," I said, holding her as best I could at arm's length. "It's okay now . . . It's over."

In a minute it was, with the sheriff reading the handcuffed Sylvia Clayton her rights while the younger woman heaved sobs into my shoulder.

"Don't you dare say anything, Maria," the doctor's wife said. "I want to talk to my lawyer."

I looked at Toronto. "PI lackey?"

He shrugged, shook his head, and smiled.

The next day, Toronto and I buried Jazzman in the high clearing. It was a private ceremony, just the two of us beneath an ashen sky. Little did I know then what hawks would be in my own future, what skies, what death and life. When finished, we descended to the fire road again. I climbed into my pickup and Toronto saw me off. I like to think that in some way, beyond our understanding, his peregrine still soars there on that mountain.

It was five hours of thinking to the beach.

NOT A MONSTER OF A CHANCE
A Scumble River Mystery Story

Denise Swanson

Denise Swanson introduced readers to the fictional small
town of Scumble River in *Murder of a Small-Town Honey*.
Her heroine, Skye Denison, returned in *Murder of a
Sweet Old Lady*.

S cumble River, Illinois, located seventy-five miles south of
Chicago in distance, and at least seventy-five years behind
the city in attitude, had one claim to fame—a beautiful recreation club. It featured a sandy beach, shady picnic spots, and
sparkling lakes for fishing and water-skiing. This particular
summer the Scumble River Recreation Club seemed to have
an additional feature—a monster.

"A monster," Skye Denison snorted as she climbed the
metal steps of the lifeguard's chair and scanned the water. All
clear. Seven-thirty was too early for any swimmers. "No
doubt someone got drunk and watched a TV program featuring Loch Ness last night."

Officer Quirk took off his hat and wiped his forehead with
his handkerchief. The dark blue uniform had not been designed to be worn standing in the sun on hot sand. "Could be,
but the chief told me to inform the lifeguards, and ask them to
keep an eye out. And since you're a shrink and all, I thought
it might be best if you talked to the others. So they don't panic
or nothing."

Ordinarily, Skye was employed by the Scumble River
School District as their school psychologist. But since she had
the summer off, and needed the money, she was moonlighting
as a lifeguard at the recreational club.

"What exactly happened?" She tucked a stray chestnut curl
into her French braid.

"Some high school kids were messing around out here last

night after the beach closed. On a dare, one of the boys swam past the rope, meaning to swim all the way across the lake. He was about three-quarters there when he spots something. The kid claims it was a spiked fin as long as a Chevy truck."

"What did he do?" Skye's mind flashed to a picture of a teenager being chased by the Munsters' pet dragon, Spot, and she fought the giggle that was trying to bubble to the surface.

"He raced back to shore. He says the thing followed him to the rope, and then turned back into the deeper part of the lake."

"Probably a big old catfish or something. Liquor tends to magnify things in our perceptions. What are you doing about it?"

The officer settled his hat back onto his crew cut. "Just notifying the lifeguards for now."

"You don't think we should close the beach and the lakes?" Skye narrowed her emerald-green eyes. The chief of police, Wally Boyd, was furious with her because of her actions while investigating her grandmother's recent death. She wondered if this was a hoax he had dreamed up, hoping she'd make a big fuss about the incident and look stupid.

"Hell, no!" A voice bellowed from behind them. "We let people think we actually believe this crap, and all those Chicago folks will be dropping out of the club faster than you can say, I want my money back."

Charlie Patukas stood under the pavilion several feet back from the water. Skye grinned. She should have known her godfather, whom she called Uncle Charlie, would be involved. Not only did he own the only motel in town, he was on every board and committee that had any influence—including the one for the recreational club.

"Hi, Uncle Charlie, can you come down here? I'm not supposed to leave the beach." Skye shaded her eyes so she could see the man standing in the shadows.

He hitched up his gray twill pants and adjusted his red suspenders. "No, I gotta get going. Just wanted to ask you to sniff around a little, and see what the truth is about this monster business." Charlie turned to go, speaking over his shoulder. "It's probably just a bunch of teenagers wanting to stir things up."

Quirk shook his head. "Charlie's probably right. But make sure no one swims past the ropes today."

"No problem. It's against the rules anyway."

The morning was uneventful. Skye spoke to the other two lifeguards, telling them to keep an eye out, but not to spread the rumor around.

During her lunch break, Skye sat with her best friend Trixie Frayne. She too was moonlighting: a swimming instructor during the summer, but the high school librarian during the rest of the year. "So, did you hear about the monster?"

Trixie stopped with her sandwich suspended midway between the table and her mouth. "What monster?"

"The monster of Scumble River. It was spotted last night at the beach."

"Right. What's the punch line?" Trixie took a bite.

Skye explained what Quirk had told her.

Trixie ran her fingers through her short cap of brown hair. "You don't think there's anything to it, do you?"

"Just too much liquor, too many hormones, and too active an imagination."

"You know, that's probably what they said in Loch Ness—at first." Trixie's brown eyes twinkled. "Maybe we should look into it."

Skye shook her head. "Nope. I think that's exactly what Wally wants us to do."

As they threw away their trash and headed back to work, Trixie said, "I have a funny feeling about this."

The beach filled up as the afternoon progressed. Skye and the other lifeguards were busy keeping everyone where they were supposed to be—the little kids seemed to want to go off the high dive, and the teens wanted to congregate in the kiddy area.

At three, Skye blew her whistle for a break. Everyone reluctantly headed toward shore. Everyone, except a woman doing laps out by the rope. She wore a bright pink swim cap covered with rubber flowers. Skye knew from experience that it was almost impossible to hear anything with that type of head gear, but she blew her whistle again anyway. The swimmer showed no sign of having heard the signal.

The other lifeguards had already left the beach for their

break. Skye swore under her breath and waded into the water. When she reached the ropes, she popped her head up and scanned the area. Great. The woman must have realized the break had been called, and swam back to shore.

Skye took one more glance around, and was about to go back, when she spotted the swimmer. The woman was halfway between the ropes and the opposite shore. What to do? Shouting was useless, and Skye herself was not supposed to swim past the ropes, unless it was an emergency. She decided that the best course of action was to go back to the beach and radio for someone to pick up the lone swimmer on the other side.

As Skye started back, she heard a scream.

"Help! Oh, my, God! Help me!"

Skye splashed to a stop and frantically scanned the lake for the swimmer. She spotted the woman flailing in the water. Skye immediately headed in her direction, keeping her eye on the woman as she swam.

Just before she reached her, the woman went down as if she had been sucked into a giant straw.

Skye redoubled her efforts and arrived at the spot less than a minute later. She took a deep breath and dived. She stayed under as long as she could, but there was no sign of the woman. She dived again and again.

Apparently no one noticed the activity, because no one came to help. Finally, too tired to make it back to the beach area, Skye dragged herself to the opposite shore and collapsed on the sand. She had seen a woman drown and been unable to save her. She felt hollow inside.

When she got her breath, Skye started the long walk back around the lake. She briefly considered swimming across, a much shorter distance, but after what she had seen, decided against it. As she trudged down the dirt road, she noticed a pickup inching its way in her direction.

The truck stopped as it neared her; the window was rolled down. It was her cousin Ginger's husband, Flip. "Hey. What you doing?"

Skye explained as she was climbing into the cab. "Hurry and turn around. We've got to report this, and get a search team out there."

He reached into his jeans pocket and, handed her a leather case.

"What are you doing with a cell phone?"

He shook his head, a sneer on his broad, flat face. "Everyone's got a cell phone. Even small-minded, stupid people like the folks in Scumble River."

She sighed. Although she had been back in her hometown for eleven months, the twelve years she had been gone were a big gulf to cross. Especially since right before she left, she told off the whole town in her valedictorian speech. Most of the community were still reminding her of her youthful transgression.

Skye dialed the police. Unfortunately, her mother, May, was the afternoon police dispatcher. After lengthy reassurance that Skye was fine, May finally took the report. Skye's next call was even worse. It was to Charlie.

Flip had continued around the lake and pulled into the beach area, only a couple of minutes before the police car, boat truck, and ambulance arrived. Charlie's white Cadillac was close behind.

Despite Charlie's objections, the police closed the beach. Although they dragged the lake for the rest of the day, there was no sign of the woman, the creature, or anything unusual. No one knew who the swimmer had been. Skye had only gotten a brief look from a long distance. Her description of the woman was vague, at best. The gaudy bathing cap had drawn most of her attention.

While the fire and rescue squads worked, Charlie muttered about lost membership, and worried what would happen if the Chicago people pulled their money out of the club. Skye sat next to him under the pavilion and tried to soothe him by pointing out the five-page waiting list they had of people wanting to join.

The police chief called a neighboring county for divers, but they wouldn't be available for several days. It had been a rough week for swimmers in Illinois.

Charley left at five to make some calls, but Skye remained at the club until the police packed it in for the night. Wally had told her more than once that she should go home, but she felt somehow responsible and refused his escalating commands to leave.

After her last adventure, she was again without a car. One of her many relatives had lent her a scooter to get back and forth from the beach. She hadn't planned to be driving it in the dark, and was still trying to figure out how to turn on the light after the police left.

As her fingers flipped the different switches, she heard a sound from the beach. Great. It was probably kids who had heard what happened and were now daring each other to brave the water and face the monster.

She knew the police didn't have enough manpower to post a twenty-four-hour guard—two officers were sick and one was away on vacation. That only left Chief Boyd, Officer Quirk, and a part-timer to cover three shifts, seven days a week.

Reluctantly, Skye got off the scooter and walked toward the sound. At the top of the stairs leading down to the sand, she stopped and drew back. Sitting on the beach was a man dressed in work clothes.

The only illumination was the moon and whatever spilled over from the lights in the parking lot, but he appeared to be upset. Skye hesitated. Good sense told her that she should hop on her scooter and go home. However, her training as a psychologist made it difficult for her to leave someone in such obvious distress.

She opted for a compromise and cleared her throat, while remaining at the top of the steps. It took a couple of tries, but the man's head finally turned in her direction.

"Ah, hi, is there anything I can help you with?" Skye thought she sounded more like a grocery clerk than a psychologist.

"No, go away." The man turned back to staring at the water.

"Sure. Ah, but I need to tell you one thing," she persisted.

"Don't you hear so good? Get the f—" His back was rigid and his hands were fisted by his sides.

Skye swallowed her fear and interrupted him. "This afternoon someone drowned here under mysterious circumstances, so don't go in the water."

She turned to leave, but the man swiftly rose and called, "Wait a minute."

As he drew nearer, Skye got a better look at him. He was a medium-sized man with muscles that were just starting to soften with age. His face was acne-scarred, and the scraggly mustache obscured the expression on his lips.

He spoke from the bottom of the stairs. "What do you know about what happened this afternoon?"

Skye backed up a little. "Why do you ask?"

"Look, I'm sorry I yelled at you." The man ran a hand through his thinning brown hair. "Please tell me what you know."

"Only if you stay down there."

"Deal. By the way, my name's Mark Petty."

"I'm Skye Denison, head lifeguard." Skye told him about the so-called monster, the woman, and what had happened. She concluded with, "So, the police are trying to figure out who the woman was, and what happened to her."

The man sank down on the bottom stair. "I think it was my wife, Karleen."

"Oh, my. I'm so sorry." Skye sat on the top step. "Why do you think it was her?"

"I usually work the seven-to-three shift at the quarry, but today I was forced to do a double. I tried calling to tell Karleen, but I kept getting the machine. When I got home, a couple of hours ago, I found a note she had left me saying she was going swimming at the club and that she'd be back by three. But she wasn't there."

Skye scooted about halfway down the stairs. "You must have been worried."

"Yep, it isn't like her not to be where she says she'll be."

"I see. So what did you do?"

"I called everyone I could think of. No one had seen her all day. Finally, I went to the police station, but the only one there was the dispatcher. She wouldn't tell me nothing. Just said I should come out here to talk to the chief. But I must've missed him."

"He left about twenty minutes ago." Skye stood up. "You should probably go back to the station."

"Yeah." He got to his feet and started up the stairs.

When he reached the top, Skye could finally get a good look at his face. He appeared numb. "Could I ask you a question?"

He shrugged. "Sure. I guess."

"Do you have any idea why Karleen would swim past the ropes?"

"Well, she wasn't one to follow the rules." They continued to the parking lot. "She said only old people did that."

The man got into an ancient gray pickup and pulled away. Skye finally found the light switch on the scooter and followed him. She watched him pull into the police station, then turned and drove home.

Her cat, Bingo, met her at the door, demanding his supper.

By the time she fed him, showered, and put on her nightgown, it was nearly ten. Too late to call anyone and ask if they knew anything about Mark and Karleen Petty.

She fell asleep, stroking Bingo's shiny black fur and listening to his deep-throated purr.

When her alarm rang at six-thirty the next morning, Skye wondered if she should report for work or not. Would the beach remain closed? She was reaching for the phone to call Charlie and ask, when it rang.

She snatched up the receiver.

"Skye, I need you down to the club right now." Charlie's voice boomed in her ear.

"Oh, are we opening the beach back up?"

"No, but the newspeople got a hold of the story and are swarming by the gate. I'm going to give a statement at eight, and the board decided you should be there to answer questions, since you're the only witness."

"Are you sure that's a good idea? Maybe we should stick with no comment."

"Hell, I don't know. I'll pick you up in twenty minutes. Just look pretty, and don't mention the monster."

Skye looked down at the green tank suit she had slipped on. About six months before her return to Scumble River, she had quit dieting. By eating healthy and getting a reasonable amount of exercise, Skye let her weight go to its natural set point, which meant she had gained weight. Most of the time she was comfortable with her more generous curves, but no way was she being photographed for newspaper and TV in a swimsuit.

She changed to a pair of khaki slacks and a black polo top. It was too late to subdue her curls with hot rollers, so she scrunched them with some mousse, and pushed the whole mass back with a faux tortoiseshell headband. Slipping her feet into sandals, she thought, *I'm ready for my close-up, Mr. DeMille.*

Charlie was waiting when she walked out of her cottage. An unlit cigar was clamped between his teeth, and he barely responded when she kissed him on the cheek. His concession to the upcoming media event was a freshly pressed white shirt with his usual uniform of gray twill pants and red suspenders.

They drove in silence to the club's gates. Several vans and cars blocked the entrance. People carrying cameras and microphones were shoulder-to-shoulder with those dressed in suits. The sun beat down relentlessly. The temperature was already eighty-seven, with matching humidity.

Charlie parked the Caddy on the side of the road. The car was immediately swamped by reporters shouting questions.

Wally materialized in the midst of the swarm and escorted Charlie and Skye through the melee and to the front of the gates. The chief handed Charlie a bullhorn. The crowd quieted down.

Charlie summed up the events, and handed the bullhorn to Skye.

Before she could speak, the reporters starting yelling questions. "Is it true you saw a dinosaur eat the victim right in front of your eyes?"

Skye opened her mouth, but another newsperson shouted, "Is it true you wrestled the monster trying to save the victim, and have marks on your body where you were bitten?" She was sorely tempted to drop her pants and flash them her unblemished bottom.

Several more questions in that same vein were screamed at Skye in an endless stream, with no break allowing her to answer. Finally, she broke in and said, "I saw a swimmer in distress and swam toward her. Unfortunately, she sank before I reached her, and due to the muddy conditions of the lake, I was unable to spot her below the water's surface. I saw nothing else while I was attempting the rescue."

Wally took the bullhorn back and said, "We've sent for divers. When they arrive here in a few days, I'm sure all our questions will be answered. This drowning is unfortunate, but not unusual. We generally have one or two drownings a season."

Skye narrowed her eyes. She knew for a fact that those drownings were usually near the dam on the river, or off of a drunken party pontoon boat, not at the swimming beach. What was Wally hiding?

A reporter asked, "Does that mean you're going to open up the beach today?"

Charlie, the chief, and Skye exchanged glances. Charlie answered. "We'll be keeping the beach closed for a few days."

The same reporter countered, "So you are worried that there is a danger?"

Skye noticed Charlie's heightened color and stepped in. "Of course not. We're closing the beach out of respect for the victim. We'll reopen in a couple of days."

Wally took Skye by the elbow and Charlie by the shoulder, and escorted them through the mob, back to the Caddy. He leaned through the open window and said to Charlie, "Drop her off and meet me at the station."

Skye raised an eyebrow when they pulled into the police department. "I thought you were instructed to get rid of me before coming here."

Charlie smirked. "Just because Wally's got a bug up his butt about you double-crossing him last month when your grandma died doesn't mean I got to do what he says."

"Okay. Well, when he kicks me out of his office, I'll wait for you in the car." Skye was afraid that Charlie seriously underestimated Wally's outrage.

They waved to Thea, the daytime dispatcher, as she buzzed them in, and climbed the stairs to the chief's office. Wally was already there, but on the phone. He absentmindedly waved at them to sit down.

Skye sat at the edge of her, chair, waiting to be dismissed. While Wally talked, she studied him. The chief was a handsome man seven years her senior. In the midst of a divorce, his usually even temper had shortened, and lines were forming around his mouth and on his forehead.

He caught her staring at him and ran his fingers through his crisp black hair, ruffling the waves and bringing her attention to the gray at his temples. He slammed down the phone and said, "What did you bring her for?"

Skye loved being referred to in the third person, but bit back the snappy comeback as penance for her previous sins.

Charlie snapped, "Because Skye's solved the last two murders in this town. What's your batting average?"

She didn't think it was possible, but Wally's brown eyes turned colder. They usually reminded her of liquid chocolate, now they resembled a Fudgsicle.

The men stared at each other. Neither one was willing to blink. Skye took a breath and said, "Wally, I'm sorry about last time. Can't we just forget it and move on?"

"No." The chief turned his attention to her. "You just don't get it, do you? I can't forgive what you did. Ever."

Charlie crossed his arms. "You're mad at Skye. I get it. But whatever your opinion of her personally, she's good at working out puzzles. So let's put our heads together and figure out this monster thing, before Scumble River loses the few tourists we have."

Skye added softly, "Or before the monster eats someone else."

Wally stared at her. "You don't believe that monster crap, do you?"

"No." She felt her face redden. "But that woman didn't just drown. Something pulled her down."

"Do lakes have whirlpools?" Wally mused out loud.

Charlie and Skye shrugged.

"Did you talk to Mark Petty last night?" Skye asked Wally.

He nodded, then added in a disgusted tone, "After you had already questioned him."

She ignored his gibe. "Do you think the woman I saw was his wife, Karleen?"

Wally shrugged, a stubborn look on his face.

Charlie leaned forward and said quietly, "Look, son, you know it's in everyone's best interest if you cooperate."

After a long pause, Wally blew out a breath and said, "Yeah. Okay. She owned a bathing cap like the one you described."

"I suppose it's pretty distinctive." Skye drummed her fingers on the desk. "Or do they sell them around here?"

"No," Wally answered. "Petty said he bought it for her in Florida last year."

"Something's been bothering me about what Mr. Petty said last night." Skye chewed on her lip. "He said Karleen didn't like rules, but that she always let him know where she'd be. If I didn't follow rules, would I willingly account for every minute of my time?"

Wally answered her, "You might, if you thought your husband would beat the crap out of you if you did otherwise."

"What?" Her eyes snapped wide open.

"We've had a couple of domestic calls from the Petty residence. Never an arrest, but Quirk's had to break up fights a few times."

"Mmmm. Maybe it was suicide." Skye bit her lip. "No, I saw the way she went down. It looked like a vacuum cleaner was sweeping her up. She couldn't do that herself?"

The three sat in silence until Charlie spoke. "Karleen Petty. Why does that name seem so familiar? Do you have a picture of her?"

Wally flipped open a file folder and handed Charlie a photo. The older man studied it silently before handing it back. "She's been at the motor court, but Karleen wasn't the name she registered under."

"So why did Karleen Petty sound familiar to you?" Wally questioned.

"Last week she checked in again, but this time she dropped her purse while she was paying. When I helped her pick things up, I noticed a credit card in the name of Karleen Petty." Charlie smiled without humor. "She saw me noticing and hemmed and hawed something about it being her friend's card, but I been in the motel business a long time. She wasn't the first woman playing house with someone that wasn't her husband."

"So, Mrs. Petty was having an affair." Skye arched a brow. "Always the same man?"

"Yeah, nice-looking kid. I'd say at least ten years younger than her, maybe more."

Wally read from his notes, "Her husband said she was twenty-nine. The people in Scumble River would have been up in arms with a woman that old messing around with a teenager."

"Very interesting. An abusive husband and a really young boyfriend. What does this all tell us?" Skye studied the ceiling.

After a long silence both men answered at once, "Nothing."

Wally added, "It has nothing to do with this drowning. You were there. No one was around. No one pushed her under, or forced her into the deep water. It was an accident."

"But something doesn't add up," Skye insisted.

"Accidents rarely do." Wally got up, and ushered Skye and Charlie to the door.

Charlie drove Skye home. It was past noon, and after eating a hasty lunch, she changed back into her swimsuit. She put a pair of denim shorts over the tank, and laced on an old pair of tennis shoes before hopping on her scooter. It was time to visit the scene of the crime—or accident.

Skye didn't attempt to get into the recreation club by the front entrance, not wanting to run into either reporters or police. Instead, she made her way to the back, where a metal gate blocked a dirt path. A barbed wire fence surrounded the property.

The gate was fastened with a shiny new padlock, and Skye could see no way to open it without the combination. She sized up the fence. Maybe she should just go around front. She was both a member and an employee, and had every right to be on the property. But visions of reporters made the barbed wire seem less threatening.

Skye carefully stuck one leg through the opening she had created by stretching the wire with her hands. Then she bent over and heaved her torso through. All that was left on the other side was her right leg. She cautiously lifted it and pulled.

She made it, and with only a few scratches. Skye tried to remember the layout of the club from the map she had seen

on the wall in Charlie's office. There were three main lakes.
One for swimming, one for fishing, and one for water-skiing.
But if she remembered correctly, all the lakes were connected
by narrow inlets that weren't accessible by the roads.

Where was the closest one to the swimming area? To the
left. She walked slowly, trying to catch a glimpse of water
through the trees. After a half mile, she spotted a glimmer of
blue and left the road.

Tire tracks. Skye caught her breath. Someone had been
off-road here. Could she be right? She followed the trail of
flattened grass through the trees until she came to a tiny
beach. The sand showed signs of recent occupation.

Skye picked her way carefully around the marks. Caught
in the underbrush was—a bright pink rubber flower. And the
final clue was two sets of footprints leading away from the
water. She smiled and headed back to town.

Wally sat silently and listened to what she had to say. Without comment, he picked up the phone and issued instructions.
Finally, he looked at her and said, "We'll take care of things
now. You can go on home."

Skye nodded, knowing that was as much as she would get
from him. It saddened her, because he was usually such a different person. She shrugged as she walked down the stairs.
Maybe after the divorce was final, and he'd had time to stop
being mad at her, he'd go back to his old self. The one she'd
had a crush on since she was fifteen.

Later that evening, Skye's doorbell rang. Her mother and
Charlie were on the steps.

May was talking as she entered the house. "You were right.
Karleen didn't drown. It was all a plot, so she could get away
from her husband, and be with her teenage lover."

"What? How did Wally prove it?" Skye was floored at
how fast things had been resolved.

Charlie sank into Skye's new recliner. "Wally had me look
at the high school yearbook. I found Karleen's honey, in last
year's. His name was Joel Hadley. Police showed his picture
around at diving shops in Joliet and Kankakee. Sure enough,
he had rented equipment two days ago and returned it yesterday."

"Then I was right. Karleen and her lover planned the

whole thing. She made a spectacle of herself with that stupid bathing cap so someone would see her. Then when they had a witness's attention, her lover, using scuba-diving equipment, pulled her under. They shared the oxygen mask and swam underwater to that little beach I found. Joel had parked his vehicle there, and they went out the back gate."

"How did they get out the back gate? I thought you said it was locked," May demanded.

Skye sat next to her mother on the sofa. "That was another tip-off. Why would the padlock be shiny and new? It should be old and rusted. Unless Joel cut the original one off and replaced it with a new one, so no one would notice. Joel must have been the monster that chased the teenagers. It was all a setup for Karleen to drown, and have her body not found."

"That's my goddaughter. Smart as a whip." Charlie beamed.

"Did they find out how he did it?" Skye asked.

"You stopped looking after you found the spot that Joel and Karleen used. Wally checked the rest of the places where someone could get into the water and swim to the beach area. He found the so-called monster." May sniffed. "It was just an old canoe painted green. Joel had nailed triangle-shaped pieces of metal to the bottom, so when it was turned upside-down, they stuck out of the water like a fin."

Skye shook her head. "Did they catch Karleen and Joel?"

"Yeah, they were using a credit card of his that she had signed for." May shook her head. "Those two are a few nuts short of a Payday candy bar."

"Too bad they couldn't charge them with anything." Charlie leaned back and clasped his hands over his stomach.

"Why?" Skye asked.

"Think about it," Charlie commanded. "What laws did they really break?"

Skye narrowed her eyes. "Well . . . there's got to be something. They caused us all a lot of headaches."

Charlie sighed. "Too bad you can't arrest people for being a pain in the as . . . er, butt." He put his feet up and closed his eyes. "Of course, if you could, half the town would be in jail."

CORPSE ON A HOLY DAY

A Sister Fidelma Mystery Story

Peter Tremayne

Peter Tremayne is the author of six mysteries of ancient Ireland, including *A Shroud for the Archbishop*, *The Spider's Web*, and *Valley of the Shadow*. All of them feature Sister Fidelma.

The day was hot in spite of the breeze blowing off the sea from the south. The procession of pilgrims had left the sandy beach and were beginning to climb the steep green hill toward the distant oratory. They had stood in reverent silence before the ancient granite stone of St. Declan, a stone that, it was said, had floated to that spot across the sea bearing on it vestments and a tiny silver bell. It had floated ashore on this isolated part of the Irish coast and was found by a warrior prince named Declan who knew it was God's way of ordaining him to preach the new Faith. So he began his mission among his own people, the Décis of the kingdom of Mumhan.

There the stone had stood since the moment it had landed bearing its miraculous gifts. The young brother who was conducting the pilgrims around the sites sacred to Declan had informed his charges that if they were able to crawl under the stone then they would be cured of rheumatism but only if they were already free from sin. None of the band of pilgrims had ventured to seek proof of the stone's miraculous property.

Now they followed him slowly up the steep hill above the beach, straggling in a long line, passing the gray abbey walls, and moving toward the small chapel perched on the hill top. This was the final site of the pilgrimage. It was the chapel that St. Declan had built two centuries before and in which his relics now reposed.

Sister Fidelma wondered, and not for the first time, why she had bothered to join this pilgrimage on this stifling summer's day. Her thought was immediately followed by a twinge of guilt, as it had been before. She felt an inner voice reprimanding her and pointing out that it was her duty as a religieuse to revere the life and works of those great men and women who had brought the Faith to the shores of Ireland.

Her peripatetic journey, fulfilling her main duty as a *dálaigh,* or advocate, of the law courts of the five kingdoms of Ireland, had brought her to the subkingdom of the Décis on the south coast of Mumhan. When she had realized that she was staying a few days at the great abbey of Ardmore, which St. Declan had founded, coinciding with the Holy Day set aside for his veneration, she had attached herself to the band of pilgrims being conducted around the principal sites associated with his life and work. Fidelma was always keen to acquire knowledge. She pressed her lips in a cynical grimace as she realized that she had answered her own question as to why she was part of this pilgrim group.

Brother Ross, the young man in charge, had been prattling on about the life of Declan as he preceded them up the hill. He was an intense young man, scarcely more than the "age of choice," hardly out of his teenage. Even the steep climb did not seem to make him breathless or cause him to pause in his enthusiastic monologue.

"He was one of the four great saints who preached in the five kingdoms of Ireland before the coming of the Blessed Patrick. They were Ailbe, the patron saint of our kingdom of Mumhan, Ciarán also of Mumhan, Ibar of Laigin, and Declan of the Décis of Mumhan. So we may boast that this kingdom of Mumhan was the first to convert to the new Faith . . ."

Brother Ross was naively passionate as he began to enumerate the miracles of the saint, of how he raised people who died of the Yellow Plague. The pilgrims listened in a respectful and awed silence. Fidelma had assessed the dozen or so men and women who were trudging up the hill and came to the conclusion that she appeared to have nothing in common with them except a membership of the religious.

They were now approaching the brow of the bare hill where

the small oratory of gray granite stood. It was perched on the top of the round hump, surrounded by a low stone wall. From a distance, it had appeared a small speck of a building. As they drew nearer Fidelma could make out its rectangular dry-stone walls. It was scarcely thirteen feet by nine feet in dimensions and its steep sloping roof was in proportion.

"This is where the earthly remains of the blessed saint repose," announced Brother Ross, halting and allowing the pilgrims to gather around him by the gate of the low wall. "After the end of his arduous mission through the countryside he returned to his beloved settlement of Ardmore. He knew he was not long for this world and so he gathered the people and the clergy around him and counseled them to follow in his footsteps in charity. Then, having received the divine sacrament from Bishop Mac Liag, he departed this life in a most holy and happy fashion, escorted by a chorus of angels to the kingdom of heaven. Vigils were held and solemn masses celebrated, signs and wonders were seen, a conclave of saints gathered from all corners of the land."

Brother Ross spread one hand toward the oratory, his voice warming to his theme.

"His earthly remains were escorted to this, his first little church, to be laid to rest within it. I will lead you inside. Only three may accompany me at a time for, as you can see, it is very small. In the oratory lies a recess in the ground in which is a stone built coffin. This is the resting place designated by Declan himself at the bidding of an angel. His relics are there and great signs and miracles are worked through the invention of the Blessed Declan."

He stood with bowed head for a moment while the pilgrims mumbled their respectful "Amens."

"Wait here for a moment until I enter the oratory and ensure we are not disturbing any worshiper. This day is holy to the saint and many people come to pray here."

They paused by the wall as Brother Ross instructed while he turned inside the enclosure and crossed to the lintel door and disappeared inside.

A moment or two later, the young man burst out of the oratory, his face flushed, his mouth working yet uttering no sound. Sister Fidelma and the others stood staring at him in total surprise. The sudden change from the quiet respect to such agitation was bewildering. For several moments, the young man could not utter a word and then they came out in a spluttering staccato.

"Uncorrupted! A miracle! A miracle!"

His eyes were wide and rolled as if he had trouble in focusing.

Fidelma stepped forward in front of him, "Calm yourself, brother!" she demanded, her voice rising in sharp command to quell his excitement. "What ails you?"

Brother Ross seemed finally to focus on her with his wide staring eyes.

"The body of the saint . . . it is uncorrupted!"

"What do you mean?" Fidelma demanded in irritation. "You are not making sense."

The young man swallowed and breathed deeply for a moment as if to gather his composure.

"The sarcophagus! The stone has been swung aside . . . the body of the blessed Declan lies there . . . the flesh is uncorrupted . . . truly . . . a miracle . . . a miracle! Go and spread the news . . ."

Fidelma did not waste time on trying to make further sense of the young man's incoherent claims.

She strode quickly by him, shaking aside his restraining hand, and went into the oratory, crouching a little to pass under the lintel. There was only one small window to give natural light and she paused, blinked, and waited a moment for her eyes to adjust. Two tall candles on an altar at the end of the small chapel were unlit but, surprisingly, a small stub of candle stood splattering on the tomb slab.

This stone slab had been pushed at an angle from the recess in the ground revealing the contents of the shallow grave. She strode forward and peered down. Brother Ross had been right in so far that a body lay there. But it was not the body of someone who had been interred two centuries before. She bent down to examine it. Two things she noticed: the blood was still glistening and wet, and when she touched the forehead, the flesh was still warm.

When she emerged, she found Brother Ross still lyrical

with excitement. The pilgrims were gathered excitedly around him.

"Brethren, this day you have witnessed one of the great miracles of Declan. The saint's body has not corrupted and decayed. Go down to the abbey and tell them and I will stay here and watch until you return with the abbot . . ."

He hesitated as the eyes of the pilgrims turned expectantly as one to where Fidelma exited from the oratory with a grim face.

"You saw it, didn't you, Sister?" demanded Brother Ross. "I told no lie. The body is uncorrupted. A miracle!"

"No one is to enter the chapel," Fidelma replied coldly.

Brother Ross drew his brows together in anger.

"I am in charge of the pilgrims. Who are you to give orders, Sister?"

"I am a *dálaigh*. My name is Fidelma of Cashel."

The young man blinked at her brusque tone. Then he recovered almost immediately.

"Lawyer or not, these pilgrims should be sent to tell the abbot. I will wait here . . . This is truly a miracle!"

Fidelma turned to him cynically.

"You who know so much about the Blessed Declan may provide the answers to these questions. Was Declan stabbed through the heart before being laid to rest?"

Brother Ross did not understand.

"Was the Blessed Declan, in reality, a young woman?" went on Fidelma, ruthlessly.

Brother Ross was outraged and said so.

Fidelma smiled thinly.

"Then I suggest you examine your uncorrupted body a little further. The body in the grave is that of a young woman who has recently been stabbed in the heart. It has been placed in the grave on top of old bones which presumably is the skeleton of Declan."

Brother Ross stared at her for a moment in horror and then hurried back into the oratory.

Fidelma instructed the pilgrims to wait outside and then hurried after the young man, pausing just inside the door.

Brother Ross kneeling by the tomb turned and glanced up toward her. His face, even in the semigloom, was white.

"It is Sister Aróc, a member of the community of Ard-more."

Fidelma nodded grimly.

"Then I think we should dispatch the pilgrims back to Ardmore and ask them to inform the abbot of what has been found here."

The band of pilgrims were spending the night in the hostel at Ardmore anyway.

"Shouldn't we go . . . ?"

Fidelma shook her head.

"I will stay and you may stay to assist me."

Brother Ross looked bewildered.

"Assist you?"

"As a *dálaigh,* I am taking charge of the investigation into how Sister Aróc met her death," she replied.

When the pilgrims had been dispatched down the hill toward the monastery, Fidelma returned into the chapel and knelt by the tomb. Sister Aróc was no more than twenty years old. She was not particularly attractive; in fact, rather plain-featured. A country girl with large-boned hands whose skin was rough and callused. They lay in a curious clawlike attitude at her sides, as if the fingers should be grasping something. Her hair was mouse-colored, an indiscernible gray-brown.

As Fidelma had previously noticed, there was one wound on the body. There was no need to ask what had caused it. A thin knife blade with its rough worked handle still protruded from it. Her habit was ripped just under the left breast where the knife had entered and doubtless immediately penetrated her heart. The blood had soaked her clothing. It was not dried and that indicated death had not occurred long before. In fact, she thought the time could probably be measured in minutes rather than hours.

A thought had occurred to Fidelma and she examined the floor of the chapel, tracing her way carefully back to the door and outside. She was looking for blood specks but something else caught her eye—droplets of wax near the sarcophagus. The fact alone was not surprising. She would imagine that many people over the years had entered with candles and bent to examine the stone that had covered the relics of the saint. What was surprising was the fact that the tallow grease lay in profusion over the edge of the sepulcher on which the flat covering stone would have swung shut.

Fidelma, frowning, seized the end of the flat stone and exerted her strength. It swung. It was not easy to push it but, nevertheless, it could be moved with a rasping sound back into place across the tomb. Thoughtfully, she returned it to the position in which she had found it.

She let her gaze wander back to the body to examine the knife again. It was a poor country person's knife; a general implement used for a variety of purposes.

She made no effort to extract it.

She turned her attention to the accoutrements worn by the girl. A rough, wooden crucifix hung around her neck on a leather thong. It was crudely carved but Fidelma had seen many like it among the poorer religious. Her eyes wandered down to the worn leather *marsupium* that hung at the girl's waist.

She opened it. There was a comb inside. Every Irish girl carried a comb. This one was made of bone of the same poor quality as her other ornaments. Long hair being admired in Ireland, it was essential that all men and women carried a *cíor* or comb. She also found, rather to her surprise, there were half a dozen coins in the *marsupium*. They were not of great value but valuable enough to suggest that robbery was no motive in this killing even if the thought had occurred to Fidelma. It had not.

The more Fidelma looked at the corpse, at the position of it, the more she realized that there was something bizarre about this killing; more peculiar than even the usual aberrant fact of violent death. She could not quite put her finger on it. It was true that the corpse's facial muscles seemed slightly distorted in death as if there was a smile on its features. But that was not what bothered her.

By the time she left the oratory, three senior religious were entering the low gate to the oratory grounds. Fidelma immediately recognized the pale, worried features of Rian, the Abbot of Ardmore. With him there was a tall woman, whose features were set and grim, and a moon-faced man, whose features looked permanently bewildered, who she also recognized as the steward of the abbey. What was his name? Brother Echen.

"Is it true, Fidelma?" greeted the abbot. He was a distant cousin and greeted her familiarly.

"True enough, Rian," she replied.

"I knew it would happen sooner or later," snapped the tall sister with him.

Fidelma turned inquiring eyes on her.

"This is Sister Corb," Abbot Rian explained nervously. "She is the mistress of the novices in our community. Sister Aróc was a novitiate under her charge."

"Perhaps you would be good enough to explain the meaning of that remark," invited Fidelma.

Sister Corb had a long, thin, angular face. Her features seemed permanently set in a look of disapproving derision.

"Little explanation needed. The girl was touched."

"Touched?"

"Crazy."

"Perhaps you might explain how that manifested itself and why it would lead to her death?"

The abbot interrupted anxiously.

"I think it might be better explained, Fidelma, by saying that the girl, Sister Aróc, isolated herself from most of us in the community. Her behavior was . . . eccentric."

The abbot had paused to try to find the correct word.

Fidelma suppressed a sigh.

"I am still not sure how this manifested itself. Are you saying that the girl was a half-wit? Was her behavior uncontrollable? Exactly what marked her out as so different that death was an inevitable outcome?"

"Sister Aróc was a fanatic about religious beliefs." It was the moon-faced steward of the abbey, Brother Echen, who spoke up for the first time. "She claimed that she heard voices. She said that they were"—he screwed up his eyes and genuflected—"she said they were voices of the saints."

Sister Corb sniffed in disapproval.

"She used it as an excuse not to obey the Rule of the community. She claimed she was in direct communication with the soul of the Blessed Declan. I would have had her flogged for blasphemy but Abbot Rian is a most humane man."

Fidelma could not help the censure that came into her voice.

"If, as you say, the girl was touched, not of the same mental faculty as others, what good would a flogging have done?" she asked dryly. "I still do not see how this behavior would have led to her death . . . her death *sooner or later* was the phrase I think you used, Sister Corb?"

Sister Corb looked disconcerted.

"What I meant to say was that Sister Aróc was otherworldly. Naive, if you like. She did not know how . . . how lecherous men can be."

The abbot seemed to have a coughing fit and Brother Echen seemed to have taken an intense interest in his feet.

Fidelma stared hard at the woman. Her eyebrow rose in automatic question.

"I mean . . . I mean that Aróc was not versed in the ways of the world. She let herself enjoy the company of men without realizing what men expect from a young girl."

The abbot had regained his composure.

"Sadly, Sister Aróc was not possessed of good sense but I think that Sister Corb might be overstating the attraction that Aróc could stir in the minds of any male members of our community."

Sister Corb's lips twisted cynically.

"The Father Abbot sees only the good in people. It does not matter the extent of the attractive qualities, a young girl is a young girl!"

Fidelma raised her hands in a gesture indicating hopelessness and let them fall.

"I am trying to understand what is implied here and how this is providing a clue to how and why Sister Aróc came by her death in such bizarre circumstances."

Sister Corb's eyes narrowed slightly and she stared across the chapel ground to where Brother Ross was leaning against the low dividing wall, still looking pale and shaken.

"Have you asked him?"

"Brother Ross? Why?"

Sister Corb's lips compressed.

"In fairness, I should not say another word."

"You have either said too much or too little," Fidelma replied dourly.

"Where was he when the killing took place?"

"That I can answer," Fidelma replied. "Brother Ross was conducting the band of pilgrims around the sites associated with the Blessed Declan. I was part of that band."

Sister Corb was not convinced.

"How can you be so sure?" she demanded.

"Brother Ross had been with us during the last two hours."

"So why could he not have killed the girl before he met you?" pressed Sister Corb, refusing to be budged from her suspicion.

"Because"—smiled Fidelma—"she was killed not long before we arrived at the chapel and found her. In fact, I would say she was killed only minutes before."

Sister Corb's mouth snapped shut. She seemed irritated at Fidelma's logic.

"Why would you accuse Brother Ross anyway?" asked Fidelma with interest.

"I have had my say," muttered the mistress of novices, her lips forming into a thin line of defiance.

"I will tell you when you have answered my questions to my satisfaction," replied Fidelma softly. The fact that there was no belligerence in her voice made it that much more imposing. Sister Corb was well aware of the powers of an advocate of the law courts.

"It is well known that Brother Ross desired the girl," she replied defensively.

"Desired?"

"Lusted for her."

Brother Echen snorted with derision.

"That is, with all respect, only Sister Corb's interpretation. Her jaundiced view of the intention of men in any situation leads her to make leaps of imagination."

Fidelma swung round to him.

"You do not share Sister Corb's view?"

"Ask Brother Ross himself?" the steward replied casually. "He liked the girl's company. They were often together and he did not ridicule her, as some did. But he had no lecherous intentions."

"How do you know this?"

"As steward of the community, it is my job to know things, especially to keep a watch for anything which might lead to a disturbance among the brethren."

"What, in this matter, might have led to a disturbance?"

Brother Echen glanced at Sister Corb meaningfully.

Fidelma turned and smiled at the abbot.

"Father Abbot, if you and Sister Corb will wait with Brother Ross . . . ?"

She waited until they had moved out of earshot before turning back to Brother Echen.

"Well?" she prompted.

"Sister Corb was creating trouble for Brother Ross. She was jealous."

"Jealous?"

Brother Echen shrugged eloquently.

"You know . . ."

"I don't know. Tell me."

"Corb was jealous of Ross because she wanted Aróc for herself. Sister Corb is . . . well, that is why she has a peculiar attitude to men and ascribes lust as their only motive."

"Did Aróc respond to Corb's advances, if that is what she made?"

"No. Aróc was otherworldly, as I have said. She did not care for any physical contact. She was one of the aesthetes sworn to a life of celibacy. She rejected Corb even as she would have rejected Ross had he thrust his attentions on her."

"What makes you sure that he did not?"

"He told me that he did not. He enjoyed her company and speaking to her of the saints and of the Faith. He respected her too much."

"How well did you know Sister Aróc?"

Brother Echen shrugged.

"Not well at all. She had been six months with the community. She was still technically under the instruction of the mistress of the novitiates—Sister Corb. Truth to say that I spoke only once to her and that was when her case had come up before the council."

"Her case?"

"Corb had been asked to report on her novitiates by the abbot when we sat in council to discuss the affairs of the community. That was when Corb talked of Sister Aróc's eccentric behavior. It was decided that I should question her about the voices she claimed to hear."

"And what did you decide?"

Brother Echen shrugged.

"She was not mad in any dangerous sense, if that is what you mean. However, her mind was not sound. She was 'otherworldly,' as have said. I have met one or two religious who claim to have spoken with Christ and his Holy Saints and known many who have claimed as much and more who have become saints themselves."

"Just one point more, where were you during the last hour?"

Brother Echen grinned broadly.

"With ten witnesses who will account for my presence, Sister. I was giving a class in calligraphy to our scribes for I am considered to have a good, firm hand."

"Ask Sister Corb to come to me," Fidelma dismissed him.

Sister Corb came but was still belligerent.

"Why haven't you spoken to Ross?" she demanded without preamble. "There is some way he must have killed her . . ."

"Sister Corb!" Fidelma's sharp tone quelled her. "We will speak of matters of which you are competent to give evidence about. Firstly, where were you during this last hour?"

Sister Corb blinked.

"I was in the abbey."

"And you can prove this fact?"

The mistress of the novitiates frowned for a moment.

"Most of the time I was instructing the novitiates this morning."

Fidelma picked up her hesitation.

"During this last hour?"

"Are you accusing me . . . ?"

"I am asking where you were and whether you can prove it."

"After instructing the novitiates I spent some time in the

abbey gardens. I do not know whether anyone saw me there or not. I was just returning when I heard the pilgrims coming to tell the abbot what had happened here and so I joined him and Brother Echen."

"Very well. How long did it take you to climb the hill to this chapel?"

Sister Corb looked surprised.

"How long . . . ?"

"Approximately."

"Ten minutes, I suppose, why . . . ?"

"That is most helpful," Fidelma replied, cutting the woman short. She left Sister Corb, ignoring the look of anger on her angular features, and walked across to Brother Ross.

"Death is not a pleasant thing to look on, is it, Brother?" she opened.

The young man raised his light blue eyes and stared at her for a moment.

"It was gloomy in the oratory. I did not see too well. I thought I saw . . ."

Fidelma smiled reassuringly.

"You made it plain what you thought you saw."

"I feel stupid."

"I understand that you knew Sister Aróc quite well?"

The youth flushed.

"Well enough. We . . . we were friends. I could say that . . . that I was her only friend in the abbey."

"Her behavior was described as a little eccentric. She heard voices. Didn't that bother you?"

"She was not mad," Brother Ross replied defensively. "If she believed it then I saw no cause to question her belief."

"But the others thought that she was insane."

"They did not know her well enough."

"What do you think she was doing up here in the oratory?"

"She often came to the oratory to be near to the Blessed Declan. It was his voice that she claimed that she heard."

"Did she tell you what this voice told her?"

Brother Ross gave the question consideration.

"Aróc believed that she was being chosen by the saint as his handmaiden."

"How did she interpret that?"

Brother Ross grimaced.

"I don't think that even she knew what she was talking about. She thought she was being told to obey the will of someone two centuries dead."

"And what was that will?"

"Celibacy and service," replied Brother Ross. "At least, that is what she said."

"You say that she liked to come to the oratory to be close to Saint Declan. Did you help her remove the lid of the sarcophagus and then grease it with tallow candle wax to allow her to swing it to and fro at will?"

Brother Ross raised a startled face to meet her cool gaze. Fidelma went on rapidly.

"Do not ask me how I know. That is obvious. I presume that you did help her for there was no one else to do so."

"It was not an act of sacrilege. She just wanted to look on the bones of the Blessed Declan and touch them so that she could be in direct contact with him."

"Did you know that Sister Aróc would be here this morning."

Brother Ross quickly shook his head.

"I had told her that the pilgrims would be coming to see the oratory this morning—it being the Holy Day."

"It sounds as though she was strong-willed. Maybe she did not care. After all, today would be a day of special significance for her. As the feast of Saint Declan, the day on which he departed life, it would be obvious that she would come here."

"Truly, I did not know."

"What I find curious is, knowing her so well as you did, even knowing her habit to open the tomb and gaze on the relics of the saint, why you came rushing out crying the saint's body was uncorrupted. Had you not known what the relics were like, had you not known what Aróc looked like, it might have been explicable . . ."

"I told you, it was dark in the oratory and I truly thought . . ."

"Truly?" Fidelma smiled cynically. "Not for one moment did you consider any other option than to rush forth and proclaim that Declan's dusty relics had been suddenly translated to incorrupt flesh?"

Brother Ross wore a stubborn look.

"I have told you all I know in this matter." He folded his arms defiantly.

Fidelma's lips thinned and she gazed an inordinately long time on him; examining, particularly, the front of his robe.

"Do you have any suspicion of who killed Sister Aróc?" she finally asked him.

"I know only that she died a violent death here when there was no need for such an end to her life," he replied belligerently.

Fidelma turned away toward the agitated figure of Rian, the Abbot of Ardmore.

"I am grieved, Fidelma. I am the head of my community, the shepherd of my flock. If there was violence brewing I should have felt it."

"You are only a man and not one of the prophets, Rian," Fidelma admonished. "There is no need for you to take any blame for this onto your shoulders."

"How can I help resolve this matter?"

"By answering a few questions. Did you know Sister Aróc?"

"I am abbot," he responded gravely.

"I meant, know her on a personal level and not merely as one of your flock."

The abbot shook his head.

"She was brought to me six months ago by Sister Corb, who wished to induct her into the school of the novices. She was of the age of choice. She struck me as a religious girl although not overly bright. Apart from my one interview with her, I have only seen her at a distance."

He paused and then glancing swiftly across the chapel ground toward Sister Corb he continued.

"Sister Corb came to me a few days ago to lodge an official complaint. It was only then that I heard of her curious behavior; what was it that Brother Echen described it as— 'otherworldly'? Echen was sent to speak with her but he reported that she was eccentric but not dangerous."

"Do you know whether Sister Corb might have other motives for complaining about Aróc?"

The abbot flushed slightly and then grimaced.

"I know what you mean. I had not thought that applied in this case. But Sister Corb does have several liaisons which I would not approve of. But, as abbot, sometimes it is diplomatic to feign a lack of knowledge."

"Several?" Fidelma's brows arched. "Could it be that some of her—her liaisons, as you call them, might have been jealous of Sister Corb?"

The abbot looked startled.

"Do you mean . . . ?"

"Questions again," snapped Fidelma. "Every question I ask, I seem to get answered by a question!" She repented at once as the Father Abbot seemed to wince at her outburst. "I apologize. It is just that it is so difficult to extract information."

"No, it is I who should apologize, Fidelma. There are several members of the community who would be angered by Corb's attention to Sister Aróc, if that is what you are asking. But I do not think that they would be worth considering in this case."

"Why not?"

"If my meager knowledge of law is anything to go by, as well as being a suspect by motive, you must also be suspect by opportunity."

"Your knowledge is correct," affirmed Fidelma.

"Well, you indicated to Brother Echen and to Sister Corb that this murder took place shortly before your group of pilgrims arrived at the hilltop. Look around you."

The Father Abbot spread his arms.

Fidelma knew what he meant without looking. The hill, as they wound their way up the only track, was just a round grassy hump without trees, without bushes, and only the small oratory on top. Anyone, leaving the oratory shortly before the arrival of the band of pilgrims, would have no place to hide.

She smiled quickly.

"No, Father Abbot, I suppose it was not a sound thought to imagine someone sneaking up from the abbey and killing

Sister Aróc and then sneaking away moments before a party of pilgrims arrived at the oratory."

"Then what are you saying? Who killed Sister Aróc?"

Sister Fidelma turned to the others and waved them to come forward.

"My investigation seems to have drawn to its close," she said, addressing the abbot.

He looked bewildered.

"Then I must ask you again, who killed Sister Aróc?"

Fidelma glanced toward Brother Ross.

Sister Corb was smiling in grim satisfaction.

"I knew it," she muttered. "I . . ."

Fidelma raised her hand for silence.

"I made no accusation, Sister Corb. And you should know the penalty for false accusation."

The mistress of the novitiates was suddenly silent, staring at her in bewilderment.

"But if Brother Ross is not the murderer . . . " began Brother Echen helplessly. "Who killed her?"

Fidelma glanced again to the young religieux.

"Brother Ross will tell you," she said quietly.

"But you said . . ." began the abbot.

Fidelma shook her head impatiently.

"I said nothing. I implied he did not murder Aróc but I did not say that he did not know who killed her."

Brother Ross was regarding her with frightened eyes.

"You would not believe the truth," he said quietly.

"I know the truth," Fidelma replied.

"How? How could you know . . ."

"It was not that hard to work out, given the time factor and the situation of the oratory where no one could hide."

"You'd better explain it to us, Sister Fidelma," the abbot said.

"Our group of pilgrims came to the oratory and, as I have pointed out, Aróc's death occurred, judging by the condition of the corpse, moments before," Fidelma explained. "Ross went into the oratory first. Moments later he came out. He might well have had time to stab Aróc and then return to us to pretend that he had discovered the body. But the evidence is against that. Such a stab wound would have caused blood to spurt on his robes.

"It was obvious that Aróc was killed while lying in the open tomb. She was not killed elsewhere and dragged to the open tomb. There were no blood splatters leading to the tomb which would have been made. If Brother Ross had killed her, then his robes would have been drenched in spurting blood from the wound. Instead, he has some spots of blood on his right hand and his sleeve. They were made when he bent to touch the corpse."

She pointed to his robes so that they could verify her statement.

The abbot was worried.

"You have presented us with a conundrum. Tell us the answer. The killer was hiding in or behind the oratory, is that it?"

Fidelma sighed shortly.

"I would have thought it obvious."

Brother Ross gave a little groan.

"I confess! I confess! I killed her. I did it."

Fidelma looked pityingly at him.

"No you did not."

Sister Corb was indignant.

"That will not do, Sister. The man has confessed. You cannot deny his confession."

Fidelma glanced at her.

"Brother Ross is even now trying to save his friend's soul. He believes that the Penitentials would prohibit Sister Aróc being accorded the last rites, a forgiveness of sins and burial in sanctified ground in a state of spiritual peace. It is time to tell the truth, Brother Ross."

"The truth?" pressed Brother Echen. "What is the truth?"

"She killed herself."

Brother Ross groaned piteously.

"When you have eliminated every other explanation as being impossible, that which remains must be the truth," Fidelma said dryly. "Am I right, Brother Ross?"

The young man's shoulders had slumped in resignation.

"She . . . she was not of this world. She heard voices. She thought she was being instructed by spirits, from the other-

world. By the Blessed Declan. She had visions. She made me
open the tomb so that she could touch the holy relics. I
greased the stone so that she could swing it open by herself
when she wanted. She often spoke of joining the holy saint.
I did not think she meant to kill herself."

"What happened?" demanded the abbot.

"I brought the pilgrims to the oratory and went inside before them in case there was a worshiper at prayer. I had no
wish to disturb anyone. I saw her body lying in the open
grave with both hands gripping the knife in her breast. I realized with horror what she had done. There was no time nor
place to hide the body from the pilgrims. If I had attempted
to swing the tomb shut those outside would have heard me.
I forced her hands from their grip on the knife and put them
at her sides. I tried to remove the knife but it was buried to
the hilt, that was when the spots of blood stained my sleeve
and hand. I think I panicked, believing the pilgrims would
come in any moment. The only thing I could think of was to
pretend the saint's body was uncorrupted and hope it would
distract the pilgrims to run down to the abbey to report the
news, giving me time to dispose of the body. I did not count
on . . ."

He glanced toward Fidelma and shrugged.

"The crime of suicide forbids her being laid in hallowed
ground," pointed out Sister Corb. "The suicide is classed as
a *fingalach,* a kin-slayer; a person no better than a murderer."

"That is why I tried to protect her so that her soul could
journey on to the otherworld in peace," sobbed the youth. "I
loved her that much."

"There is no need to worry," Fidelma assured him gently.
"Sister Aróc can be buried in consecrated ground."

Here the abbot began to protest. Fidelma cut him short.

"Sister Aróc, for legal purposes, was classed a *mer,* one of
unsound mind. The law states that the rights of the mentally
disturbed should take precedence over other rights. A lenient
view is taken of all offenses committed by them."

"But Brother Ross lied," pointed out Sister Corb, angry
and determined that someone should be punished.

Fidelma countered her anger softly.

"The law also looks kindly on those whose concern it is

to protect those unable to protect themselves. Brother Ross may now rest assured that Sister Aróc's soul can now depart in peace."

The abbot glanced around hesitantly before heaving a low sigh of acceptance.

"Amen!" he muttered softly. "Amen!"

LIGHTNING STRIKES TWICE

A Claire Reynier Mystery Story

Judith Van Gieson

Judith Van Gieson's new series, featuring Claire Reynier, began with *The Stolen Blue*. Claire has since reappeared in *Vanishing Point*.

It was raining the day Claire Reynier met her old friend Lynn Granger, a hard summer rain that bounced as it hit the sidewalk. They spent the morning in the Albuquerque Museum wandering through an exhibit devoted to Dale Chihuly, a glass artist from Seattle whose work Claire admired. Lynn had never heard of him before, but she agreed with Claire that he was magical. Chihuly's work was mounted in clusters on the walls. The room was pitch-black, but the glass was spotlighted. The shapes reminded Claire of jellyfish. The underwater effect was enhanced by the darkness of the room.

Claire and Lynn had been friends for forty-five years ever since they spent their childhood summers in nearby houses on Hawley Lake in northeastern Arizona. Claire was divorced now and lived in Albuquerque. Lynn was living with her third husband near Phoenix. They visited whenever they were in each other's cities and occasionally shared late-night phone calls. Although Lynn was Claire's oldest friend, they didn't talk about their childhoods. There was a secret they had never shared, a secret that had become the foundation of their friendship. Originally Claire thought of the secret as a dark cellar with a locked door, but as time passed it began to resemble a concrete slab, so impenetrable, so taken for granted that she had almost forgotten it was there.

"I'm hungry," Lynn said.

Claire, who could be compulsive about time, glanced at her watch. It was only eleven-thirty, not yet lunchtime in her opinion.

"Is there anyplace nearby to eat?" Lynn asked.

"There's the Church Street café," Claire said.

"Let's go," Lynn replied.

They left the gallery, walked down the lobby, looked out the door, and saw rain pummeling the sculptures in the sculpture garden. Even though it was June, the rainy season, it was unusual for it to rain so hard so early in the day. Usually the thunderheads built up in the late afternoon and the rains followed. It had been a long, dry spring full of dust and wildfires, and it refreshed Claire just to watch the rain. She could have stood in the glass doorway and watched it all afternoon, but Lynn became impatient.

"Let's *go*," she said.

"We'll get wet," Claire replied. No one ever thought to carry an umbrella in New Mexico.

"So we'll get wet. Let's go."

"All right," Claire said. "Follow me."

She pushed open the door, ran across the sculpture garden, through the gate, and turned the corner into a courtyard where the roots of a gnarled wisteria snaked across the bricks. She exited onto San Felipe Street, quickly glanced both ways, then raced across, hearing Lynn's shoes pounding the pavement behind her. The hollyhocks in front of the café—works of art in their own right—hung their heads under the force of the rain. There was a flash of lightning followed quickly by a clap of thunder, just as they leaped through the door of the café.

"That was close," Claire shivered.

Lynn didn't answer. The restaurant was full of empty tables draped with ghostly white tablecloths. The hostess told them to sit wherever they liked, and Lynn picked a table in the corner near a window.

"Can I get you something to drink?" the waitress asked.

"I'll have a glass of Chardonnay," Lynn said.

"Iced tea," said Claire.

Once they were seated she realized how wet she was. Her dress clung to her back, water from her hair dripped onto her shoulders. The restaurant was dim and quiet, but outside the window rain splattered and lightning flashed, reminding Claire of one summer she and Lynn spent at Hawley Lake.

"Do you remember the time we were running from your house to mine on the path beside the lake and there was a clap of thunder and a flash of lightning so close we could see it enter the ground and smell the ozone? I'll never forget that smell." Claire shivered. "It was the summer we were twelve years old."

Lynn stared out at the rain and shook her head. "I don't remember most of the things that happened that summer." The waitress brought the drinks and Lynn took a large sip of Chardonnay. Her eyes turned toward Claire. Usually Lynn was immaculately groomed, but the rain had washed the curl from her hair, and her mascara ran down her cheeks. "On Labor Day weekend I was raped."

The truth that had been hidden all these years suddenly lay between them on the table. "I know," Claire said. "But I never felt I could talk about it until you did."

"I was waiting beside the road for a ride to a Girl Scout meeting when he grabbed me. He kept me for three days in a remote cabin in the Gila Wilderness. My only defense was to curl up in a ball like a small animal." Her voice rippled across the pain like water on a rocky riverbed.

Claire remembered the days when Lynn was missing and the pall hanging over Hawley Lake as acrid as the smoke from an out-of-control fire.

"Did you know that they never found him?" Lynn put her empty wineglass down hard and it thumped the table. "He heard the police dogs barking in the distance and he got away. The state police found me all alone in the cabin. After they questioned me and brought me home, my mother said, 'You must never talk to anybody about this ever again.' I told my husbands and I told my therapist, but nobody else. Maybe if I had talked about it more, I would have excised it, but as it is, I can remember every detail. I took a drawing class recently, and I discovered that I could still draw his face. After I drew it, I began to see it everywhere. On every blank, white surface I can see that man's face."

She took a pencil from her purse and began drawing on the white tablecloth. While she did, Claire thought that if the rape happened today, police artists and computer simulation would reconstruct the face and it would appear in newspapers and on television making it far easier to catch the rapist. But when Lynn was raped, in the late fifties, it was believed that a girl raped would become a girl scorned and the truth was hushed up. Lynn had always been artistic and it only took a few strokes to draw the rapist's face.

While Lynn drew, Claire listened to the rain dripping from the eaves strangely apprehensive that she might recognize the man. She was fifty-one now, and though she occasionally forgot a name, she hadn't yet forgotten a face.

Lynn finished her sketch and put down her pencil. Claire stared at it, and though she was relieved to see a face that she didn't recognize, she was disturbed by the power it had to haunt and to terrify. The man's hair was thin and shoulder length. He had high, sharp cheekbones, small, mean-spirited eyes, and a deep cleft in his chin. Claire pondered how computer simulation would age the face. There would be even less hair today, the cheekbones wouldn't be as sharply defined, but the small eyes and the cleft in the chin would remain.

"I don't recognize him," Claire said with relief.

"I didn't think you would. He was from out of the area, I'm sure. Hawley Lake was a small community. If anyone suspicious had been around, someone would have reported it. I believe that he had raped before and probably continued raping wherever he went until he was either killed or caught. That was a man who hated girls and women. He robbed me of my childhood. He robbed me of my memory. I know you and I were friends and shared wonderful moments before he raped me, but I can't remember any of it. Sometimes I feel like my memory was struck by lightning and all of my innocence is gone. I won't get my childhood back until I know he is dead or incarcerated or has a terminal illness." Lynn finished her wine and put the glass down. "He said one thing I will never forget which was that he went into the darkness looking for light."

The chill that Claire had anticipated before she saw the face affected her now. She became aware that the room was cold, that her clothes were wet. She was a librarian. Words were the tools of her trade, and she didn't forget an evocative phrase. She didn't know precisely when or where, but she was sure she had heard it before.

"That sounds familiar," she said to Lynn. "I haven't ever heard you use that phrase, have I?"

"I doubt it," Lynn said. "I listened to what my mother said and rarely said anything about the rape." She put her pencil eraser to the rapist's forehead. "Seen enough?" she asked.

Claire nodded, convinced this was a face she would never forget.

"Good." Lynn began rubbing the rapist out. "Enough about this son of a bitch, let's talk about your life."

While Claire told Lynn about her new life in Albuquerque, and her job at the Center for Southwest Research, she watched the face of the rapist turn into a smudge on the tablecloth.

That afternoon she drove Lynn to the airport. She stood on the observation deck and watched her friend's plane take off into the rain. Rain was still falling when she got into bed that night, but the thunder and lightning had stopped. It had turned into a gentle, soaking rain, the kind the Navajos called a female rain. Claire wished it were cold enough to start a fire in the gas stove. She still felt damp and chilled from Lynn's story and from being out in the rain. It was cool enough to bring her cat, Nemesis, into bed and he snuggled against her feet while she pondered the phrase "into the darkness looking for light," wondering where she had heard it as she fell asleep.

She woke up, as she often did, at two in the morning, in the middle of a dream full of written words, words with a meaning she couldn't quite decipher. It occurred to her at that moment that she hadn't heard Lynn's phrase, she had read it. Her memory was photographic in the sense that she could remember exactly where she saw words on a page. Those words appeared to her now as she must have seen them then, on the right side of a book, near the bottom of an odd-numbered page. Many of the librarians she knew developed unusual skills. One, who had asthma, could tell where a book had been by its smell. Remembering exactly where on a page Claire had read something wasn't a particularly useful skill. It would have been far more productive to remember which book she had read it in. The only thing that was useful in this memory was that she knew the words were in a book that she had read in recent memory. All she had to do was search the odd-numbered pages in every book she had read in the last few years to find it. Nemesis had departed, and she felt alone in her bed. The rain stopped, the night was still, she fell asleep again.

In the morning she did her tai chi exercises, finishing by imagining her mind was an empty bowl. Pieces of paper with words typed on them drifted into the bowl. The words she saw were darkness and light.

When she got to the library she searched through *Bartlett's Familiar Quotations,* but didn't find the quote there. She did a search of quotations on the Internet and didn't find it there either.

Her friend and coworker Ruth O'Connor poked her head through the door to say hello. Ruth had the quick motions of a small bird. "Ruth," Claire asked, "have you ever heard or read the phrase 'into the darkness looking for light'?"

Ruth was the librarian who believed she could smell the origin of a book. She sniffed the air before she replied, "I don't believe so. Why?"

"An old friend of mine was raped when she was twelve years old. It was something the rapist said to her, but we never talked about it until yesterday. I know I read that phrase, but I can't remember where."

Ruth tilted her head as she always did when thinking. "Someday soon the Internet will get to the point where the content of every book will be available and you will be able to search for any phrase—like that." She snapped her fingers.

"Someday," Claire agreed, but that didn't help her now.

"Do you read true crime?"

"Not much," Claire said.

"That's where I would start."

"Thanks," replied Claire.

Before she left the library that night, she searched the database for true crime books. Fortunately that was one category in which she had done limited reading. She didn't find a single book about a rapist. But it didn't surprise her to find numerous books about serial killers, most of whom were men who preyed on women. It was quite possible that men who started out as rapists turned into killers. It was also possible that Lynn's rapist had already been a killer. Her life had been scarred by the attack, but she was fortunate she had survived. In the serial killer category, Claire discovered three books that she had read. She went to the shelves, found the books, and checked them out.

When she got home that night, she fed the cat, cooked dinner for herself, then sat down on the sofa in her spare living room with the books. True Crime was not her favorite genre. She got enough of that on the evening news. If she was going to read about crime, she preferred to do it in the format of a mystery. Still for her purposes, true crime books had an advantage; they all contained photographs of the killer. Unfortunately none of them resembled the face Lynn had drawn on the tablecloth. One notorious serial killer had actually been in operation at the time Lynn was attacked. Yet physically there was no resemblance. He had a plump face that was almost good-looking, making Claire wonder, as she had when she first read the book on a plane, what had set him on his twisted path. She recalled buying the book in an airport and reading it on a plane trip she took with her ex-husband, mostly to annoy him.

The photographs in the books gave Claire little hope that she would find the quote she was looking for in the text. Nevertheless she skimmed them, checking the exact spot on the odd numbered pages where she remembered seeing the quote, paying particular attention to anything in quotation marks, the words of the killers. Her search produced only dark thoughts, which she tried to eliminate by staying up late playing solitaire on her computer. After she had a couple of easy wins, she went to bed, but her dreams were haunted by the faces of the serial killers.

"Find anything?" Ruth asked when she peered through the door the following morning.

"Nothing but bad dreams," Claire said.

Ruth tilted her head as if she were trying to locate the right vantage point in her trifocal lenses. "'Into the darkness looking for light.' It has a poetic ring, doesn't it?"

"You could say that."

"Is there any possibility you read it in a poem?"

"I doubt it. I have a visual memory and I see it as prose."

"A prose writer with a poetic style."

"Possibly." With the speed and intensity of a lightning flash, the thought occurred to Claire that she might have read the phrase in a mystery. She read a lot of them. It was a genre with room in it for poetry. "Maybe I read it in a mystery."

"Ah," said Ruth.

She went back to her office, leaving Claire to consider which mystery. Since her bookshelves at home were full of mysteries, she tried to narrow the field. First she made a list of the mystery writers she considered poets. Several best-selling mystery writers had been crime reporters. She believed it was their realism and their knowledge of the criminal mind that made their work so popular. Then there were the mystery writers who had been in law enforcement—cops, rangers, private eyes. Could one of them have had some contact with the rapist? Could the phrase have stuck in his or her mind and made its way into a book? She thought of the former crime reporters Michael Connelly and Patricia Cornwell. Fortunately for her search, Claire hadn't read all of their books. Tony Hillerman had also covered the crime beat. She *had* read every one of his books and going through them was a formidable task. She knew of no mystery writers who were criminals, although she supposed that was a possibility, too.

She spent a long weekend flipping through the odd pages of the Cornwells and the Connellys she had read, all of the Hillermans, the cops, the PIs, the poets. She saw a great deal of crime and some good writing, but she did not find the phrase she was looking for.

"How did it go?" Ruth asked her on Monday morning.

"I didn't find it. I went through forty books over the weekend. I looked at the books that I thought showed a flair for poetry as well as the mystery writers who had been crime reporters and the ones I knew had been in law enforcement."

"You read forty books over the weekend?"

"I didn't actually read them. I skimmed the odd pages; that's where I remember seeing the quote."

"You left most of the books unread and half of them un-skimmed."

"I know, Ruth, but I remember where on the page I saw those words."

"You trust your memory? How old are you?"

"Fifty-one."

Ruth threw up her hands. "I rest my case." Ruth was sixty-five herself, retirement age, although she enjoyed her work far too much to ever consider retirement.

"You still remember smells, don't you?" Claire asked.

"Not as well as I used to," Ruth replied.

She walked out of the office leaving Claire to wonder if she could trust her memory. It hadn't failed her yet, but she supposed that sooner or later it would. What if she hadn't read the phrase where she thought she had? What if her memory was playing tricks on her and she hadn't read it at all? She relied on her memory and didn't want to consider that one day it might fail. She knew that as people aged, they might no longer remember a face or what they had eaten for breakfast, but their memory of early events became sharper. Someday she might be lying in a retirement home remembering the dolls, the dogs and cats, the games and friends of her childhood. Yet when Lynn tried to return to her early years she would find a door locked tight.

Librarians were known as the keepers of memory. Memories of the childhood summers on Hawley Lake were precious to Claire, and she wanted to be able to share them with her friend. It would also please her to know that justice had been served—if it had been served—but she didn't know how to proceed. She hadn't told Lynn of her search, not wanting to cause disappointment if she came up empty. In a way, any search that involved memory was a race against time, but she was too stubborn to take Ruth's advice and read every page of the books she had skimmed. She decided to table her search for a while. Perhaps if she emptied her mind, the solution would appear.

It took a few weeks, but one night she woke up at 2:00 A.M. to see that the streetlight had etched the shadow of a tree branch on the wall of her bedroom. She thought about what Lynn must see in the shadows of her blank walls. She realized that in her mystery search she hadn't considered the books that were set in the time and/or the place the rape occurred.

Claire got up, turned on the light, and went to her floor-to-ceiling bookshelves. The shelves were full of books and searching them was a forbidding task even when it wasn't the middle of the night, but the fact that her books were shelved by category made it easier. There were shelves devoted to mysteries, shelves devoted to the Southwest, even a subsection devoted to Southwestern mysteries. She found a book there by a woman writer who lived in Tucson, a paperback original Claire had read a few years back that she found undistinguished in plot and in style. She hoped it wasn't that attitude that had kept her from considering it before. The title of the book was *The Salt River Killer*. The Salt River wasn't near Hawley Lake, but it was in Arizona.

The author's name was Kate Lamar. The bio on the inside back cover said she had lived all over the country and worked at various jobs to support her writing habit. She had taught, she had been a waitress, she had driven a truck. She had not, apparently, been a crime reporter or a cop. The photo on the inside back cover was grainy. It showed Kate Lamar had long black hair and wore jeans. She looked to be in her mid-thirties, but Claire knew that jacket photos were often deceiving.

She sat down and began flipping through the book from back to front as if it had been written in Japanese. It only took a minute to find what she was looking for. It gave her some satisfaction to discover that the quote was exactly where she had remembered reading it, on an odd-numbered page near the bottom. The female protagonist, a detective, was confronting the murderer, a serial killer.

"Why did you do it?" she asked him.

The killer gave a rambling, incoherent answer, but in the middle of the paragraph Claire found the phrase she'd been looking for, "I go into the darkness looking for light."

"Yes," she said. Her hands trembled as she closed the book. Sleep was impossible after that. She got up early, went to the library, got on her computer, and tracked down Kate Lamar's phone number and address on her search engine's

White Pages. While she waited until it was a reasonable hour to call, she searched the phrase Salt River Killer to see if there had actually been one. Amazon.com listed Lamar's book for sale, even though it was out of print. There were Web sites that mentioned the Salt River, but none that mentioned a Salt River Killer. Claire logged off the computer, called Kate Lamar, and got voice mail advising her to leave a message after the tone. She left her name and number, said she worked at the Center for Southwest Research and wanted to talk to her about her book, *The Salt River Killer.*

Lamar did not call back. Claire waited a few days, called again, and left another message. When there was still no reply, she wrote a letter explaining that there was something in *The Salt River Killer* she wanted to discuss with the author but not saying exactly what in fear of scaring her away. Claire waited a few weeks. There was still no answer. She was considering going to Tucson and knocking on the woman's door when she noticed in the Sunday paper that Lamar had a new book out and a signing scheduled at a Santa Fe store. The evening of the signing Claire drove up to Santa Fe.

The event was not well attended. The owner of the bookstore had set up twenty seats in rows in front of a table. Only three people had sat down, and Claire suspected that two of them worked at the store. She had been hoping to study Kate Lamar in anonymity and considered lurking in the bookshelves listening to what the author had to say, but then she decided that if the author saw her buy a book, she might be more disposed to answer her query.

Claire sat in the second row. The manager indicated it was time for Kate to begin and she read in a nervous monotone without lifting her eyes from the page. Claire saw that the jacket photo had been deceptive, and she changed her estimate of the author's age to early fifties. Her hair was too black to be real and, in fact, a thin line of gray showed at the roots. It occurred to Claire that she could have been raped by the same man who raped Lynn. If that was the case, how deep was her memory buried? Would it do her any good to revive it now?

While the author read, Claire debated going home after

the signing and leaving Kate Lamar to whatever peace she had found in her life. But her need to know was overpowering. When the reading was over, she approached the author with the new book in her hand. "I'm Claire Reynier," she said as Kate signed the book. "I've been trying to get in touch with you about something you said in *The Salt River Killer.*"

Kate looked up and Claire saw fear swirling in her dark eyes.

"It's important to me and to a very good friend of mine," Claire continued.

"Sure," Kate said. "Whatever." She made a show of looking at her watch. "I have to leave here immediately after the signing. Give me your number, and I'll call you when I get back to Tucson. All right?"

It wasn't all right, but Claire gave the author her card and left the store feeling that Kate was watching her every step of the way. For a person who had to leave immediately and who had a limited number of books to sign, she took her time about exiting the store. While she did, Claire circled the lot looking for a car with Arizona plates. She suspected Kate's car would be an older model subcompact with dents and dings, and she was right. Her task was made easier by the fact that the car had a bumper sticker promoting the author's latest release. Claire was struck by the conflicting desires an author would have to protect her privacy and her solitude in order to create, as opposed to the self-promotion required to sell books.

Her own vehicle, a truck with New Mexico plates, was inconspicuous in this parking lot. She drove it to the shadows near Kate's car and waited for her to come out. Lurking in the shadows was out of character for Claire, but she reminded herself that she was doing this for her old friend Lynn.

Eventually Kate Lamar left the store. As soon as she entered the parking lot, she dropped any pretense of animation. Her shoulders slumped and she hung her head as she walked. It seemed obvious to Claire that this was an author who sold very few books and was worried about where the next royalty check was coming from. Nevertheless, when Kate reached for the door handle of her car, Claire stepped in front of her.

"I'll only take a minute of your time. This is very important to me," she said.

The author appeared too dispirited to resist. "What is it you want?" she sighed.

"In *Salt River Killer* you used the phrase 'into the darkness looking for light.'"

"So?" Kate asked.

"My oldest friend was raped in Arizona when she was twelve. The rapist used that phrase."

"Oh, God," Kate said. Her hand fell away from the door. She dropped it to her side and clenched it into a fist.

Her misery invoked compassion in Claire. "You weren't raped by him, too, were you?" she asked softly.

"No." Kate shook her head. "That wasn't it. I once taught a creative writing course in prison."

"In Arizona?"

"No, in Illinois. Joliet. I may have inadvertently picked up that phrase from a prisoner. Sometimes when you're writing, you're not quite sure where a phrase comes but it seems right so you use it. It wasn't my intent to plagiarize."

Artificial light beamed into the parking lot. There were many deep shadows, but the places that were lit were unnaturally harsh and bright. The whiteness of Kate's face emphasized the darkness of her eyes. Claire looked into them and knew that she was hiding something.

"You know which prisoner, don't you?"

"No, honestly I don't."

"That rape erased all memories my friend had of her childhood. You have the power to give her her memory back, to let her know that the man is in prison, that justice has been served."

Kate reached for the door handle again. "I have to go," she said.

"I don't intend to use this against you in any way," Claire replied, knowing that a writer could get in trouble for plagiarizing a student. "I only want to know for the sake of my friend."

"You won't tell anyone?"

"No one. Just give me his name. Please."

"It's Richard Kirsch."

"What does he look like?"

"He's an old man now who suffers from arthritis, a lifer who has been in prison for thirty years."

"For what?"

"Rape, murder."

"Was he a serial killer?"

"It's possible, but he was only convicted of one murder."

"Did he ever spend any time in Arizona?"

"Yes. He wrote about Arizona in my class."

"Does he have any distinguishing facial characteristics?"

"He has small eyes and a deep cleft in his chin."

"Ah," said Claire. "Has he found any light in his darkness?"

"I doubt it. Richard Kirsch is a man who spent his life in darkness. I think he finds energy there, but light? Not likely. I'll tell you something. Even though he is an old man now, I believe if he ever got out of prison he would rape again. He sat in the back of the room and the way his eyes burned still gives me the chills. I write under a different name than I used then, or I wouldn't have dared say a word about it."

She had more or less admitted that she had plagiarized Richard Kirsch, but Claire didn't bring that to her attention. She thanked Kate and said good-bye.

On the lonely drive back to Albuquerque in the hour she had to think about their encounter, it occurred to her that elements of Kate's story could be fiction. She didn't want to tell Lynn about it until she was positive.

In the morning she found the address for Joliet Prison on her computer and wrote to Richard Kirsch creating a fiction of her own by saying she was writing a book about rapists. She wanted to know if Kirsch had anything to say about his case, and if he would contribute a picture.

The answer came back sooner than she expected, almost by return mail. Claire supposed he had little to do in prison and any attention was better than none. His letter was handwritten and rambling. Her eyes went immediately to his picture. Like some authors, the face he presented to the world was that of a much younger person. It worked better for Claire's purposes than a more current photo would have.

Richard Kirsch's hair was thin and long, his eyes were small and mean, and he had a deep cleft in his chin.

It's him, Claire thought. She forced herself to read the letter. The man had a flair for words, but there was no wisdom behind them. He didn't try to explain or justify or apologize. All he said, basically, was that he had never found what he was looking for.

She called Lynn and invited herself over to Arizona for the weekend. It was a good time to come as Lynn's husband intended to be out of town on business. They lived in the mountains north of Phoenix in a house surrounded by saguaros. Claire arrived in the evening and they sat on the terrace watching the sun drop behind the mountains and listening to the coyotes yip. It was the hour known as civil twilight. Claire was about to break the surface civility in hopes of restoring it at a deeper level.

"I have something to tell you. I think I found your rapist," she said.

"No! How?"

"The phrase you quoted about going into the darkness looking for light stuck in my mind. I was sure I had read it somewhere. I searched many books but eventually I found it in a mystery by a woman named Kate Lamar who lives in Tucson. I confronted her and she told me that she had taught a rapist named Richard Kirsch in Joliet Prison in Illinois. He had once lived in Arizona. She admitted that the phrase came from him."

"He's in prison? Thank God. How can we be sure it's him?"

"I have a photo. Do you want to see it?"

Lynn closed her eyes, squeezed her fingers tight, held her breath, then whispered, "Yes."

Claire handed her the photo. "Kate said he is an old man now. This is a photo of him in younger days."

Lynn stared at it. "It's him," she said with tears in her eyes.

"I thought so," replied Claire.

"How long is he in jail for?"

"Life."

"He deserves every rotten minute of it," Lynn said.

"I got the photo by telling him I was writing a book about rapists. He also sent me a rambling letter. Do you want to read it?"

"Does he admit guilt or apologize or say who else he raped?"

"No."

"Then I don't want to read it."

They sat on the terrace until it turned completely dark. When the stars were in place, they went to bed. Claire woke in the middle of the night listening to the coyotes barking, remembering, wondering what thoughts her friend was thinking if she was awake too. When she got up in the morning, Lynn was sitting on the terrace, drinking coffee. Claire joined her.

"Did you sleep all right?" she asked.

"Not bad," Lynn replied. "Considering. Thank you for doing this, Claire. You're a dear friend."

"I was glad to help," Claire said. "It was my childhood, too, and you're the one I shared it with. When I woke up in the middle of the night and heard the coyotes barking, it reminded me of the neighbor's dog at Hawley Lake who barked all night. Do you remember when he snuck into your father's garden and stole his tomatoes? 'I never saw a dog before who ate tomatoes,' your father said."

"What was that dog's name? Rojo?" Lynn asked.

"Yes."

"He was a big dog with a reddish coat?"

"Yes."

Lynn smiled. "I remember," she said.

UNDER THE BIG BLACK SUN

A Filomena Buscarsela Mystery Story

k.j.a. Wishnia

k.j.a. Wishnia was nominated for the Edgar and the Anthony Awards for his first Filomena Buscarsela mystery, *23 Shades of Black*. He has since written *Soft Money* and *The Glass Factory*.

The first few days out of detox are always the roughest. But if you can get through them, you're on your way to being all right, and creeping along the well-traveled road from ruin to recovery. At least that's what I told the guy who wandered up from the shoreline and began what seemed like a nice enough conversation, until he found out we were from New York.

"New Yorkers are very intelligent," he says, scratching at the sandy stubble around his chin.

"Well, they have to be—" I begin, trying to be polite.

"Even the way they drink out of the bottle," he says, pointing at the row of tourists posing on the hotel deck fifty yards down the beach from us. "It's a certain angle. Not a wasted movement."

Oh. Why don't the Miami Beach police just issue every visitor a deranged-psycho-is-talking-to-me locator you can activate every time this happens? Then you can sit there smiling and nodding your head, secure in the knowledge that men with tasers and butterfly nets will be turning up in less than three minutes.

He says his name is Trane, and I give him a couple of quarters so he can "call his doctor," then Antonia and I shake the sand out of our threadbare beach blanket and start walking up the sandy slope towards Ocean Drive.

What is it about South Florida? This place is like the filter in the bottom of a drain, collecting all the gunk that comes sluicing down the coast, having run out of other places to befoul.

There's a dip in the dunes, and my daughter is the first one over the top and down into the trough, where a little boy is happily digging with a green plastic shovel. He's all alone. Antonia plants her knees in the sand in front of him to say hi, and the boy looks up. He's got dark brown skin and wild, wavy hair, big rolling eyes, a runny nose, and the bulbous forehead characteristic of some kind of birth defect. Then he waves hello. The arm not holding the shovel is stunted, three fingers where the elbow should be. Something tells me he's not supposed to be out here alone.

I ask him his mother's name, and get a bunch of meaningless syllables: "Cooo-cooo-cooo, giggleegeee, giggleegeeee."

Antonia's very mature for a preteen. She doesn't recoil or make a face. She starts helping him dig, while I climb up the rim of the sand pit, shielding my eyes from the sun, and start searching the horizon for a missing parent.

I must have left my scanners on the default setting of "female," because I pass by a male figure three times before realizing that he's probably the one. Tall and elegant, he is walking away from the hotel deck turning his sharpened gaze to the east and west, an agile urgency conveyed by his avian movements. You don't need a Ph.D. in body language to know that the man is frantically looking for someone, and he has the same deep-brown skin color and dark wavy hair as the boy. Antonia's watching the kid, so I pad along the dunes towards Mr. Missing, who looks quite cool in a pair of loose white shorts and a light blue polo shirt without a stain on them. I'd be sweating through burlap if I lost sight of Antonia.

"Are you looking for a little boy?" I ask, beads of moisture forming on my upper lip.

"Yes! You have seen him?"

"He's right over there."

"Thank God," he says, setting off in the direction of my outstretched arm. I try to keep up with him, but in flip-flops on hot sand, I might as well be wading through Jell-O.

"How'd you lose sight of him?" I'm talking to his back.

"Pande! Pande!" His shadow skims over the crest of the sand pit and drops off my radar screen and out of sight.

I come upon the man resting on his heels in the sand with one arm around his son, speaking in a language whose words I do not know but whose pitches are unmistakable as the soothing, universal tones of parental nurturing, interspersed with the sharp, strict tones of a thousand years of parental warning, while Antonia looks on, invisible from four feet away.

"Is that where you're staying?" I ask, pointing at the huge glass slab of the Redmont, the luxury hotel from which he appears to have emerged.

"No." I'm clearly an intrusion in his life, but after staring at me he adds a phrase out of courtesy. "We are in a cheaper place."

"Us too. We get a week in a prefab on Fifth Street—with cement stairs that somebody painted green—for the price of a bed and room service for one night in that place. But hey, you don't come to Miami Beach to stay in your room, right?"

"No, you don't," he agrees.

"Look at them," I say, watching the wealthy sun-worshipers starting to clear a trail into the cocktail hour with ice tongs and mosquito torches. Some of them are excavating with the precision of paleontologists, others are bush-whacking with the bravado of drunken Ostrogoths. One guy seems bent on clear-cutting his way through with a bulldozer and a log chain. He's a fifty-five-year-old frat boy, well tanned, chest hairs going gray, upper body muscular but sagging, and he's pinching plenty of bikini bottoms and snapping towels at the Speedo-rumps that go with them if they happen to raise a fuss.

Pande grabs my attention by repeatedly smacking his shovel against the sand as if he were swatting at a sudden plague of flies and loudly trilling with his tongue.

I'm not going to ask, What does he have? So I ask, "So where are you staying?"

"We are just around the corner."

You're more than around the corner if you're in a cheap place, buddy, I think to myself. Antonia and I have a five-block walk to our plebeian accommodations.

"Are you from India?" Antonia blurts out.

"Yes."

"Where in India?"

"You wouldn't know it."

"Where?" she insists.

"So many questions from a little girl," he says, but I guess he feels that he owes us an answer. "We are from Vidisha."

"Where's that?"

"It is near the Betwa River," he replies, an answer that would normally prompt a deluge of follow-up questions but this time it strangely satisfies Antonia's inquisitiveness.

Not mine, however.

"Where's his mother?" I ask politely, glancing around as if I expect to be introduced to her.

He's too educated and polite to tell me to do him a favor and drop dead, but I can see a quiet, smoldering pain darkening his features.

"My Unnati died of complications three months after giving birth to Pande."

"Oh. I'm so sorry." The Third World syndrome. "I didn't mean to pry—"

"Of course you did." It's just a flat statement. No anger. "But I also chose to answer you. I thank you for watching over my Pande, but now I think it's time to head back to our rooms."

He straightens up, and I have to tilt my head up to meet his gaze and study his angular Aryan features. He could pass for Robert Redford dipped in cocoa.

Now there's a thought.

And he's another single parent . . .

We're headed in the same direction, skirting the sandy walkway between the palm trees and the benches filled with the last of the left-wing Jewish workers who fought for the unionization of the garment industry sixty years ago so they could retire here and complain about the weather in Yiddish.

"Ot geyt an andere kubanitse," says one of them as I walk past.

I want to turn to him and say I'm not Cuban, I'm an Ecuadorian-American living in New York City, where I also happened to pick up a little of the *mameloshn*, but I don't want to spend time chatting up a former Stalinist hard-liner—as inviting as that is—and lose sight of my new friend, Mr.—

"Hey, I don't even know your name," I say, skipping to catch up with him.

He doesn't break his stride, or even slow down, but keeps going as if trying to shake off a clinging odor in the air. I pull up even with him and introduce myself.

"I'm Filomena. This is my daughter, Antonia. I already met your son, Pande."

He's too well bred to ignore this.

"My name is Vishal. Now please let me take him home."

"All right, but our children were playing very nicely together."

He stops.

"I'm sorry," he says. "I am being rude after you were kind enough to help me. I'm just upset about Pande wandering off and—well—"

"And making you look like a bad parent." I finish his sentence for him.

"Well, yes," he admits.

"That's nothing," Antonia starts to say, but I stop her before she can tell him about the time she watched me burn a hit man's face with a red-hot piece of iron or the time I nearly knifed a government thug who was chasing us through a tropical swamp, or any of the other inappropriate things she has witnessed as part of my demented life as a crimefighter.

I noticed that the Redmont Hotel has a public bar overlooking the water.

Zero hour.

"Would you like to have a drink with us?" I ask.

He follows my gaze towards the hotel, his lips tightening nervously as if he were weighing his chances of being thrown out of the place for having the wrong pedigree. We don't have a caste system here, exactly, but we still have our lords and serfs.

And I still don't know which one is the dessert spoon.

"How about a plain tonic water?" he asks.

"That's fine with me."

They stick us near the maintenance shed, but the ocean

view is broad and inviting. Pande behaves very well, sitting quietly the whole time, gently rocking his head back and forth and sucking on the last of his soda with a straw. I wish I could say the same for the Class of '65 Spring Breaker, who's graduated to slapping babes full-handed on the butt, a move I haven't seen a guy get away with in twenty years—but then, I've been dutifully yoked to parenthood for a dozen years myself.

The junior execs seem to sense this alien presence, this motherly office, and throw themselves in deeper, partying while they still can before one of the party girls snags them and they end up chained to a weekly paycheck and a thirty-year mortgage.

I'm just beginning to get lulled by the sound of the waves concussing against the wooden pylons beneath the deck, when the big man crosses over the line and ends up in a T-shirt-grabbing scuffle with one of the junior silverbacks. I start to rise out of my seat but Vishal puts his hand across my forearms and cautions me against getting involved.

"You better watch who you mess with!" threatens the young male animal.

"I don't see your name on her," says the dominant male.

Nobody's asking *her* opinion.

The bartender and the pool man dash in and pull the two men apart, the hotel steward appears, pleading "Mr. Johnson, Mr. Clancy, please don't let this get out of hand, this is a friendly place, there are children present."

Mr. Johnson looks up and apparently registers us for the first time, smiles and says, "Sure thing, José. I wasn't going to start anything. It's the kid's problem, anyway, trying to keep his girl."

Mr. Clancy—"the kid"—performs the ritual of struggling to break free so he can slug Mr. Johnson squarely on the jaw, but with two burly men holding him back, he soon has the excuse of cooling off and smoothing out the bunched-up marks made by several fists on his Ralph Lauren shirt.

Mr. Johnson directs the bartender to serve him: "Get me a whiskey sour, Charlo—with plenty of ice this time." And he comes right over and sits down with us as if he were part of the family.

"How you folks doing today?"

"Why, you planning on reading us the specials?" I ask.

"Huh?" he snorts.

"What's your name, anyway?"

"Johnson."

"I heard the Johnson part."

He smiles. "Wally. Wally Johnson." The letters W and J are sewn together on his shirt and shorts. He holds out a big meaty hand for me to shake, gets a few of my fingers and crushes them, as if that's supposed to impress me.

I tell him my name, then he pulls the same act on Vishal, who meets the man's cast-iron grip with surprising stoicism, and says, stiffly, "Vishal. Vishal Chanderdatt," enunciating each syllable clearly as if he expects to have to repeat it several times.

But the guy just turns to me and says, "What are you drinking there?"

"Just club soda with a twist," I explain.

The waiter puts Johnson's drink on the table in front of him and starts to leave. Johnson grabs the waiter's arm and says, "And a Coke chaser—in the bottle."

"Yes, sir."

"So what do you do when you're not fondling women's asses?" I ask.

Johnson laughs as he takes a big gulp from his drink and answers so quickly a fine spray of whiskey sour spatters my shoulder. "I'm a beach bum," he says. "My company went belly-up and I jumped aboard a dot.com—but they're getting ready to toss all the dead fish like me overboard any day now, so I figure I'd better get in shape for my retirement, huh?" and his jaw cracks open in a wide-mouthed lion-hunter's laugh.

"So what do you do?" he asks.

Vishal answers that he is a technician for a local television station. The waiter serves Johnson his bottle of Coke, and I'm thinking, "Beach bum" my ass. This is a guy who's used to ordering people around. He's probably just down here getting away from his wife and spoiled-rotten teenage children. I bet he told them he's on a business trip. Probably took off his wedding ring, too. I check for a light band of skin on the fourth finger of his left hand and—yes, indeed—there it is.

He's leaning a little closer to me, his leg hairs are tickling me like a swarm of fever-bearing mosquitoes, and he's suggesting that some kind of get-together should occur later on when the moon is out and the kids are in bed, when Trane, the beggar who bugged me on the beach earlier, looms over us, having miraculously evaded the hotel staff, and asks for a dollar.

"You want something?" says Johnson. "I got something for you."

Trane thrusts out his hand because the security staff have spotted him and he's only got about three seconds left to clinch the deal, but before I know it Johnson is giving the Coke bottle a vigorous shake and popping his thumb off the top as if we're in a junior high school cafeteria and spraying Trane with dark bubbly sheets of sticky brown liquid.

"Har-har," bellows Johnson, while Vishal cringes with embarrassment.

I tell Johnson that I'll probably be seeing him later, and the two of us get to our feet while the security staff close around Trane and hustle him out of there like a dope dealer at a Catholic school pep rally.

A few hours later, the kid's in bed, and I close the flimsy self-locking door on our sparsely furnished by-the-week vacation apartment, relishing a moment of solitude and what passes for freedom these days—a quiet walk under the stars with the damp, gritty sand crunching between my toes and grating pleasantly against the soles of my feet, which have been thickened from pounding the hard pavement of city streets for far too long.

I walk north along the shore until the tension and anxieties start to ease, until my mind stops contracting around all those what-I-should-have-told-this-or-that-client scenarios I thought I left behind and opens up to the vastness of the warm breeze coming across the water. I guess you can carbon-date me by the fact that I still remember the latter-day *Jackie Gleason Show*, which always began with an aerial shot of this beach, and ended with the burlesque house–trained comic's bellow, "The Miami Beach audience is the greatest audience in the world!"

Somewhere between sea and sky I turn about and head back, steering towards my little spot of four-walled solidity and the ever-fixed star of parenthood and all its attendant responsibilities.

But I linger for a moment, anchoring myself at the water's edge and marveling at the wide and unknowable expanse of ocean, its vast blackness seeming all the blacker in contrast to the pinpoints of white light reflected upon its dappled surface, clusters of twinkling white globules suddenly tinged with red and orange and red.

I turn and see an EMS crew scrambling over the deck chairs at the Redmont Hotel, their chaos muffled at this distance by the forceful wind spiriting over the face of the deep.

I'm on my feet, the brightly tinted scene floating closer to me over the dark and featureless void of sand. And into the melee:

"—no response!"

"—dilation?"

"—no pulse at all—"

"Ma'am, could you stand back, please?"

"Everybody off the deck!"

"Ma'am, could you keep back?"

"Everybody off the deck! Now!"

A hard fist closes around my arm as the Miami Beach police remind me that no matter what my other creditable accomplishments may be, I'm still just a greasy *latina* standing in the way of some big white men. I pick up some splinters as I'm dragged against the dried wooden railing.

"Come on, move it!"

"Everybody inside!"

"—move it, move it, move it!"

"—freakin' ghouls."

The bunch of us are shoved inside the main tavern and the glass doors are slid shut, leaving us to gawk like fish in a tank at the ghastly underwater ballet unrolling before our bulging eyes. A crew of four EMS workers come gurgling out of the maintenance shed, angling a stretcher between them that harbors a semihuman object swathed in plastic wrap and tubes.

Tight hands press down a light green oxygen mask over most of the face, but the hair and coloring look like my old schoolmate, Mr. Wally Johnson.

"What happened?"

"I don' t know."

"The guy who cleans the pool found him."

"In the shed?"

"He hit his head or something?"

"I don't know."

"Must've passed out—"

"—had three or four martinis—"

"—more like five or six—"

The flurry of excitement and speculation goes on for a few minutes, until the sightseers get bored with watching a few yellow ribbons of accident scene tape fluttering around the empty deck and begin to cluster around the bar on the opposite side of the room. I notice the junior exec from this afternoon stretching his elbows out like he's ready to call it a night. He's heading for the door when an unfriendly-looking cop comes in and announces that the victim, who has been identified as Mr. Wally Johnson, has been pronounced dead, and that henceforth, "nobody goes in or out until we talk to them."

Oh, God. This'll take about five hours, with this crowd.

"Oh, that's terrible—"

"Poor *Señor* Johnson—"

"Was it an accident?" asks a concerned middle manager.

"How did it happen?" asks another.

"Did I ask you to say anything?" answers the cop, leaving out the epithet that would normally follow as surely as spring follows winter. I guess he's got to keep it in check when he's dealing with the tourist trade, because he manages to be both rude and crude while keeping the actual obscenities to a minimum, a finesse some New York cops could take a lesson from.

The cop snags the junior exec, since he was the one trying to leave just as they came in. The guy squirms a bit in his chair when it comes out that he was involved in an altercation with the deceased earlier in the day, but it only takes about ten minutes to clear him after nearly twenty witnesses place him in the bar from 7:00 P.M. on.

"Don't go anywhere," they instruct him.

I'm still picking splinters out of my elbow when they call my name.

"Are you just trying to find accident witnesses, or are you treating this as a suspicious death?" I ask.

The guy looks at me like he's going to toss me into the hold of the next banana boat back to South America for that one, but he manages to say, "Damn right we are."

"Then why the hell is a precinct cop conducting a murder investigation?" I say, drawing attention to the insignias on his shirt.

"Buh, this is just a preliminary," he blusters, and is saved from further exposure by the timely arrival of two *real* detectives, who tramp in like their heavy footfalls are the only things keeping the building from floating away. They dispatch a forensics team to the pool shed with cameras, tape measures, air quality monitors, evidence bags, you name it.

Suddenly I think about my kid. I've been here so long, I hope she doesn't wake up and panic when she sees I'm not there. On the other hand, she's used to my disruptive schedule. Just a little while longer.

Naturally the detectives try to keep it from us, but from what I can make out of their movements around the shed and the partial phrases that drift over to me I can piece together that Johnson's blood-alcohol level was high enough to cause him to pass out—although why he should choose to do it in the pool shed is a bit of a mystery—and that someone disconnected the pool's heating vent, which caused the shed to fill up with lethal amounts of carbon monoxide gas in about three minutes, which is what actually killed him.

They find all kinds of stuff in the shed indicating that someone was living in there, and shortly thereafter they discover Trane cowering under the boardwalk and arrest him on suspicion of murder.

"I was only stayin' there a couple days, man," Trane protests.

"That's the least of your freaking problems, dirt bag. Let's go," one of the cops says.

The detectives come back inside and tell us we're free to go, so naturally I go right up to them and say, "The suspect was living in the maintenance shed?"

"Yes, ma'am," says Detective Thomas, whose name I have picked up through my hypersensitive eavesdropping skills.

"Why kill a man and leave him in your crib?" I ask.

"He's not rational," explains Detective Clarke, as if that covers everything.

Thomas's turn: "Plus we have witnesses who say that earlier today the deceased sprayed him with soda in an attempt to humiliate and degrade him," he says, already translating it into police report language.

"I think he's been treated worse than that over the years," I suggest.

"Yeah," says Clarke, "that's why he'll get five years checking out the nurses' asses in some treatment center instead of fifteen getting reamed in Starke. It'll be good for him."

"Maybe the best thing that ever happened to him," says Thomas, and they both get a good laugh out of that.

So that's it, huh? They've got a body they can shove in front of a judge, and their work is done? Even if it doesn't make too much sense?

I corner the junior exec, who's ordering a drink out of relief.

"Boy, they sure had me sweating, and I don't even have so much as a speeding ticket hanging over me," I say jovially, sighing as if a hugely stressful moment has finally come to an end.

"That's how they work it," he says, matter-of-factly.

"Yeah, I saw them putting the screws to you."

His smile curls up and dries like a time-lapse photo of a withering flower.

"I guess it was on account of what happened between you and Johnson this afternoon over what's-her-name—"

"Tricia can take care of herself," he says sharply. "She could've broken the guy's arm if she wanted to. She was just being *polite*." He makes the word sound like a crippling Kung Fu move.

"The name's Filomena," I say.

"Chris," he says, not divulging more than he has to. Then, in a shift, he adds his last name as if it were a gentlemanly duty akin to laying his velvet cloak over a mud puddle for me, "Chris Clancy."

That old Southern charm.

We chat for a while, biding my time until he gets moderately greased, then I let it slip what a dirty old pig Johnson was, and Clancy lets the whole world know that, sure, Johnson was a pig, "But I wouldn't a gassed him, I'd a strangled him."

He only met Johnson two days ago, and he already wants him dead. Hmmm.

That gets my wheels turning. The method was gas. The opportunity was that Johnson was a boorish lout and falling-down drunk. What's left? Motive. I think I'll try to find out a bit more about Mr. Wally Johnson, businessman, who was spending a little time down in Florida trying to get away from—from what?

I excuse myself from the gaiety of the tavern and head for the comparatively grim and chilly reception desk, where a lonely male in his twenties is watching the minutes tick away, slogging his way through another endless graveyard shift.

"Excuse me," I ask, cocking my head to read his ID tag, which says his name is Roy. "Do you have an Internet terminal I can use?"

Roy says, "Are you a guest at this hotel?"

"Of course I am."

"Room number?"

"Oh, I don't know which number, Chrissy has the key." I get just the blank stare I wanted. "Mr. Chris Clancy?"

Roy punches up Clancy's name on the screen. "Ms. Tricia Lynn?

"That's me!"

Ask a stupid question . . .

"There's a computer with Internet access in the conference room, but you need the password to log on."

"So give me the password."

"I can't. It's against our policy."

Then why'd you make me go through the process of identifying myself, you jerk?

I mean: "Then why don't you log on for me? I promise I
won't peek at your precious little password."

"I can't leave the front desk unattended."

"Why not? I can watch the desk for two minutes. Nothing's going to happen, I'll be fine."

"I'm sorry, I can't allow that."

"Listen, Roy, you want a wrongful arrest to be blamed on
one hotel clerk's irresponsibility? You want the real murderer
to get away? How would Mr. Redmont feel about that?"

"Gosh, I—I thought—"

"You thought I just wanted to do some after-midnight
shopping for lingerie on the Internet. Now go hook me up."

"Yes, ma'am."

Gee, maybe I should've started out that way.

I finally sit down in front of the terminal and send Roy on
his way with a scooting motion of my hand, itching to type
in my subject's statistics. First I enter the hotel registry and
call up Wally Johnson, Room 1165, and see that he paid with
cash, not credit card, and gave his home address as 146 Ev-
ergreen Terrace, Springfield, MA, and I'm not laying any
money on finding a W. Johnson listed there, folks.

I close the registry and enter a standard ID search and—
surprise, surprise—can't get a match for that name and address. I try Wally Johnson, all states, date of birth "before
1950," and get several hundred possibilities. Nuts. I've got to
narrow the search fields, but to what? What else do I know
about him? I exit the standard search and link to a high-
security private investigator's site that charges by the minute
(maybe I can find a way to bill this to *somebody*), type in the
passwords and my account number and call for a search of
Wally Johnson, same as above, business executive, married,
height and weight estimates, eye color and other descriptors,
and then request the option for field matches for a history of
alcohol usage and possible disorderly conduct. Unfortunately, there are no subject headings for a chauvinist pig with
colonialist tendencies (since he seemed to have no trouble remembering the first names of all the hotel staff).

You know how many business executives named Johnson there are, in their fifties, with drinking problems?

But no match for Wally. I try Walter and Wallace, getting a couple of hundred matches, but only a few dozen who recently retired or were downsized, and most of them are too old to be my guy. There are a few possibles that I print out and set aside, but there always seems to be something that eliminates each potential subject from my list of possibles. You know: Walter Johnson, age 56, of Columbia, MO, recently retired as VP of Marketing at Cyclodyne Corp., so he could spend more time with his grandchildren and work in the nearby soup kitchen at St. Phillip's Episcopal Church every Sunday. Doesn't sound like my guy, right?

Still nothing, and the meter's clicking away.

I've got no reason to believe that Johnson is his real name, either. He gave a fake address, and paid in cash, so what's to keep him from giving a fake name, too? But he didn't seem like the kind of guy who'd put a lot of thought into some diabolical, double-edged pseudonym. He'd probably just turn his name around so he could keep using all those monogrammed shirts.

I try "John Walters" and get more of the same useless garbage. Then I punch in "John Wallace." Score.

There's enough sources on him for me to get off the expensive pay-per-view site and link to a standard who's who.

John Wallace, former chairman of Amalgamated Compounds, which recently changed its name to AmalCom to erase the association with the old name (so I guess he was only half lying when he said he worked for a dot.com), has been the subject of a police search for several months now, ever since the legal authorities repeatedly failed to locate him at his last known address in Delaware. After all, you can't serve a summons to an empty house.

AmalCom claims to know nothing of his whereabouts, and furthermore dismisses the summons as warrantless, since "all claims were settled" in the case of—CONTINUED ON NEXT PAGE.

Click.

UNABLE TO DISPLAY PAGE. *Arrgh!*

Okay, it's a big enough story. I ought to be able to find it elsewhere. No, not on the AmalCom site. Maybe from the Wilmington *News Journal*. Or the RainBeau Network. Hmmm. What's www.India.vs.AmalCom.org?

A field of digital gray-and-white squares gradually resolves into thickly billowing somber clouds as the graphics load first—which is certainly unusual—then the words and the rest of the site build over that.

Of course.

How could I forget?

Fifteen years ago, in one of the world's worst industrial accidents, an explosion at the Amalgamated Compounds pesticide plant in Sehore, India, released forty tons of hydrogen cyanide, monomethyl amine and *carbon monoxide gas* into the atmosphere, killing over 3,000 people within minutes and causing permanent, crippling injury to more than 200,000 others. Although Amalgamated Compounds settled for $470 million, which comes to only $600 for each of the injured survivors, the Indian government issued an arrest warrant for Mr. Johnson, charging him with "culpable homicide," after a memo was found in the smoldering ruins of the Sehore plant in which Mr. Johnson instructed the senior staff, who were all Americans, to cut corners at the highly profitable facility by letting the safety systems fall into disrepair, or even, in some cases, to shut them off completely. In response to the charge that he had "demonstrated a depraved indifference to human life in his delegation of operational and maintenance procedures at the Amalgamated Compounds of India location," Johnson blamed the disaster on sabotage committed by a "disgruntled employee," and refused to provide crucial scientific data, claiming that the exact chemical composition of the leaked gases was a "trade secret."

It also notes that, after all these years, about a dozen victims of the disaster are still dying every month.

I call up a map of north central India. Sehore is about forty miles from Vidisha, where Mr. Chanderdatt told me he comes from. But I bet that's not the whole story. I click and return a few times.

Well.

He comes from a place that woke up one hot, heartless

morning to find that the very air had turned against them, a place where there was no refuge under the big black sun, which was blotted out by the thick stinging clouds of night and fog courtesy of Death, Incorporated.

I've been on the machine for far too long and my eyes are getting bleary. I log off and wander bandy-legged out the door, down the hall, and back to the tavern to stare out the sliding-glass doors at the naked deck, roped off and guarded until daybreak brings a relief crew to sift the scene for further evidence linking Trane to Johnson's death.

Finding the side exit, I grasp the handrail extra tightly and clomp down the wooden stairs to the beach, the wind blowing my mussy, late-night computer-search hair into my face. I head for home, stumbling with occasional blindness on the uneven sands, until I catch the glow of two bright eyes lurking like a tiger's in the shadow of a low-lying palm tree. I look again and they're gone. But a sudden break in the cloud cover lets a few radiant droplets of moonlight fall earthward, silvering the dark outline of the mysterious stranger's footprints retreating up the beach.

I run after him, pushing the fear of smacking facefirst into a palm tree trunk to the back of my mind, feet digging into the cool sand, legs silently pumping and closing the distance between us. In a moment I'm there, at the corner of Fourth Street, but he's gone. Flying on instinct alone, I race five blocks west to a row of cheaper places with neon signs blazing the word "ROOMS" into the night. There are dozens of cheap rooms on the block, but twenty minutes later I've learned that only two have current registrants with polysyllabic Indian names. The first one is an extended family of itinerant pilgrims—three aunts, two uncles, six little kids, and the hundred-year-old grandfather—all staying together in one room, much to the irritation of the manager.

The second one has a single room rented to "Chirakall V. Shiva and son."

Hmmm.

I find him sitting by the window, staring out at the now-starry, now-cloudy sky.

I wait.

"Now what?" I say.

"Now it's finally over," he answers.

"It's not over. You have to help Trane."

"Who?"

"Trane. The guy Johnson sprayed with soda. He's going down for this murder if you don't—"

"Don't what? Give myself up? Who will take care of my son? You? Take a look at my son!"

And I do look at him, sleeping the deep sleep of the innocent, his huge head crowded between two carefully arranged pillows.

"The people's justice has been served," Vishal insists.

"Not completely. An innocent man is going to be charged with this crime."

"What crime? Johnson didn't even feel any pain," he says disgustedly. But soon, deep breaths dispel some of his anger. "What do you want me to do about it?"

There's no easy answer.

"You'll find a way. You've obviously been wrestling with plenty of demons," I say, walking out. "I'm sure you can subdue one more."

And I go back to my own child, my own innocent child, and cradle her until the glorious rosy dawn comes up and banishes all my fears of sudden, fleet-footed airborne death to that murky place where the shadows retreat to when the bright bands of daylight erase their presence, where they lie in wait for yet another opportunity to pierce my mortal shell with their poisonous spines of doubt and paranoia.

Happy holidays.

Wish you were here.

SERVE AND VOLLEY
A Jacob Burns Mystery Story

Matt Witten

Matt Witten's series character, Jacob Burns, made his first appearance in *Breakfast at Madeline's*. He has since made return engagements in *Grand Delusion* and *Strange Bedfellows*.

There's a lake in the Adirondacks we go to every summer. On the map it's called Jones Lake. But everyone who summers there calls it Lake Chutzpah.

The Lake Chutzpah story began over eighty years ago, when a hardy crew of Jewish schoolteachers and union activists from the Bronx pooled their meager resources, bought up the lake, and built cabins there. For two months every year, they escaped the capitalist rat race and rode the milk train up to the Adirondacks to live out their utopian socialist dreams. They sunned themselves on the beach, experimented with "free love," had lively all-night debates about how best to educate the workers, and held campaign rallies for Eugene V. Debs and Norman Thomas.

Now, at the dawn of a new millennium, those socialist dreams are as faded as an old campaign poster. Nevertheless, the descendants of the old Jewish leftists—sprinkled now with *goyim* and even, horror of horrors, the occasional Republican—keep on coming to Lake Chutzpah each year with their children and grandchildren.

Five years ago my family started coming, too. My wife Andrea knew someone in the community, so we were able to rent a house. This was no mean feat. Whenever a Lake Chutzpah-nik goes to that great Bundist Convention in the sky, and her descendants decide to rent out the house, there is always a mad scramble by potential tenants. We've rented the same place for five years, and we count our blessings.

Lake Chutzpah is as close to utopia as we'll ever find on this earth. In addition to the perfect sandy beach, there's a clapboard Community Center overlooking the water where you can go to Jewish folk dancing on Friday evenings, kids' game night on Sundays, and concerts and lectures on Tuesdays. Ping-Pong is anytime.

I mean, Lake Chutzpah does have its flaws. The Latts and the Pitkins have barely spoken to each other since the early sixties, when they got into an obscure tiff about landscaping. And harsh words are sometimes exchanged when octogenarians get bonked on the head by little children's wiffleballs at the beach.

But still, you should see the lake on a sunny July afternoon. No motorboats are allowed. The parents relax on beach chairs or sail their boats around the lake while the kids build sand castles and splash in the water. The teenagers swim out to the raft and flirt with each other, and the grandparents and great-grandparents hang out in the shade and tell stories that date back to the Great Depression—and beyond.

Another thing about the beach: I have never, ever seen a cell phone there.

Yes, in a world bereft of tradition, where we are reduced to searching for meaning on the Internet, Lake Chutzpah quietly and simply provides its lucky residents with a gift that people once took for granted, but has now become incredibly rare: a sense of community.

For members of our confused species, I can't think of anything more important.

It's so important, some people will kill for it.

It happened last year, on the Friday of July Fourth weekend. That's the first big weekend of summer, when most of the sixty Lake Chutzpah families arrive. The beach that day is awash with pale-looking folks hugging and shaking hands and *kvelling*.

"So how was your year?"

"You're looking great . . ."

"Did you hear Irving Bloom died . . ."

"God, your kids are so much bigger . . ."

I only see these folks for two months out of the year, but

I feel closer to them than I do to almost anyone in the "real world." That Friday I reconnected with Lenny, a Boston psychotherapist who told me all about his new mental health Web site, where you can get diagnosed for depression online; Stu, an old codger from Phillie who's the world's leading expert on Jewish boxers, and also has every album the Kingston Trio ever made; and Bennett, a bushy-bearded Connecticut professor who was compiling a dictionary for an ancient American Indian language that only has two native speakers still alive—and they're both about to kick off any day now.

Bennett's dictionary project seemed akin to all the other idealistic quests that have floated around Lake Chutzpah for the past eighty years. "You're a true Lake Chutzpah-nik, Bennett," I told him. "I'll bet you'd have made a great Trotskyite theorist."

"I really *am* a Lake Chutzpah-nik now, Jake," Bennett replied. "Gloria sold me her house."

"Wow. *Mazel tov,* buddy." Bennett was positively beaming. For seven years, he and his wife and daughter had rented a place from Mel Klavens's widow, Gloria. Every summer, Bennett would politely ask her if she was ready to sell. Evidently she had said yes at last.

I was jealous as hell. Like Bennett, I wanted to buy the house my family was renting. Our landlord lived in Seattle and hadn't been to Lake Chutzpah for twenty years. But for some reason, he still wasn't ready to sell. Sometimes I didn't mind being a renter, but on a gorgeous cloudless day like today, when the water sparkled, the fish jumped, Andrea and the kids were happy, and I was surrounded by friends, I wanted to be an *owner*. An official, permanent Lake Chutzpah-nik.

I wanted to fix it so today would last forever.

A couple of hours later, around four o'clock, my two sons Shaq and Kobe were in the water playing blindman's bluff with about twenty other kids. I hasten to mention that my boys' real names are Daniel and Nathan. But they like to give themselves nicknames, and Shaq and Kobe——for Shaquille

O'Neal and Kobe Bryant—were their new monikers this summer.

Our kids were being watched over by Debby, the new lifeguard. She was only sixteen, and she'd been on the job for just a week, but she seemed competent. She had a long nose and a body that wouldn't have looked good in a bikini, but she had a shy sort of cheerfulness that was very winning.

Meanwhile Andrea was sunning herself by the water with the other women. They were talking about whatever women talk about when men aren't around. Over by the trees, at the far end of the beach, sat the old-timers.

And as for the men under age sixty . . . we were all playing volleyball.

But when I say "volleyball," please don't think some laid-back California game. Lake Chutzpah volleyball is an entirely different animal. And that's exactly what we became as soon as we stepped onto that sandy court: animals.

Most—if not all—of the Lake Chutzpah men have very cerebral jobs out in the real world. We're professors, writers, lawyers, doctors. We don't get much chance to let out our base physical aggressions during the year. So when volleyball season finally arrives, we cut loose.

The first game of the year is especially riddled with raging hormones. That's when we begin establishing the new pecking order for the coming summer. We learn which forty-year-old guys have lost a step, and can't jump and spike with the same authority anymore. We learn which teenage boys have become men, and can now hold their own with the big guys.

Saddest of all, we learn which oldsters are no longer up to playing. On this particular Friday, when we were rounding up the players, Hal Arnold turned us down. "Sorry, guys," he said regretfully, shaking his balding head. "Don't think I'm up for it."

"You sure?" Eric Chansky asked. Eric was a volleyball stalwart, in his mid-forties but still one of the best players on the beach—arguably *the* best. He was in great shape, going on hundred-mile bike rides at the drop of a hat. Not only that, he was six feet two, with extra-long arms for spiking.

"Maybe I'll play a little later," Hal replied. But something in the way he said it told us that he wouldn't be playing much this year, if at all.

"Okay, Hal, hope you change your mind," I said. I didn't like seeing Hal go down. Five years ago, when I was first introduced to Lake Chutzpah volleyball, he was still a tough player. The guys said that fifteen or twenty years ago, Hal had been the king of the beach.

Everyone else that we asked to play said yes. We were afraid Chuck Tabatznik would turn us down, since he had a brace on his knee and had made noises about a strained ligament. But he assured us nothing short of death would keep him off the volleyball court. "Hey, I'm only forty-seven," he said. "Not time to crap out on volleyball just yet."

For years, Chuck had been the other main contender for Lake Chutzpah MVP. He and Eric were pretty evenly matched, and they were better than any of the young teenage boys who were starting to build up their strength and volleyball savvy. Chuck was only six feet tall at most, no taller than myself, but he had a fierce competitive spirit and letter-perfect timing on his spike. He always hit the ball at the exact moment when it was at the top of its arc, and his hits had so much power that the player facing him could rarely block them. I couldn't count the number of times Chuck had stuffed me.

Myself, I'm a pretty average player. On a good day I can spike with some regularity; on a bad day, my spikes seem to either hit the net, go long, or get blocked right back to me. Five years ago, when I started playing volleyball, I was already thirty-seven. I figure by the time I get enough experience to play really well, I'll be too old.

Ah well, such is life. In the meantime, I'll enjoy being average.

"Good to see you," I told Chuck as he joined Eric and me on our rounds of the beach, picking up players.

"Likewise," Chuck replied, and then quickly turned to Eric and asked him something about the volleyball net.

Chuck and I had an odd, strained relationship. I say "strained" because we basically never talked to each other, beyond volleyball pleasantries. I say "odd" because we used to talk to each other all the time.

Like me, Chuck was a screenwriter. The first three summers I went to Lake Chutzpah, Chuck and I used to spend a lot of time sitting on the raft, dangling our toes in the water, and *kvetching* about the incredible foolishness of all those Hollyweird dingbats who failed to recognize our true greatness.

But then, two years ago, a strange thing happened: I actually sold a screenplay. Even stranger, I sold it for a million dollars. Ever since then, Chuck had steered clear of me.

My other old artsy friends were pretty cool about my sudden rise to fame and fortune—or even if they weren't, at least they pretended to be. If they were secretly rooting for me to write a sequel that bombed, or get addicted to meth, they never let on.

But Chuck was different. He never even congratulated me on my big sale. Once, when we found ourselves alone on the raft together, I tried to talk to him about the change in our relationship. But he mumbled something about having to take his teenage son sailing and dove off into the water.

Maybe one day Chuck and I would be friends again. Until then, we always had volleyball.

We wound up with fourteen players that day, enough for seven on a team. That was more crowded than we would have liked, but we couldn't very well tell anybody no. That would be a scandal.

Once we got everyone together, it was time to choose up sides. This was always a delicate task, fraught with emotion. You want even teams, but you don't want to be too obvious about saying which players are good and which are lousy.

Eric usually took the lead in tough situations like these. A high school principal from Long Island, he was a natural leader. Also, he'd been coming to Lake Chutzpah all his life, and his great-grandparents had been among the Original Settlers back in 1913, which gave him an automatic air of authority in our community. Even Chuck, who'd been coming to Lake Chutzpah since he was two, was a newcomer compared to Eric.

So it was Eric who stood by the net and summoned an air of studied casualness as he said, "Well, let's see, I guess we should choose up sides."

Jay, a rabbi from Brooklyn, spoke up. "Just don't put me on Barry's team, he practically broke my ribs running into me last year."

"Are you kidding?" protested Barry, a famous defense lawyer from Newton. "You ran into *me*!"

Similar joshing broke out among several other players, but it all felt forced. Despite our jokes and exaggeratedly relaxed postures as we stood around, we all knew this was the beginning of the Big Test. Our physical skills were about to be measured against those of the Other Men. Our rank in humanity was about to be assigned.

Of course, Eric was only one guy. And maybe our play in the ensuing volleyball games would change our ranking, and we'd be viewed differently by Eric and everyone else next time, and our standing in the community would go up.

But for now, this was where we'd start off. We were about to find out how good, how *manly*, we were considered to be.

We stood waiting with bated breath.

Now at this point, you may be wondering—especially if you're of the female persuasion, and have always found guys puzzling—why in the world a bunch of grown men with such obvious accomplishments out in the professional world would take a mere game of volleyball so darn seriously.

Well . . . what can I say? The moment brought back primal memories from elementary school, of waiting for the team captains to call out your name when they chose up sides, and praying that you wouldn't suffer the abject humiliation of getting picked last.

Unfortunately for socialism, there's something about raw competition that just plain hits the spot.

So there we stood, awaiting Eric's verdict. He lazily scratched his ear, trying in vain to downplay the terrible importance of what he was doing. "Well, I guess me and Chuck should be on different sides," he drawled. "And then how about David, Jay, and Barry with Chuck . . . and Bennett, Jake, and, Joel with me . . ."

Note how he picked six guys at once. This was an excellent maneuver on Eric's part, the sort of masterstroke that made his leadership role more than merely hereditary.

You see, now any of us six could secretly imagine that he

was being labeled the third-best player. Eric had succeeded in smoothing the hard edges of our competition—

My admiration for Eric was rudely interrupted when Joel, a seventeen-year-old who must have shot up a foot in the past year, spoke up. "Eric, you sure you and me should be on the same side?" he said. "Wouldn't that make the teams unfair?"

Everyone stared at him. What the heck was this kid saying?

Actually, we knew *exactly* what he was saying. He was claiming to be as good a player as Eric—and claiming it would be unfair to the opposition if he and Eric were teamed together.

He was also supremely dissing Chuck. He was saying to him, you're history, baby. I have hereby supplanted you in the Lake Chutzpah hierarchy as Eric's main opponent.

We all looked over at Chuck. His lips tightened. He didn't say a word.

Nobody else knew what to say, either. Joel was being incredibly gauche. We Lake Chutzpah-niks are not a trash-talking bunch—not in the way Joel did it, anyway. We don't just tell somebody, hey, you're no good anymore.

Finally Eric found his tongue. "I think the teams will be okay this way," he said, and then moved on quickly to choose up the rest of the sides.

Joel's arrogance shouldn't have been so surprising, given that he came from a wealthy, self-centered, Upper East Side family that felt they were entitled to the world, and then some. The father, Gordon, had inherited a multimillion-dollar business from *his* father. The mother, Sylvia, had inherited a multimillion-dollar business from *her* father. Their skill at picking rich parents seemed to have convinced them that they were the smartest, best-looking people in the world.

They did have the best-looking house in Lake Chutzpah, I'll give them that.

As for Joel, he had apparently blossomed into some kind of amazing baseball star during the past year. Or at least that's what his parents had been noisily proclaiming on the beach that afternoon. According to them, eight major league scouts had already come to watch him pitch for his high school team.

Well, hopefully his baseball skills wouldn't translate to volleyball, because I wanted to see Chuck whup his ass today—even if Chuck was on the other team.

The game began pretty well for our side. We were playing 3-2-2—three up, two middle, two back. Eric started out in the front row, and he put Joel in the back, no doubt as an unspoken punishment for his rudeness.

Meanwhile Chuck started out in the back, too. This decision surprised me at first. Why hadn't he put himself in the front, so he could face off against Eric, like he always did? Then I understood. He was fixing it so he'd have a chance to spike it down Joel's throat. The two of them would hit the front row at the same time.

The only problem with this strategy was, it left no one of Eric's caliber on their front row. Jay, the Brooklyn rabbi, was tall and gangly and not bad, but he couldn't fight Eric off. Eric got us started with a spike and a block to make it 2 to 0.

At that point Eric showed his characteristic generosity, passing up a couple of half-decent spiking opportunities to give me two beautiful sets right at the net. I was able to hammer it home both times, and felt like a champ. Okay, so I was faced off against a five-foot-nine fifteen-year-old, but still. Four, zip.

We lost the serve when they hit the ball into a no-man's-land between three of our guys. Any one of them could have hit it, but they all let it go. Typical first-game-of-the-summer miscommunication.

Then their server found a hole in our game—namely Steve, the microbiologist in our back row. He served it to Steve repeatedly, and Steve kept hitting the ball sideways, backward, downward . . . any way but forward. Before we knew it, the game was tied at four.

From then on it was a hard-fought battle: a spike here, a dink shot there . . . a point for us, a point for them, a change of serve . . .

And now the score was 13 to 12. They had the lead but we had the serve. We were playing to 15, so it was crunch time.

Our team rotated into position. Eric was with me in the back row. Bennett, the Indian language expert, was in the middle row. That was ideal—he was our best setup man.

And smack dab in the middle of our front row was the up and coming whippersnapper Joel. Standing opposite him was the old lion, Chuck.

It was my turn to serve, which is the strongest part of my game, if I do say so myself. I generally aim for the far right corner, giving the other guy, if he's right-handed, an awkward shot. Sometimes he'll miss; more often he'll hit it, but saddle the next guy with a somewhat awkward second shot. Then their team will have a tough time setting up a good spike.

I was serving to the fifteen-year-old, so I had a pretty good feeling about it. I got myself ready and whacked the ball.

The kid had to scramble. He managed to hit the ball straight up in the air. Somebody raced over and kept the ball alive, but it stayed in their back row. The best their third guy could do was hit a nice easy floater over the net. It went straight to Bennett.

Bennett had all the time in the world to get right under the ball. He lofted it, soft as a balloon, to Joel's sweet spot—a foot above the net and a foot to this side of it. A perfect set. The whole thing was like slow motion. Joel jumped up . . . Chuck jumped up to block . . .

And Joel rammed it right down his throat.

"Nice shot, Joel," Eric said.

Joel let out a noisy war whoop.

Chuck just pursed his lips.

Not wanting to congratulate Joel, who was starting to really piss me off, I congratulated Bennett instead. "Great set," I told him.

Of course Joel didn't even think to thank Bennett. He was too busy carrying on.

The ball came back to me. I served again. This one was even better than before. Once again the other team had to scramble to get the ball over, and once again it eased down lazily toward Bennett's waiting arms. He gave Joel another perfectly placed balloon.

This time Chuck timed his jump perfectly, and I thought he'd have Joel's shot blocked. But Joel smashed the ball so hard and so fast, it caromed off Chuck's arm and went way out of bounds into the woods. The fifteen-year-old kid had to run to retrieve it.

Joel pointed his finger at Chuck, as if to say, "Don't mess with me, old-timer." A couple of the other teenagers on the court whooped it up. "The new generation!" one of them shouted as he slapped Joel five. Usually they were sweet kids, not given to trash talking, but Joel brought out the worst in them.

Meanwhile Chuck just looked down and pawed at the sand with his toes.

"Good play, Joel," Eric said, but then pulled him aside, as surreptitiously as possible—which wasn't very surreptitious—and said quietly, "Look, go easy on the celebrating, all right?"

Joel just shrugged and went back to his position. The score was 14–13, us. One more point and we'd win.

Bennett called out encouragement to me. "One more, baby!"

"You got it," I replied. I planted my feet and served again to their far right corner . . .

You'd think the fifteen-year-old would have figured out my game plan by now and made some adjustments. But no, once again he was out of position, and once again they were unable to give Chuck a set. This time, though, instead of the ball sailing down toward Bennett like a giant soap bubble waiting to be blessed, it sailed toward me.

And in that nanosecond when the ball hovered above me, I made a decision.

I decided I didn't want that jerk Joel to get another easy spike—even if it meant my team losing the game.

So instead of setting up Joel, or hitting the ball to Bennett so he could set up Joel, I took a third option. I gave a nice set to Tommy, a sixteen-year-old kid in our front row.

The ball was well placed, and Tommy was big enough and athletic enough to drive it home. I could feel him getting ready to do just that. But at the last moment, Joel shouted "Set me!" Tommy, no doubt intimidated by the older boy, changed course and lofted the ball to Joel.

But it wasn't a great set. It reached the apex of its flight right above the net itself. In other words, it was an equally good set for both Joel and Chuck. In fact, it was slightly better for Chuck, because the ball was coming straight toward him and therefore easier to judge and smash.

Chuck jumped high in the air.

Joel jumped, too.

The ball floated above them.

Chuck reached out to slam it.

Joel's arm flicked out. He gave the ball a little sideways tap.

Chuck's arm hit nothing except the net itself. He fell down to the sand and screamed.

The ball landed next to him. We'd won the point—and the game.

Chuck was writhing in agony. We all ran up to him, or at least all of us older guys did. Joel was busy celebrating his glorious victory.

"Chuck, you all right?" Eric asked.

"Damn knee," he groaned. "I'm fine." Then he looked up and pointed an accusatory finger at Joel. "You were over the net!"

Joel waved his arm dismissively. "No way. That was a clean hit."

"Bullshit!" Chuck jumped up, wincing with pain. "You were a foot over the fucking net!" He turned to the rest of us. "Come on, wasn't he over the net?"

Eric, Bennett, and I looked at each other. None of us was sure if Chuck had a legit beef or not. It had happened too quickly.

Ordinarily, with a game on the line, we would have shown team spirit and acted like we were sure Chuck was wrong. "Forget about it! He was on this side!" we would have yelled. We'd have insisted on taking the point, and the game.

But with Chuck injured and Joel acting like a first-class jerk, our team spirit was a little shaken. "Why don't we do the point over," Eric said.

Joel paused in his high fives with Tommy. "What, are you crazy?"

"You were three feet over the net!" Chuck yelled.

"Come on, you got beat!" Joel yelled back.

"Joel, enough. We'll do it over. Get back in position," I said.

"We won the game," Joel complained loudly. "Why should we do it over just because he feels bad?"

"Fuck you," Chuck said.

"Hey," Eric cut in, "let's all try to act like grown-ups. Go ahead, Jake, serve it again."

"Time out," Chuck interrupted. He turned to the fifteen-year-old. "Listen, play on the line. That's where he's serving it."

The kid dutifully moved over to the line. It took away my best play. But the kid might very well be too psyched out by now to make a decent shot. Maybe I should just hit it to him anyway . . .

Or maybe I should turn traitor.

And that's what I decided to do. I hit the ball high and straight to Jay, the rabbi in the back row.

The rabbi had plenty of time to loft it to the defense lawyer in the front, who set it up for Chuck, just as nice and easy as you please. You could practically feel Chuck salivating. The volleyball wafted through the air toward him . . . Chuck leaped . . . his long, powerful right arm smashed the ball—

—right into Joel's forearm, high above the net. The ball came crashing down on Chuck's side. It rolled away on the sand. We'd won.

Joel had won.

"He did it again!" Chuck yelled. "He was on my side!"

"You're dreaming," Joel shot back. "I killed you. It was a perfect block!"

Both of them looked to Eric for his verdict. Eric turned to Chuck and just shook his head slightly. It was the only possible decision. We'd given Chuck a break once, we couldn't do it twice in a row. "Good game, guys," Eric said. "You ready to go again?"

"No, screw this," Chuck said. "Kid's an asshole. I'm going sailing."

He limped off the court. I wondered if his knee was hurting, and that was the real reason he was taking off.

Joel got in the last word. "Anytime you wanna try again," he told Chuck, "I'm ready for you."

Chuck stared at him, then limped away. Eric and I turned to each other and rolled our eyes. Chuck was right. What an asshole.

That night was the big July Fourth campfire. This being a semisocialist kind of place, we didn't go too big on the patriotic end of things. There were no fireworks, for instance. But we had plenty of marshmallows and folk songs.

In addition to doctors and lawyers, the Lake Chutzpah community boasted a fair number of talented musicians. One guy had even won an Oscar for his music composing, and another was a violinist with the Philadelphia Symphony Orchestra. But the way they both acted that night, strumming their guitars by the campfire and leading us in the old tunes, you could see that "Kumbaya," "We Shall Overcome," and "Union Maid" still meant more to them than any fancy music they'd heard since then.

Andrea, myself, and the rest of the Lake Chutzpah grownups sat on logs and sang along, while Shaq and Kobe played Capture the Flag with the rest of the preteens. As for the teenagers, I'm not sure but I think they were skinny-dipping down at the beach.

The fire was crackling, the moon shone brightly, Andrea was sitting beside me, and the songs of my youth were just as beautiful as ever. All was right with the world.

After a rousing rendition of "Puff the Magic Dragon," I got up to hit the bathroom at the far end of the community center. I ran into Chuck coming out. It was the first time I'd seen him up-close and personal since the big game.

"Hey, how's it going?" I asked. "Gonna sit by the fire and pretend we're kids in summer camp?"

"First I gotta go over to the Katebs and get more firewood."

"Need help?" I offered, a little unwillingly, since that meant I'd miss precious music time. On the other hand, it would be nice to spend a few minutes with Chuck, see if we could smooth out our relationship.

"No, I can do it, they have a wheelbarrow. Fucking Joel,"

he continued without a pause, as if that had been the real content of our conversation all along. "Can you believe that guy?"

I don't know why I came to his defense, but I did. Some perverse ornery streak. "He's young, he doesn't know any better. He'll grow up."

"No, he's a prick and he'll always be a prick, just like his father. You know what Gordon did last year?"

Gordon Marx was the father. "No, what?"

"Wanted to buy my house. How much do you think my house is worth?"

Chuck's place was just a small two-bedroom, though it did have a big backyard you could build an addition in if you had the bucks. I figured it was worth fifty or fifty-five thousand, but I guessed high to flatter him. "I don't know, sixty or seventy?"

"Yeah, well, the scumbag offered me a hundred. Thought he could just *buy* me."

"Hey, you can't get mad at him for trying to throw money at you."

"Arrogant shit thinks I'm gonna trip all over myself bowing down to his money. Just because I didn't make a million bucks on some screenplay doesn't mean I'm desperate."

This was the closest we'd ever come to discussing my movie sale. "Listen, Chuck," I began—

"Skip it," he said roughly. "All I'm saying, Joel's a fuckhead from a long line of fuckheads. I better go get that wood."

Then Chuck went off without another word.

Next time I saw him, he was in police custody for murder.

What happened, we were in the middle of the old John Lennon ditty, "Give Peace a Chance," when we heard police sirens come screaming toward us. We assumed they were heading down the road toward the town of Lake Luzerne, to deal with drunken revelers who'd set off one firecracker too many. But then the siren stopped close by, and we could see the bulb atop the cop car flashing through the trees.

"Looks like they're at the Marx place," someone said. Gordon and Sylvia Marx jumped up from the fireplace, where they'd been singing along too, and ran back to their house. Sylvia was yelling "My God, what happened?" the whole way.

Andrea, myself, and several others followed behind to see if we could help. But by the time we got there, it was too late.

Joel was already dead.

He lay on the ground in the Marxes' driveway, right by their BMW. A rivulet of blood ran from Joel's cracked head to the ground. A small fawn made of wrought iron, one of the Marxes' kitschy yard decorations, was facedown on the driveway, beside the body. It looked like the fawn had been the murder weapon.

As for Chuck, he was in the police car with a cop guarding him.

Sylvia was kneeling by the body, weeping hysterically. Harry Kateb's elderly wife Barbara was holding her. Gordon was doubled over, looking like he was about to pass out.

"How could he die?" Sylvia screamed. "He's my boy!"

Shivers ran down my spine. I felt horrible about disliking Joel and his parents so much. Nobody deserved this.

"Sit down, honey," Barbara said.

"It's not fair! He was gonna play for the Yankees one day!" Sylvia said plaintively.

Barbara hugged her as she sobbed.

Harry Kateb was there too, talking to the police. He was eighty-five years old and frail, with long unruly white hair, but still mentally sharp. He was a retired dentist, but looked a little like Einstein.

"I figured I'd just bring the logs down to the fire myself," Harry was explaining. "It's not too hard, I have a wheelbarrow. So I'm on my way past the Marx place when I spot the young fellow, Chuck, at the top of the driveway. I say hi to him, but he's just standing there. Then I look where he's looking. The BMW is over there with the door open. And the boy, Joel, is lying on the ground with that stupid deer on top of him. I never did like that deer."

"Did Chuck say anything to you?" the cop closest to Joel asked, his voice high and excited. In his early twenties with slicked-back hair, he looked like he was having the biggest thrill of his life.

"Yeah," Harry replied. "He just kept saying, 'Oh shit oh shit oh shit' over and over again."

Gordon spoke up. He was still doubled over. "He killed him," he said in a hoarse whisper. "The bastard killed my son!"

I moved away from them and headed over to the cop car. The window was rolled down an inch. I looked in at Chuck.

Chuck looked back at me. "I didn't do it," he said frantically, "I was just walking by."

A burly cop stepped toward me, nightstick in hand. "Away from the car, please."

"I swear to God, Jake," Chuck said imploringly, holding me with his frightened brown eyes, *"I didn't do it."*

The cop pushed me away from there. But Chuck's eyes stayed with me.

I spent a lot of time in the shower during the next couple of days, because that's where I do my best thinking. When faced with an especially thorny problem, I've been known to stay in the shower for literally an hour. Terrible for the environment, I know. I try to make up for it by being extra conscientious with recycling.

But besides making me squeaky clean, my long showers didn't do me any good that weekend. Neither did my long swims at the lake. I just kept pondering the same question, over and over: Would a guy really commit murder because his manhood was challenged?

Well . . . yes, I guess. Happens all the time. But I kept seeing Chuck's eyes. Call it a hunch, or call me a fool, but I *believed* them.

I'd talked to Chuck before he went for firewood. That was right around the time Joel got killed. Chuck was pissed off, sure. But homicidal?

On the other hand, if he didn't do it, then who did? Joel inspired dislike in people, no doubt about it; but who hated him enough to bop him over the head with an iron objet d'art?

I broached the subject with other Lake Chutzpah-niks at the beach, but nobody seemed to have any ideas. The mood that weekend was somber despite the blue skies. The old-timers spoke in hushed tones beneath the big willow tree. Nobody played volleyball. Shaq, Kobe, and the other little kids made a small coffin out of sand to memorialize Joel.

To make matters even worse, Debby the lifeguard was freaked out by this whole turn of events. She came to work the day after the murder as usual, but that night she called the head of the beach committee and told him she was quitting to work at the Gap in the mall. That left us without a life-guard for the foreseeable future, meaning that whenever our kids went in the water, we'd have to watch over them care-fully ourselves. No more afternoon naps or paperback read-ing sessions. I know that's not really a big deal, but it was another annoying irritation.

"This is turning into quite a summer," I said to Andrea as we lay in bed together Sunday night.

"I'm surprised Debby quit," Andrea said. "She seemed so levelheaded."

"Well, I guess murders can freak people out."

"I guess so," she said, and that was the end of that con-versation.

But the next morning, while I was soaping under my left arm in the shower, I got an idea.

I jumped out, toweled off, and left the house. I lied and told Andrea I was going into town for a newspaper. I didn't want her and the kids to know what I was up to, because they'd get all riled up. The last time I got involved in a mur-der, it disrupted the family routine for months. The thing is, they tend to get scared I'll get murdered, too.

As soon as I was out of the house and out of their sight, I switched directions and walked toward the cabin of Joel's best friend at Lake Chutzpah, Tommy. The kid was outside when I got there, pitching horseshoes by himself on the front lawn. He looked a little startled when I approached.

"Hitting any ringers?" I asked.

"A few." He pitched another one. It was way off.

"I'm awfully sorry about Joel."

Tommy nodded and pitched again. Even further away.

"Listen, Tommy, would you mind if I ask you a couple of questions?"

"About what?" he said suspiciously.

"I'm wondering how long Joel was here this summer before he got killed."

Tommy turned to face me. "I've heard about you. You
think you're some kind of Colombo. You're gonna try to get
Chuck off somehow."

"Only if he didn't do it."

"But he *did* do it."

"How do you know?" Tommy didn't answer. "Come on,
just answer my question, okay?"

Tommy sighed, then said, "He was here a week."

"So he must have gotten to know Debby."

"A little," Tommy said warily.

"How little is 'a little'?"

"I don't know," Tommy said. "Look, you were at that
volleyball game. You *know* Chuck killed Joel."

Then Tommy's lip started to tremble, and he walked away
from me into his house.

By the time I got back home, Andrea and the kids were
gone. They left a note that they were crayfishing in the
nearby creek, and I should feel free to join them. Instead I got
in my car and had breakfast at a nearby diner, then went out
to the mall.

It was ten-fifteen when I got to the Gap, and except for me
there were only two other customers. There were two store
clerks: a prim-looking young woman in her early twenties
and Debby.

"Hi, Debby," I said.

She didn't look too happy to see me. "Hi."

"Listen, I need to talk to you for a few minutes."

She glanced uneasily at the other woman, probably her
boss. "I'm busy."

"It's about Joel's death."

"Why are you asking *me*?"

"Why don't you take a short break? I'm sure your boss
won't mind. The store's not exactly crowded."

"I can't. This is only my second day."

The hell with it. I'd ask my questions right then and there,
if I had to. "Debby, how well did you know Joel?"

Her shoulders hunched up anxiously. "Not that well."

I'm not the world's most perceptive guy when it comes to

body language, but this time I could tell. She was lying through her teeth. I decided to lie, too. "Tommy says you were Joel's girlfriend."

No quiet lip trembling for this girl. She burst straight into tears. Then she walked away from me. I followed her. She went into the women's bathroom. I followed her in there, too.

Debby blew her nose, then gave me an aggressive look through her wet eyes. "So I went out with him, so what?"

"And what happened? Did he break up with you?"

"No. Look, it was just a casual summer thing."

"If it was so casual, then why'd you quit your lifeguard job?"

"I was bored. You have to sit there all day and do nothing."

"You'll never make me believe working at the Gap is more fun than being a lifeguard. Don't lie to me, Debby. You were with him that night, weren't you?"

"No, I was with my brother."

I tried to make my voice gentle. "Look, if you got in a lovers' quarrel, maybe he hit you, you hit him back, that's not murder, that's just an accident. What are you, sixteen? You won't even have to go to jail."

Debby blew her nose again.

"You can't carry this around with you all your life. You have to come clean."

"I told you, I was with my brother," Debby said emphatically. "We were seeing a movie."

And then she left the bathroom and walked back to the cash register, where she rang up a customer's purchase. I couldn't get another word out of her.

Fortunately I had a pretty good idea where her brother was. Beach gossip had spread the word that he worked at Von's Ice Cream and Miniature Golf, just down the road from Lake Chutzpah. So I drove over there right away, hoping to get to him before Debby called and asked him to confirm her alibi.

There was a teenage boy at Von's with the same long nose that Debby had. I asked him for a scoop of soft vanilla, then said, "You must be Debby's brother."

"Yup," he replied.

"I'm from Lake Chutzpah. We really miss her there."

This time he didn't even say "Yup." How could I get him to open up?

"I guess she was pretty upset about Joel. She was going out with him, wasn't she?"

The brother shot me a look filled with sudden anger. "Debby told me you might come. Look, we were at a god-damn movie that night."

"What was the movie?"

"None of your business."

"You want me to go to the cops?"

"You're crazy," the brother said. "Debby would never have killed Joel in a lovers' quarrel. She knew it was just a fling. You think she's stupid enough to get all wrapped up in a guy like him?"

"Evidently she was."

"Look, we're *locals*, okay? Debby was having some fun with him, but hey, he's from a different planet. I mean, his parents were buying him a house, for God's sake. You think our parents could ever buy us a house?"

This was the first I'd heard about this. "What do you mean, his parents were buying him a house?"

"Right at Lake Chutzpah. His parents made the deal last week. I'm surprised you didn't know."

I was surprised, too. Usually any house purchases become instant fodder for Lake Chutzpah gossip. What was going on here? Had Joel's parents been playing it close to the vest for some reason?

Then all of a sudden it hit me. *Oh, Lord.* I hoped to hell I was wrong. But I had to find out.

I went to the pay phone outside Von's. First I called Joel's mother, Sylvia. Then I made another call.

Both calls confirmed my suspicions. My stomach churned. I was pretty sure I saw a way to clear Chuck of mur-der. But what I was about to do was dreadful.

Still, I had no choice. I got back in my car and drove to Joel's murderer's house.

I parked in his front yard. Then I walked up the path and knocked on his door.

His wife answered. She said he'd just gone up to the lake

to go sailing. I wished I didn't like the wife. I wished I didn't like their eight-year-old kid.

I ran to the lake, my heart pumping like mad, so I could catch my prey before he went out into the water. I needn't have hurried. He was sitting in the lifeguard's chair, looking out over the lake. Just sitting there, thoughtfully scratching his beard. He was alone. It was only eleven-twenty, and people generally didn't hit the beach until after noon.

"Hi, Bennett," I said.

He gave me a nervous look, then composed his face into a placid expression. "Hi, Jake, what's up?"

"Still excited about buying the Klavenses' house?" I asked.

He turned away from me. "Yeah," he said.

I stepped closer to him. "I hear it was a close call."

His body tensed. "What do you mean?"

"I talked to Sylvia Marx today. She said she'd been planning to buy the Klavenses' house for Joel."

Bennett didn't say anything.

I steeled myself to continue. Playing hard-ass doesn't come naturally to me. "Kind of a good thing for you Joel got killed, isn't it?"

Bennett's face started to crumple. Some people make good murderers, some don't.

But he tried to cover. "What a terrible thing to say."

"Not as terrible as killing him. Where were you Friday night?"

He blanched. "Are you insinuating something?"

"You weren't at the campfire."

"Sure, I was."

"Not till after Joel got killed."

"Look—"

"Bennett, I just called Gloria Klavens. She says you were on the phone with her Friday night. You were going ballistic because she was backing out of her deal with you. She was selling the house to the Marxes instead."

Bennett just sat there on the lifeguard's chair with his mouth hanging open.

"Here's what happened. You got off the phone with Glo-

ria. You were in a rage. You went straight to the Marxes'
house to confront them."

"No—"

"You ran into Joel. You had words. You picked up the
deer. Then you killed him."

"That's—that's not true."

"Yes, it is. There's an innocent man in jail right now, suf-
fering for your crime. And the cops will be able to prove it.
There's your phone records, and I'm sure you made other
mistakes, too. You should have stuck to philology."

Bennett started to cry. I seemed to be good at making people cry. His tears fell into his brown beard.

"I'm sorry, Bennett," I said sincerely. "You really should
turn yourself in. Maybe they'll give you a break."

Bennett's shoulders were heaving with sobs. I put my
hand on one of them. "What happened, Bennett?"

He finally looked up at me. "I didn't . . . mean to," he
said, gasping for breath. "I just wanted to . . . talk to Gordon.
But he wasn't there . . . and Joel drove up in that white BMW
of his . . . and I asked him where Gordon was."

Bennett started to get his breath back as remembered fury
surged back into him. "That goddamn kid. He said to me,
'You're too late, pal. We already bought that house you
wanted.' So I said something, and he started giving me shit,
like, 'Hey, we're richer than you, and we offered more
money, so screw off.' I was just so upset, I mean, we rented
that house for seven years. Gloria *promised* us that house. It
was *ours*. And Joel got this really snide look on his face, and
he said, 'Don't feel bad, maybe we'll rent it out to you for long
weekends sometimes.' And I just couldn't take it anymore.
I . . . picked up that stupid deer and I . . . I hit him."

Bennett grabbed at his hair. "I didn't mean to kill him, I
swear. You really think they'll give me a break?"

I had no idea. "Sure, they will."

"All I wanted," said Bennett, "was a house. So I could be
part of the community. That's all."

Bennett turned himself in later that day, and the legal
wheels began turning.

I guess Bennett was already more a part of the community

than he realized, because a lot of Lake Chutzpah-niks pitched in to help him. Barry, the hotshot lawyer from Newton, took charge of his defense, and a psychiatrist from New Rochelle testified that Bennett had been extremely emotionally disturbed. A bunch of other Lake Chutzpah-niks, including myself, testified on his behalf as character witnesses.

In the end, the Newton lawyer plea-bargained it down to second-degree manslaughter, three to six years.

Not only that, Bennett is serving his time in a minimum security facility at Mt. McGregor, not far from Lake Chutzpah. It's not such a bad place.

I hear they even have volleyball.

SWEET REWARDS
A Dr. Watson Mystery Story

Wayne Worcester

Wayne Worcester's two mysteries featuring Sherlock Holmes and Dr. Watson are *The Monster of St. Marylebone* and *The Jewel of Covent Garden*. In this story he provides a fitting last line for the collection.

Until Lady Pembroke suddenly keeled over in the lobby of our hotel, Sherlock Holmes had more or less resigned himself to having a bad vacation.

One moment the dowdy old lady was standing directly in front of him, waiting for the concierge to present her with a bill; the next, she made a sound much like a gasp, dropped the outsized leather traveling bag she had been holding tightly to her bosom, clutched her throat with both hands, and fell stiffly backward flat onto the floor.

Holmes had been standing directly behind her, scowling and impatiently shifting his weight from one foot to the other. When the woman began to fall, he did nothing to prevent it. In fact, he twisted sideways, turned his head sharply, and followed her rapid progress all the way to the floor. The back of Lady Pembroke's head hit the highly polished wooden surface with a crack like a rifle shot.

The detective winced slightly. He made a quizzical and tight throaty noise, something like "Hmm," and bent over even farther for a closer look.

As he did so, his expression changed quite dramatically. His gray eyes were wide and alive with anticipation where only a moment ago they had seemed hard and almost lifeless.

Sherlock Holmes despised taking a holiday, you see, and I understood why: he enjoyed his work so thoroughly, found it so invigorating and engaging, that the prospect of several days' inactivity was downright loathsome.

I had broached the idea of a brief vacation months earlier, but he had balked from the start.

"The criminal elements would have a field day in my absence," Holmes said.

"We won't tell them you're gone," I replied. He did not catch the sarcasm in my voice, or if he did, he chose not to respond to it, which was rather more likely.

"They will know."

"Really, Holmes," I protested. "We are only talking about a few days' respite at the shore. You will be back in town before anyone knows you're gone."

"Hhmph!"

Despite his many protestations, I persisted. I looked for ways to raise the issue, and by mid-July, even the weather conspired to help me. The temperature climbed to an oppressive height and stayed there for five consecutive days. Fetid air sat heavy and listless like a noisome blanket all over London.

After supper one evening in our quarters at 221B Baker Street, I told Holmes flatly that I thought he looked more worn and tired than I had seen him in years. I could not actually see his face at that moment because it was hidden behind a newspaper, but that changed abruptly. Holmes sat up, crumpled the newspaper in anger, and dropped it on the table.

"All right, Watson," he announced. "All right. I give up. I will take a brief vacation, but only because I can think of no other way to end your infernal nagging."

"Very good, old boy," I said. "Just getting out of this heat will do us both some good. Where will it be, then? What do you fancy?"

"This is your idea, Watson," Holmes said pointedly. "You decide."

"Brighton, then," I said.

Holmes rolled his eyes.

"Very well. Shoreham By Sea, then. It's just west of Brighton, and right on the Channel, but not nearly as popular or crowded as Brighton. Yes, that will do nicely."

For most of the train ride down, the great detective had sat looking forlornly out of the window.

I did not care. The farther we traveled from London, the

brighter, clearer, and sunnier the day had become, and I found my own disposition changing accordingly.

From the train station in Brighton, we hired a ride to Shoreham By Sea. I asked the driver for a recommendation and it was not long before our hansom pulled up outside a grand-looking old hotel called The Arms Royale. A long fine beach lay directly across the way. I stepped from the hansom, took a deep breath, and exhaled loudly.

"Aah!" I exclaimed. "Wonderful! Give yourself half a chance, my good man, and you will love vacation, I assure you."

"Once more, Watson, you have missed my point entirely. I abhor inaction. The locale does not matter. Why is that so difficult to comprehend? Hmm? Why?"

"Even a fine machine must rest, Holmes."

"Not if it's properly made, Watson, and I . . ."

"Excuse me, gentlemen . . ."

It was the driver.

"If'n you'd take your bags, I could be off."

"Oh, yes, of course," I said. "Sorry about that."

The interruption effectively ended our argument, at least for the moment. Holmes waved off the porter, and we gathered up our few bags and marched to the front desk with a knot of other arriving guests.

I heard the concierge say, "Ah, Lady Pembroke, just one moment." I saw him turn away and the next sound I heard was the poor woman's head hitting the floor.

Before I could move to her side, three people who very obviously were part of the hotel staff hustled through the patrons milling about the lobby and gathered beside the fallen woman. They shouldered her upright with an efficiency born of experience, and quietly half walked, half dragged her to an overstuffed chair in a sitting area off the lobby.

I started toward them. "I'm a doctor," I said. "I'll give you a hand."

The concierge spoke quickly. "No need sir. Lady Pembroke . . . well, our responsibility. She's been a guest many times and, you see, she is prone to such spells. Hot weather and, well . . . tight laces. I'm certain that you understand. She looked a bit under at breakfast, too, but I am sure she will be fine in a bit. The staff will care for her. Really, sir."

"Very well," I said.

Holmes was watching Lady Pembroke's removal in silence. His lips were drawn as tight as the strings of a purse. His brow was furrowed. He appeared caught between pensiveness and puzzlement.

"Your names, please, gentlemen," the concierge said. "Sir, your names pl . . ."

Before I could answer, Holmes turned to him and said, "Goodrich. John W. Goodrich. My companion is Dr. James Winston. Accommodations for three nights."

I was startled, of course, but I said nothing. Clearly, something was amiss. Holmes picked up the bag nearest him, the porter collected the rest, and we followed him to our rooms, a spacious suite on the first floor facing the sea.

The instant the door closed, Holmes opened the suitcase he had been carrying and unceremoniously dumped its contents on the floor.

"Quickly, Watson," he said, "bolt the door."

As I did so, Holmes set the empty suitcase on the bed, opened it wide, and began kneading the lining of the bag with the tips of his long, nimble fingers. He stopped at a point midway up the side, opened the blade of the pocket-knife that he always carried, and then slowly and carefully slit the lining of the bag open along one entire seam.

I was watching, trying to make sense of it all, when Holmes exclaimed, "Aha!"

From under the lining of the bag, he withdrew a small painting. It was rectangular and not much larger than the span of Holmes's hand. There were five figures in the painting, four of them were grotesque-looking crippled men.

"Extraordinary!" Holmes said. "Yes. Yes, indeed. Flemish. Without a doubt. I need more light. Let me get my glass."

"It belongs in a museum," I said.

"Yes," he replied. "In fact, until rather recently the painting *was* in a museum. The Louvre, I believe. Now, the artist would . . ."

"Good Lord," I said.

"Mmm, no," Holmes said, "not nearly that old. Probably sixteenth century."

Holmes raised his magnifying glass to the small canvas and focused on the lower corners, first the right, then the left, which was darker.

"Aha. Here's the signature, Watson, on the left. Bruegel. Yes, of course: Pieter Bruegel. He even was kind enough to date it for us. Roman numerals. Let me see: M: 1,000. D: 500. L: 50. That makes it 1550, then X, which brings the total to 1560, and then V, and I, I, I. Yes, 1568. Didn't I say, 'Sixteenth century'?

"Oh, this is an extraordinary piece of art, Watson. I believe this is the work known as 'The Beggars.' I have never seen it, but I have read descriptions. This almost certainly is it."

"I presume you have read newspaper accounts to the effect that this painting was stolen from the Louvre," I said, intending my statement more as a question than an observation. Holmes was on the scent, however; nothing interfered. He was preoccupied and remained silent. The detective set the painting against the back of the nearest chair and continued to stare at it while removing his briar pipe from his coat pocket. He thumbed a couple of pinches of shag into the bowl without taking his eyes off the canvas, struck a match, and inhaled deeply a couple of times.

I cleared my throat loudly. "I say, Holmes, I suppose that you have read news . . ."

"What? Oh, I heard you the first time, Watson. No, there have been no such stories. No respectable museum would announce such a loss if there was any way to avoid it. That bit of arrogance should make our work a bit easier."

" 'Our work,' Holmes?" I said with a start. "What do you mean, 'our work'? What work? I really must take exception to this."

Grayish-white smoke curled silently to the ceiling. Holmes turned from the small painting to me.

"We are on holiday, or at least I am," I said. "You do as you see fit, but do not presume to involve me in this, this . . . whatever this is. I see absolutely no reason why you can't simply turn it over to the authorities. I am sure they are quite capable of handling the matter."

"Oh, I rather doubt that, Watson," Holmes said. "I doubt that very much. If this were merely a single theft, then perhaps the local constabulary could handle it, but I assure you that is not the case. These are much deeper waters. By the way, did you happen to bring along your revolver? No? Pity. Well, we will have to make do. Perhaps it won't come to that, but really old boy, like it or not, we are both already involved."

Holmes's words stopped me, which is, I am sure, precisely what he intended. I scowled at him with the last vestige of anger that I had to offer and then shook my head in resignation.

"Let me get my pipe," I said, and went about collecting the necessary implements. I sighed deeply, almost theatrically I'm afraid, but I couldn't help it. I was bone tired and I felt a sudden sense of despair to think that I had embarked on a holiday to have my rising spirits dashed by a new mystery of some magnitude, and apparently a dangerous one at that. I sat down heavily in the nearest chair, lighted my pipe, and said to Holmes, "Explain, please."

"Well, we haven't much time, Watson," Holmes said. "Where should I begin?"

"Oh, how should I know, Holmes? What about that old lady who fainted dead away in the lobby?"

"That's not a beginning, Watson; that's an ending, I'm afraid."

"What do you . . ."

Holmes raised his right hand, palm toward me.

"You're right," he said. "You are right. Sorry. I'll be direct. First, Watson, that was not a lady; that was a man got up as one. You will recall that I was standing behind him, and very close at that. It was clear that he was wearing a wig, a good one. I could not help but note that hair strands of an altogether different color and texture were sticking out from beneath his coiffure.

"That aroused my curiosity. I looked for other suggestive details and quickly found them. Makeup, for example. It was so heavy as to extend around to the nape of his neck, obviously to mask skin that was coarse and leathery. The gambit was becoming clearer, you see. Then I noted that his hands appeared to be callused, and there were half-moons of dirt beneath at least two of his fingernails. That cinched it, really, for no lady of our association ever would appear in public so unkempt. I'm sure that if you sort through the contents I emptied out . . ."

Holmes's attention drifted to the items he had dumped on the floor, men's clothing mostly, and several tins. He nudged one with the toe of his boot.

"There, Watson. You see? Makeup."

"Listen, Holmes, I don't mean to be indelicate, but I am quite certain this Pembroke figure wouldn't be the first man to dress up in such a fashion. Some chaps are that way, you know. There was that ugly business with that Oscar Wilde fellow and . . ."

"Much different, Watson, and I am not a recluse: I am aware of such things."

"Well, if that fellow had not fainted, would you still have thought . . ."

"Ah, that," Holmes said. "Yes, point number two. There was no fainting. 'Lady Pembroke,' or whoever he is, most certainly was dead by the time his head hit the floor."

"You can't be serious, Holmes."

"Oh, but I am, Watson. Most assuredly, I am. I caught a slight scent of almonds as I was standing there, the merest trace, so slight that I could not be sure. That's why, after he toppled, I leaned so closely into his face: to see if I could confirm my suspicion. And I did."

"Cyanide?"

"Unmistakable," Holmes said. "Had you been allowed to examine the victim, you would have picked up on it at once. And even if you had not done so you would have noted that the person was dead . . . probably."

"Oh, probably," I said.

"That's why the staff so quickly declined your offer of help," Holmes said.

"That does make sense," I allowed, "but how did you know about the painting?"

"I didn't," Holmes said, "though I am flattered that you

would think I might have been able to divine such a thing. I assure you, I did not know. How could I?"

"Well, why did you snatch the bag?"

"Ah," Holmes said, "that's a different question. It seemed reasonable that the man was carrying something of exceptional value. How else to explain why he was clutching that bag as if his life depended on it? It did, you see."

"We must inform the police at once," I said.

"And how do you suggest we do that, Watson? Have the concierge send a telegram?"

"Well, we could do that, yes," I said with some indignation. "Why not?" I regretted the question the very instant that I asked it, for the answer was suddenly all too clear. The hotel staff was involved in whatever foul business this was, and the concierge would have to be included.

"Ah," Holmes said. "I can see the bright light of understanding shining on your face, doctor." My old friend paused, took a deep pull from his pipe, and smiled.

"By the way, Watson, I don't want you to take my reference to our being in 'deep water' as any kind of rub. Really, this is a splendid locale. It was a fine choice, indeed. This is turning into quite a holiday. How ever did you know to select . . ."

"Oh, stop it, Holmes," I said with a smile. "You have made your point. We do seem to have fallen into it. So, what now?"

"Now, Watson, we act quickly. Much depends on it."

We collected the dead man's clothing and makeup, returned it to the bag, and set it in the back of a tall wardrobe. We removed our own clothes and sundries from their suitcases, and Holmes talked as we got situated.

"The hotel 'staff' suggests organization, Watson, and experience; you saw how quickly and matter-of-factly at least four people responded to what must have been a crisis: the loss of one of their own couriers. So, there's no telling how many people actually may be involved, but it is at least clear that the Bruegel is not the first painting to have been spirited through this hotel."

"All from France?" I asked. Holmes took notepaper from the desk and began writing while we talked.

"Some, undoubtedly," Holmes said. "France is closest. Spain and Italy also seem likely, but the continent has no shortage of repositories for great art. We've no way to know the sources. Some of them may even be private. None of which matters at this instant," he said.

The detective folded the sheet of paper on which he had been writing and handed it to me.

"I want you to return to the Brighton train station by way of at least two cab rides, three would be better. See that this message is cabled from the station to the director of the Louvre. Be certain that it is sent in your presence and that the verbiage is precisely what is written here. Meanwhile, I will use the time to do some investigating of my own."

"Very good, Holmes," I said.

I left The Arms Royale at once. The hotel was especially busy and the lobby was a hub of activity. No sooner did I find myself out-of-doors, however, than I realized I had not eaten since breakfast, which had been a good many hours ago. I bought a meat sandwich from a vendor by the beach, and ate it lustily while keeping my eyes open for a cab. Several minutes passed, but before long I was alone in a hansom and bound for my first destination, a tavern for which I had spotted a large advert near our hotel.

Seeing that it was several miles off the direct route back to the train station, I settled in for the ride and rather quickly dozed off. I awoke at my destination, paid my fare, had a leisurely pint of ale at the tavern, and then resumed my journey. By the time I realized I had not yet read Holmes's message, there was not enough light to do so. I waited until I arrived at the station. In anticipation of another fare, the driver cheerily agreed to wait for me. Inside the station, I unfolded Holmes's note and quickly read, "Have recovered a work that begs your attention. Please dispatch nearest reliable agent to meet for late tea at The Arms Royale, 5:00 P.M., two days hence. Agent must use word 'drosophila' upon introduction to John W. Goodrich and companion."

"Drosophila," I repeated in a half whisper. A fly, specifically a fruit fly. I remembered it from my medical studies: *Drosophila melanogaster* was routinely used in laboratory experiments. I shook my head. I could not pretend to understand the workings of Holmes's mind.

A scant few minutes later, I was back in the hansom, and a while later, I was walking through the front doors of our hotel. Given the time, there was little activity. A porter recognized me and nodded, and I went to our rooms straightaway. Holmes had already retired. "Naturally," I said to myself, grousing a bit, for I was weary.

The detective arose well before me the next morning. I knew this because I awoke to his pounding on my door. It seemed to me that I had barely gotten to sleep.

"Get up, Doctor," Holmes called. Then he marched into my room and threw open the curtains.

"There, see! The sun is bright. There's a fine breeze freshening off the water, and all in all it looks to be a marvelous day."

I griped and grumbled, but managed to feign wakefulness.

"I'll meet you out front when you are ready, Watson," he said, turning to leave.

"Wait, Holmes. I'll meet you in the dining room for breakfast," I said. "How's that, eh? I'm famished."

"No. Outside. We can neither eat nor drink here," he said. "Not unless you want to risk joining Lady Pembroke, wherever he is."

"They know who we are?" I asked.

"I don't think so," Holmes said, "but they know we're not right. I'll explain downstairs." With that, he closed the door.

A while later, I found Holmes leaning against the front railing of the hotel. A knapsack was slung over his shoulder and in his right hand he was holding a rather long and stout walking stick.

"I've packed provisions for us, Doctor," he said, rather loudly I thought. "Let us take advantage of the day; it's perfect for a hike along the coast, don't you think?"

"Oh, perfect," I said.

"Well then, let's be off." So saying, Holmes began walking at a pace that a good many men, myself included, would quickly find tiring. Some thirty minutes later, when we were well clear of the downtown, I told him to stop.

"I really must have some food, Holmes."

"Oh, yes," he said. "Of course. Forgive me. Let's go on just a bit farther though."

We walked for another quarter hour, and then Holmes struck off the path. I followed him until he had found a small clearing. Holmes lighted his pipe and smoked while I ate a breakfast of half-cooked sausage and two dried-out scones.

"Sorry, old man," he said. "It was the best I could do at the carts by the beach."

I mumbled around a mouthful of greasy meat, "Glad to have it. There. Now tell me what you meant back there. Are they on to us or not?"

"For all intents, yes. They came for the painting some time last night."

"What? Did they get it? Did you confront them?"

"No, to all those questions. After you left, I went downstairs and became the most garrulous guest this hotel has had in years. I was charming, if I do say so myself. In the span of an hour, I must have met half of the guests and nearly all of the staff. A motley bunch they are. The concierge, by the way, assured me that no sooner had we repaired to our rooms than Lady Pembroke came to, had another cuppa with the staff, and went on her merry way."

"Humph!" I grunted. "Not since Lazarus."

"Indeed," Holmes said. "I was able to learn that only a minute or two before she was stricken, Pembroke had, in fact, sat down to tea . . . two sugars, no milk. Barbaric, eh?" Holmes smiled.

"Without milk, you mean? I should say so." Holmes was still smiling, but even more broadly, which was not at all like him.

"Watson," he said through his teeth. "We're being watched. Two men behind you. About fifteen paces. One to the left, one to the right." With the toe of his boot, he nudged a rock the size of an orange toward me, and looked away, feigning a yawn. Under his breath, he said, "I'm going to stand, turn, and run. That'll draw one of them off. Man on the right is closest to you. Throw hard," Holmes said. Rising slowly to his feet, he added, "Don't miss. Yours is the one with the pistol."

"Now!" Holmes shouted, and he turned and ran.

Immediately, I heard rustling, curses, and footsteps behind me. I grabbed the rock, sprang to my feet, turning, looking for my man. He already had closed half the distance between us. I barely had time to cock my arm. He was raising his pistol when I let fly overhand as hard as I could, aiming straight for his head. I let my momentum carry me forward and down to the ground. I half expected to hear the gunshot and feel the bullet any second. When neither event occurred, I looked up and saw my target spread-eagled on the ground. My rock lay by his head. His pistol lay on the ground, only inches from his hand.

I scrambled to my feet, grabbed the weapon, and charged after Holmes. I heard a scream and shifted my course toward the sound. In a smaller clearing than the one I had left, Holmes's assailant stood hunched over before the detective, his face a mask of pain. He was holding his right arm. Sunlight gleamed off the keen blade of a long knife on the ground by his feet. The ruffian's hand dangled at an awkward angle. Holmes raised his walking stick, and rapped the man smartly on the side of the head. The thug collapsed in a heap.

Holmes turned to me. "Ah, Watson. I didn't think your assailant would risk firing this close to the walking paths. Glad to see that I was right. Let's go back and collect our things."

My felled assailant had not stirred. A large red bump half the size of a hen's egg had risen on his forehead. I carefully checked the man's wrist for a pulse.

"He'll live," I told Holmes.

He nodded, stowed the pistol in his knapsack, and we quickly regained our path.

"I think we have earned a drink, don't you?" I said to Holmes.

"By all means," he replied.

At the edge of town, we put the sea to our backs, found a tavern, and stayed awhile before resuming our walk. Our leisurely trek used up the rest of the day and the early part of the evening, and by the time we returned to The Arms Royale I felt somewhat rejuvenated, despite the trouble we had encountered.

"Holmes," I said when we were back in our suite, "you knew we would be followed."

"Certainly. But if we had stayed put, we'd have been at their mercy. This way, we at least stood a chance."

"What about the painting? You said they came after it."

"Ah, yes," he said. "Pembroke's small suitcase was missing by the time I returned to my room. But I had kept the painting with me all evening."

"How so?" I asked.

"The lining of my jacket," he said. "It fits quite nicely."

"Then you have been wearing it all day?"

"I made a cardboard sheath for it. I could think of no way to be more certain of its whereabouts."

I laughed, shook my head, and bade my comrade good night.

The next morning, Holmes informed me that he had an errand to do and he asked that in his absence, I send another telegram to the director of the Louvre. He handed it to me saying, "Only this time, Watson, simply give it to the concierge and leave."

The message read: "Have recovered a work that begs your attention. Please dispatch local agent to meet for late tea at The Arms Royale 5:00 P.M." The note was signed John W. Goodrich.

"No code word?" I asked.

"None required," Holmes said. I did not understand, but neither did I question the detective. He rarely erred in such matters.

I will meet you in the tearoom at 4:00 p.m.," Holmes said. "Meanwhile, my good friend, do watch your back. I will leave the, uhm, knapsack, though I don't expect you will really need it."

"Very well," I said. I accomplished my assigned task and whiled away the morning and the better part of the afternoon walking along the beach, getting progressively wetter as the tide came in and then finally giving myself over to an invigorating dunk and a vigorous swim. I returned to the hotel refreshed and ready to take on all comers.

I walked to the door of the tearoom, which was crowded with diners, but I immediately spotted Holmes at a table in the far corner. His chair was situated between two large windows through which the late-day sun streamed. He was holding something on the table in both of his hands, a smallish glass decanter, or so it appeared from my vantage point, and he was studying it as though it were the most fascinating object he had ever seen. As I got near, I realized that he was examining a glass flycatcher. This one was a bit on the fancy side, a bell-shaped jar of the lightest shade of blue. A decorative stopper protruded from the top. Water sweetened with sugar, honey, or a few drops of molasses was poured into the jar and allowed to pool at the bottom around a raised hole that looked much like the mouth of a small volcano. Three small feet kept the base of the jar elevated, so that flies had room to find their way inside. From the looks, a new victim had entered recently; it was still flying around inside.

"From the other side of the room I could not imagine what had you so enthralled," I said to Holmes, pulling up a chair.

"Hello, Watson. Yes, a flycatcher."

"Well," I said, "I've had a grand day, just grand. Plenty of sun and fresh . . ."

"The design is simplicity itself," Holmes said.

"What? Oh, you weren't . . ."

"Simple, but deadly, Watson. The trap is predicated on the notion that the insect's insatiable appetite contains the seeds of its very own destruction. The fly is drawn in by the promise of sweet rewards, only to get so enveloped and overwhelmed by it that escape becomes impossible."

I noticed that as Holmes spoke, the fly in the bottle seemed to be acting out the detective's narrative. Finally, it fell into the bottom of the trap and drowned.

"And so it goes," Holmes said. "And so it goes." He lifted the flycatcher from the table and returned it to its home on the broad sill of the window.

"Well, Watson," the detective said, looking at me for the first time. "You appear to be as refreshed as you sound. This holiday business does seem to suit you."

"My only regret, Holmes, is that we did not get away sooner. I . . ."

"Excuse me, gentlemen."

I turned to the intruding voice and saw that it belonged to a tall and thin, well-dressed, mustachioed man with small and rather thick eyeglasses. His black hair was combed straight back, which emphasized the severe angularity of his face.

"Which of you would be Mr. Goodrich?"

"You needn't be overly polite," Holmes said. "I saw the concierge point us out. You know that I am the person you seek, so do sit down."

The man nodded curtly and sat. "I believe you have recovered something that, uhm, 'begs' my attention, or rather my employer's attention."

"Are you always so coy?" Holmes asked.

The man's dark eyes flashed. He looked straight at Holmes, leaned forward over the table, and lowered his voice. "The Bruegel, then. Do you have it? The painting really must be returned to its rightful home. And let me say in advance that we do truly appreciate your generosity. Would that everyone were as public-spir . . ."

"There must be some misunderstanding," Holmes said. "There is a price."

Our visitor cocked his head slightly and raised his eyebrows.

"Seventy-five thousand pounds," Holmes said.

The man blinked three times. He looked as if he had been slapped.

"Nonsense," he said. "Even for such a work, that is . . ."

"Oh, perhaps I should have explained," Holmes said. "The price also buys my silence. Ah, here is our tea."

The man leaned back in his chair, but did not take his eyes off Holmes for an instant. Our hostess was an attractive brunette, and she seemed to have singled me out for her most engaging smile. The woman set down a crystal plate of warm almond biscuits. The aroma was heady and intoxicating. She moved gracefully and poured the milk and tea unobtrusively. She removed the lid from a small china bowl of sugar cubes, used small silver tongs to pluck one of the cubes, and held it just above our guest's cup.

He said nothing, just held up two fingers. Two sugar cubes followed. He nodded, stirred, and sipped deeply as the waitress moved to us.

"Thank you, no," Holmes said. "For either of us."

She nodded and left.

Our guest sipped some more of his tea. And said nothing for a few long moments. He was still staring at Holmes.

"You were saying?" Beads of perspiration had appeared on the man's forehead.

"Paintings such as the Bruegel are always noticed," Holmes said. "You can't flog them off just anywhere. I would guess that most of them are going to private collectors in America or Australia, probably the latter, given that nation's remoteness from our shores."

Our guest suddenly appeared sick. He reached for the collar of his white shirt with one hand, dropped his teacup from the other, grabbed at his throat, and fell to the floor, noisily upsetting the chair.

A woman at a nearby table shouted in alarm.

"Good grief," I said.

Holmes threw his linen napkin onto the table. "Do you see, Watson? They're drawn to sugar." He rose quickly to his feet.

Other diners arose and began moving toward our table and the fallen visitor.

"Well, I think this brings our little vacation to an end, don't you?"

"Our bags . . ."

Holmes was prepared. He reached into the corner, snatched up my suitcase, and handed it to me. He picked up his own bag, and with a signifying nod, threw me the knapsack. He turned sharply and headed for the door. I was right behind him. We pushed and elbowed our way around the edge of the room so as to avoid the hotel staff, which was forcing its way through the diners toward our table. I noticed that one of the rushing staff had his forehead tightly wrapped in a bandage. I didn't doubt that were we to stay, I would have found another staff member with his arm in a cast.

Our sudden presence in the lobby seemed to stun the concierge.

Holmes waved nonchalantly as we sped past the man and out the front door.

A hansom cab was pulled up near the entrance. "Talk about luck," I muttered under my breath. Holmes shouted,

"Brighton Station," to the driver as we climbed in. I slammed the door and the hansom lurched forward.

"The painting?" I asked.

Holmes tapped his chest.

The ride was quick and sure. Neither of us spoke until we had boarded our train for London and settled into a compartment.

We cracked a window, sat opposite each other, and lighted our pipes. Holmes removed his coat, used his penknife to re-open part of the lining, and then extracted the cardboard squares that concealed the small masterpiece. He quickly put the package in his suitcase, locked it shut, and stowed it under his seat.

No sooner had he done so than the compartment door slid open and a woman stepped quickly inside. It was our tea hostess, the brunette with the warm smile, only this time she had a pistol in her hand. She motioned us to move farther toward the window, which we did.

"You seem to have recovered something that begs my attention," she said. Then with that warm smile, she added, "Oh, yes. I believe I am supposed to say the word 'drosophila,' too."

"Quite," Holmes said. "I have been expecting you."

"Where is the painting?"

"In a moment," Holmes said. "First, a question, if you please.

"The museum directors to whom you answer. I presume you have employers all over the continent, not just at the Louvre?"

The woman nodded. "The Prado pays well, too," she said. "Theft is such an enormous problem."

"But not murder, I gather."

"My employers pay to have their art returned. I do what I have to do, and they never ask questions. I'll take the painting now."

"It's in the suitcase under the seat," Holmes said.

"Get it," the woman said. She cocked the hammer on her pistol and trained it directly at the detective.

"Certainly," Holmes said.

He reached beneath the seat, pulled out the small suitcase, and in the same upsweeping motion slammed the bag into the underside of the woman's outstretched hand, driving it toward the ceiling. The handgun discharged. In the small compartment, the sound was deafening.

The door flew open and before the woman could do anything, Inspector Lestrade had his right hand locked around the woman's wrist and his left forearm braced hard across her windpipe from behind.

I pried the gun from the woman's hand. Lestrade twisted her arm down behind her back, and in an instant had the bracelets on her.

"For a minute, I thought I was too late," Lestrade said. "We had our ears tight to the door so we could get down that helpful explanation she was offering, and then I heard the shot, Mr. Holmes."

"Holmes!" the woman said. "Sherlock Holmes?"

The detective smiled at her. "Your humble servant."

The woman sagged. "My luck!"

A patrolman appeared in the hallway at that instant, and Lestrade pushed the woman through the open door. The officer took her in hand.

"Your timing was impeccable, Inspector. And by the way, I have newfound respect for your abilities with a horse-drawn cab."

"That was you waiting outside the hotel, Lestrade?" I asked.

The hatchet-faced policeman smiled.

"Guilty as charged, Doctor. Mr. Holmes was kind enough to send me an urgent cable first thing this morning. He had the plan all laid out. I was just playing the part."

"Not so," Holmes said. "We have had our differences, Lestrade. That's so, but execution was absolutely crucial. Watson and I are in your debt."

"Oh, I think that bill's more'n paid up," Lestrade said. "By now, my boys have got that concierge and his crew in hand, and I expect that when I get back to the Yard, there'll be a couple of French policemen waiting for me. I gather we'll be talking to the Spaniards pretty soon, too; Lord knows who else. This is going to take some time, and it looks like we'll have a chance to twist the noses of some pretty snooty museum folks. 'Tween you and me, I'm looking forward to that. Well, I'd best be off."

"Don't forget this," Holmes said. He opened his suitcase, removed the Bruegel, and handed it to the inspector.

"Details, eh?" Lestrade said, mocking his own forgetfulness.

We shook hands and the inspector left.

Holmes and I relighted our pipes and sat in silence for a few minutes. I gazed blankly out the window and watched the countryside speed by in what seemed an ever-hastening and increasingly tiresome blur. *Too fast,* I thought to myself, *much too fast.* Holmes's voice startled me.

"You know, Watson," the detective said, "I think you may have had the right idea all along."

"How's that, Holmes?"

"Vacation. I have to say the change of scenery actually was refreshing in a way."

"You're serious?"

"I am, indeed," Holmes said. "In fact, if you would like, we can choose a new destination right now and change trains in London."

"Not bloody likely," I said.

"Excuse me?" the detective said.

"You may continue on, Holmes, but I've had it," I said. "I haven't the stamina for another holiday."